RENEWAL

RENEWAL

A DAUGHTER OF FATE
BOOK ONE

J. L. Rabone

Podium

Published in 2024 by Podium Publishing
www.podiumaudio.com

RENEWAL

Viridian North
Forgotten Woods
Ingalham Town
Ingalham Woods
Ghost Bay
Restless Sea
Ridge Town
Ridge Pass
Wayward
Talbour
Deadlands
Ordil
Ordil Woods
Layland Tower
Bay
Prairie Expanse
Oran Lake
Jagged West
Zromore Capital City
Barrows Tower
Haro Woods
Rastar Mine Town
Kaytar Bordercity
Dry East
Crestel River
Frost Sea
Zandar Bordertown
Talin
Gelid Woods
Frozen South
Zopan Empire

CHAPTER ONE

Life changes fast.

My stomach swooped as my hands scraped against the ground I was shoved onto. The fabric of my torn dress clung to my skin as it soaked up the rain, chilling my body. Turning my head, I didn't hold back from glaring at the man who sneered in satisfaction at my pitiful form. His red hair fell before his dull brown eyes, leaning towards me and grabbing my chin.

"Now you look at me with such passion?" Garret Asher stated as though he had achieved his goal.

"It's more than you deserve, husband," I spat back before he could yank me to my feet with the chains dangling around my wrists.

"Ha, you never did use my name, Lynette." He dragged me across the gravelled pathway at the front of his mansion. One of my shoes fell, revealing the terra-cotta skin of my bare foot.

A wooden platform had been staged at the centre of his dreary garden, a single post looming. Soldiers lined up behind the post, standing tall, glancing our way as the rain pattered on their black armour. Finally, one of them broke from their line and headed towards us.

Quickly, the soldier yanked the chains from my husband's grip, leading me up the platform steps and towards the post. I didn't bother resisting as the soldier tied a rope around my waist, securing me to the pole and letting my arms fall loosely. My raven hair clumped in the rain.

"How does it feel to know that they all hate you?" Garret asked me with genuine curiosity in his voice as he approached the stage.

"Not much different than my feelings for you." I smirked, knowing how angry it would make him. His hatred for my indifference towards him all these years had only grown. Baron Garret Asher had never been able to hold his temper without an audience. Usually, he would have started beating me by this point, but the soldier's presence deterred him.

He didn't hesitate to slap me, though. The sound echoed throughout the estate's yard.

"This wouldn't have happened if you had shown me affection. I can still make it go away. Just admit to being guilty of murder, and I'll have you imprisoned instead." Garret lowered his voice as he spoke close to my ear. His warm breath against my cheek felt clammy.

I couldn't hold back my laughter.

"Oh, husband, do you think so little of me? You have no power to change my sentence any more than you do to gain my affection." I sighed, looking at his foolish face.

I had considered him quite handsome once, as many young ladies do. However, after ten years of marriage trapped within his small estate, I had seen the darkness within his heart. My bruises and scars were a testament to that.

Yet I had never considered him cruel enough to frame me for murder.

How he had done such a thing when I barely left his estate still baffled me. My trial had left me with more questions than answers. My reaction to their claims had probably solidified my guilt.

Our arranged marriage was insufferable for both of us, but a divorce would have been sufficient, not this.

"Lynette." Garret gritted his teeth as he glanced towards the soldiers standing nearby, hesitant.

"Step aside, Baron Asher. The family is here for last rites." A guard stepped forward, his golden spear standing tall at his side, symbolising the royal guard. They didn't usually turn up for executions, but the murder of royal blood was an exception. Even if that blood was far removed.

They had at least granted my request for a private execution—a privilege of law granted to those in my situation. I was surprised they accepted. However, the crown did not want to publicise the death of their distant relatives. That would show weakness.

"Tch," Garret muttered. "Consider this my way of granting mercy. At least now you won't have to suffer as your soul wastes away." He gently rubbed my neck, causing me to shudder before he leaned close to my lips. "Goodbye, sweet wife." He pressed his lips against mine before pulling away.

I felt nothing as usual in his interactions with me.

Did he think this was a better death for me? Ha, what thoughtlessness. Though perhaps it might be better than wasting away from my disease; I had already done that once.

"Viscount Heversham." A guard bowed towards the older gentleman approaching the platform. His boots were shined to perfection. His aged white hair was slicked back, untouched by the rain as the droplets avoided him altogether, creating a canopy above him. Father had always been a skilled water summoner.

"Disappointed?" I asked as my adoptive father approached me, stamping his black cane. A small snake curled around it, slithering towards his palm, its body made up of moving water.

"Surprisingly, I am not," he said, raising an eyebrow as he inspected my bedraggled appearance.

"You say that as though you were hoping for this." I sighed. I knew we didn't have the best relationship, but Roger Heversham was still the man who had raised me.

"I didn't know what I had hoped for." He shook his head in thought. "I had always thought this marriage would be good for you. You always were unruly, but murder? Lynette." He narrowed his eyes at me.

"As I've said, Father, I had no involvement." I repeated my statement of innocence. Viscount Heversham's eyes flickered towards Garret momentarily before returning to me.

"I wish that were true," he stated.

"Don't you all," I sneered, to hide the pang of pain in my gut. But of course, he would never believe me. He had never had much faith in me since the beginning.

I was nothing but a weak mortal. A commoner.

"I had thought selling you into marriage to the baron would help you grow up, but this? This is a curse from the gods you brought upon our family. It's the gods' grace that Cassandra is no longer here."

"What do you mean, 'selling' me into marriage?" I asked, my eyes narrowing, trying to forget the comment about my adoptive mother.

"I suppose you should know," he sighed. "The baron had always requested your hand, Lynette."

"Father, what are you saying?" My voice involuntarily rose. "I married the baron so Kara didn't have to. I did this for her." I tightened my lips to hold the lump forming in my throat.

"Lynette, what I told you was untrue." He paused, seeing the shock on my face. "When I received the baron's proposal, I thought the marriage would be what you needed. It was doubtful you would get any other suitable requests, and he was a good suitor. But, knowing your temperament, I knew you wouldn't accept. So I did what I thought would get you to the altar." Father looked away, his wrinkles folded on his brows: a face he often showed me when he was disappointed by my actions.

"So you lied to me." I spoke with little emotion as I absorbed this. All this time, my decision to marry the baron so Kara wouldn't have to had been based on a lie. It wasn't Kara he had requested. It had always been me.

"I did," Father said as his water snake slithered up his arm to wrap around the collar of his tailored jacket. "To convince the baron not to rescind his offer after learning of this, I sold him an iron mine as part of the marriage."

I couldn't help but look over at Garret as he shifted from one foot to another, uncomfortable standing near so many guards.

So he still married me even knowing I accepted under false information and took an iron mine to profit?

Garret's frustration over my indifference towards him somewhat made sense now. He must have originally had feelings for me, but that wouldn't change the fact that he was still a monster.

"Kara. Where is she?" I asked, feeling a rush of emotion at this betrayal.

I had been such a fool.

What would this life have been if not for this marriage?

Was Father only telling me this now as a way to redeem his own actions? Or was he hoping to make me more miserable?

"She's at the palace as usual. I haven't told her what's happening today. I couldn't have her seeing such a stressful event." Father's expression hardened.

"Good," I muttered. It would be difficult to do this knowing Kara was watching.

"Eduard sends his regards."

"I'm sure he does." My oldest brother had always been open in his dislike for me. I had doubted he would have much to say.

The guards began to sound the drums they had brought. I looked up at the gate of Garret Asher's estate and saw the man who would be my executioner.

A silver mask covered his face, two horns attached slightly higher than his forehead. They had neat spirals, the silver glinting in the rain. The only visible feature through the gap in his mask was his purple eyes of the royal bloodline. His formal armour rattled with each step as he walked down the line of guards holding their golden spears at attention.

Duke of the Frozen South, Azriel Elkhart. It was the first time I had ever seen the man I had heard the maids gossip about. They said he was undefeated in war. His power was second to none other than his second cousin, the empress. He was born with the aether of his bloodline, the Draygon race.

"Is it time already?" Father asked, watching Duke Elkhart step up onto the stage.

"Yes, Viscount Heversham." Duke Elkhart's voice was low.

"Very well then, I shall remove myself." Father bowed in respect to the general. Walking closer to me, he whispered his final words. "I hope it shall be quick for you," he said, lightly patting my soaked hair.

I followed him with my gaze as he moved to stand beside my husband, watching us from the sidelines.

That might have been the only time he showed me any semblance of sincerity.

Duke Elkhart stood before me now. He was tall, taller than I had imagined him to be. No one had seen his face since he was a boy. No one knew why he always wore the mask, but it was well known not to ask him.

I doubt I would have ever encountered this man if not for the fact I was here for the crime of murdering his twin nephews.

"Baroness Asher, I am here to carry out the punishment for your crimes. Do you have anything to say before I carry out the sentence?" the duke asked me formally.

"No, Duke, I have already stated all I had to say at my trial." I half smiled towards him; it had been a trial of lies and deceit.

"Understood." He nodded and picked up the sword handed to him by one of the guards. The handle was adorned with intertwining dragons, their eyes dazzling blue diamonds. I recognised it as the sword of dragons' breath, one of the famous weapons of power. Well, this death might not be as pitiful as my last if he was using that.

"Any final requests?" he asked, raising the sword high, his eyes glancing at the black veins on my neck.

"Only one, please make it quick. I do not want to give anyone the pleasure of my slow death." I looked up at the sky as rain fell onto my face. Grey clouds hid the sun, and no birds flew by.

When nothing happened, I looked back towards the duke and was surprised to see his eyes on me.

"Don't worry. If not today, I will die soon." I didn't know why I needed to comfort him during my execution. The telltale signs of my disease probably paused him.

"I will make it quick." The duke nodded, signalling before swinging his sword towards my neck.

CHAPTER TWO

My hands instinctively rushed to my neck as I gasped awake. My heart beat so fast it could have escaped my chest.

Looking around, I noticed the fluffy warmth of quilts covering me as I lay in a simple four-poster bed. The walls were made of stone plastered in a pale purple paint, a few cracks in the corners sheltering spiderwebs.

A small wooden desk was pushed up at the right side of a door. An oil candle and scattered papers littered it. Opposite was a dressing table with a mirror hung on the wall above. The room itself was pretty small.

It was my old room at the Heversham estate, where I had lived before my marriage to Lord Garret. My heart calmed down as I recognised this familiar scenario.

Hauling myself out of bed, I rushed to the dirtied mirror and wiped it clean with the cream sleeve of my nightgown.

This face, this shoulder-length raven hair, and dark forest green eyes looking back. It was me. But not the woman I was, the girl I used to be.

The only difference was a noticeable scar that now stretched across my neck.

My body relaxed as a sigh left my lips.

So, it had happened again. I thought it might.

Moving away from the mirror, I turned towards my desk, picking up the scattered papers. I rummaged through them, only finding notes on the math and literature books piled neatly on the shelf above.

Until finally, I found something.

It was a note written in my hand, they all were, but it was clear, and it was dated.

Turning back round to the mirror, I stared at myself again. It was 1567, the year I turned twenty-one. I married Lord Garret when I was twenty-two and died in my thirty-second year in the autumn of 1578.

I had gone back in time again.

Feeling the strength drain from my legs, I returned to the bed and fell onto my back. That would make three deaths, and this was my fourth revival.

I never returned to the same moment.

It was always slightly forward in time from my last return.

My memories were fuzzy, but I knew my most emotional moments. They were burned into my mind. I closed my eyes to try to recall precise details of less essential memories, but my head immediately hurt.

Ow, I should know better than to do that.

I knew from experience in my last repeated lives that my emotions and habits gained from maturing reverted to the mind of my younger self.

I had seen a mature version of myself in my dreams. So I knew I had lost something of that part of myself whenever I regressed. My memories always returned fully to my dreams.

Lifting my arm, I glanced at the silver bracelet dangling from my thin wrist. The black gems that had been set in it were now all gone. Every death resulted in one disappearing; I had my suspicion on my first death, but the second confirmed it when a gem vanished again. Now there weren't any left.

So was this my last life?

A slight knock on the door made me stiffen.

"Lynette?" The person who spoke in a bored tone didn't waste time in opening the door. I turned my head slightly to look at my visitor, careful to pull the collar of my nightgown up enough to cover my neck scar. It wouldn't be easy to explain why that had suddenly appeared.

A maid dressed in a simple black dress and white apron opened the door; her ginger hair was pinned up in a loose bun, and it bobbed as she searched my room before settling on my figure upon the bed.

"Here, my lady, water for your morning face wash." She sighed as her blue eyes looked at me on the bed. She walked over the hardwood floor to drop the freshwater basin on my bedraggled desk. Water splashed out onto some of my papers from her clumsy handling.

"Thanks, Freda." I waved my hand at her to leave. Freda Parsons was officially my personal maid. We were well acquainted enough now that I no longer addressed her as Miss Parsons.

She was chosen after losing a bet with the other maids. I didn't mind much, as Freda wasn't all that bad. Maybe a bit neglectful, but she did not actively go out of her way to bully me.

After all, no one wanted to be close to the Crazy Cerue Lady who was me.

I couldn't stop my snicker as I thought of the nickname the other nobles in Talbour had given me.

A cerue was a tiny demonic beast coated in black fur resembling a feline. They tended to go rabid for no apparent reason and were considered pests.

I didn't know how to handle my emotions in my first life. So I lashed out a lot, which resulted in my reputation. I think I once brought a weapon to a social event and threatened the hostess. It might have been one of Father's jians. That did cause a stir.

"Clean up quickly, my lady. His lordship wants to eat breakfast early today so he can meet your brothers," Freda informed me before ungracefully closing my door on her way out.

I stared at the door briefly before finding the will to pull myself up. This wasn't the first time I had come back in time after death, but this time?

I was tired.

Tired of doing this all over again.

Slowly I made my way to the washbasin and dipped my finger into the water. It was lukewarm, better than the stone-cold water my last maid used to bring me.

At least when I was married to Garret, the maids took care of me. However, it might have been out of pity from all the beatings I received rather than that they liked me. I was lucky Freda was my maid in this household. She at least somewhat did her job well.

Taking the plunge, I splashed the lukewarm water onto my face, scrubbing my eyes and the fresh scar on my neck as though I could clean it away. Pulling my collar down a little further, I inspected it some more. It was reasonably smooth and straight. The blade had made a clean cut. Following it, I found that it stretched around the circumference of my neck, so there was no hiding it with makeup.

I sighed again. *I guess I'm going to have to start wearing choker necklaces from now on.*

Did I even have any?

Opening the desk drawer, I picked up my red velvet jewellery box and hunted for something I could use. After pulling out numerous pearls, I finally found a plain, dark green ribbon. It would have to do for now. As I was about to put the box away, I paused, glancing again at the bracelet on my wrist. The dainty silver chain had three empty gem settings. It was still beautiful, but perhaps useless now.

Nevertheless, after consideration, I decided to keep wearing it. This bracelet was the only thing I had of worth on me when Cassandra, the viscountess, found me wandering the streets of Wayward Town as an urchin.

I didn't remember where I got it or how I ended up in Wayward Town as a child. My first memories are of starving and begging for scraps from the town baker's shop. If the viscountess hadn't decided to adopt me, I'd have probably died as a child.

Most of the townsfolk in Wayward had ignored me, afraid of my raven hair, green eyes, and terra-cotta skin—common traits of people from Dramoria, the neighbouring empire.

There had been speculation about how I ended up in the Zopan Empire. However, with my lack of memory and scraggy torn clothing, it was determined I must have come from the forgotten woods splitting the two countries.

The aether in those woods was so dense and ancient that anyone caught wandering into them either never returned or, if they did, had no recollection of who they were. If that truly was where I came from, it was a miracle I came out the other side into the Zopan Empire at all.

Sitting on the stool at my desk, I studied the bracelet more. It was made up of three separate silver chains twisted together. Three small charms dangled from it where the black gems once sat.

I had often thought about how it worked. However, no matter how much I tried to research the books I had access to, I never found anything. Nothing could explain how it granted me the ability to cheat death. At least, there was nothing in the books that were permitted to the public.

No known aether has that power. Not that I know of. No summoner has ever contracted a time beast. That would have been highlight gossip.

I had only one conclusion: the only possible answer must be with the gods. Gods that I had never paid attention to in any of my previous lives.

Honestly, I didn't think they were plausible enough to be worth considering.

The pain I had suffered had created a seed of distrust in them. I often avoided them in conversation and never visited the temples.

Perhaps this time, I should.

Moving to my wardrobe, I picked a simple green dress to match the green ribbon I had tied around my neck. It was one of the few items I owned that wasn't inlaid with jewels or fancy expensive cloth. I didn't feel like wearing those anymore. Stepping into the skirt's ruffles, I lifted the dress over my head, the bell sleeves hanging over my shoulders as I bent my arms to fasten the buttons of the bodice.

Usually, my maid would assist me with this, but because I was a forgotten lady in this house, that was a whimsical dream. Freda had offered once, but I hadn't trusted her enough. Besides, no one should see my death scars. That would raise too many questions I really couldn't explain.

I got about half of them buttoned before I couldn't reach the rest. Then, dropping my arms, I turned at an angle to see the buttons in the mirror.

Closing my eyes, I slowed my breathing to centre myself. It was challenging to do this after reviving.

Looking into myself, I visualised my blood running through my veins, then concentrated on the feeling, calming my heart some more to slow down its pace.

I tried to pick up on the sense of something foreign to my blood, something small and almost nonexistent.

After a few minutes, something finally sparked within me as a tiny white mote flickered in my mind's eye. Grasping it, I tugged, and it sprang to my fingertips swiftly. Though small and alone, it was enough for what I wanted.

Opening my eyes to look back into the mirror, I moved my fingers, directing the mote of white towards the buttons at the back of my bodice. It fluttered, almost fizzling out at my weak control, but finally attached to the buttons, and I watched as they were tied together with aether.

Core aether. I possessed it, but it was frustratingly weak.

I could only manage to do simple tasks like buttoning my dress or stirring a spoon in my tea. It was so weak. All the tests I had done as a child revealed no core at all. As a result, I was considered a mortal like the majority of commoners in the Zopan Empire.

I couldn't sense my core at all in my first and second lives. To the dismay of my family, this meant I wasn't worth much. Just another useless mouth to feed. My only value was in my marriage.

Only in my third life, married to Garret, did I learn I had a core. For many days I shut myself up in my room in his mansion. Alone, with nothing else to do as I avoided that man, I meditated to occupy my time.

No books were legally allowed to be sold regarding aether and mote cores. So my discovery during my meditation on its existence was pure chance. I still do not fully understand what aether is.

Only soldiers, summoners in the royal army, are taught such knowledge.

This time alone allowed me to practise what I could from the little I had seen of aether used by my father. Eventually, I learned how to sense the aether in my blood. The many hours and days of learning this seemed to have stuck with my mind when crossing over to my fourth life.

However, the power was the same, a single insufficient mote of aether. Most average commoners who had a core could at least control twenty motes of aether. This was just how weak I was.

Dragging a brush quickly through my wavy hair, I pinned a pearl to the side to hold my fringe back. Then, happy with my simple overall look, I left my room, gently closing the door into the empty hallway.

My room was at the back of the manor, away from the main floors my family resided on. Only empty rooms were beside my own.

As I stepped down the echoing hallway, I looked at the paintings hung on the walls. Each was a portrait of one of the various past heads of the Heversham family. Some were painted with their wives and children, some posed valiantly with their swords, and others flourished their feathered pens symbolising their political skill.

I neared the end where the most recent painting hung. Roger Heversham, the current head, his deceased wife Cassandra, and their three children were together with happy smiles. It was a stark reminder that I wasn't blood-related to this family, excluded from the picture.

It was painted on the day my oldest brother, Eduard, had confined me to my room for lashing out in public at a party. I can't remember the details now. It was so long ago. It meant little now after three lifetimes. Perhaps that was the day I insinuated that another noble had been unfaithful to his wife?

Leaving the hallway of paintings, I descended the mahogany stairs. Mage lamps hung on the pristine white walls, illuminating the foyer below. It had been many years since I was last in this manor, and I had somewhat forgotten its grandeur. My heeled shoes echoed on the wooden floors as I turned the corner to head to the dining room.

Standing in front of the doors was an elderly man dressed in a fine black suit and white gloves, with a pocket watch nestled in his right hand.

Henley Ruopold, our butler, watched me approach with a frown on his face.

"His lordship has been waiting. You're late," he tutted, putting the watch away.

Well, doesn't he have such a sour face on him today.

"I'm here now, aren't I?" I responded, refuting Henley's rudeness. I was an honourary lady of House Heversham, and it wasn't a butler's place to tut at me or get annoyed at my actions. Before, in my first life, I had never picked up on his disdain for me, but now it was apparent.

Henley cast me a curious glance. "This way," he said, opening the doors.

Bright morning light hit me as I entered the dining room. A rectangular table was in the centre of the room, draped in an expensive white cloth.

Three sets of plates were arranged at the far end of the table, and cutlery was placed neatly on light blue napkins.

At the head sat Roger Heversham. His piercing dark blue eyes glared at me under the shroud of his light brown greying hair. He had a strict face with deep-set wrinkles stemming from a permanent frown. His look was unnerving, but I ignored it.

To his left sat Kara, my adoptive sister. She beamed at me, her blond ringlets bouncing as she turned her head. She was a pretty young girl with many admirers.

"Lynette! There you are! Come sit, sit." Kara waved her hand to the seat on her left. I returned her smile and moved to sit.

None of the maids standing at the edge of the room had stepped forward to pull the chair out for me. Typical.

"What took you so long, sleepyhead?" Kara giggled at me, picking up one of the napkins to place on her knees.

"I had an issue with my jewellery." It wasn't exactly a lie, but I wasn't about to say that I was late since I took my time adjusting after being killed. Not that they would believe anything I had to say anyway.

"Your jewellery?" She cocked her head with innocent blue eyes. They were the same as her father's, yet not the same at all.

"Yes, I will head to town after breakfast to buy more. I have discovered I don't own enough chokers." I spoke as the maids began to head towards a cart of food the chef had just brought in.

"Not enough?" My father finally spoke. He observed me, slowly placing down this morning's reports.

"Yes, not enough. I require more," I said, knowing his disapproval. He had never been happy with my spending.

I often bought many things in my first life I didn't need. I know now that I did it to try to make myself feel like I was one of them, as though I had received gifts from my family.

Instead, I only ever saw them bestow gifts amongst themselves. I had never received anything from them.

This made it difficult to hold back my pain when our brothers showered Kara showered in gifts, whilst they ignored me.

So, to numb my feelings, I took it upon myself to buy extravagant things with the money Roger gave me. Resultingly growing exceedingly upset if he disallowed me funds.

On this occasion, though, I truly needed some more chokers, and acting like my once-spoilt self wasn't a bad way to get them. That was the Lynette my family was currently familiar with, after all.

"I will grant enough for only five," Roger said, turning his attention to Kara, deciding that that conversation with me today was enough.

"Kara, honey, how did your embroidery of the handkerchiefs go?" He smiled at her, something I had never experienced.

Kara's pink dress stood out against the blue-painted walls as she eagerly picked up her fork and began to tuck into a plate of freshly cooked poached eggs and toast.

"Oh, Father, I'm almost done! And in time for Eduard and Callan's return. They should be finished by this afternoon."

"That's wonderful. I've made sure to prepare a welcoming meal for them. You can present it to them then." Roger placed down his newspaper as the maids gave him his plate of bacon, eggs, and toast.

I couldn't help the stiffening of my hands at the mention of my brothers. Was today when they returned home? So . . . it must be the day of the parade.

"Here, my lady." Freda quietly approached me to put down my meal. It was scrambled eggs, just that alone, no bread, nothing else.

I felt my eye twinge; they always gave me measly portions, but this was a child's portion. It was no wonder my body was malnourished. At least Garret had fed me well.

"Do you think they will like my new dress?" Kara asked, proud of the pink frills puffing from her oversized skirt.

"You look stunning, sweetie. They will both love it," Roger said, merrily complimenting her. It was always like this when I was summoned to eat at the table. They spoke happily together, ignoring me. The kitchen staff would give me pitiful meals, and eventually, at the end of it, when I left, the tension would leave the room.

Kara was always nice to me. She had been the same—sweet, innocent, and utterly oblivious to my suffering—in all my three lives.

Poking my fork into my eggs, I found numerous bits of shell left, for an extra touch of inedible torture. It was well hidden from the eyes of others.

"Really?" Kara exclaimed. "It was so difficult to decide. It was either this one or the one you bought m—"

"I'll be heading out now." I interrupted her, standing up. "With your permission, my lord." I was going to leave regardless.

"You've not finished your breakfast?" Roger questioned my full plate.

"It wasn't to my taste." I smiled at the maids, and they froze. "It had too much seasoning in it."

"Too much seasoning?" Roger furrowed his brows but did not attempt to look at my plate.

"It's nothing you should worry about." I smiled innocently. He had had plenty of time to notice the numerous meals I never ate. There was no point in mentioning it to him. I had already tried that before, and he hadn't believed me. Or, as I was beginning to suspect, he did not really care. He never had.

"Freda?" I called.

"Yes, my lady." Freda nervously approached me, her eyes darting to Roger and back to me.

"Fetch my satchel, will you, and the money the viscount has granted me for shopping." I pushed the plate into her fumbling hands. "Deal with this as well." I waved a hand, stepping out of the room before my father could respond.

CHAPTER THREE

reda quickly brought my brown leather satchel as I waited at the double front doors. Henley was waiting with me. He had already summoned a young boy from the stable to fetch me a carriage.

"Which shop will you be visiting today?" Henley asked as Freda handed me the satchel.

"As it's the festival, I may browse some of the stalls," I answered, tucking the strap over my shoulder.

"That is not allowed. You do not have permission to roam the streets," Henley narrowed his eyes at me.

"I don't have permission?" This wasn't the first time I had been given restrictions, but I didn't know what reason had prompted this today.

"After you caused a scene last year, you were banned from exploring any festivals on your own," Henley informed me, causing me to sigh.

Of course, my actions in my first life.

I was jealous of the attention Kara received from my aloof brothers and had threatened to have an entire street of stalls removed for selling "ugly" things. I think I had even pointed a lit piece of wood at a stall as part of that threat.

Eduard saw it as a stain on the family's pride and had me housebound for a month. I missed everything, including the fireworks. It was probably a fair punishment for my actions.

"Fine. I'll just go to Hanson's shop," I mumbled, resisting the urge to roll my eyes. I really did earn my nickname: the Crazy Cerue Lady. "I shall likely return in the afternoon," I said, pushing the doors open to find the carriage being pulled up—perfect timing.

"Likely?" Henley countered.

"Yes, likely. I'll be sure to come back before Eduard and Callan arrive."

"Very well, I shall inform the viscount." Henley bowed his head slightly towards me in forced etiquette. "I hope you have a pleasant outing, Miss Lynette," he said, seemingly reluctant.

Jeez, does he ever smile?

"As do I," I said before heading out. It wasn't hard to miss how he never called me *my lady*.

The young boy that Henley had sent to fetch the carriage sat in the driver's seat, having driven it around. It was a rickety thing, small and shabby. A single kreshna demonic beast was saddled to pull it.

A servant's carriage.

I hadn't ridden in one of these since my marriage to the Garret Asher.

The large creature pulling the carriage huffed as it neared me. Its shoulders were wide, its skin a tough flaky brown. Two curved horns protruded behind its floppy ears, much like a ram beast, as it shook its head to rid itself of the flies attracted to its eyes in the heat of the summer.

It was heavier than most farming beasts and often startled but easy enough to breed domestically. After all, it was a subservient demonic beast used to pull carriages in the Zopan Empire. Only nobles could afford to use horse-drawn carriages. It was one of the few animals that didn't possess aether.

"S-sorry, miss," the young boy said, a little embarrassed. "The stables told me to use this carriage for—for the miss."

"It's fine, don't worry," I said, to set him at ease. But of course, only my father, Kara, or my brothers would use the horses. As a non-blood-related commoner, I didn't qualify despite being adopted by Cassandra as a child. That was the way Father wanted it. I was not worthy enough.

Freda didn't say anything on the matter. She only tried to look away, embarrassed after this morning. She often tried to avoid the dining room. I suspect she knew what the chefs did to my food, but as my personal maid, she held no power to protest against the head chef. I was thankful she sometimes brought me sandwiches without being asked.

"Er, where do you want to go today?" the young boy asked, getting down from the driver's seat to open the carriage doors for me. Then, like a mini gentleman, he held out his hand for me to use, which made me genuinely smile. He was a nice kid.

"The temple." I took his hand, stepping up into the carriage. Unfortunately, the seats weren't cushioned, and the floor was mucky. I sighed, knowing my butt was going to suffer today.

"The temple?" Freda finally made a sound. "My lady, you told Henley you were going to Hanson's shop." she said, following me into the carriage. A lady can't ever travel without her personal maid, after all.

"We will. We are just going to the temple first," I said, settling into the hard seat. Freda settled opposite me.

"But my la—" she tried to protest.

"It's not a lie, Freda, only omitted truth." I shrugged. "The temple, please," I repeated, nodding to the young boy.

"Right, the temple, of course, miss." The young boy was very chipper.

"I'm in your care, young man," I said with a smile.

"Ah, I—it is Miguel Kesat, young miss." He blushed before closing the door and returning to the driver's seat, leaving me alone with Freda.

The carriage began to move, the sound of gravel crunching under the kreshna's heavy feet. The journey to the temple would probably be delayed if Talbour had crowds today, so I had some time to myself—if I ignored Freda.

The tension in my body began to ease as I saw the manor moving farther and farther away down the neatly pebbled path, around large crisp-cut gardens. Finally, we passed the large ornate gates that blocked the manor and its hidden luxury from the citizens of Talbour. The guards the viscount employed closed the gate behind us, their eyes watching warily as they saw me.

"My lady, if Mr Ruopold finds out . . ." Freda began tugging the brown cloak she wore tighter. If Henley found out that she didn't stop me, he would chastise her.

"He won't find out because we won't tell him," I stated bluntly.

"But—but the boy . . ." Freda hesitated.

"Don't worry. He won't say anything if we ask him not to. He's probably just as aware of how much trouble he would be in for taking us to the temple once he finds out I didn't have permission." I grinned at her, which startled her.

"O-of course, my lady." Freda was visibly uncomfortable with the idea.

"Relax, Freda. If anything happens, I'll take the blame." I finally relented.

"T-take the blame, miss?" Freda seemed genuinely surprised.

"Yes, I don't want to deal with a new personal maid anytime soon," I remarked, which reddened her cheeks. Was she embarrassed again?

"Thank you, my lady," she said after a bit of silence. Was she contemplating that?

"It's nothing I can't handle anyway." I shrugged. It wouldn't be the first time I had taken the blame for something. However, this situation was by my demand, not Freda's. "If you don't mind, could we sit in silence for a while? I need to think."

"Yes, my lady." Freda seemed happy with that idea as well. She probably disliked spending time with me as much as I did being babysat by a servant. I had been rather awful to her in the past. She had once asked to clean my room, but my past relationship with my maids had soured any trust in the manor staff. I had thrown a glass at her, convinced that her request was another scheme to make my life miserable.

Maybe I had been too paranoid.

Quietly I looked through the window, watching the buildings of Talbour City pass by. It was strange to see the city after so many years. Cassandra Heversham had first brought me here from Wayward Town when I was seven. She was a kind woman who had taken pity on me when she found me. A rare kindness I haven't experienced much of in my three lifetimes.

I miss her, a lot.

Every regression had always been after she had already passed away. Every life, I had to re-endure the home of the Hevershams without her. She had been the only member of the family who wanted me there. Of course, Kara was just as kind, but she was so sheltered she never really saw how I was suffering.

Cassandra would have seen it and wouldn't have stood for it, but her death was untimely.

I was left behind as unwanted baggage.

Roger Heversham hadn't been pleased when Cassandra returned home from her trip to visit her family in Wayward with me at her heels, but he couldn't say no to his wife. Roger loved her dearly, as did Eduard, Callan, and Kara. It was only at Cassandra's insistence that my name was added to the family register.

The carriage bumped a little as it moved onto the cobbled streets of Talbour from the smooth road of the nobles' plateau. The mansion estates lining the road thinned, their towering gates and walls replaced by unconcealed smaller homes, conjoined against one another in neat rows. Commoners briskly carried out their daily morning chores, hanging washing from windows and sweeping dirt from doorways. White spires towered in the distance above their homes.

I still remembered the day we got the news of Cassandra Heversham's passing. We received it a week after the event, which devastated us all. I was only thirteen. That seemed like half a century ago now. Nevertheless, it was still a vivid memory when Talbour guards stopped at our door. They told us of the tragic accident that occurred when she was travelling through Ridge Pass on her annual trip to Wayward.

Nemions had attacked her carriage, dangerous prowling feline demonic beasts with midnight fur and talons sharper than knives. They were not native to Ridge Pass. They had managed to travel there from the deadlands.

It was a simple case of being in the wrong place at the wrong time.

Every time I returned after my death, there was always a part of me hoping to have come back before the accident, so I could prevent it somehow, but that was never the case.

I died at age thirty-three in my first life. My second life ended when I was twenty-eight, and in my third life, I was thirty-two.

It was becoming exhausting.

I had already resigned myself to death in my first life. I had accepted it, in fact. Yet, despite that, I returned and returned again.

Why?

Why send me back?

Suddenly the carriage bumped, causing me to grab the seat for security.

"S-sorry, miss! The kreshna was startled by the crowd," Miguel shouted to me, his voice barely audible over the increased sound of the town centre. Pulling the drab curtain aside, I saw the streets littered with people as they bartered their items for sale. Buskers playing their instruments, stalls competing for the best food, and crowds happily chatting. It was a busy summer's day, and the festival was in full swing. Far different from the quiet I had grown used to locked away in Lord Garret's manor all those years.

Our marriage hadn't been pleasant. He had always worried about my appearance in society, fussing over the bruises his beatings would leave on my skin. So I became a bird in a cage, never stepping outside those walls except for special occasions, such as a visiting guest or a ball that we could not refuse to attend.

I had to learn from secondhand gossip from the maids about what was happening in the empire. I even employed someone to spy on my family and report to me anything worth knowing. All just so I could feel some connection outside that ugly home.

At first, I argued with Garret. I fought back and attempted to defend myself. Gradually, I knew I was tumbling further into a hole within myself. A mortal couldn't defend against an aether user.

Then, one day, I locked my heart away.

Nothing bothered me anymore; indifference was my best friend and only defence against his cruelty. When Garret learned of my illness, he strangely left me alone. It was brief relief for a year or so before the Draygon boys were murdered.

I should have thought about it more.

Maybe I would have picked up on Garret's unusual behaviour around me. But never had I expected the royal guard to barge into the mansion to arrest me as a murderer.

Garret was a fool.

He was not capable of murdering someone. Especially two children distantly related to royalty. He was too cowardly for that. He had definitely been used by someone else who did. I had been a barter in their sick conspiracy. No doubt Garret would have been killed next to keep their secret.

"We're here, miss." The carriage had pulled to a stop at the front of a large building that dwarfed the houses beside it. The temple's steeple could be described as touching the sky; built from rare white stone, it sometimes looked like a sharp cloud from a distance.

Stone steps led up to a courtyard where a fountain with a crossing water feature attracted young children to throw copper coins in exchange for wishes.

Behind the fountain, an archway into the temple, nearly four men tall, beckoned its followers into its embrace.

I had heard that all temples were built with the same structure. Only the capital's temple was on a grander scale.

Miguel opened the carriage door, offering me his hand again, which I took gratefully. As I stepped out, a few people looked at us curiously but didn't remain long when they saw my clothing. The dress I wore wasn't something a noble would wear. The deep green, tightly buttoned bodice was far too simple for someone worth watching. It was definitely less flashy than my usual attire. I always used to wear clothes adorned with jewels in my first and second lives.

"Thank you, Mr Kesat. I will be heading into the temple for a while. I can't say how long I may be. Where shall I find you?" I asked, brushing some of the dust from my skirt. The carriage had been rather dirty.

"I-if it's okay, miss, after I move the carriage, I thought I might go get some street food whilst I wait?" He nervously scratched his small hand.

"Of course, that's fine. I shall meet you at the square, then?" My agreement surprised him. I doubted the viscount would have allowed any of the servants at the manor to do as they wished.

"My lady, Mr Kesat should wait for our return. We can't walk the streets to the square," Freda said, reprimanding me, twitching a bit as she looked around at the crowd around the temple.

"We?" I raised my eyebrows at her. "Freda, I shall be going to the temple alone. You're free to join Miguel at the festival."

"My lady!" she exclaimed. "I cannot leave you alone. That is not . . . is not how it's done." She tried to argue her point, afraid for her own safety if she was discovered to have left me alone.

"Freda, it may not be how it is done, but it's how this is going to happen." I shook my head. "Like it or not, you're not coming with me." This was something I had to do on my own. "I doubt you have time off to go to the festival, so just use now to enjoy it whilst you can. I promise I won't be reckless." I added the last part as a compromise.

I could see the cogs working in her brain as she considered my words. Then, after a moment, she solemnly nodded and stepped back into the carriage.

"That's a plan, then, miss!" Miguel exclaimed with delight, returning to the driver's seat. "I hope your prayers are answered, miss," He smiled at me with a boyish charm before waving goodbye.

It wasn't so much my prayers, but questions I hoped would be answered today.

Picking up the hem of my dress, I began my climb of the stone steps towards the fountain. It was weird to feel this much energy in my body again. Before, my body had become beaten and tender from Garret's mistreatment. Climbing up steps like this, I likely would have required help halfway, but now it was a breeze. Even with my malnourished body, I no longer ached with movement.

Nearing the arch, I spotted several children throwing coins into the fountain. They happily ran around playing games. A few elderly folks beckoned them over to talk about the fables of the gods.

Two monks stood at the entrance to the arch, dressed in long white cloaks; they greeted each follower with warmth and guidance. I thanked them as they asked if I wanted directions, but I knew whom I wished to seek today. The maids in Garret's mansion had taught me much about the gods in my previous life.

As I stepped into the archway, the sunlight dissipated, replaced by mage lamps on the domineering white stone walls of the dome's entrance. The dim glow they produced created a myriad of shadows against the walls as people passed them.

Pretty, it's like stars against clouds.

Eventually, the domelike cave opened up to the hall of the gods, their statues arranged in a circle as they enveloped the people equally. Monks were lighting mage lamps. Their fingers snapped towards each lamp before they bowed in prayer, facing the statue of their god or goddess. They would have been members of the army once. Without strong enough cores to remain and become summoners, many aether users joined the temple. Most were commoners who were gifted with small cores, wanting to be of use in some way with their talents. On rare occasion, nobles who did not wish to fight demonic beasts would give up their claim to their heritage and join a temple, though they usually became templars, protectors of the bishops.

Many men were scattered in the hall today. They were dressed formally and quietly, making their prayers to the gods. Most of them had gathered near Ragnor, the god of strength and war. Maybe they were hoping to become foot soldiers.

A few others, dressed in noble attire, stood before Trinsa, the goddess of spirit and knowledge, who was commonly followed by those who wished to wield aether. She gifted us our cores at birth and guided us in the use of aether, or so they say. I only knew what the maids had taught me in my third life.

A pair of elderly women bowed deeply at the feet of Herishma, the goddess of fertility and health.

A lone monk prayed to Urish, the god of justice and exchange.

Only two gods were alone without prayers being made to them: Yune, the god of creation and death, and the goddess Vishka. Both were deemed not as important as the rest, as they affected only the beginning and the end of our lives. People prayed to Yune at funerals, mostly discounted by many as the god of creation. He created all that we know, but that also included demonic beasts—the very creatures that caused so much death.

Vishka was who I had come to see.

Yune and Trinsa were fabled to be the parents of Vishka, so the three held unique ties. When I was married to Garret, I had a lot of time to consider my situation with the information the maids had told me. If the gods were real, it would be only Vishka who could have sent me back at the moment of my death.

She was the goddess of rebirth and time. Her role was to take care of our souls when we die.

Looking around, I saw a table of unlit wax candles that people were collecting to light at their god's feet.

The maids had said that gods communicate through the candles we light during prayer. I had always believed that to be myth and more a tradition than truth. I definitely couldn't see any movements in the flames of the lit candles scattered around.

"Excuse me." I approached a monk standing nearby at the edge of the room. His white hood dropped below his eyes, so I couldn't see his face properly in the mage light.

"Yes, child of aether?" He smiled, opening his arms in greeting.

"I would like a private prayer with Vishka." I fumbled my words, unsure if I should have replied with something about aether. I had never been much of a worshipper.

"This way, child," he said, gesturing to the right, towards a set of doors built into the circular walls of the dome. I followed him as he took me to the third door behind Vishka's statue and opened it for me.

"Uh, thanks." I awkwardly bowed my head to him before stepping inside. I guessed there was no queue for Vishka.

"Knock twice when your prayers have been completed." His lips twitched before he closed the door behind me, and suddenly the room was engulfed in darkness.

"Crap," I sputtered, trying to find a light source. Moving my hands along the stone walls, I gently tapped the floor with my feet to ensure I didn't step on anything. Eventually, I felt a tiny lump in the wall that stuck out unevenly. Grabbing it, I flicked it up, igniting a collection of mage lamps at the very end of the small rectangular room. An aether tool for mortals. It wasn't often that aether tools were in Talbour. I guessed the temple got special privileges. Normally, only aether users could recharge mage lamps.

A smaller version of the statue in the main hall stood in the centre of the room. Burnt-out candles littered the base of her feet; only a few remained lit, nearing the end of their wicks. "Vishka," I said hesitantly, taking a step forward.

Her eyes were covered in bandages, her hands close to her chest but cupped together, pointing up to symbolise her catching souls for rebirth. It was a beautiful if not an eerie statue.

I tried not to feel uncomfortable in the small room alone with it, but it was hard not to.

Picking up one of the unlit wax candles on the floor at her feet, I held it against the flame of another, igniting the wick before placing it back down in front of me.

"Oh, great gods," I began, a little uneasy. Was this a silly idea?

"I regret to say, this is my first time visiting." I had never been much of a religious person before.

"I have many questions I fear will remain unanswered." I sighed, looking up at Vishka, solemn and quiet as a statue always is.

"If you are real, I'm sure you know my plight. This is the fourth time I find myself twenty-one again. Did you have a hand in this?" I asked earnestly.

"If you hear me, if at all possible, please answer," I said again, feeling a little stupid at the silence.

The flame of my candle began to dim. It was odd as there was no wind in the temple. It was built with no windows to prevent wind.

All of a sudden, the flame grew. I held my breath as it changed to a hue of blue.

The gods, they were answering! The candles hadn't been a myth! Did this mean they were real?

Perhaps this would have been more surprising if I hadn't returned from the dead. I guessed I was more composed towards the impossible now. Before, I would never have thought that the gods could interact with people, or were even real, for that matter. Now? I guessed anything was possible.

"Is there a reason you granted me this chance?" I asked, my eyes glued to the candle. It returned to the dim flame it had started with, then flickered blue again. I scrunched my face, confused.

What did that mean?

"D-does a large flame mean yes?" I asked, and the flame bellowed again, heat licking my skin. I needed to confirm before asking more questions.

"So large, yes, small, no?" The flame bellowed, answering my confusion. That limited me to yes and no questions. I pinched my lips. I would not be able to find out why I had been brought back with such questions. I had no idea about why I had regressed, so I did not know what I should ask to understand why. However, I could confirm how, maybe.

"Were you the one who sent me back?" The candle remained dim again, making me frown, but then it grew a little bit before falling. So did that mean Vishka had a hand in it?

"Were you involved in sending me back?" I altered my question, and the flame grew large this time, a definite yes.

"Was my bracelet a part of that?" I asked, and the flame glowed blue, confirming my suspicions. The bracelet surely must have been a conduit of some sort for my rebirth. Why else would the stones vanish?

"Now that the gems have gone, is this my last life?" I asked, my heart stopping for a moment. The flame grew large, a bright blue, a yes. The fear creeping into me made my hands shake.

I couldn't screw this life up, then. This cycle wasn't going to continue.

Slowly I dropped to my knees at the feet of Vishka as the realisation of the truth began to set in.

"Is this chamber soundproof?" I whispered, and the flame flickered blue in answer.

The lump I had been holding in my throat all this time rose as I released the knot in my heart and tears began streaming down my cheeks.

It was never easy when I regressed, but I had grown numb to it now.

Trapped in a marriage of abuse for years, stuck alone in a mansion with no one but a man I hated. Sold to that life by a father I thought I could somewhat trust. Then used in a conspiracy and framed for the murder of two young boys I had no interaction with. Finally sent for execution at the hand of the general whose very nephews I had supposedly killed. It was only one of the endings I had experienced in my three lifetimes.

I sat there for some time, crying, as the pain of what had happened to me took hold.

For so long, I had shut myself off from feeling my emotions when married to Garret. It was the only way I mentally got through my days, but now?

What was I to do now? Relive that pain again, just in some different way? I had died every lifetime, each worse than the last. Was I doomed to die again in my last life?

"Vishka," I said, my voice shaky from crying. "Can I change my fate?" The statue loomed above me as I held my breath, looking at the flame. It flickered at first, then rose to a glorious blue.

My heart leapt in hope.

"So there is a way I can lead a different life than before?" More tears began to fall. "Will you show me the way?" I asked, my hands shaky, but the flame didn't move. There had to be a reason the gods had brought me back. They surely couldn't expect me to figure it out alone. I hadn't in three lifetimes already. Was my only purpose to suffer? I had to have faith that it wasn't; that would be too cruel.

My chest tightened as no response followed.

So they weren't going to help me. A sharp laugh left my lips, echoing in the silence of the room.

That would be too easy, too simple. Of course they wouldn't help; they hadn't so far, so why would they now?

It was up to me to change my fate.

Vishka couldn't help me with this. I was on my own to figure this out.

I sat alone with Vishka for some time before pulling myself back together. Wiping my cheeks with the back of my hand, I tried to lessen the appearance of my no-doubt red eyes. Then, as the monk instructed, I raised my hand to knock twice on the door to signal the end of my prayers.

Vishka has heard your prayers!
Welcome to your guidance system. For a short time, this system will help guide you in the path of fate.
Use it wisely!

I screamed, falling backwards onto the cold stone floor at the box appearing before me.

CHAPTER FOUR

W hat the hell is that?" I shouted in shock at the box before my eyes. I waved my hand in front of it, but the box had no physical substance. It just floated there. Could other people see it? There was no one else with me to check. Suddenly the words began to change.

Vishka's Guidance System

Hi there, beloved child. It is me, Vishka. I cannot answer why you were reborn. My guidance will provide assistance. Look out for your likeability meters. If they drop below −50%, you risk death!

Keep vigilant, my child.

I stared at the message for some time. I was sure if anyone walked into the prayer chamber, they would see my mouth agape.

Likeability meters? What even did that mean?

I held my hand to my chest to try to calm my breathing.

Was I hyperventilating?

Suddenly a loud creak echoed as the door opened, causing me to squint at the brightness of light after being in the dimly lit room for so long.

"May the gods' grace hear your prayers, child of aether," the monk said in greeting, bowing his head before pausing at my pose on the floor. "May I help you up?" he asked curiously.

"Y-yes, please," I said, checking to see if he looked at the box still floating there. He didn't, not even as I took his hand to pull myself up. So other people couldn't see it.

"Are you all right?" the monk asked, checking me over as I brushed the dust from the back of my dress. That fall really did a number on my rear. It was definitely going to be sore tomorrow.

"I'm all right, thank you. I believe my prayers have been heard." I half smiled, averting my gaze, aware it was apparent I had been crying.

"Of course," he said, kindly not asking me about my red eyes.

The monk guided me back through the temple towards the dome entrance. A few more people had been gathering in prayer since this morning. I spotted a few more nobles mingled amongst the many commoners as they offered flowers and gifts to their chosen gods. They glanced my way in recognition but didn't approach. Who would approach the Crazy Cerue Lady?

Perhaps it was so busy today because of the army parade festival, or was this the usual crowd for a temple? I wouldn't know.

"May we have the honour of your visit again." The monk nodded as we reached the spot where I had approached him before. He gestured towards the dome tunnel I had come in from, assuming I had finished my visit. "Your patronage is valuable to us." He bowed to me before leaving to assist someone else.

At the side of the entrance was a table with a large embellished wooden bowl and a couple of monks standing nearby. Inside, I spotted numerous gold, silver, and copper coins.

"Many thanks for your help." I tugged open my satchel and pulled out two silver coins to drop in the bowl on my way out of the temple. The two monks thanked me for the donation as I left the archway and went back outside.

I couldn't help but look up at the sky, free of clouds in the summer's heat.

The box had faded when I left the prayer room, so it either didn't stay long or only worked in the temples. I guessed I would find out . . .

Vishka! She heard me! I didn't understand what guidance she had given me, but it was the help I had requested. I would have been less accepting of what had just happened if not for the fact that I had already died three times.

She had said she couldn't tell me why I had been cursed to relive my lives. However, that did not mean there wasn't one. There must be a reason.

Maybe I needed to find that out myself.

There had to be a reason for my suffering.

Either way, I was free to choose my own path now. I just had to find it.

I took my time climbing down the steps, strolling by the people of Talbour as they laughed with one another, enjoying the festivities. Some people waved small flags on sticks with the emblem of the Zopan Empire, others ate street food out of napkins, and children ran with kites gently moving with the breeze.

It had been years since I had been alone to enjoy the sights of the city like this, and I felt a little spring in my step today after Vishka's gift, whatever it meant. There was hope I wouldn't suffer in this life, and that was all that mattered.

Following the crowd, I happily watched the families celebrating the annual festival. Every year the capital sent its army to the deadlands to cull the demonic beasts from encroaching on the Zopan Empire. It was a dangerous job, but not doing it resulted in casualties, like my adoptive mother, Cassandra.

On their return, the army always passed through Talbour. It was a slight detour, but it allowed the capital to interact with its people and the army to pass messages and pick up supplies. So the people of Talbour decided to make it into a yearly festival to celebrate the soldiers' safe return.

Noticing a wooden sign with a jeweller's pick and chisel, I detoured from the crowd to a shop I knew reasonably well: Hanson's Jewellery. The shop window had many fancy designs today. Some were even themed for the festival, their jewels in the colour setting of the Zopan Empire, black and yellow. They shone particularly well in the summer sun.

I had said I wanted to stop by for some more chokers. So, true to my word, I opened the shop door, and the jingle of a bell alerted the shopkeeper to my presence. But, of course, he had plenty of customers already, so he barely noticed me.

In my first life, I would have complained about the lack of service. I likely would have shouted and demanded something free of charge. I really had been a spoilt brat. My adoptive family's lack of care for my life as they abandoned my existence in the quiet corner of the mansion had truly festered my emotions. I knew now, after my marriage to Garret, there were worse people in life. In some situations, being ignored was preferred to unwanted attention from people I hated.

Happy to browse, I sauntered towards the leather and ribbon goods. They were usually the only items commoners bought. However, I didn't think a jewelled necklace would hide my scar. I needed a thick band, comfortable to wear and sturdy. I couldn't have it falling off in a tumble.

Picking through the pile of ribbons, I eventually found what I was looking for, a solid brown leather piece with lace ties on the back, similar to those on a bodice. It could have been more pretty, but it was durable. I also picked out some coloured ribbons with sewn-in clasps for fancier occasions. Hauling my pile to the counter, I waited for the shopkeeper to be free before bargaining him down to only three silver for the five chokers. It was far less than the initial five gold Roger had given me. I supposed he expected me to buy the most lavish items in the shop. That was what I usually did in my first life. I often filled the empty void of my heart with the luxurious items I could buy.

Exiting the shop, I rejoined the crowd. Most of them were heading to the side streets filled with numerous stalls. The smell of the food drifting towards me made my stomach growl; I hadn't technically eaten yet with that disaster of a breakfast, but I'd promised I wouldn't go to the stalls alone. I should keep that promise. Knowing my luck, I'd probably only get caught.

Vishka's Guidance System
Smart! Stay away from the stalls for now.

I held my hand to my mouth to hold in my scream. Was this thing just going to keep popping up out of nowhere? But, as before, it dissipated after a few moments, and no one was wiser. So it was definitely only me who could see it. Otherwise, I was pretty sure many people in the crowd would have said something.

Sticking with my decision and the guidance of Vishka, I avoided the stalls and followed the crowd heading towards the main square.

Eventually, I came to the square, where I agreed to meet Miguel and Freda. The festival was centred here, and the bustling noise of people overwhelmed my senses.

Barricades had been set up, creating a path for the army to walk through when they arrived. Many people were already gathering at the edges of the barricades, saving their friends the best spots to get a good view.

Looking around, I soon spotted a line of carriages above the heads of the crowd in the distance to my left. Gripping my satchel tighter to my chest, I began to push my way through towards them. I apologised every now and then to anyone I bumped. A bitter smile tugged my face; I would never have apologised in my first life. I would have announced my presence and demanded that people move out of my way as a noble.

When I finally made it to the carriages, I saw a mix of them, from kreshna-pulled run-down carriages to the fanciest horse-drawn carriages glittering with gold. Their adult drivers chatted together in a circle laughing, some even smoking cigars.

"Miss Lynette!" I heard a voice call out to me on my right. "Miss Lynette! Over here!" Miguel jumped and waved frantically, standing on our carriage nestled between a few others at the back.

I smiled, grateful that he had spotted me. I wasn't sure I would have found him.

He should work on his etiquette, calling me miss instead of my lady would have gotten him scolded by Henley, if that man even cared.

"There you are." I relaxed, approaching the carriage and loosening my grip on my satchel.

"Did you have a good time at the temple?" Miguel asked, climbing down from the driver's seat.

"I did, thank you. Did you have a good time at the festival?"

"Yes!" he exclaimed. "I got to eat a crepe with strawberries and cream. Then I found some hard candy, and then I had some cheese with cranberries! There's so much I still haven't tried," he said, beaming.

"Did you eat all of that? Are you not full?" I laughed.

"I wish. I also saw some fantastic acrobatics. The performers flew in the sky and landed perfectly. I had no idea how they did it!" Miguel giggled. Clearly, he had had a good time enjoying the festival. I was a little jealous.

"And where is Miss Parsons?" I asked, looking around.

"Ah, she's been waiting inside the carriage, young miss." Miguel shrugged. "She ate some of the crepes with me and watched the acrobatics but didn't stay for too long."

"I see," I mused. Freda must have been somewhat nervous about getting caught leaving me alone.

I tapped on the carriage door, and she pushed it open gingerly. Then, seeing my raven hair, she quickly moved it open, a sigh of relief clear as day on her face.

"My lady, thank goodness you are back!" Freda exclaimed, deflating the stress she must have been holding.

"Quickly, get in. We should be heading back. It's already past the second bell," she said, trying to usher me inside.

A blast of horns sounded from a short distance away. We both turned our heads towards it, as did most of the crowd, with a cheer of excitement.

"They're here! The army is here, miss! But, ah—" Miguel paused. "I suppose you will want to be heading back now." His voice didn't hide his disappointment.

"Yes," I said, seeing his face fall. "But maybe we can watch the parade first." I stepped back down, to Freda's frustration.

"Really?" His smile widened to his ears.

"Well, it's hardly a time to leave now, is it?" I smiled, climbing onto the driver's seat.

"My lady! Where are you going?" Freda exclaimed, clamouring out of the carriage after me.

"It's better to see from higher up, don't you agree?" I tucked my dress under my knees before sitting and placing my satchel on my lap.

"Very true! I guess I just didn't expect the miss to sit here. It's not something a noble would do," Miguel said.

"That's correct, my lady, it's not proper," Freda complained.

"I'm not a true noble, so it's fine." I shrugged as the horns grew louder, the army approaching.

"Ah!" Miguel covered his mouth with his hand, realising his mistake. "I'm s-sorry, miss, I—I—" he stammered as Freda's face paled.

"It's fine, Mr Kesat. I'm not a true Heversham." I said, trying to settle him. The prospect of not being a part of this family had long since become a reality for me.

In my first life, it was a constant emotional struggle trying to be accepted by them, and I found time and time again that I could only screw it up. In my second life, I threw myself into parties, avoiding them and trying to live outside the manor as a socialite, only to be scorned by them. In my third life, I did what they asked of me to help the family and suffered for the longest time under Garret's beatings.

This life, I was through with caring about them.

"I see." Miguel lowered his head, twiddling his fingers.

"My lady . . ." Freda was lost for words.

"It's fine, jeez, let's just enjoy the parade, okay? And keep it our secret." I held up my hand, zipping my lips and throwing away an imaginary key.

Miguel half smiled, deciding to join me in the driver's seat, and Freda looked away from me before struggling to get up and join us. Then, after a little scooting down, we all sat at the front of the carriage, raised above the crowds, waiting for the army to arrive.

A small bump on my side made me look to Freda; she looked away from me, holding a square wrapping of paper. She lightly brought her fist to her lips and coughed.

I smiled at her hesitation as I took the parcel from her; the smell of a lukewarm crepe filled with strawberries made my stomach growl as I opened it.

"Can I ask you a question?" Miguel mumbled as I took a bite of the crepe.

"Sure," I sighed.

"Um, h-how did you come to be a Heversham? No one tells me much." He looked away so I couldn't see the embarrassment on his face, which made me smile.

Freda immediately coughed loudly into her hand, staring daggers at Miguel. It shouldn't be such a taboo subject, but I understood his curiosity. Rarely were commoners adopted by nobility. It was likely a dream many had, to become nobility.

"Cassandra Heversham picked me up as a child. It's not something you say no to when you live on the street begging for food to survive." I rested my head in my hand as drums started to play, announcing the army getting closer. The strawberries in the crepe were delightfully sweet.

Freda turned away again, unable to look me in the eye.

"I understand." Miguel turned back to me, thoughtful. "I would probably do the same," he confirmed, swinging his legs over the side of the carriage. Sweet kid.

The crowd's cheers exploded as music bellowed into the square. The sound of armour clanging in unison with the beat of drums caught Miguel's attention. He stood up to get a better look as the soldiers of the Zopan army came into view.

The first squad marched dressed in grey linen tunics with the Zopan emblem at their centre of their capes. They beat against drums, and some blew into trumpets as they led the march. Those who stood at the edges held large flags of the black and yellow Zopan emblem, featuring two dragons connecting their claws. The flags towered three men tall.

Next were the generals, their horses adorned in gold plating.

Three of them sat waving to the crowd, all relatively older gentlemen. The man in the middle wore a dark red hooded cloak with golden gauntlets and leg bands. Upon his shoulder sat a bird, its wings tucked, its black beak sharp against the flames of its fiery feathers, his summoned beast. He must be the general of the summoners, Jared Baler. He was well known to the people as the hero of Ridge Pass. Alone, he had saved the lives of fifty soldiers trapped under the rocks of a landslide whilst defending against mountain golem demonic beasts.

"Look, a summoner!" Miguel pointed at him, his eyes growing larger. "Someday, I want to be a summoner."

"A summoner? You want to join the army?" I asked as the next squad came into view.

It was the summoner squad.

They mirrored Jared's clothing, all wearing dark red hooded cloaks with the exception of black brigand armour on their chests instead of gold. The small metal studs glinted in the sunlight.

They all marched in unison, each with creatures seated upon their shoulders, held in their hands, or walking beside them. The creatures ranged from as small as mice to the size of large dogs as their forms flickered in flames. Behind them followed a group wearing grey cloaks hemmed with red thread. Future fire aether summoners. I had to admit that it was fascinating to watch.

"Of course, in the army, I could fight those nasty Dramoria invaders, win victories, and earn glory." Miguel punched the air to show his mightiness. I couldn't help my slight flinch as he mentioned Dramoria invaders. He must not have known that my features were Dramorian.

Freda caught on to it, though, and she hastily glared at Miguel, but he looked back at her, confused.

"What if you are not able to summon?" I watched him shrug Freda off and proceed to fight an imaginary enemy.

It was only possible to become a summoner with a core, but not everyone with a core could become a summoner. I didn't know the full details. However, I did know you were either born with a core or you weren't. Commoners rarely had them, and those who did weren't powerful enough to become summoners. They joined the temples as monks.

"Then I'll join the foot guard. They are just as strong." Miguel sat back down, tired out. "Have you ever tested if you could summon?" he asked in child-like wonder.

"No, I haven't, but the likelihood that I can is slim." I watched as the first summoning squad moved past us and the next squad arrived.

Each squad seemed to have the same elemental summons. The second was earth creatures, their forms made of soil and rocks. The soldiers wore brown tunics instead of red beneath their black brigand armour. Their brown cloaks flourished behind them. Some had gold embellished thread at the seams. Again, they were followed by a group wearing grey cloaks hemmed with dark brown thread.

"What do you mean?" Miguel asked.

"Do you see any women in those squads?" At my question, Miguel moved to inspect them.

"Not many . . ." He watched them as the third squad arrived, their creatures glittering in the sunlight as water shimmered on their bodies, their tunics and cloaks dazzling blue followed by those wearing grey cloaks with blue hemming I lifted my hand to hide my face as they passed, knowing my brothers would likely be in that squad.

"A woman becoming a summoner is very rare. Women of nobility run their households, not risk their lives to fight demonic beasts. It's also very rare that commoners can become summoners since they often do not have strong enough cores," I explained. "Nobles are born with strong cores because of their ancestors. Their bloodlines are controlled to produce children with strong cores."

"But you've never tried, so how do you know you can't become a summoner?" Miguel shrugged, unfazed by this information.

I opened my mouth to reply but found nothing to say. He had me there.

I couldn't say I knew for sure I couldn't become a summoner. It wasn't anything that had ever occurred to me to even try. Heck, I didn't even think I had a core until my third life, stuck with Garret. The likelihood was slim, though; I doubted I had a core strong enough.

The final squad passed by, their creatures a little harder to see as they billowed in the wind, their bodies ethereal as the wind they controlled. This squad wore pale green, which was striking against the black armour. Their squad was also followed by a group in grey cloaks but with green hemming.

"You make a good point." I half smiled as the next part of the parade arrived.

The crowd cheered louder as a man riding alone on a horse approached.

He led a marching squad dressed in lamellar armour and grey cloaks not covering their faces. The layered black scales looked heavy as the squad stood straight, proudly following their commander. Without the hooded cloaks the summoners wore, it was easier to see the mix of the races amongst the soldiers: human, beast-kin, and even the rare daemon. Some women could even be spotted in the foot guard as they followed the man wearing a silver mask with horns.

My body tensed as I watched him closely. Azriel Elkhart, the leader of the foot guard, was one of the few left from the Draygon race. They were the same as humans but bore white hair and unnatural purple eyes. They had the strength of two men and possessed the ability to use lightning aether. Azriel wore a purple cape that contrasted against the steel lamellar on his chest, his silver mask hiding his features. He didn't glance at the crowd once as they cheered for him.

The man who had killed me.

"Doesn't he look so intimidating," Miguel cooed. "I wonder why he wears that mask. It's all my friends talk about. We have theories. Maybe he burned his face with the lightning. Maybe he's just ugly." He giggled.

"Perhaps," I mumbled, struggling to look away from Azriel Elkhart, the young duke at this point in time. His father was the duke currently. My hand rubbed my neck instinctively. The man who controlled lightning, the rarest of elements. The royal family's power.

"I heard they are looking for sign-ups tomorrow," Miguel said as we watched the last of the foot guard pass by, followed by another squad playing instruments to signify the end of the march.

"They are recruiting?" I said, fairly certain they did so every year.

"Yeah, something about gathering strength for the Zopan Empire. There are lots of notices about it on the boards around town." Miguel pointed to one nearby, and sure enough, I could see a group of young men reading it with interest.

Freda glanced at them as well, a blush on her cheeks. I guess she was at that age.

"I would sign up if I was old enough." Miguel sighed in longing.

"One day, you will get your chance." I patted his shoulder, standing up so I could climb down from the driver's seat. Freda immediately followed.

"We should be heading back to the estate now," Freda said, ushering me to the doors of the carriage.

"Yes, I know, it won't be long before the young lords come back, and I should be there before they do." I sighed in defeat. I had put off going back long enough.

"Oh, right, of course! Let me open the door for you." Miguel scrambled after us, making sure to open the carriage door before we got to it.

"Thanks." I stepped onto the rickety carriage and back onto the grubby seat just as another message popped up.

Vishka's Guidance System
Quest Received!
Sign up for the army

CHAPTER FIVE

ign up for the army? Seriously? Me? But I could barely grip a sword! I
pulled on the sides of my hair as I paced back and forth in my room.

"Vishka, you can't be serious," I exclaimed for the sixth time without a
response. Finally, giving up, I flopped onto my bed face first. I had a few minutes
until the planned meal for my brothers' return.

Plenty of time to freak out.

What could I even do in the army? I was a weakling considered mortal. I
could barely control my core's singular mote of aether, let alone summoning
aether, which probably requires thousands.

I was underfed and my arms were frail, with no muscles for using a sword,
bow, or dagger. I was utterly useless at combat . . . perhaps I could be a designated
cleaner? Yeah, that I could do. It would be gross, no doubt, but something I was
capable of. I glanced around at my dark and dusty room for a moment.

"Arrgh." I huffed into my pillow, turning over onto my back. Who was I kidding? I had never done domestic chores; I would be useless at that too.

Maybe this was where I was going wrong in my previous lives. Was I too weak
to survive? Was this Vishka's way of saying I didn't belong as a regular citizen?

I released a long breath, staring up at the ceiling. I had planned on leaving
this house. But I wasn't sure what I would do when I did leave. Perhaps this was
it? The path I was meant to take?

A quiet knock on the door made me jump.

"Lynette?" a female voice called as the door opened. "Are you ready yet?"

"Kara . . ." I stared as my sister entered my room. Her hair was in ringlets, her figure dainty, and her eyes shaded with light pink makeup. She looked as she did when she was eighteen and was buzzing with excitement from the look on her face.

"What are you doing on the bed?" she asked, tutting, seeing my appearance. "What happened to your hair? Here, let me fix it." She motioned to my shabby desk.

I rolled off the bed with a moan, dragged my feet to the stool, and sat down obediently. I would do many things for Kara I wouldn't for others.

"It just kind of happened," I sighed, looking at the mess in the mirror. I had really stressed out about Vishka's quest.

"Oh yeah? Looks to me like you were upset about something." She smiled knowingly.

How did she read me so well, yet remain oblivious to my misery?

"I'm just nervous about seeing Eduard and Callan after so long." I lied but also didn't. I was nervous about seeing them again. My two older brothers, who hated me, were nothing for me to be excited about.

"What's there to be worried about?" Kara tipped some pins onto the desk and began to twist my hair up into a bun. Down was probably too messy now. The frizz wouldn't go away without washing it.

"You know they won't be happy to see me." I sighed as she began to prod the pins into place.

"Nonsense! They will be delighted to see you, Lynette. You are their sister just as much as I am," she sternly told me, fighting a stray strand of hair that kept escaping.

"All right, I won't argue." I bit back the frown on my lips. I wasn't their sister or Kara's by blood. As much as Kara thought of me as though I were, they definitely didn't.

"Good," she said triumphantly. "There, perfection." She made a gesture with her hand, kissing the tips of her fingers before pulling them away. It was definitely an impressive bun. She had even used the green ribbon I used as a choker earlier to tie around the bun. It did match my dress.

She glanced at my desk and her small nose wrinkled. "You should open your window more; it's getting dusty in here."

"Maybe," I said with a grim smile. I often did open my window for that reason; it was just such a dark room that everything looked worse than it was. There was a mage lamp installed on the wall, but Roger never visited to maintain it with his aether, so its light had vanished long ago; the dust would be more obvious if he did.

"Must you wear this?" She poked the leather choker I had swapped for the green ribbon. It had an engraved swirl pattern, so it wasn't downright dull.

"I must. It's my new fashion choice," I told Kara, full of fake confidence. It technically was, even if it was out of necessity.

"It just seems so . . . not you." She slumped, clearly not liking the lack of jewels. She was a spoilt child, after all. Much as I had been in my first life, though she had the love of her family.

"I like it, so I'm wearing it." I smiled, making her cave.

"Fine, but there's no way that's a trend." Kara accepted my choice, linking her arm through mine as I stood.

"Perhaps not yet," I said teasingly.

"Perhaps never." She rolled her eyes. "Is that what you bought today? Nothing else?" she said as she expertly led me from my room down the hallway of paintings.

"I bought a couple of ribbon ones, but this one was my favourite, alongside a black version of the same design."

"You didn't get them at the temple, then?" As she spoke, I froze on the spot, narrowing my eyes.

"How do you know I went to the temple?" I asked, already knowing it was Freda. She must have told her. Miguel wouldn't know who to tell. Not only my personal maid, Freda was also my personal spy—Kara's spy. That much I had learned in my second life. Kara was always worried about me when I left the manor; she liked to keep up to date with my life.

"I have my ways." Kara winked at me. "So tell me, were you praying for a lover to appear?" She wiggled her eyebrows.

"Kara," I deadpanned, continuing to walk forward.

"One day, someone is going to choose you, you know."

"I know, that's what worries me," I muttered as we left the hallway.

"Again worrying, you need to relax more," she said, scolding me playfully. "I won't tell Father or Eduard, so relax. It's not like you broke a statue of the gods whilst you were there," she joked before giving me a pointed look.

"No, I didn't cause any trouble." I smirked back at her, letting her lead me down the stairs and eventually towards the dreaded dining room.

As we entered, the first person we saw was Viscount Heversham. He looked up only at Kara as we entered, ignoring me altogether.

"Father!" Kara released me, running up to him to envelop him in a hug, causing him to chuckle.

"Kara dear, and here I was about to get the servants to fetch you." He patted her shoulder as she broke the hug to take her seat on his left.

"I finished the handkerchiefs. Do you think Eduard and Callan will like them?" Kara pulled out two light blue squares of silk. Delicate embroidery of blue snakes had been worked on the material, along with their initials.

A snake was the crest of the Heversham family; nearly all of their ancestors produced the same type of summoned aether spirit. Using a snake on garments, carriages, and other items had become a tradition. Thus, the colour blue also followed as the symbol of water, the Heversham's dominant affinity as summoners.

"They are beautiful. Your brothers will think the same," Roger said, complimenting her as I silently chose a seat at the other end of the table.

I would have liked to sit beside Kara, but either Eduard or Callan would make a stink about that, as they always had in the past. It was best to sit away from them when they were here, so I chose the opposite seat to Roger's at the head of the table, the farthest away.

"Your lordship." Henley stood at the doorway, his black suit pressed neatly. "The young lords have arrived." He bowed as heavy steps echoed behind me, my back facing the door.

Please ignore me, please ignore me, please ignore me.

"Kara! Father!" Callan's loud voice erupted first as Kara squealed, pushing her chair out and running up to him for a hug.

Callan stepped into view beside me, his tousled light brown hair like his father's, his steel grey eyes like Cassandra's. He stood close to six feet tall, with tanned olive skin after being in the deadlands' dry heat.

My eyes widened, however, as he hugged Kara; there above his head . . . was it a number?

Vishka's Guidance System
Callan Heversham
Likeability: −25%

The box popped up to confirm what I saw, likeability . . . was this what it was?

A literally numbered index of how much someone liked me? So if Callan's rating ever fell to −50%, I could risk death? Well . . . my second life's death just became somewhat more transparent.

A dry cough to my right startled me. Hesitantly, I turned to see Eduard staring at me impatiently. He had steel grey eyes like Callan's, though their hostility almost seemed sharper. In the proper lighting, his hair was a much darker shade of brown, almost black. He had a strong jaw, and many women in Talbour saw him as the most eligible bachelor. But, to me, he was the most frustrating jailer.

"Eduard." I nodded simply, eyeing the slithering water snake curling around his arm. Like Father, Eduard was a skilled water summoner. Callan was an experienced aether user but hadn't been able to summon a spirit yet.

Floating above Eduard's head was another likeability meter. My guidance system confirmed it for me again.

Vishka's Guidance System
Eduard Heversham
Likeability: −13%

I was surprised to see that his meter was lower than Callan's. I would have thought Eduard hated me the most. He sure acted like it.

"Have you been well?" Eduard asked me, his voice calm, not taking his eyes off me. Calculating as always.

"Well enough." I forced a reply, feeling the urge to pinch my fingers. Eduard always made my chest tighten in anticipation. I never knew when he would punish me, confine me, shout at me, do something that made me feel small.

"How were the deadlands?" I sensed he wanted me to continue rather than opting for silence, my usual response. Was it six months he had been away? That was usually the length of time they were both gone. Sometimes it was longer, leaving me alone with Roger and Kara. Did Eduard miss torturing me?

"It was as expected," Eduard replied dryly, stepping closer as the hairs on my arms rose.

"Expected? It was magnificent," Callan said, beaming as he rushed over to sit beside Kara. "Lord Azriel was fantastic, a true beast under that mask of his. I swear he could take on anything with just his sword alone. He barely used his lightning aether."

"That would have been a sight to see," I replied to Callan in an attempt to veer Eduard's attention away from me. Eduard stopped moving closer. I could almost feel the frown on his face as I dismissed our conversation.

"I got to kill a few fire scorpions and even a couple of overgrown cerue." Callan raised an eyebrow at me with a slight grin.

Good for him. Too bad I'm not bothered by that joke anymore.

"Cerue? How interesting. Did the Lord Azriel train you?" I asked Callan, not reacting to his taunt. The smirk on his face quickly fell as I became less fun for him. Callan had always been easy enough to deal with. It was his temper that I had struggled with in the past.

"It was certainly successful, Father." Eduard finally left my side to sit beside Roger at the other end of the table, leaving me to my solitude.

"I'm glad to see you both home safely." Roger greeted them proudly as we settled for the special dinner Roger had planned. "Even if it is only for a day or two."

I wonder what I'm going to get served?

"You must tell me all about it. I've been so excited about you coming home. We can go to the festival together! It's on for a few more days." Kara excitedly began to chatter to Callan as he told her of his exploits.

I wasn't interested in listening to his exaggerated tales of sleeping in a tent for a few months or the gruesome combat they faced with the demonic beasts in the deadlands. I had heard it all before, but also a lump formed in my throat at the mere thought that it could be me next year if this quest of Vishka's had me joining them.

Zoning out, sipping my tea, I leaned my head on my hand as the three chatted away. Eduard glanced at me a few times but didn't really pay attention to anything I was doing. This was the easiest way to survive most dinners. In the past, when tried to join the conversation, I would only get scowled at, sent to my room, or flat-out ignored. So it hurt less to not say anything at all.

I watched the happy thanks Callan and Eduard gave Kara when she presented them with their handkerchiefs. Callan proudly folded his into his uniform's front pocket so it was visible. Unfortunately, it clashed horribly against his grey standard tunic. The small flowers Kara had added around the snake were too girly for his usual attire.

Because he couldn't use summoning aether yet, Callan was a part of the training unit in the army, which specialised in weapons combat and basic aether techniques. His tunic and cloak were lined with blue thread at the hem to symbolise his element, but because he hadn't summoned a spirit yet, he could not wear the same blue cloak Eduard did.

Eduard neatly tucked his gifted handkerchief inside his black jacket. He had somehow found the time to change out of his uniform before joining us. Typical of him.

Even though Eduard was a summoner, he wasn't a part of the army's main fighting force. Instead, he had chosen to join a different division, laying the foundation for the skills he would need to become the next viscount someday. I wasn't sure exactly what he did. However, I had never lived long enough to see him become the viscount. Maybe I could join a noncombat division like he had.

A clatter of wheels announced the food carts' arrival; a delicious smell drifted to the table, perking us all up. I had only eaten the crepe Freda brought me, so I was rather famished. The maids wasted no time leaving their assigned places at the edge of the room to pick up the plates of food. I saw freshly cooked steaks and baby potatoes, making my mouth water.

Finally, it was my turn, and I was left disappointed.

Freda was hesitant as she came over, her hand shaking a little as she put the plate down. The smell of eggs and fat wafted to my nose; wrinkling it, I looked at my meal of lumpy white slop.

Gruel. They were seriously serving me gruel. They had hidden it well under a layer of steak. Without a closer look, it might have looked like mashed potatoes. The steak was seared and burnt on the underside but looked perfectly fine on top.

Snapping my head towards the chef, I saw his satisfied grin at my reaction. His eyes laced with ridicule and mirth as he left the room, having brought in the food cart. No wonder Freda had been nervous. She had no control over what the chefs served. I would have liked to think she would not give me something so foul willingly.

Begrudgingly, I didn't bother to pick up my cutlery, continuing to sip my tea instead. It was better than the trash in front of me, no doubt mostly made of lard from the looks of it.

Across from me, Roger happily tucked into his medium-rare steak, oblivious. Eduard and Callan enjoyed their fresh meal. After months of living on rations, they barely had time to look up from their own food.

Pleasant as always, Kara flashed me a quick smile before continuing to chat away, just as oblivious as her father.

The past me would have stood up by now, raised my voice, and accused the chef of trying to poison me. Eduard would then get mad at me for ruining the atmosphere, telling me to stop being ridiculous and appreciate the food they provided without ever looking at it.

Next, Callan would storm out, taking his food with Kara, upset with me for ruining their meal. Finally, Roger would quietly sit at the head of the table, happy to listen and watch the event unfold without interference, leaving it all to Eduard.

Frustrated at their lack of understanding of the reason for my outburst, I would have flipped the table, which would have sentenced me to confinement in my room. I would likely then be brought nothing but mouldy bread for a week by the kitchen staff, Freda sometimes sneaking me a decent snack. I had been through this scenario too many times.

I would leave this house soon.

"I have an announcement to make now that we are all together." Roger interrupted the meal, causing us to pause. This hadn't happened before. I had usually left or already ruined the meal by this point.

"An announcement?" Kara asked, looking to her brothers for hints, but they were just as surprised. Of course, they would be. They had only just gotten back after their expedition to the deadlands.

"Yes, my dear." Roger smiled affectionately before looking directly at me.

I stilled in my seat, my teacup poised near my mouth.

"We have received a marriage proposal for Lynette from Baron Elliot Asher on behalf of his son. I have decided to accept." Roger beamed at me as though it were a gift.

"A proposal! Oh my gosh, how exciting! Lynette, did you hear? You're getting married!" Kara clapped in glee, the thoughts of a wedding dress no doubt filling her mind.

"Ha, Lord Garret? Seriously? When did he even meet Lynette?" Callan asked, continuing to cut his steak.

Eduard remained quiet but didn't move to continue eating, looking at his father for his response to Callan's question.

"They m—" my father began.

"It was at Sarah Gangley's ball two months ago," Kara interrupted, giggling.

"I knew Garret Asher had taken a fancy to you, Lynette! He was terribly eager to ask her for a dance, and he ended up asking her three times before she finally let him." She winked at me, popping a potato in her mouth.

"Sarah Gangley? Her coming-of-age ball, was it?" Callan said.

"Yep, they looked so gorgeous together. Let me tell you, I was jealous, as only Steven Gangley asked me. Many of the other ladies told me how jealous they were of Lynette as well." Kara continued to tell them of the ball as my blood ran cold.

Slowly, I lowered my cup of tea, trying to keep my hand as steady as possible.

But, of course, I had returned later this life than last time, so there was no way to fix my initial meeting with Garret Asher. I had forgotten how we met in the years living with him, a memory I had succeeded in burning from my mind.

Was I going to suffer at his hand again?

The tea began to shake with my trembling. I quickly grabbed my right wrist with my left to lower the teacup properly onto the table.

"Lyn—"

What was I going to do?

Roger could definitely make me marry like he had last time, though before he hadn't announced this. Before, I had already stormed out, so Roger had told me about the proposal alone in his study where I could protest. That was when he lied to me about Kara being the person that Garret wanted to marry, to convince me to agree in her stead. However, Roger didn't need to do that. As my adoptive father, he had the right to choose my husband. He had only wanted to make it so I wouldn't protest as much.

Was this why I had to join the army? Was that my way to escape?

I needed to hurry.

Tomorrow wasn't soon enough. I needed to pack a bag and leave first thing in the morning. The longer I stayed here, the stronger my chances of getting remarried to that bast—

"Lynette!" My body was abruptly shaken. I blinked and found a pair of calloused hands on my shoulders and steel grey eyes as Eduard stared at me in concern.

"Lynette? Are you all right?" he asked me, his voice heavy.

"I-I'm fine," I said, taken aback by how close he was. When did he come over to me?

"You're as pale as a sheet," Eduard remarked, loosening his grip on me with a furrowed expression.

"It's fine. I just haven't eaten yet," I absently answered, touching my forehead. I was sweaty.

"Haven't eaten? We were just having a meal, idiot." Callan rolled his eyes at me as though I were talking nonsense. Kara, I noticed, was cocking her head curiously.

I stilled in Eduard's hands. Were they going to shout at me as they did in my past lives when I mentioned the food?

"I—I need to go," I said, pushing my chair back and attempting to stand. However, when I tried to, my legs betrayed me.

"Lynette!" Eduard caught me in a swift movement. I felt the pressure of his hand on my waist as he lifted me to my feet.

What was wrong with me?

Shock, I must be in shock.

The trauma Garret had left me. I guessed hearing his name invited fear now.

"I'm fine," I lied, trying to pry Eduard's hand away, but he held firm. What was up with him? Usually, he avoided touching me.

"Maybe she needs to lie down, Miss Parsons?" Kara stood this time, trotting over to me and signalling my personal maid. Whatever good she was going to be.

"Psh, she's just overreacting again. Let her go, Eduard," Callan said, annoyed with me.

"I'm fine, Eduard," I repeated, trying to pry his hands away again.

"Miss Parons, fetch her some water." Eduard ignored me and the open hand Freda offered. Freda bowed and quickly moved to do as she was told.

"Really, I'm okay. It's just a light dizzy spell." I sighed.

Kara placed her hand on my forehead. "You do feel a little hot. Maybe you caught a fever?" She pouted. "On such a good day like today too! We will have to celebrate Lord Garret's proposal tomorrow instead."

My body flinched as she said his name.

I wondered if Eduard noticed.

"I'm sure she's fine," Callan mumbled, finally placing his fork down. "I wouldn't be surprised if she's doing this for attention." His smug look towards me shot daggers.

"Callan, don't make assumptions." Roger scolded him as Freda brought me my water. I didn't reject it because, frankly, I probably needed it.

"Assumptions? You know she's exaggerating." Callan's tone grew increasingly annoyed.

"I think I will excuse myself," I said, hinting at Freda.

"Yes, run away now that you've made a scene." Callan shook his head.

"Callan." Eduard firmly frowned at him, eliciting a snarl.

"I'm fine, really," I sighed, my mind reeling. "I just haven't eaten in a while. That's probably why I'm so faint."

"What?" Eduard frowned down at me. "That's the second time you have mentioned not eating."

"Huh." I looked at him, confused. What had I just said?

"What do you mean, Lynette?" Roger said, now finally standing up from his chair. "Explain. What do you mean you haven't eaten in a while?" He slowly walked towards me.

My face flushed as I realised my mistake. Crap. I said that out loud, didn't I?

"Um . . ." How could I deescalate this? Eduard was definitely going to put me under house arrest again.

"What a farce," Callan said, interrupting my response. "Saying she hasn't eaten all day. Pah," he grunted. "What a ton of lies." He stood and began towards us.

"We feed her extravagant meals like thi—" He stopped midsentence, having picked up my bowl of trash for the first time and looking at it closely.

"What is it?" Roger said, seeing the widening of Callan's eyes.

"What the hell is this?" Callan shouted "Bring Mr. Orca in here right now!"

"Y-yes," a middle-aged maid stuttered at the outburst and left the room.

"What's . . . ah!" Kara peeked at the bowl and gasped. Eduard's gaze bore into me, scrutinising me as he held me in place.

It was then that the maid returned, closely followed by the chef whose eyes darted around the room followed by a gulp.

"Is this supposed to be a joke?" Callan narrowed his eyes at the chef as his face went white in a matter of seconds. His previous ridicule vanished.

"M-my lord, i-it's not what you think," the chef stammered, unsure what to do with himself.

"Oh? What exactly do I think it is?" Callan's voice never lowered as he threw the bowl at the wall beside the chef's head. It smashed on impact, gruel and steak trickling down the walls as the chef ducked. Callan had always been quick with his temper.

"Callan, enough." Roger stamped his cane on the floor, his water snake slithering around it.

"Father!" Callan complained, but a hard stare from Roger made him lower his hands and settle.

"Mr. Ocra, explain." Roger directed his attention to the whimpering chef.

"Yes. Please do," Eduard added.

"I—I—" The chef wrung his hands, lost for words.

I watched his lip tremble under the pressure in the room. Even the other staff watched him expectantly, most probably afraid for themselves as well.

Reluctantly Eduard released his hand from my waist as I finally pried it off.

This whole situation was escalating. Yet, as unwell as I felt from the news of my marriage proposal, the ridiculousness made me chuckle.

All eyes turned towards me as the laughter grew.

"Really, now? I'm surprised you care at all, Callan." I wasted no time gripping Freda's hand to steady myself. I much preferred her support to Eduard's.

"What?" Callan frowned.

"You're acting like this is unusual. The meals I eat are none of your concern."

"None of my concern?" Callan scrunched his face. "Of course, it's my concern, yo—"

"It's never bothered you before." I leered at him. "It's never bothered any of you, so there's really no point in caring now." I shook my head at their stupefied stares.

A cold silence filled the dining room as my meal dripped slowly down the walls and my utensils sat on the table perfectly clean.

I hadn't eaten anything as they merrily chatted away earlier. None of them ever bothered to notice, though, to check on me or ask my opinions on my life.

"If you're finished, I think I'll return to my room now to rest," I said, breaking the silence. "Freda, if you could help me to my room, I'd appreciate it." I turned to open the dining room doors.

No one tried to stop me from leaving as I walked away, supported by Freda. The moment the doors closed, I heard the muttering of voices ignite, and two boxes appeared before my eyes.

Vishka's Guidance System
Callan Heversham
Likeability: −20% (+5%)

Vishka's Guidance System
Eduard Heversham
Likeability: −16% (−3%)

CHAPTER SIX

The evening sky grew dimmer through the purple curtains shading my window. There was still enough light for me to see the papers on my desk as I sat quietly eating a sandwich Freda had brought me. I tapped my pen against the wooden desk as I contemplated what I needed to do.

Vishka wanted me to join the army. The idea was fairly simple. They were recruiting in the square during the festival, after all. Every year when they passed through the towns of the Zopan Empire, the army recruited at each city on their way back to the capital. Then they brought the new intakes to the facility based there. The problem was getting accepted.

Commoners with large cores were always accepted, and nobles with recommendations from their families.

Commoners considered physically able were also accepted as foot guards even if they didn't have a mote core. Because I was a woman with barely an existence of a core, my chances were incredibly slim. Getting a recommendation from my family was also a no-go. There was no point in even asking, as that would tip them off to my plans. I didn't exactly have the physical prowess to be considered a foot guard, either.

My only chance was to increase my mote core.

Could I do that within the next two days before the army left?

The quiet in my room surrounded me as the light tapping of my pen echoed.

Perhaps . . . there was that one method I could try? I read about it once in the library of Garret's manor. A newly accredited researcher had discovered a type of root that, when consumed with mistwood tea, dramatically increased the size of untrained cores. The discovery was extraordinary, and many weak nobles used it to empower their children. Even commoners used their life savings to purchase the roots for a chance to improve their core. This method wouldn't be revealed until another five years or so. What was the root called again . . .

Jabascus! It was a jabascus root.

It was a reasonably unpopular vegetable in the commoner circles because it tasted bitter without any apparent benefits. The corners of my mouth tugged. I should be able to purchase it relatively cheaply, then. Maybe I could try taking it a few times to raise my core?

I quickly noted it down on my paper so I didn't forget the name.

Now for my second problem: Garret Asher's marriage proposal.

Father had already announced his intention to accept the proposal, and Kara was excited by the prospect.

I sighed, dropping my head onto the table. Even if I successfully joined the army, it wouldn't cancel the wedding, only postpone it until I finished training in the army. Once Father decided on something, he never went back on his word, without me having my name crossed out of the family records or begging at his feet, which I had already tried in my previous life. There were slim pickings of options. Maybe postponing the wedding at least would open some opportunities for me to find another way out.

No.

That was too risky. Knowing Garret, he would just push the issue. He would likely join the army at the same time as me if he found out. That was a guarantee, in fact. He joined after our first year of marriage, so it was fair to plan that he would join a year earlier if I did.

I had to do something else, something that would make Father cancel. . .

That was when it hit me, something that would make Father cancel the marriage, something that would also irritate Garret and make him avoid me if he did join the army.

My lips upturned even further.

I needed a scandal.

Vishka's Guidance System
Quest Granted
Create a scandal to escape your marriage to Garret Asher

"My lady." Freda pouted, quietly following me down the dark hallway. "This isn't a good idea. What if you get caught? The young lords . . ."

"The young lords aren't your concern, Freda. Your only concern is what I want, and right now." I stopped and looked around the corner, checking that it was empty before continuing. "I want to go out."

"B-b-but it's past your curfew, my lady. If young Lord Eduard finds out you snuck out at night . . ." She continued to follow me as we secretly crept through the manor. Eduard and Callan had already retired for the night. I had checked with Freda before making my escape. It hadn't been too hard to convince her to help me after I showed her a gem for her troubles. I had never rewarded her before, so she was fairly surprised at my offer.

"Freda." I stopped and faced her. "This is the least you could do." I pointedly stared her down, watching her shrink with guilt.

She has been spying on me for Kara; she should hopefully feel some guilt about that.

"Okay," she whispered with a slight nod. Hesitantly, she went in front of me and checked ahead as we had planned. Once she gave me the signal, I quickly joined her at the front doors.

"Good, now, remember, in the morning, just act like you usually do, and if anyone asks, just say I didn't answer when you knocked on my door." I pulled the hood of my black cloak over my head.

"Yes, my lady, but what if . . . what if something happens to you?" she asked, smoothing down the cloak around my shoulders.

"Don't worry, I'll be fine." I smiled. I had no way to guarantee that, though.

"I shall pray for you to stay safe." Freda grimaced as I stepped outside. "I prepared a kreshna outside the gates," she mumbled, surprising me. I hadn't asked her to do that. I had fully expected to walk, expecting getting into the stables unnoticed to be too big a risk.

"Thank you, Freda." I smiled at her genuinely.

"My lady." Freda bowed slightly before silently closing the manor doors.

Not wanting to waste time, I hugged my cloak close and hurriedly walked as quietly as possible towards the gates in the stone wall surrounding the mansion. Mortal guards would be guarding them, men who didn't have cores, commoners.

Mortal was a term used for anyone without a core or access to aether. Nobles often used it to look down on someone as such, and they had often insulted me with it. Most mortals did not worry about such things, though we knew better than to be concerned with the insults of nobles.

Reaching the wall, I pushed my body against the cold stone. The night sky made it difficult to safely navigate the rocky ground in the moonlight. Carefully, I slid against it until I spotted a particular bush I was familiar with. Dropping to my knees, I pushed it apart to reveal a small hole in the stone wall. It was a gap created by Callan last year when he got overzealous whilst training. I planned to take advantage of it.

Lying flat on my stomach, I began the short crawl through the gap. The jagged stone scraped across the back of my cloak before I finally pulled through to the other side. Quietly I looked to my right, towards the main gate, and watched for the mortal guards.

A pair of guards were avidly chatting with each other, not looking my way.

Taking my chance, I quickly rose to my feet and sprinted to the tree line just ahead. I didn't know if I had made any sound, so I rushed to hide behind a tree, peeping back at the guards. Thank the gods I did, as they were now walking towards the hole I had run from and looking around.

Gently, I moved farther back into the trees, watching not to step on any twigs before returning to the pathway farther down out of sight.

As promised, on the pathway was a lumbering kreshna tied to a tree; its cloven feet stomped in impatience, its floppy ears swishing as it snorted at my presence. Kreshna were well known to be incredibly stubborn creatures. Their attitudes towards people were always reluctant and often required specialised stable hands. However, as Freda would have known, I never had such problems with the beasts.

Raising my hand towards it, I approached slowly, holding my hand steady for the kreshna to complete the distance. He paused momentarily, looking at me intently, then butted my hand with his nose in contact.

"There, there, boy." I smiled and patted his head between his curled horns. "Will you help me get to town?" I asked him, moving my hands along his neck towards his back. His nodded snort gave me the signal I needed.

Gripping onto the raised ridge of scales at the base of his neck, I pulled myself up and onto his back, my feet dangling comfortably over his broad frame. With a small squeeze of my legs, he huffed but began to walk forward towards the lights of the town a distance away.

It was hard to hide the smile on my face as the kreshna carried me forward. It felt freeing, riding the beast in the night like this. I hadn't had this much freedom before: to be alone, to be outside, to be crazy enough to do what I was planning. I laughed out loud, holding my hands out in the air. Perhaps I should have given up my care for this family long ago. It was very freeing.

Vishka's Guidance System
Well done on escaping the mansion at night!

After about thirty minutes, we arrived at the centre of Talbour, having left the nobles quarter. It was completely different at night.

The streets were quiet, devoid of families. Only a few beggar children ran amongst the adults who gathered around the stalls of the night market held during the festival. Shopkeepers bellowed about their unique products, primarily different alcohols, games of chance, and even some gambling.

The acrobats Miguel had mentioned danced with fire at the square as a man held a hat to collect the crowd's coins. I stopped the kreshna, watching them for a while. Their performance was spectacular. A thin, flexible woman balanced on a large wooden ball on her tiptoes whilst juggling balls of fire. Her fellow acrobat, in the meantime, created a whip of fire, flicking it into patterns in the sky around her as he coordinated the dance of flames. It was incredible, especially as they weren't using aether.

As I watched, a few of the crowd pointed towards me as I rode the kreshna. Some raised eyebrows, and others whispered in confusion. It wasn't often someone was seen riding a kreshna. They almost always exclusively pulled carriages, a beast of stubborn hostility to riders. Keeping with the merry mood, I gently waved to a few who stared, changing whispering into smiles as they watched in awe as I moved the kreshna through the square. It seemed my presence was becoming a commodity of the festival.

Ever since I was little, I had always had an understanding of kreshna. I didn't know why or how to explain it. I just always knew the best way to approach them, how to calm them and gain trust. Callan had called me a freak for it; Eduard had banned me from ever approaching the idea of riding them in public. They treated it like a dirty secret I had to hide. Well, I'd had enough of hiding.

Directing the kreshna away from the square to the dismay of my onlookers, I rode down the streets past tightly packed wooden stalls towards my destination. It was hard not to notice the increase of soldiers in the town with the army's arrival. More men happily drank from their mugs as they traversed in groups of three to five through the stalls, their coloured cloaks standing out amongst the commoner mortals.

I was fascinated by the few beast-kin amongst them, their stature that of a human but each with different tails and animal ears poking out of their hoods and below their cloaks. I hadn't seen many beast-kin in the predominantly human Talbour before.

The daemon were even vaguer. I had only ever read about them in books; they were similar to the beast-folk but different. They, too, had the stature of humans, but their eyes sported slits for pupils, with irises in colours unnatural to humans, such as red or yellow. Their hair often matched the unusual colour of their eyes; sometimes they had been described as having spikes like bone on their bodies, but I had never seen one. It was impossible to tell under the cloaks of the few I thought I spotted.

Easing the kreshna to a standstill, I grabbed the raised scales on its back and jumped off, taking the rope around its head towards a wooden pole set up for horses to be tied. The stallions there baulked a bit at the kreshna's presence but soon calmed down with a few pats to their noses.

Turning, I made my way into the swinging doors of my destination, a local inn called the Traveller's Rest.

Immediately as I entered, a gush of noise rushed through my ears; crowds sat around various tables drinking and laughing, and many of the army's soldiers hollered, clanking their mugs in merriment. I looked around and struggled to see an available table, but there was a free barstool, so I made my way over, raising the hood of my cloak.

"What will it be?" A young woman approached me as I sat down. Her dress was laced so tight that her chest was pressed upwards. I couldn't help the blush on my face as she chuckled at my gaze. "I recommend the Talbour Ale. It's our best since it's fresher than the imported stuff." She winked, clearly an advocate for her town's products.

"One of those, then, please." I dragged my eyes away from her chest, thankful for the suggestion. She promptly brought a wooden mug over, and I gave her a bronze coin as I took my first sip. It was a smooth drink with a harsh aftertaste, but bearable.

Glancing around, I watched the patrons as they enjoyed their evening. If this was going to work, I needed someone gullible enough to gamble with; a small part of me was also a little bit picky about my target if it worked. The blush returned as I considered my gamble, slight hesitation making my heart pump faster.

Was I being foolish with this?

If it didn't work, Eduard would probably lock me in my room for years, repeating my first life.

I released a heavy sigh as I looked at the mug in my hands. What other choice did I have? I had tried most of my other options before, but they didn't work out so well.

Eduard was probably going to lock me up regardless for sneaking out.

Standing, I straightened my cloak in preparation, then made my way to a particularly rambunctious table of young men.

"I raise you two bronze." A gentleman dressed in grey slammed his hand down on the splintered wooden table, his scraggly brown beard twitching with his glare at his fellow gamblers.

"Bring it on, Hugh." A young gentleman opposite Hugh grinned. He had short blond hair and was smoothly shaven compared to the other men at the table, who all looked similar to Hugh. His bright red robes stood out against their bland grey, and he was also reasonably handsome.

He will have to do.

"I'll take that bet," I interrupted, causing silence to descend as they all paused to look at me.

"What?" I sat down next to Hugh. "Afraid a girl might beat you?" I smirked, purposely picking up a set of cards.

"Bold." The man in red leaned back into his chair. "We might let you join, but isn't it rude to hide your face in a game of cards?" he asked, raising eyebrows.

"Fair enough." I shrugged, pulling down my hood and taking out my dark hair to settle against my shoulders. They all stared at me again. I expected that much. Soldiers were often on guard around me because of my Dramorian features, and terra-cotta skin wasn't common in Zopan. "How about I buy a round to apologise for my rudeness." I smiled, signalling for the barmaid.

"Aha! Welcome, girlie! The more, the merrier when drinks are offered." Hugh slapped my back, causing me to jolt forward, chuckling as the rest of the table grinned.

Commoners are definitely more rowdy than the nobles I know.

"Happy to help." I laughed, making an order with the barmaid for the table.

"So what do we call you?" another gentleman dressed in grey with tawny hair asked, taking my two bronze to add to the pile at the centre of the table.

I shouldn't give them my full name. It would be best if they think I am a commoner.

"Lynette." I checked my cards and began to devise a plan. "And you?"

"I'm Jacob, and this is Hugh." He nodded to the gentlemen beside me. "That's Richie." He pointed to the older man beside the blond in red. "And that's Nate." The man in red gave a showmanship bow towards me.

"So what's earned us your presence tonight, Miss Lynette?" Nate asked, placing down a card.

"What brings anyone to a tavern? Gambling." I placed my own card down with a grin.

"Good answer, girlie." Hugh leaned into his hand, folding.

"Well, you're definitely good at it," Nate observed, his eyes flicking to my cards as Jacob and Richie folded.

"I'll take that as a compliment." I pulled out another bronze coin. "I'll raise you."

The night grew weary as empty mugs scattered around the table. Hugh was facedown on the table, passed out from the alcohol. Richie and Jacob were slightly better but had long lost their coins and were now just watching as Nate and I competed for the large pile at the centre.

"Are you sure you're not cheating?" Richie exclaimed as I placed another strong card.

"Don't blame me. You got bad hands." I laughed, waiting for Nate's turn. He sighed in exasperation.

"You're killing me here, Lynette!" Nate moaned, taking a large sip of his ale. "Come on. I can't afford to lose this much. There's gotta be something, a compromise," he whined.

I couldn't stop my smirk as I leaned my head on my hands; I had avoided drinking as much as they had, but Nate wasn't really that drunk either, despite the many mugs he had consumed.

"Hmm, maybe there's something you could do." I grinned. "A favour of sorts." This was what I had been waiting for. I didn't spend years in my room with absolutely nothing to do other than study books. It turned out I had a talent with cards.

Nate narrowed his eyes. "What sort of favour?"

"How about you let me share your room tonight? Everywhere is full with you guys in town, so I'm in somewhat of a pickle."

"Ehhhh." Richie perked up a bit, his eyes widening, turning his head to Nate and back to me numerous times. Nate was quiet, looking at me. It was a little unnerving compared to his attitude for most of the night.

Oh gods, Nate's face looks serious.

"Sir . . ." Jacob tried to talk to Nate, but he cut him off with a shake of his hand.

"Take Hugh up to his room, will you? I think he's had enough." Nate's voice lowered. Richie and Jacob glanced at Nate before nodding and moving to each take one of Hugh's arms and haul him towards the stairs to where the rooms were.

I felt a chill run through my spine at Nate's look.

Crap.

"What's your aim?" he asked, picking up the cards to reshuffle the deck.

"I told you I need a room for the nigh—"

"Don't play dumb with me, Lynette. We both know there's no good reason a noble daughter would approach a table of men to play cards."

"I—" I felt a lump forming in my throat. Double crap. "How did you know?"

"Your cloak is pristine, with a few scuffs but otherwise barely worn. Your boots are clearly expensive leather with tight stitching, you appear to have money to burn, and you've not tried to flirt once, which most mortal commoners do when chatting with a summoner." He dealt us each six cards.

"What's your aim?" he asked again, following my silence.

Well, I guess there's no point in hiding my intentions. It will affect him too.

"I have an issue I need to resolve." I placed down a card.

"Such as?" Nate placed his own.

"Marriage," I sighed, taking a hearty gulp of the ale this time. Its burn was pleasant.

"Marriage? What's so bad about that? You're a nice girl. I'm sure you'd make a great wife," he said, frowning whilst placing his card.

"Hah." I laughed sarcastically. "That may be true, but is it fair for me to have a husband who'd cause me nothing but misery? I think not."

"How do you know? Is he that much of a scumbag?"

"Trust me. He is." I shivered a little, thinking of Garret's face.

"Who are you?" Nate asked after a pause. "If I agree to anything, I need to know the repercussions."

"Lynette Heversham," I whispered, hoping he didn't know of the name.

"Heversham?" Nate suddenly looked at me with a new expression. His defensive body language relaxed, and I could see the cogs working in his mind. "Eduard and Callan's relative?"

Crap. Of course he would know of them despite the size of the army. I had hoped he wouldn't. Small hope.

"Sister, actually," I mumbled.

"Sister? I thought their sister was called . . . what was it . . . Kayla?" Nate leaned forward, now scrutinising my face.

"Kara; don't worry. I doubt they mention me much." I pulled back, a little embarrassed by his stare. "I'm adopted, not real blood."

"You say that with such resignation." He raised an eyebrow, ultimately abandoning his cards now.

"I guess I'm used to being an existence they don't mention." I shrugged.

"And they're forcing you into a marriage you don't want?" Nate asked, linking his fingers on the table.

"What choice does a girl have against her father's decision?" I was nothing but a burden Father wanted to pawn off to the worst man possible. He did once. He'll do it again.

"All right." Nate suddenly stood up.

"Wha—" I straightened in surprise.

"All right, I'll share a room with you." Nate held his hand out towards me with a smile. His lips were smooth, and I could see the cut of his sharp jawline from this angle. He really was handsome.

Hesitantly I placed my hand in his and let him pull me to my feet. However, he quickly dragged my body towards him, enveloping my waist in his arms. I felt the heat in my cheeks and couldn't stop the small gasp from escaping my lips.

What is he doing?

"Shall we make a show of it?" He leaned his head against my cheek, whispering as a few of the patrons began wooing at us, many of the soldiers bashing their drinks in laughter at his actions.

"Uh—um," I gulped as he pulled away, his face so close our noses touched. "Thank you," I whispered back, my nervousness swirling in my stomach.

He didn't think I was going to actually . . . No, he couldn't . . . could he? Should I? It wasn't like I hadn't been with a man before, having been married to Garret in my previous life. Technically I was still a virgin in this life, but I'd never experienced it with a man I didn't hate.

"Don't worry about it." He leaned even closer, causing my heart to thump faster than I knew it could. I felt his breath on my skin; it was warm and soothing, and then suddenly his lips were against my own. I jolted at the action. My skin didn't tremble in disgust. It was pleasant, nice even. I could swear the nerves in my stomach fluttered with every lip movement.

As he pulled away, I heard the patrons hollering and quickly raised my hands to cover my beetroot-red face. Nate gripped them, though, and pulled them away with a slightly apologetic smile.

"Shall we?" He hinted towards the stairs, and I could only meekly nod, letting him lead me hand in hand up towards his room for the night.

Well, I guess the scandal was successful.

CHAPTER SEVEN

Pain thrived in my skin as black veins littered my body. They pulsed, bringing with them waves of agony as I lay on my bed scrunched in a ball, hoping the tighter I squeezed my arms, the less it would hurt. Wincing, I forced my eyes to open at the sound of my door and footsteps approaching.

"Eduard." I breathed heavily, fighting the spasm of pain that currently struck me. It would come and go but was always worse when the black veins grew, the disease that haunted my body.

"So sweaty," he remarked, glaring down at my pathetic form, the fabric of my ruined nightgown.

"Eduard . . ." I reached a hand out to grab the bottom of his jacket. "Please . . . let me see a doctor," I begged.

"Lynette, we've spoken about this." His voice was quiet, or was it just that I couldn't hear over the pain? A cold, wet thing sank into the skin on my forehead. Everything was so blurry, so dizzy. "We can't let you see a doctor, Lynette. There's nothing they can do," he murmured, watching me crumble.

"Please . . . just once. Please," I rasped.

"Lynette, stop." He raised his voice slightly, pulling away so my hand dropped, unable to reach anymore. "This is for the best," he said before closing the door, leaving me alone to suffer.

Light brushed against my eyes, forcing me to pull awake from my nightmare. I momentarily gazed at the boring white ceiling for a moment whilst my brain caught up to where I was.

"Ah!" I gasped, shooting up in my bed and tucking the covers closer. Quickly looking to my left, I found no one beside me. I was alone. "N-Nate?" I hesitantly called out, then heard the sound of running water in the small en suite.

"Here," he called from behind the closed door, settling my nerves. He hadn't just left, then. Contrary to my thoughts last night, once we entered his room Nate had offered me the bed whilst he opted for the small settee in the dingy room. I had refused to allow him to sleep in such a small space since he was far too tall to have a comfortable night. After some arguing, we agreed to share the bed with no intimacy.

Stretching, I hauled myself up and grabbed the plain white blouse and leather trousers I had been wearing the night before. Pulling them over my undergarments, I rushed, a little worried Nate might finish up in the bathroom. I was comfortable enough to sleep in my underthing's alone after Nate's promise and insistence that he wouldn't do anything. The wall of pillows I made between us made me more comfortable, but it was nice to meet a gentleman for once in my life.

A rare occurrence. Or maybe mortals just didn't interest him. We were exceptionally squishy in comparison. What might cause me grievous harm would only scratch a fully trained summoner.

The latch on the bathroom door clicked as he entered the room, rubbing a towel through his wet honey-blond hair.

"Ah—um—hi," I said, unsure how to approach him. This wasn't a situation I had exactly experienced before.

"Hi." He chuckled, stepping aside. "All yours if you want it."

"I'm fine." I nervously pinched the hem of my shirt. "Thank you, again, for doing this. I know you had no reason to, so thank you."

"It's no problem." He smiled, sitting down on the settee. "To be honest, I'm fairly excited to piss off Eduard. That dude has a real stick up his butt." He grimaced jokingly, making me chuckle.

"Do you know him well, then?" I asked, running my hand through my hair since I lacked a brush.

"Well enough; he's got a bit of a reputation with the soldiers for being a stickler for rules."

"That doesn't surprise me," I sighed, sitting down on the bed. "He's always punishing me at home."

"Punishing you?" Nate frowned this time.

"Oh, it's nothing that bad!" I quickly raised my hands and shook them. "He just doesn't let me leave the mansion when I've . . . upset him," I say, trying to choose my words carefully. I didn't want to get Nate involved in my cursed life more than necessary.

"I see." Nate silently looked away. I wasn't sure what he was thinking. How could I? "It's Nathaniel Hudson, by the way." He broke the silence, making me cock my head.

"Nathaniel?"

"Nate's my nickname the lads use when we're off-duty. Figured you ought to know if anyone asked you questions. You should probably know who I am, right?"

"Right! That's true." I nodded. "So, may I ask you a question?"

"Sure, what is it?" Nathaniel raised an eyebrow.

"What made you . . . what made you agree to this?" I waved around the room, indicating my request to make it seem like we had shared an intimate night. It was a surefire way to create a scandal for any noble. An unmarried woman sleeping with a stranger she met in a mortal commoner inn was no behaviour for a lady. I suppose some would call me crazy, living up to my Crazy Cerue Lady nickname, I guess.

"It was simple, really." Nate stood up and moved to sit beside me on the bed, his shoulder touching mine. It was . . . weirdly comforting. "If there was another way out for you, I figured you would have taken it; approaching a tavern, and a group of men, summoners, took guts. It was fairly obvious you had no other choice, so"—he looked at me with a smile—"I knew I had to help the woman so daringly trying to make her own path."

I blushed. "Th-thank you."

"Enough with the thank-yous." Nate suddenly rubbed the top of my head playfully. "Just use the opportunity to do what you want." He smirked. "Besides, I got something out of this too."

"What do you mean?" I asked.

"I know a thing or two about being pressured into something you don't want." He sighed. "My mother is very demanding, insistent I get married myself." He looked at me sadly. "But I have the luxury of denying that request, unlike you. As soon as she hears of this, it will keep her at bay for a while. If she finds out I held some interest in a woman for once, she will be ecstatic."

"You don't want to get married?" I asked.

"No." He laughed. "Not to a woman."

"Huh?" I scrunched my mouth, slightly confused, awaiting his answer, but Nate only looked at me pointedly. My mind blanked on his meaning for a moment. "Oh!" The penny dropped. "So you . . ."

"Yes." He laughed again at the surprise on my face, leaning back on his hands. "I have no interest in any women, so you were always going to be completely safe with me." He winked, making me blush again. "You picked wisely, little cherub."

"I think I was just lucky for once." I smiled, pulling my legs up to hug them. This was the first time in a long while that my heart and stomach felt settled around someone. It was nice not being afraid.

That calmness immediately vanished as the box appeared.

Vishka's Guidance System
Quest Update
Congratulations! You have successfully completed a scandal that has lowered
your reputation
WARNING
Be wary of the fallout, and stay low for a while to let tempers subside

I stilled, reading Vishka's latest message and warning. Did that mean the news of where I was and what had happened had already reached the mansion? It might be possible. Most of the mortal commoners knew who I was. I had caused enough public scenes in my childhood, and my distinct Dramorian features stood out, so it was obvious who I was to most locals. I guessed Freda wasn't successful in biding my time this morning. I knew the news would reach the Hevershams fast with Father's surveillance in Talbour, but not this fast.

Damn it.

"I should go, it's already morning, and I probably should leave before I'm found here." I stood, grabbing my black cloak.

"You in a rush to be somewhere?" Nate asked, also grabbing his red cloak to wrap around his shoulders. It covered the pristine black leather brigand armour he had already put on before I awoke, hiding the well-toned arms that were obvious in his tight red tunic.

"Yes, actually, I've no doubt my family has probably heard the news of this by now, and it's probably best neither of us is here." I didn't hesitate to grab his wrist to lead him towards the door.

"Whoa, calm down. I doubt they know already."

"Not worth the risk of getting caught here if they do," I said, opening the door. "My father has connections everywhere in Talbour."

"You really think they know you're here already?"

"Yes, I really do," I sighed. "I don't know how I'm ever going to repay you for this. Truly, thank you."

"Seriously, what did I just say? Stop thanking me." Nate removed his hand from my grip and instead placed it around my shoulders as we descended the stairs.

"Sorry." I smiled, making him shake his head warmly.

"It's fine. By the sound of the tower bell, I should probably get going anyway, summoner duties and all that." He held out his hand for me at the last step, and I gladly took it, allowing him to lead me through the tavern. A few grey-cloaked soldiers were gathered around the bare tables looking the worse for wear, but they watched us curiously and whispered.

"Right, you must have a lot to do?"

"You would be surprised, Lady Lynette." He spoke my name loudly enough for the people whispering to hear, playing the scene well. "So, this will be fare-well," he said, stilling my hand in his.

Slowly I released him, straightening myself. "Right, of course. You probably have to report in or something," I mumbled, feeling a little silly. He was a summoner. He wouldn't be worried about getting caught by Eduard or Callan, like me.

"Something like that," he mused. "Stay safe, Miss Lynette. May we meet again." He dipped his head and back in a showman's bow, causing a few people to look our way again.

"Stop it," I whispered, motioning for him to stop drawing attention to my embarrassment. "Stay safe, Nate." I smiled, feeling a pang in my chest.

It wasn't often I met someone who didn't treat me with displeasure.

"May we meet again." Nate held the door for me as I shyly curtsied to my new friend.

"May we meet again." I repeated his farewell before turning and leaving the tavern behind.

The pang in my chest numbed the moment I did so.

I already missed the feeling of calm he gave me. I had never met someone so kind. It hurt, to leave it, but there was no choice if Vishka's warning was anything to go by.

I had to stay out of sight for a while. Not easy during a festival.

The morning streets of Talbour were full of people, many stragglers still nursing hangovers, others setting up their morning stalls. Walking, I led my kreshna through the crowd by the rope tied to his horns.

Hiding in plain sight, that was my plan.

It was sort of working. Now and then, I spotted some of the guards from the Heversham mansion. They were alert, restless almost as they pushed their way through the crowd, clearly searching for something. I made sure to stick to the edges of the main street so I could dip into the alleys when I spotted them, using the kreshna to block my view. It had been successful so far.

Given the way they looked flustered, the viscount must have heard of my scandal already; there was no way they would be that stressed unless he had given them explicit orders to find me. Too bad for them. I didn't plan on being found for a while.

The viscount was most definitely furious right now; I had done a lot of disgraceful things as a result of my pent-up emotions when I was growing up, but I hadn't ever done something like this.

For a noblewoman to be caught with a stranger alone for the night was beyond disrespect, and the other nobles of Talbour would likely look down on our family for my actions.

Honestly, though, I was past the point of caring what they thought a lifetime ago—literally. My only concern now was the vegetable market, which was only a few blocks ahead.

As I weaved my way through the crowd, the hustle and bustle of vendors shouting over one another soon drowned out most of the conversations I passed. It was incredibly lively here at the vegetable market.

Farmers travelled from the lands outside the city to sell their goods at the final sixth day of a week, on the day of light when their crops were good. Some would remain for the next—the first day of fire for the new week—but many would return if they sold well enough.

During the festival, it became even more crowded. Every farmer came for the entire three days of the festival, the days of wind, darkness and light. They came even if they did not have any crops to sell just to catch up with friends, buy seeds, and exchange trade. It was a lively place to be.

Taking my time so as not to stand out, I glanced at the stalls looking for what I had come for: jabascus.

If I was going to try to improve my core, I would likely need it, how much I did not know.

I saw many variations of wheat, carrots, cabbage, and even a stall of medical herbs, which caught my attention for a while.

I ended up purchasing some dried valerian root, bloomvine, and willowspire. All useful when prepared properly. They were fairly common around Talbour and easy enough for most commoners to find but not so much for me as I didn't have the luxury of wandering the nearby fields to gather them.

Garret's library hadn't had many subjects to study in my third life; it had mostly been history, politics, and war tactics, but I did find a large collection on herbology collecting dust on his shelves. I had spent a lot of time there reading the volumes, hoping to find something that could help with my disease. It was a fruitless effort. There was no mention of anything similar to the black veins that sprouted on my skin, slowly draining my vitality every life.

The disease always appeared in my twenty-fifth year. I had found a way to slow its spread from my experimentation with herb powders, but nothing close to a cure. It didn't make sense to bring me back plagued with this curse.

Eventually, I neared the end of the street, where the crowd was thinner and the stalls bare.

It wasn't here.

What could I do now? I couldn't exactly grow some jabascus. I wasn't a farmer. There wouldn't even be enough time. I began to pace back and forth as my anxiety increased. Just what choice did I have? I couldn't improve my mote core in two days. If I went back to the manor, Eduard would lock me away in my room again. If that happened, would I even be able to leave to take the recruitment test for the army before they moved on?

"Arghh!" I exclaimed, slumping my head against the kreshna. "Peta, what am I to do?" In our time together, I had found that the name Peta suited him.

The kreshna snorted, a wisp of my hair tickling his nose, and shaking his head, he stomped. When I didn't react, I noticed he did it again, so I finally looked up at him and saw his eyes watching me keenly. He shook his head again, so I gave in and patted his nose, calming him down. "I know it's not easy," I sighed.

"Vishka, should I just try to join now?" I asked, hoping for a box to appear, but it did not. It seemed her messages were entirely unpredictable.

"Fine." I frowned, leading Peta forward again, this time towards the square. I wouldn't be able to avoid the viscount for long.

Better now than never.

The square was very different to last night. The acrobats were still here performing again with the fire whips. However, at the centre of the square now stood a long table. Behind the table were stationed several summoners, and guards stood nearby, awaiting the army assessment for new candidates. I gulped, fear growing in the pit of my stomach.

Two lines of young men and a few women had formed at the front of the first table.

The first line had many with clothes either dirty or ripped. Their hands were cracked with lines of mud, their bodies thin, the poorest of Talbour. The second line had a mix of people with sturdy but plain clothes and commoners who had better luck in life. They all stood to the back whilst at the front were people wearing only the finest leathers, silk, and velvet in colours so bright and joyful, they could only be nobles.

As the line moved, I silently fell into step at the back of the second line, pulling my hood up. I was too well dressed for the first. I would stand out. As with the others who rode here with horses, a grey-cloaked soldier offered to take Peta to the water trough they had set up. I thanked him with a nod, afraid to use my voice here. He gave Peta a funny look before shrugging and taking him away.

I leaned slightly to my right to get a better look at the front of the queue. Immediately I recognised some of the nobles who queued ahead. I had no doubt they would recognise me too.

I watched as the line moved; each person would step forward to the first table, where two summoners dressed in blue cloaks stood, one for each line. The summoners asked candidates to place their hands on a glass ball. As soon as they did, the ball would glow, and each time the intensity of the glow changed for the nobles up front.

However, the first line of poorer commoners often only got very low emittance of light or none at all. It must have been an aether core evaluation tool.

After a candidate had been tested with the tool, they moved along the table to a summoner dressed in a green cloak. There were about four green cloaks, so that part of the test seemed to move fairly quickly, as four candidates were tested at a time rather than just two like the first test.

I didn't understand what they were being tested for; the people in green cloaks all had check boards, and for some candidates, the summoners asked them something, and then the candidate would lift their hand in response, palm facing forward. For others, mostly the poor commoners, the summoners asked them to first place their hands flat on the table, and a red flash happened, with evident pain on the candidate's faces.

It didn't look pleasant.

The candidates then moved to the final table, where red-cloaked summoners were sitting rather than standing, and they were handed the papers from the check boards the green summoners had been writing on. Some of the candidates had big smiles when they left. Others looked sullen. That must have been where the results were evaluated for acceptance or denial.

I couldn't help but nervously shuffle on my feet as the line grew shorter in front of me, my turn growing closer. It was then that I spotted Rian Thornfax, daughter of the Earl of Thornfax. She was with Kit Balburn and Harold Eastmond, both baron's children, and Lacey Weadall, the daughter of the only other viscount in Talbour.

Slowly I pulled my hood further down to try to hide my face more.

Rian Thornfax was the youngest of three girls. She was someone I had often fought with in my past lives. She often managed to say just the right things to hurt me to the point of reaction and was the cause of many of my scoldings from Eduard. She was also the reason for my nickname, the Crazy Cerue Lady. Her father's rank of earl was above that of a viscount and only underneath the Marquess of Talbour, the ruler of this town.

I was foolish enough in the past to have gotten caught up with her, not just in my first life but my second as well. I am fairly confident that my second life had gone drastically wrong because of the influence of Rian Thornfax's and my clashes during social gatherings. Callan had been very unhappy with me whenever we fought. He only seemed to despise me more when I reacted to Rian's insults.

I had no intention of catching her notice this time around.

I watched as Rian stepped forward, her expression confident as the others cheered behind her. She was going to pass the test, as she always had done in my past three lives, though this was my first time witnessing her assessment. It was something she had bragged about often, claiming that the summoners welcomed her with open arms because of her skills and potential. Her family never held reservations about making women enrol.

I frowned, thinking back to those days at the social gatherings in my second life. I mostly sat alone during them, listening to her explain this day so proudly whilst simultaneously insulting me for being so useless that all I could do was buy dresses. It was weird watching it now for myself.

She flicked her brown, medium-length, neatly braided hair back behind her shoulder. She was of fairly average height and an athletically built, fair-skinned woman with a goal-oriented feel about her. She had wide-set brown eyes and an oval face. She was an average-looking woman, but maybe I was just biased. Her poise and confidence often made her the centre of attention in our peer group.

Stepping forward towards the glass ball, she placed her hand upon it. As expected it flashed so brightly that a few people at the front of the line had to shield their eyes. Triumphant, she moved to the next table when the green-cloaked summoners asked her to raise her hand and began taking notes on their check boards.

I could see they were pleased with whatever they saw from the expressions on their faces. As expected of someone from an earl's bloodline, she had an incredible mote core.

Finally, after she moved to the last table where she was questioned, I was too far away to hear what they were saying, but the result was her stepping to the right, heading to a large tent behind the assessment tables. The place where successful candidates were to await.

I sighed, slumping my shoulders. I supposed if I did pass, I would likely have to interact with her. She was a very proud woman, from what I remembered of my second life. We clashed so easily because I was incredibly stubborn. I hadn't interacted with her in my third life as Garret's wife. Perhaps this one might be different?

Lacey Weadall was next, the daughter of the viscount Mitchell Weadall. I was surprised to see her here; not many women applied to the army, and I didn't remember her speaking of being a part of it. I knew her older brother Zachary had joined when Eduard did.

Lacey was nervous as her hand shook, touching the glass ball. It glowed but not as brightly as Rian's had. She was a meek, petite girl with frizzy auburn hair worn up in a ponytail, narrow lips, and a turned-up nose. She had never been very talkative, choosing to watch rather than get involved from what I witnessed.

I hadn't spoken to her very much, so it could be she just didn't like a conversation with me as the Crazy Cerue Lady. I saw a hesitant smile, almost reluctant when the ball glowed, before she moved on to the next table to be assessed by the green cloaks for the test I didn't understand.

Kit Balburn was next, the son of Francis Balburn, a baron of Talbour. He was a plump man with light brown eyes, puffy lips, and neat eyebrows. His curly brown hair was styled with wax as he walked forward towards the glass ball. As expected, it glowed at his touch but less so than for Lacey or Rian.

Ranks were assigned based on the power of your bloodline, so it would be unusual for a baron's child to have more aether than the child of a viscount or an earl. Kit Balburn grinned happily at the result before heading over to the green cloaks to stand beside Lacey as she finished her assessment. I saw her nervously wringing her hands as she discussed the results at the final table with the red cloaks. It didn't take too long, but she didn't seem all too pleased as she dragged her feet towards the tent for successful candidates.

Finally, Harold Eastmond, the son of Rheese Eastmond, another baron of Talbour, approached. Like Kit, the glass ball glowed for him but not as brightly as it had for Rian or Lacey. It was a little bit brighter than it had been for Kit, in my opinion. He was a tall and slender man, dark-skinned, with stern, black eyes, a triangular face, and a stubble-covered round chin. He wore immaculate, high-end clothes and seemed relaxed with the result as he moved on to the next table, his long dark brown hair styled in decorative cornrows.

I had never interacted with Harold before. He hadn't stuck around for the social season in Talbour in my second life. I remembered him as someone who preferred his own company. He had witnessed my harassment of others more than once, though he never got involved. Perhaps that was why I remembered him.

It appeared that they all had passed. I watched as each of them finished the final assessment with the red cloaks before moving to the tent at the back. My palms had already begun to sweat. That was already four people who hated me that I would have to deal with if I passed. Why exactly did I have to join the army again?

I sighed, my feet moving forward as the rich commoners took their turns. Some had very weak reactions to the glass ball. Others were on the same par as the sons of the barons, which delighted them. Not everyone passed, though.

I saw that a couple of other children of barons I didn't know too well were accepted; however, there were many who didn't pass at the final table. Quite a lot of the commoners kicked up a fuss before storming away. It felt like I had been waiting a century with the unease in my stomach, but eventually it was my turn.

"Step forward." I looked up at an older gentleman dressed in a blue cloak, who waved his hand at me impatiently. I gulped, stepping forward as requested.

"Name," he asked, not looking up from a piece of paper his pen hovered over.

"U-uh, Lynette Heversham," I whispered, afraid someone else might hear me. I was sure that news of the viscount's guards searching for me had spread by now.

"What?" He finally looked at me. "Speak louder, girl. I haven't got all day," he tutted.

"Ly-Lynette Heversham." I spoke a little louder, panicked by his tone.

"Rank?" he asked, raising an eyebrow.

"Um, daughter of Viscount Heversham," I mumbled, which made him frown, so I said it again a little too quickly, making him sigh.

"Get on with it, then. Place your hand on the mote core evaluation globe." He nodded to the glass ball sitting on the wooden table before me. Up close, I saw a shimmer of murky liquid swirling on the inside; it flowed slowly in fascinating patterns, and it was a little entrancing.

This was it.

My heart hammered in my chest as I moved towards it, raising my hand. Slowly, I lowered the palm of my right hand onto the globe.

CHAPTER EIGHT

An intense cold sensation crawled into my skin the moment I touched the globe. My fingers stiffened in place from the shock, refusing to move as I panicked and tried to pull my hand away. It wouldn't move an inch, stuck in place firmly. The coldness trickled up my arm, reaching my shoulder, then travelled towards my chest and stomach. It was a sickening feeling. It felt like dead fingers were clawing at my insides. The sensation changed as soon as it reached the bottom of my stomach. It was replaced with a strong tugging upward. I thought I might be sick with the sudden uplift back to my chest, releasing finally through my hand that lay on the globe.

I grimaced as it did so, relieved it was over. To my utter surprise, the globe's liquid swirled and began to flicker with faint wisps of light. It was incredibly dim and lasted barely five seconds before disappearing. When it was over, my hand flooded once more with warmth, allowing me to finally remove it from the device.

"No light. Unfortunately, you failed this part of the assessment." The older blue-cloaked summoner crossed off something on his sheet before passing it to a grey cloak behind him.

"B-but there was light. It was faint, but it was there," I replied on autopilot, still in a little disbelief. Nothing had ever happened in all the past tests I had done when I was younger. This time, even though it was brief and dim, I saw it.

"There was no light. Accept that and move on, or are you saying that I, a fully trained summoner, don't know what I saw?" He scowled at me, annoyed that I was still standing here.

"N-no, of course not." I sighed, moving to the right to step out of the way for the next candidate.

"Good. Now move along over there." He pointed towards the second table with the four green-cloaked summoners.

"Jerk," I mumbled, moving over to the table as instructed. I knew what I had seen. There was some light. It might not mean much to him since it was a pathetic amount, but to me, it meant a lot.

Approaching the next table, I looked for one of the four green-cloaked summoners with an empty place; the third one along was waiting patiently, so I made my way over. As I got closer to him, the young man sneered at me.

"Crazy Cerue Lady. Never thought I would see you here," he scoffed, scratching the light dirty-blond stubble on his chin.

"Zachary," I stated with a dip of my head to be polite. Of all people, it just had to be Zachary Weadall, the older brother of Lacey Weadall and, coincidentally, Eduard's closest friend.

"What on earth made you attempt to sign up for the army? Don't you cause enough hassle at home? We don't need you," he tutted, picking up my chart from a grey cloak.

"I have my reasons. Do I need to explain them as part of the assessment?" I asked, raising an eyebrow. Zachary narrowed his pale blue eyes, his short, curly blond hair parted at his brow.

"No," he said curtly. "Let's get on with it, then. Show me your skills." He held the board up along with his pen, watching me.

I looked back at him, confused. "Skills?"

"Yes, skills. Bring up your blood sign and say 'Show skills.'" He seemed as confused as I did.

"Um . . . what's a blood sign?" I said, my head tilting.

"What's a . . ." He repeated my words, somewhat baffled, before a heavy sigh left him. "Of course, why would they give you a blood sign? What would be the point? Is that why you're here? To get a blood sign?" He put down his board and instead picked up a vial of strange red liquid, shaking it.

"How could I come for something I don't know about?" I retorted at his accusation. This only made his expression become frustrated.

"Why don't you know about blood signs? As a viscount's daughter, you should know that much. It's expected that commoners don't know, as they don't have the same education."

I shrugged. "I wasn't told." It was all I could say without going into the lack of care my family had for me. Zachary didn't need to know that. I doubted he would believe me anyway. No one ever did. It was interesting to learn that there was something like this I had purposely not been told about, though.

"Surprising," Zachary murmured before continuing. "A blood sign is something an individual needs to show the level of mastery they have obtained with either certain knowledge, physical skills, or crafting skills, or for summoners, their level of aether and their abilities. It's a prerequisite for being a part of the army, to grow your core, and for most crafting professions. It also provides an identification and basic layout of your health that trained medical professionals can access."

I felt my blood rush. "So . . . without one, I can't join?" My hand began to tremble a little bit. What could I do now? If I couldn't join, I couldn't get away from my family.

"I never said that." Zachary smirked, taking the cap off a bottle of red liquid. "That's what this is for. We don't expect commoners to have one unless they are practising crafting professionals who are already part of a guild. Now, give me your hand." He gestured to my right hand, holding out his own.

Was this the thing that the commoners looked to be in pain over? I hesitated, but Zachary grabbed my hand with a grin.

"This will hurt," he said before quickly pouring the liquid onto the back of my hand and chanting, "Blood of this one, gods, reveal their truth." A flash of red burst out from my hand, followed by a hot burning of my flesh sizzling on contact with the liquid. My face stiffened, biting my lip at the pain, but as soon as it was there, it was just as quickly gone again. In its place was now a red circle. Within it was a triangle, the point facing towards me when I lifted my hand to inspect it. From the sides of the circle, two lines crossed through the triangle, forming an X. The skin didn't look burnt; instead, the red outlines looked like the work of skin art I had sometimes seen on people, almost painted.

Vishka's Guidance System
Detecting blood sign implantation
Initiating melding

Suddenly Vishka popped up, and immediately the box flickered, fading and reappearing as it stuttered in and out of existence. I felt my hand begin to burn again and winced at the surprise, the box flickering faster before it almost pinged.

Vishka's Guidance System
Melding complete
The blood sign has been altered as per Vishka's guidance

"What does that mean?" I whispered, looking at the air the box used to be in.

"What?" Zachary picked up his board again, readying his pen.

"Uh, nothing." I blushed, rubbing the new mark on my hand. It didn't have any ridges. It was as smooth as my skin had always been. It was a mark I had seen on Eduard's, Callan's, and Roger's hands. I had asked about it in the past, but they had always dismissed my questions.

What had Vishka done?

"Whatever." He rolled his eyes at me. "Say 'Show skills' whilst holding up your palm. It will show me if you have achieved any skills that may be worthwhile to the army. I doubt it, though, with your recklessness." He shook his head.

Right. Eduard had probably told Zachary his opinion of me quite often; they were friends. It was no surprise that Zachary didn't have any expectations, not that I did either. As he said, in this life, my only accomplishments so far had been throwing tantrums for attention, threatening to destroy marketplaces, and actually destroying furniture. I once held a knife up to someone out of desperation when another noble child was abusing me; no one believed me when I told them why I did that, of course.

"Show skills!" I said, maybe too loudly, as Zachary rolled his eyes at me again.

"Why do they always shout?" he grumbled as I jumped at the see-through box that appeared between us. A bold red line edged it, and I could see writing in thick red letters but couldn't read it as it was backwards for me, probably because it was for Zachary to read, not me.

"Let's see now . . . name, yes . . . rank, yes . . . aether core null, as expected." His lip upturned, and I frowned at that. "Now skills, what *wonderful* skills do you have?" His exaggeration of *wonderful* turned my frown into a scowl. *No need for him to be so smug.*

"What . . ." Zachary paused his pen as he narrowed his eyes, looking at my blood sign, then back to me, puzzled. "Just how . . ." he mumbled to himself as he jotted down whatever it was he saw. He mumbled a lot, now that I thought about it. He pointed at the box and then flicked his finger upwards, and I saw the text rapidly move with the action, changing to something else.

His eyes widened, not in surprise, though, as he frowned through his blond stubble. He looked back at me with an expression I didn't think I had ever seen before. I was a little stunned by it.

"Give me your wrist," Zachary said, his voice quiet with none of the earlier smugness. It was off-putting, quite honestly.

"All right." I held it out for him, and he gripped my wrist with his right hand much more gently than the last time. The box showing my blood sign vanished as I did so. He put down his board, then cupped his left hand over his right on my wrist. Not that he needed to; my wrist was thin enough for him to wrap his thumb and forefinger around it.

"You will feel a tingling, but it's normal and won't hurt, so don't worry," he said softly.

"What are you doing?" I asked, unsure what was happening. What did he read in my blood sign?

"Just checking for something, don't worry," he responded cryptically, and then his hands glowed a light pale green. The tingling followed promptly after; it didn't hurt, as he had said, but it was strange, like the feeling of someone lightly tapping a fingernail nail against my skin. It flushed over my body, sending a shiver through my spine at the alien feeling. As Zachary's hands stopped glowing that pale green, the tingling subsided.

Zachary pulled away, releasing my hand as he gazed at me with a painful expression.

"You . . . I didn't . . ." He spoke but stopped, changing his mind and picking up the check board again. "You have passed this assessment," Zachary said, scribbling.

"I have?" I said, astonished. What did my blood sign say?

"Yes. But . . ." He paused, looking at me with that pained expression again. It was a little unnerving. "Would you come to see me if you pass the next test?"

His question made me stop rubbing my hand. "I—I guess?"

"Good. I suspect you will, with those skills."

"What skills?" I asked, very confused by this whole conversation. Why did he want to see me?

This time his smile seemed genuine as he passed the check board back to the grey-cloaked summoner. "You will find out soon enough. The next table is your final assessment. They will talk to you about it and ask you some questions."

"All right," I sighed. "Are you going to tell Eduard about . . . you know . . . me being here?" I nervously shuffled my feet, strands of fear sinking in. What if he turned up before I finished this?

"Does he not know?" Zachary seemed curious, rubbing his chin.

"Not technically . . . no . . . no, he doesn't," I whispered, looking down at my feet now, hoping my hair covered the fear on my face.

"I won't mention it unless he asks."

"Really?" My shock must have startled him from his expression. I would have thought he would tell Eduard immediately.

"As I said, I won't tell him unless he asks. I can't lie to my friend," he said, shaking his head as though that were obvious.

"Thank you, I appreciate it. I will be sure to come to see you when I can." I bowed my head to him.

"Please do." He nodded back to me, allowing me to move to the final stage of the test.

Well, that was strange. What on earth does Zachary want to talk about?

As with the second stage, four summoners were stationed at the last table. They all wore red cloaks and had very serious looks on their faces as they chatted with other candidates. It seemed my time with Zachary had taken longer than it should have, as there currently wasn't an open spot, so I waited around for a few minutes until the last spot was available.

"Name?" the red-cloaked summoner asked me. He was older, maybe in his forties at a guess, with a few silver hairs poking through his short, very ginger hair.

"Name, candidate," he asked again, tapping his finger on the table.

"Ah! Sorry. Lynette Heversham." I dipped my head in the usual short bow of greeting.

"Board!" the man hollered, and a grey cloak came scurrying over, happy to leave as soon as possible.

"Let's see here. The first assessment was to analyse the level of your mote core. This allows us to access your potential for growth to become a summoner, for which numerous grades and levels depend on how you train. This is factored by your determination, talent, and the innate core strength you were born with. The tool you used was called an evaluation globe. It measures your innate core strength.

"Your results"—he paused to read the board—"are unfortunately low. It did register the existence of a core. However, that core is so small I doubt it shows up on low-grade evaluation tools. This means that you failed your first assessment and likely will not be able to become a summoner."

The man heaved a sigh as though he was bored but didn't seem to recognise the glee on my face. So I did have a core! I knew it. I didn't care if it was small; I had one, and his explanation finally proved it. The previous tests I had done as a child must have been with low-grade evaluation tools, so it never showed up. That jerk of a blue summoner who tested me must have written that there was, indeed, some light.

"Any questions?" the red cloak asked me. I shook my head, a little nervous about speaking. He had a very domineering aura, and I feared saying something stupid to him. He was a large man, and I could see the toned muscles through his body armour as it clung to him.

"Very well. Your second assessment was to record any skills you may have that may be of use to us. The army is not just looking to recruit potential summoners but also foot soldiers, administrators, researchers, and medical professionals. We also accept anyone with outstanding crafting abilities to be our blacksmiths and leather workers, as well as those with cooking skills for the mess halls. The facility where we train is somewhat like a mini town within itself, so we are always happy to accept anyone who can sufficiently provide for the sustainability of our needs."

"Your skills are . . ." He looked at my board, and suddenly he beamed. "Well, well, well, this is a surprise. I didn't expect us to find a gem like this here in this backwater town." He finally looked up at me properly, taking an interest.

"Wh-what are my skills?" I asked anxiously.

"You don't know? Oh, you just got your blood sign? Surprising for a viscount's lineage." He shrugged.

"You have level fifty-seven in herbology, level seven in alchemy, level ten in poison resistance, level twenty-two in pain resistance, level twelve in research, and minus two in social skills." He raised an eyebrow at the social skills, and I meekly smiled in response. That was my past self showing through, probably.

For the rest of those skills, though, I knew I had done a lot of research in herbology in my previous life, married to Garret. I had even tried making some potential cures for the disease that would appear in a couple of years, but the poison and pain resistance? Why did I even have those skills? I hadn't done anything like that in this life. Was this what Vishka had altered on my blood sign? Had she amended it to include what I gained in my past lives?

"Are they good?" I asked, completely naïve to what levels counted as impressive.

"Your herbology is incredibly impressive. It takes most people years of research to reach past even level twenty-five. I must admit I am curious why a girl with your lineage has pain resistance with absolutely no physical battle skills, though. That's not something I would expect from someone who hasn't trained in combat, but I suppose that could be why you have poison resistance. You haven't been eating poisonous herbs, have you?"

I scratched under my ear and looked away in thought. "Not that I can recall" was my honest answer. If I had, it had definitely been an accident when I tried to make a cure.

His look told me he didn't quite believe me, but he didn't prod any further.

"As your second assessor must have told you, you passed the second assessment with these skills. You would make an excellent addition to our medical research facility if that is what you want to do. This brings me to the final assessment."

He leaned forward, resting his elbows on the table, cupping his hands together. "I am going to ask you a few questions now. I want you to answer me honestly. I will know if you don't," he said, almost threateningly. I gulped.

"We pride ourselves on excellence in the army. We pledge to serve the Zopan Empire's empress and defend our lands from the encroaching demonic beasts that plague it. We will not tolerate anyone who acts without this in mind or who thinks joining is an easy way to obtain power." His stern attitude had me standing at attention.

"Our foremost priority is to protect the people of this empire from any threat, do you understand?"

I nodded quickly.

"Good. This also means that no matter what you choose to do as a profession, when you pass the combat training all recruits are required to take, if you are called upon to fight, you will do that. There will be no refusal if you are called. If you do not go, there will be severe repercussions. Do you understand?"

I nodded again, though this time more slowly.

"Good. Now tell me, what do you hope to gain by becoming a recruit?"

"I want . . . I want to become strong, strong enough to defend myself when I need to." I spoke before my brain could process his question. I was surprised by my answer. It was the truth that I must have always felt but never knew how to achieve on my own.

"Fair answer. Now, before we conclude, this assessment is by no means an acceptance as a recruit," he stated, which confused me again.

"These assessments are to gather potential recruits. You will be a trainee if you decide to join. Your first task will be to march through the highland plains with us to the capital. This means you will be exposed to harsh weather and the demonic beasts that live in the highlands, and you will be expected to camp outside and keep up with us. If you tire, we will not come back for you, as this is how we weed out the weak." His direct gaze into my eyes made me shudder, thinking about the torture of walking that far.

"The second task, when and if you reach the capital, will be to become competent in combat. All trainees must learn to fight and defend themselves sufficiently to be of any use as recruits if they are called to combat. The training will be intense. You must pass a combat evaluation before formally being assigned a profession. You will also attend a mandatory class to learn about the army, our facility in the capital, the world around you, and the demonic beasts that plague it. There is also an optional class for potential summoners to learn to grow the foundation of their cores, but you will not need to attend that.

"Do you understand and accept these terms?" he finished.

I considered everything he told me. It scared me, quite frankly. I knew I would struggle with the march. The distance between Talbour and the capital was at least a month on foot. A lot could happen in a month, and my body was extremely weak from malnourishment. I also knew I was useless in combat, so encountering a demonic beast would be my death, again. Yet this was the path to which Vishka had guided me. My other three lives staying in Talbour had all ended in death anyway. This might be my last life, but perhaps, if I did die on this trip, it would be a death I had chosen, knowing the risks.

"I accept." I nodded, determined to choose my path.

CHAPTER NINE

The red-cloaked man beamed happily at me, ushering me to follow him. I hurried after him, his steps longer than my own. Hesitantly I looked back. No one else had been asked to follow their assessor; they had all gone straight to the tent. Why was he taking me somewhere else?

"Address me as General, General Saika," he announced as we walked behind the tables and past the big tent where candidates had gone after passing the assessment.

"Yes, General," I said as I nodded, picking up my cloak as it trailed in the dirt. He took me into a smaller tent with strips of red cloth flapping in the wind at its peak. The inside was bright, a mage lamp floating at the top, illuminating the stack of pole weapons featured on a rack nearby.

I slowed as he moved to a makeshift desk, opening a drawer to rifle through its contents. As he did so, I approached the weapons. I hadn't seen pole arms before. Eduard and Callan both used a sword called a jian, which was the favoured weapon of our family bloodline. These pole arms were beautiful. Each one had delicate carvings with unique patterns; some were made of wood, and others were pure metal from the sharp leaf-shaped tip to the bottom. Two had coloured tassels in bright, vibrant reds lashed at the hilt.

"Interested in spears?"

I jumped; I hadn't noticed General Saika moving up beside me.

"They are beautiful. The carvings are so delicate." I wanted to see them up close but knew I probably shouldn't be touching them.

"Good eye; these are part of my collection." He grinned proudly. "If you're interested, I would be happy to teach you a crash course." He chuckled at my expression.

"Oh, um, thank you, I've . . . never picked up a weapon before." I blushed at this embarrassment.

"Not to worry, most trainees won't have. It's to be expected." He jerked his head to indicate that I should follow him to his desk. "Different weapons are meant for different people, so we shall see what you are compatible with when we reach the capital."

"I look forward to it," I said, nodding with a hesitant smile, never thinking I would be learning to wield a weapon.

"Good. Now here." General Saika placed a scroll on the table. It had writing in symbols I didn't recognise.

"It's runes." The general laughed at my confused expression. "You won't learn these unless you want to get into enchanting, which I doubt. It's a profession for people who don't want lives." He rolled his eyes.

"What is it?"

"It's a blood contract for the army. All recruits sign them."

I frowned, a little uncertain; I hadn't seen any other people being brought here to sign this. They had all gone straight to the main tent after the final assessment.

"It's required for you to continue as a trainee," he explained, sensing my apprehension.

"I see," I said nervously. "What does it state?"

"This is a blood oath for the Zopan army. Every recruit is required to sign this to ensure that there are no runaways. Blood oaths are unbreakable and ensure trust in your commitment to the army. Three clauses allow your release: your unfortunate death, incapacitation, or approval from three ranked generals. Approval is usually given for retirement or noble heirs who must return home to govern their lands following succession."

"That's . . ." I gulped; so it was sign this and never leave, basically?

"Don't worry. I've signed it, all summoners have. It's a requirement that garners trust. Many blood oaths don't have release clauses, so I appreciate your apprehension, but this is standard protocol."

Vishka's Guidance system
Sign the contract, child

Vishka must have also sensed my unease, but she was telling me this was the way forward.

"Very well, General. What do I do?"

*   *   *

Blood dripped from the tip of my finger as General Saika pushed it onto the scroll laid out on the table. Then, as with my blood sign, a sudden flash of red sealed it onto the contract, cementing my place as a trainee in the army.

"Congratulations, trainee, you are now committed to your pledge." The fierce general grinned, his vibrant hair shining under the mage light.

My fate was sealed.

"Move to the tent behind us and wait for further instructions." He nodded towards the hulking beige canvas tent, two braziers placed at the entrance, their flames flickering in the calm wind.

"Yes, General." I performed the Zopan salute, holding my right hand over my heart and dipping my head in a bow before swiftly moving as told towards the tent.

I could feel sweat gathering between my fingers as I neared the viper's pit. Inside that tent was Rian Thornfax, the woman I had once considered my worst enemy during my second life. We had had a few encounters I didn't want to recall in my youth, so her opinion of me in this life wouldn't be swell either, but hopefully not as bad as my second.

Taking a deep breath, I saluted the two grey cloaks who stood outside and they nodded back to me, and then I stepped into the dimly lit tent.

Faint chatter roused my ears as I entered; a few groups of new trainees were already forming social structures. They all paused at my entry, most looking me up and down before carrying on with their conversations. A few didn't look away, the surprise on their faces obvious at my appearance. The Crazy Cerue Lady had a reputation, after all.

Looking around, I saw a fairly unoccupied spot near the back in the darker part of the tent. Not wanting to draw any more attention, I made my way there and gently sat down on a single wooden stool, tucking my black cloak under my legs. Quite a few people were already gathered in the tent. It was fuller than I expected. The majority wore ragged clothes, nervously talking to one another, trying to figure out what was going to happen next. They were commoners, likely untaught on what pertained to joining the army, much like I was. Most of them were young men. I didn't see many commoner women.

In comparison, neater-clothed women and men of various ages had gathered on the left side. They kept glancing towards me before whispering to one another in gossip, their body language showing hostility or just plain astonishment. The nobles of Talbour.

I tried to keep my expression neutral, knowing they were talking about me, but it wasn't easy, so I looked away from them, hoping that would ease my anxiety. As I did, I found myself facing the curious gaze of a petite girl wearing a plain white cotton shirt and brown canvas trousers. Her boots looked to be well-made brown leather already caked in dried scruffs of mud. She had friendly, prominent blue eyes, a wide face, and large ears. Shyly she tucked a strand of her straight blond hair behind her ear, gently smiling at me. I returned her smile, sensing that, like me, she didn't feel too comfortable in this crowd.

The change in her expression alerted me to a growing presence approaching.

"They let a screw-up like you join?" Rian Thornfax's disapproving voice made me sigh.

"Greetings, Lady Rian." I turned my head to face her, and she stood with her hands on her hips, glaring down at me.

"What did you do to convince them? Open your legs?" she sneered at me, her comment unwelcoming. So my scandal news had travelled fast.

"What did you do, flaunt your lineage over capability?" I retorted before I could think, quickly regretting the antagonistic comment as she scowled. My mouth had acted on instinct.

"Watch your tongue, Cerue. The fact that you are here makes me question the judgement of whoever tested you. What could you possibly bring to the army? That is, of course"—she smirked—"unless you joined to end your miserable life at the claws of a demonic beast?"

The pang I felt at those words struck a nerve.

"What vicious words from someone so *noble*," I spat, leaning on the back and intentionally returning her smirk. "Or are you just afraid that I might overshadow you? You didn't exactly show much bravery when I pointed a blade at you. If I recall, you screamed and ran for protection from your big sister. Not very warrior-like."

Rian visibly reddened as I brought up her cowardly behaviour when we were children. She and two younger barons' offspring had decided to play a game of pelting rocks at me. The adopted daughter of a viscount, a mockery of their noble births as someone born a commoner, insulted their existence. They had decided that I needed to be punished for daring to be adopted into nobility.

On pretence, they had invited me to play with them in the garden of Rian's estate during a party her parents hosted. Naïve and young, I was excited to make friends, so I willingly went with them to play their game, only to be pelted with sharp rocks repeatedly, chased, and pushed down as they joyfully punched my small body. Distressed, I grabbed at the dagger on Kit Balburn's belt and pointed it at them, tears streaming down my face. I don't recall what I screamed at them, but Rian had been so afraid of that blade that she and the two boys ran away quickly to the safety of their elders.

Naturally, no one believed my side of the story, only theirs. They lied, claiming they had not hurt me, trying to defend themselves when I threatened them with a dagger. Who would believe the story of one girl over three other "witnesses"?

"What choice did I have when you could have killed me?" Rian narrowed her eyes. "You're just the Crazy Cerue Lady, nothing more, nothing less. It would be better for all of us if you had never come to Talbour." She spat on the ground at my feet.

"Perhaps that's why I'm leaving." I shrugged.

"What?" She stumbled on her tongue, not expecting me to say such a thing.

"Perhaps I agree with you," I sighed. "I should never have come to Talbour." How different would my life have been if the viscountess had never picked me up from the streets in Wayward Town, where she grew up? I might have died of starvation as a beggar, or I could have grown to live a normal commoner's life. Pick up a profession, marry for love, maybe even have children, who knows.

"Maybe there's hope for you after all," Rian said, spite in her tone.

"Line up, trainees!" A man's voice suddenly boomed into the tent. It was commanding, demanding obedience. Rian shot me a glare before turning around to join the other nobles.

Everyone quickly dropped their conversations and rushed to line up as he asked. We formed five rows of ten, standing straight, our arms behind our backs as the red-cloaked assessors had shown us. Rian shoved me as she passed me to take a spot at the front, making me lose my balance. I felt my body moving backwards, my eyes widening as I began to fall, losing my footing.

"Oof." A sound hushed in my ear. My body halted as small hands gripped my shoulders, pushing me back up to my feet. "You okay?" a quiet voice asked as I breathed in relief.

"Yes, thank you," I whispered back to the small girl in a white cotton shirt. She smiled and stood beside me as we waited for everyone to find their place.

"Listen well, as I will only be saying this once." The man's voice echoed though I couldn't see him behind the bodies in front of me.

"We will leave tomorrow at the second bell, promptly after the last initiation intake in the morning. We expect you to bring clothes and shoes suitable for marching the highland plains. If you have weapons, I suggest you also bring those for your protection. If you don't have any, something can be arranged. It will be a long march, so waterskins and food rations are recommended, but you can and will hunt during the trip. We will provide standard tents that accommodate two people each, with bedrolls, but you are welcome to bring your own. However, you are expected to carry your gear, so bear that in mind. There's always one fool every year who brings a tent so large they collapse; don't be that idiot." He sighed dramatically at the scowls I saw on the nobles' faces. "The weather is expected to be mild, but it's always advisable to bring winter wear in your pack. As I'm sure you are aware, this will be a dangerous journey for you. Demonic beasts live in the highlands and have been known to attack on previous trips. So I advise you to stay alert and, above all else, watch out for your companions. From this moment forward, you are all members of the Zopan army; there are rules we expect you to follow, and one of those is not dying.

"Any questions?" he asked, and a few commoners raised their hands. They asked about the type of clothing to bring, worried that they couldn't afford the items he recommended. The man calmed their fears, advising that the army had spare clothing for anyone who couldn't afford it, but they would need to pay back the cost when we arrived at the capital. This was the same for any weapons anyone couldn't afford, which was something I might need to take up. Like the commoners, I could worry about paying it back later in the capital.

"All right, now, as I previously mentioned, your tents will accommodate two people each. You are welcome to choose your own tentmate, but if you cannot find someone, you will be assigned to a tent. If—" The man's words cut off as shouting suddenly echoed outside. He paused for only a moment before continuing.

"If anyone already knows who they wish to share with, then please inform the supply staff tomorrow to be registered."

I frowned as the shouting grew closer to our tent. I could make out some of the words now. It sounded familiar, almost like . . .

A flap on the tent was aggressively torn open, and I froze as I realized who the shouting voice belonged to. I still couldn't see above the heads in front of me, so I tried to peer around but only saw a brief flash of blue leather armour before the noise continued, and my body shook.

"Get out here right now, Nathaniel!" Eduard's roar was distinct, and I winced. So Eduard had finally found me, but why was he calling for Nathaniel?

"Lord Eduard, are you here to give a speech to the new trainees?" the summoner speaking with us said.

Wait, was that Nathaniel?

Slowly, I lowered my arms and carefully stepped left past the few trainees in my row until I was at the end and could peer around at the scene. The two young men I passed grumbled as I did so.

However, I didn't care too much about disgruntling them. Finally, I could see what was happening.

Eduard was dressed in full armour, the scales of his blue leather chestpiece layering into a dynamic image. It glinted in the light of the brazier's fire at the front of the tent. His stern grey eyes were directed at Nathaniel's pleasant smile as he stood in front of the trainees.

"You know why I'm here." Eduard lowered his voice, narrowing his eyes.

"I do." Nathaniel nodded. "However, this is not the time, as you can see." He remained calm.

"Where is she?" Eduard demanded.

"You don't know?" Nathaniel asked with a little smugness in his tone; I guessed he was being serious when he said he was excited to upset Eduard.

I could see where this was going. Quickly I tried to shrink down to hide my presence.

"Nate." Eduard was growing tired of his evasiveness.

"Trainee Heversham, would you come here, please?" Nathaniel asked, and Eduard's shock sent shudders down my spine. His head flipped towards the trainees, searching for me.

I sighed as a few of the trainees looked my way, giving away my position.

"Lynette!" Eduard didn't wait for me. Stomping forward with purpose, he made his way over towards me, the trainees' line broken as they darted away from him.

"H-hi," I squeaked as he towered in front of me in pure anger. His angled jaw twitched, eyes full of storms. Above his head floated the number I had seen before; however, it was different this time.

Vishka's Guidance System
Eduard Heversham
Likeability: −24% (−8%)

"Come," he barked, grabbing my hand and dragging me forward so fast I almost tripped over my feet. I saw the horror on the face of the petite girl in the white shirt as she watched us. Darn, the number had dropped since the last time I saw it.

"Where's General Saika? I want her released immediately." Eduard glared at Nathaniel as he pulled me to a stop beside him.

"He's retired back to his lodgings," Nathaniel informed him with a smile. "She has signed a blood contract, Eduard. So there will be no release."

I felt Nathaniel step closer, so I dared look at him directly. His gentle smile to me was warming, and I couldn't stop myself from returning it.

"You signed a blood contract?" Eduard's voice changed as he looked at me incredulously.

"Y-yes. I'm officially a trainee, Eduard." I gulped at his stare.

"What is the meaning of this? Nobody signs the contract until we reach the capital!" His uproar was aimed at Nathaniel, who only shrugged in response.

"Her skills were worth the immediate signing." Nathaniel's answer caused a stir of whispers amongst the trainees.

I stood there puzzled. General Saika had told me I needed to sign right then and there to become a trainee. Judging by Eduard's expression, he shared my confusion.

"Skills? What skills does she have that would be so important?" he asked, his voice lowered.

"That is not for me to say, Eduard, not here." Nathaniel cocked his head, hinting at the small crowd before us.

As though only just now realising how public this was, Eduard straightened.

"Don't think I'm done with you," he sneered at Nathaniel before moving to drag me out of the tent.

"Wouldn't dream of it, Eduard." Nathaniel chuckled. "I shall see you both tomorrow." He saluted in the Zopan way and winked at me, making me blush before we left the tent. The shocked look on my fellow trainees' faces was a sight.

I squinted at the change in brightness as we left, my hand still firmly in Eduard's grip. He dragged me in silence through the gathered summoners. I instinctively raised my hand to try to hide my face from the embarrassment. I spotted Zachary still standing behind his assessment table, watching us with a frown. I quickly made sure to mouth *Sorry* to him as Eduard led me farther away towards a carriage parked nearby. I wasn't going to be able to meet with him as I had promised.

A familiar butler stood at the foot of the carriage, showing disapproval at my appearance. Henley, without a word, opened the carriage door for us, and then Eduard proceeded to push me up the steps.

"W-wait!" I placed my hands on the edge of the doorway to stop him from forcing me in.

"What?" Eduard glared at me, his patience thin.

"Peta . . . we can't leave Peta," I mumbled, looking away from him.

"Who the hell is Peta?" Eduard tried to push me again.

"Our kreshna!" I quickly explained. "I came here with him."

"Mr Ruopold, deal with the kreshna," Eduard gritted through his teeth, finally succeeding in pushing me into the carriage. I sat down with a plop at the force, immediately scooting to the edge of the soft cushioned seats to try to distance myself as far as possible from Eduard as he sat down opposite me.

As soon as the door closed, I felt the surge of movement from the carriage, the horse's rhythm smooth compared to the kreshna-drawn carriage I had used yesterday.

I didn't dare speak first, choosing to draw out the silence between us for as long as possible. I could feel Eduard's gaze boring into me as I looked anywhere but at him.

"What were you thinking?" He finally spoke after what felt like hours but was likely a few minutes.

"Wh-what do you mean?"

"You know what I mean!" he roared, making me shrink in my seat. "What in the gods' names were you thinking? It was infuriating enough to learn you left the manor without anyone's knowledge, but for us to find out from gossip what you did last night? Lynette, I am ashamed of you more than I ever have been before." I swear I saw a vein on his head bulge. "With all of the people you could infatuate yourself with, Nathaniel Hudson was your worst choice. This is a catastrophe for your reputation that we are unable to fix!" His foot tapped in frustration.

"I wasn't *infatuated*," I mumbled.

"Oh?" He laughed darkly. "Then just what were you thinking exactly?"

"It—it was a necessary choice." I braved my heart and looked him in the eye.

"A necessary choice? What delusion made you think that fraternising in the middle of the night was a necessary choice?"

I sighed. It was probably easier to tell him the truth. "Do you think Father would accept my choice not to marry Lord Garret?"

"What?" he asked, a little taken aback.

"You know as much as I do, Eduard, once Father sets his mind on something, he won't change it." I smiled glumly. "If I refused, he would force my hand, and as his 'daughter' I cannot refuse his choice for my husband. So I did what I had to."

Eduard's silence made my skin prickle. He looked at me unusually, almost thoughtfully, but soon scowled again.

"You could have spoken to me. I would have convinced Father."

"Ha!" I mocked his words. "Yes, because telling you the truth has ended so well for me in the past." I rolled my eyes, which angered Eduard more.

"Lynette, I would have listened. Now you have just caused shame for our family! You do realise this means your prospects for marriage are nought."

"Listened like you did when I told you it was Rian Thornfax who pelted me with rocks first? Listened like you did when I told you the shopkeepers were refusing me service because I was nothing but a disgraceful adopted daughter? Listened like you did when I told you I never took the viscountess's necklace out of her room but that she gifted it to me? Really now, Eduard . . . the evidence speaks for itself." I sighed in resignation. "All I ever got from you listening is being confined to my room in punishment for telling the truth."

Eduard's gaze this time was hard to read. I didn't know what he might have been thinking, but silence once again stretched for some time.

"Why did you join the army?" he eventually said, though his voice was much calmer.

"I want to leave Talbour. It seemed a good way to do that." I spoke truthfully, though I would have preferred to sneak away on a merchant's caravan rather than in the army. Vishka's guidance hopefully would see me through.

"Do you have any idea what being a part of the army means? You will have to fight demonic beasts, Lynette; you could be killed. Just getting to the capital is treacherous enough without any training."

"I am aware." I half smiled. "I'm surprised you care so much about my potential death, in all honesty."

"Lynette . . ." He was about to say something but chose not to in the end.

"Why did you sign a blood contract, of all things? I can do nothing to get you out of it now."

"General Saika told me all recruits had to sign them." I rested my head on my hand. I was a little confused about that myself.

Eduard sighed, frustrated, bashing his hand on the seat beside him to vent a little. "That damn old man. Blood contracts are only used on the recruits who survive the journey to the capital. They are too expensive to waste on anyone who may die on the way there. Just what skills do you have that he would push one onto you early? Show me them," he demanded.

"My skills?" I asked, raising an eyebrow.

"Yes, I see the blood sign on your hand. Just do what you did for the exam; say 'Show skills.'"

"Fine." I couldn't find the will to argue. "Show skills." I held my palm out as I did before, and the red-rimmed box popped up again.

I waited as Eduard scanned through them, his eyes widening for a moment before settling.

"Do you have anything hidden?" he asked, still reading the box thoroughly.

"Hidden?"

"Yes, have you hidden anything so others can't see them." He narrowed his eyes.

"Eduard, I haven't even looked at them myself yet. I didn't even know that was an option." I sighed.

"Very well. I will teach you before we leave tomorrow. You can close it now." He sat back in his seat, satisfied with what he saw.

I lowered my palm, and the box vanished as it had done before.

"So?" I asked as he contemplated.

"Since when have you been interested in herbology?" he flatly asked me.

"A while, I guess." I shrugged. I couldn't exactly tell him I had nothing else to do in my last life married to Garret than to read the many books in his library, which were mostly herbology books, in an attempt to cure the disease that would appear in a few years.

"A while? I find it incredulous that you reached level fifty-seven. That must be why the old man was so eager to get a blood contract from you." Eduard pulled his hand through his dark brown hair as he leaned back into the seat.

"Why would that be?"

"The army lacks medical staff proficient in herbology and alchemy. Our staff mostly focuses on earth summoners who can heal using their aether. It's limited to physical injuries but very effective. However, anything viral or poisonous is resistant. Only herbal medicine can cure viral infections. So your skill is greatly required."

"Aether?" I frowned. How did you heal with aether?

"You will learn about it soon enough." Eduard resignedly shook his head. He paused, glancing at me as his lips thinned. "Did you eat poisonous herbs?"

I sighed at his question. "No, I haven't," I said, but I wasn't convinced myself.

There was a chance I could have in my last life. Eduard's face moved into the expression he usually gave me when he didn't believe me.

We sat in silence after that as the carriage took us to our destination.

"Come, we're home, and I need to tell Father of your new employment." The carriage pulled to a stop as Eduard spoke, and I heard the chatter of staff waiting for us at the steps.

Right, time to face Father: Roger Heversham.

CHAPTER TEN

The silence of Roger Heversham's office was stifling. I stood opposite his large mahogany desk, the room dimly lit with a mage light. I could have sat on one of the two blue leather chairs, but the atmosphere didn't call for comfort, so I decided to stay standing. Roger sat behind the desk, his hands folded, elbows leaning on the wood. Beside him stood Eduard, his arms folded behind his back. As Eduard relayed to Roger my latest employment, they both frowned upon me.

I nervously pinched my hand. Callan wasn't here, which was probably a good thing. At least Roger and Eduard were somewhat rational. Callan would have been shouting his head off already. As the second-born son, he didn't have the same responsibilities as Eduard, so his lifestyle was a little more carefree. I had at least been allowed to change before being summoned here.

"Lynette." Roger's voice broke me out of my thoughts.

"Yes, Viscount," I replied, nodding my head. It was strange to call him Father now. After everything I'd experienced these past few lives, he didn't feel like a father figure anymore.

"What you have done is of grave seriousness. But do you truly understand your actions?" Roger asked me, his tone not hiding his doubt.

"I am fully aware, Viscount."

"You are aware of sullying your reputation so badly that your marriage proposal was placed on hold?" He scowled at me threateningly. I saw Eduard flash me a look, almost a grimace, before returning to his calm composure.

"I am aware. I would be lying if I said that was not the point." Though *on hold* wasn't what I had wanted. I had hoped it would be cancelled altogether, but I'd take it.

"The point? You intentionally did this to stop the marriage?" Roger's voice grew in anger.

"I did," I confirmed.

"Do you have any idea of how stupid you are? This could have been resolved with a discussion. You can't be so foolish to expect that you can remain here for your whole life, Lynette. Women get married and raise families; that is the best you could hope for as a mortal, but now you have sunk that opportunity!"

"Ha," I said mockingly. "Sunk my opportunity? Whose opportunity is it I have sunk exactly? Is it not that you saw a way to get rid of me and jumped? You say we could have discussed it, but would you not have used lies to trick me into accepting?"

"Such spiteful words, Lynette. I am your father! How dare you accuse me of such things." Roger stood so quickly that Eduard had to step back.

"Accusations? Is it not the truth? Had you not planned to lie and tell me Kara had been the one that Garret Asher had wanted to marry? That if I accepted, I would be saving Kara from the embarrassment of turning him down so she could pursue her dream of working in the palace? Did you not prepare one of the iron mines to gift the baron to accept the marriage, knowing my reluctance?"

"How did you . . ." Roger paled as I told him things I could not know if I hadn't lived this scenario once already.

"Father? Is this true?" Eduard asked, surprisingly ashamed.

"Lynette, regardless of whether I had to lie to you, marrying a baron heir is in your best interests. You would have been lucky to get any other offers even before this *scandal* of yours. I only thought of what was best for you!" Roger ignored Eduard's question, or he hadn't heard him over his rage.

"Best for me? Is that not something I get to decide?" I sighed. "You think so little of me that I can't survive without a husband?"

"That is the way of life for mortal women, Lynette! As a noblewoman with no core, your value is in your marriage. As it is for every woman unable to protect herself, you know this!"

"So you say, Viscount, but I see many women with no core earning livelihoods with their crafts and talents not reliant on their core abilities."

"Those women are not nobles! You are the daughter of a viscount, not a commoner. Your future is to lead a household and raise your family's status in social circles, not to prattle on about items you can sell." Roger began to pace back and forth as his water snake slithered slowly, its movement halting to settle on his right arm. I saw its tongue taste the air before its hollow eyes blinked, resting its head gently on his shoulder.

"Oh, so it's fine for Kara not to lead that life? It's okay for her to follow her dreams to work in the palace, but not for me?" I rolled my eyes in exasperation.

"Kara isn't a mortal. She will find a husband in the capital during the social season who matches her core level."

"Ah yes, because her having a core makes her marriage valuable, not something to barely consider as anything but an option to get rid of her." I could feel my own voice growing louder as the small study we were in grew violent with emotions.

"Lynette." Roger stopped his pacing and finally glared at me head-on. "I shouldn't have to tell you that matching core levels is desired in marriage, as that is the only way to produce descendants with similar cores. The only occasion on which a noble marries another with a different core level is if they are second born or their family is already rich with descendants, so it does not matter what core levels their children may have. The baron's offer for his son is a rare opportunity that will not come again. As a mortal, you will have no viable offers from nobles as your children may also be mortal."

"Is that all you care about? Does my happiness truly revolve around being with another noble? Did you not once think about what my life married to Lord Garret would be like? I would rather live in squalor, going hungry, than be that man's wife."

"Do you think I would allow you to live in squalor? To marry a commoner? I would rather you stay here for the rest of your life than bring such shame to our family." Roger walked around the desk to stand in front of me, his hands moving in conjunction with his words.

"Do you think I want to stay here for the rest of my life?" I rebutted his arrogance. Would it be so shameful for me to marry a commoner if it meant my happiness? In his eyes, my happiness was clearly meaningless compared to his *reputation*.

"Is that why you joined the army?" he asked, narrowing his eyes. I could feel his breath against my face, he was so close.

"Yes."

"Foolish girl." He gritted his teeth even though he wasn't holding back his anger. "You may die."

"If that is my fate, then so be it." It wasn't like I hadn't died before.

"If you miraculously survive the trip to the capital on the march, you will be pushed more than you are physically capable of in training."

"I am prepared for it."

"Prepared? You have never undergone such exhaustion in your life. You will fail."

"I may at first, but it's what I want." I stood my ground. Vishka had said the army was my path forward, and I had to believe in that.

"You know not of what you speak." Roger finally stood back with a heavy sigh. "I will petition the courts for your release from the blood contract immediately, and Lord Garret will bring you home. That is my decision."

My hands tightened into fists at my side. "I will not marry him."

"You will do as I say, as your father," Roger stated defiantly.

"You are not my father," I spat, causing him to be still. Eduard's eyes widened, looking back from Roger to me. I saw the box above his head blur, the number vanishing.

"Eduard, take her to her room," Roger said, his voice quiet and oddly calm as he remained standing before me.

"Yes, Father. Come, Lynette." Eduard quickly headed towards the study door, holding it open for me. I picked up my skirt and stormed out without another word.

I followed Eduard quietly through the halls of Heversham Manor. My blood was still boiling from my conversation with Viscount Roger Heversham. Despite my protests, he refused to take into account that I didn't want to marry Lord Garret. He only cared about his damn reputation as a noble. There was no way I was going to repeat my third life married to that bastard, not a chance; this was my final life, as Vishka had said, but I would rather be killed by a demonic beast.

Eduard and I reached my room at the end of the hallway of paintings. He opened the door, waiting for me to enter, before closing it behind himself. I wandered over to my bed and plopped down with a heavy sigh, leaning back to face the ceiling.

"What are you doing?" Eduard's voice interrupted my moping.

"Watching the ceiling, what else?"

"Sit up," he instructed, so I complied reluctantly, pulling myself up. Surprisingly Eduard sat beside me, the bed dipping under the weight of the blue armour he still wore, not having had a chance to change since we arrived home as he had been guarding my movements.

"I meant what I said," I mumbled, looking at a particularly interesting speck of dust near the dank curtains.

"I know." He leaned forward on his knees. "I wasn't aware that Father intended to lie to you." His lips firmed into a straight line. "But you shouldn't have rebuked him." He shook his head.

"So I should just accept marriage to Lord Garret when that isn't what I want?"

Eduard sighed. "No, if that isn't what you want, but Father is stubborn. He won't listen when you pull these stunts." He eyed me directly with meaning. Those years of my youth throwing tantrums had definitely made Roger Heversham a stubborn man when dealing with me.

"He wouldn't listen to me regardless. He's made up his mind." I stood, not wanting to be next to Eduard any longer. His presence in my room was unusual enough. He normally avoided this place. I walked to my wardrobe and opened it, searching for items of clothing to bring for the march. It was a difficult task as I mostly owned dresses.

"He believes this marriage is best for you, Lynette. He's doing what he thinks is right."

"So my opinion is moot if it's what he thinks is best?" I said, pulling out a pair of old boots; there was a hole in the cuff, but it didn't matter so long as the soles were sturdy. My other boots all had heels, so they were a no-go.

"That's not what I said." Eduard now stood with a frown.

"You didn't have to." I sighed, finding a pair of brown woollen trousers, much better than a dress for marching. My leather trousers would be too stuffy. Eduard always did as Roger told him. I wasn't expecting him to take my side in this. He never had before. "I regret my actions in the past, but I'm doing what I think is best for me."

"What's best for you right now is surviving the march." Eduard picked up the boots I had pulled out and inspected the soles. "You need to know the basics as a noble. It wouldn't be good if it became apparent you knew as little as a commoner."

"And whose fault is that?" I raised my eyebrow at him as he put down the boots, not pleased.

"We never thought it was information you would need as a mortal. This situation was not expected." Eduard folded his arms, looking away with pursed lips.

"I guess not." I shrugged, finally choosing a burgundy cotton shirt. I would probably need a couple more.

"No. Now sit so I can explain what you need to know." He nodded to the bed, choosing to pull out the chair from my desk for himself.

I put down the shirt on top of the trousers near the bed and did as he asked. Sitting down on the flattened mattress, I was somewhat glad he didn't choose to sit beside me again.

"First thing to know is about cores and how aether works," he started.

"All right, well, I know I have one now." I smiled, pleased with that knowledge.

"What?" Eduard looked at me, puzzled.

"Ah, the test I took with the evaluation globe showed that I have a core. Though it's so small, most low-grade tests won't pick it up. That's what General Saika told me." I had forgotten to mention that to either Eduard or Roger.

"I see." Eduard rubbed his chin in thought. "That's unexpected. You likely have below a grade one if our tests didn't pick it up."

"There's a grading system?" I asked.

"Yes, it's a standard designation for evaluating the power grade of a core. Grade one is the lowest and most basic strength required for most skills. To put that into perspective, most barons have either grade two or three innate, a viscount is often grade four to five innate, an earl is a grade six to seven innate, and a marquess is a grade eight to nine innate. The royal family is usually a grade nine or ten."

"So mine is lower than the lowest standard?" I had expected it to be abysmal, but lower-than-standard lowest?

"Most likely; if a low-grade evaluation didn't pick it up. They can only sense grade one and up."

"So I won't be able to do much with it?"

"Doubtful." He shook his head. "These are grades of our innate cores. However, they have the potential to grow through gathering techniques designed to draw in aether. The growth is limited depending on your innate core strength, so having a small innate core will block your growth at a point. I have an innate core strength of five. With that, I can expect to grow to a strength of ten, but any further than that, I will struggle as my core won't be able to contain much more aether. Whereas the royal family, with an innate strength of ten, will be able to grow to a core level of possibly twenty, as their starting core was much larger and able to absorb much more aether."

"Um, what exactly is aether?" I asked, sort of understanding what he was saying but not fully. I had never fully understood what aether was. It was impossible to learn by standard means, as books on the topic were forbidden. I just knew it was the source of a summoner's power, and a demonic beast's, and that it was what our cores produced.

"Aether is the power our cores are made from." Eduard lifted his hand, and suddenly many small floating molecules of white balls tinier than the tip of a pin sprouted out from his fingers. My single mote of white paled in comparison to the dozens floating around his hand.

"This is aether." He moved his fingers, and the small white balls moved. "Every living being is made from aether. It is the makeup of our world. It exists all around us; plants, people, demonic beasts, all is aether. A person is born with a core when they possess more than is required. The additional aether condenses, allowing the person to control the abundance within. This condensed form can be grown when more aether is pulled in through specific techniques."

"So aether is the basis of all living things?"

"Precisely. Demonic beasts are born from aether-rich locations. Its density can vary. Talbour is low in aether, so there are few demonic beasts here, whereas in the deadlands it is incredibly rich, so many demonic beast forms thrive there. Demonic beasts also have cores, which are useful for strengthening our own for growth when absorbed."

"I see . . . So would I be able to grow my core with aether?"

"It is possible, but with your innate strength below the standard, I think you would be lucky to raise it even to grade one."

"Disappointing," I sighed, but was happy to know I could grow it. Perhaps with the mistwood tea and jabascus root formula, I could improve my chances of growing it past grade one.

"Quite." Eduard half smiled. "To become a summoner, the limitation is a grade eight core that has been trained past the initial first two stages."

"Stages?"

"Yes, the first is the condensation stage, which I just explained. You must gather as much aether as your core can accommodate from the natural world. You must refine the aether within your body to match your natural affinity until it is absorbed. Aether exists in many forms; some are water aether, and some are fire. You must filter out the aether of the affinities you are not accustomed to. Once you have condensed as much as possible, you can break through to the next stage. Each stage has layers. So before you can break through, don't try it until you are absolutely certain you have condensed your core level as far as you can. For you, that will likely be level one."

"And the second stage?"

"That is foundation establishment. After completing condensation, your core level will be set, but you can refine it through foundation along with your body. You will learn more about this if you ever reach this stage. The final stage is core solidification. Most people don't reach this, as you can damage your existing core if the breakthrough isn't done correctly. Each stage can propel your core's power greatly, affecting your skills' strength. However, someone who reaches core solidification and only grows their core to level ten in the condensation stage will be far less powerful than someone who grew it past that. Which is why innate core strength is so important."

"I think I understand. So why is the limitation to become a summoner a grade eight core?" I leaned back on the bed, curious.

"That is simple. Each core level allows you to control more aether." He flicked his fingers, and the many motes of white instantly began gathering together. "To summon a spirit of aether, you need to be able to control a set amount to supply the spirit." The motes squished together, and suddenly a bright light flashed for a moment. In their place popped a blue water snake, the motes disappearing altogether. The snake floated in place before Eduard outstretched his arm, and it clung to it, slithering around before settling.

"If you have too little aether, you cannot contract with an aether spirit safely. It will be hazardous if you try to summon one without a level eight core. The spirit will consume the aether that makes up your being rather than the abundance in your core to make up for what it requires. This can cause serious harm to the body and has often resulted in death."

I gulped. "So not something I should try." I hesitantly smiled, which earned me a hardened stare from Eduard.

"Do not ever attempt it, Lynette; with a core so small it will most definitely kill you."

"Don't worry," I sighed, "I won't." It wasn't like I ever hoped to be able to summon anyway. "So, what exactly is an aether spirit? Yours is the same as the viscount's."

"Yes, I chose the same aether spirit our household has held for generations, as many heirs do, since it represents our houses. Do you remember when I told you aether forms demonic beasts?"

"Yes." I nodded, intrigued.

"An aether spirit is more or less the same. We use a rune spell to summon a desired spirit to contract with. Rather than forming into a demonic beast, the aether is controlled to summon a creature we desire that is linked to our core, our very being. By doing this, the aether spirit cannot exist without us, as it can only feed on the aether we produce. Demonic beasts, on the other hand, can function on the aether in the world, so they do not need such a contract as they can grow stronger by consuming other living beings and absorbing the aether in their bodies. That is why they are so dangerous to us, as you know." Eduard didn't need to remind me of Cassandra Heversham's death; she had possessed a strong core, Roger often praised her for it, but she had still succumbed to a demonic beast attack. Now I knew they must have been drawn to her because of the aether in her core. They had wanted to consume it to grow stronger themselves.

I grimaced at the thought.

"So your core is at least a level eight, then? And you are at least at the foundation stage?" I asked because Eduard could summon. I wondered what stage Callan was at then, as I knew he couldn't summon yet.

"I'm a level ten core, at midfoundation stage, yes." Eduard nodded, happy I had understood that much, before stroking his water snake. As he did so, the snake bubbled before popping back into dozens of tiny white motes. "I won't be able to keep my aether spirit out constantly until I reach core solidification."

"I see, so that's why I didn't see many summoned creatures at the army tent today," I mused. I had wondered where they had all gone. Roger always had his water snake with him, so that meant he was at the core solidification stage.

"Precisely." Eduard shifted in his seat, bringing the motes back within himself so they were no longer floating around. "Now, I need to explain how to hide some of your abilities on your blood sign. I don't think advertising your social skills as a minus two will do you any good," he said, and I couldn't help the meek blush on my cheeks at the slight embarrassment.

"No . . . probably not," I agreed, noticing the box above Eduard's head. It had been blurred for a while now, but it began fizzling, and I was surprised at the new number it now showed.

Well, that was unexpected.

Vishka's Guidance System
Eduard Heversham
Likeability: −19% (+5%)

CHAPTER ELEVEN

Water dripped from the ends of my soaked raven hair, darkening patches of the pale green fabric of my ball gown. I sat bedraggled, alone, and miserable in the water fountain I found myself in. Rian Thornfax had moments before pushed me over the fountain's edge before leaving me in the dark of night as she returned to the party inside.

"Get out of there." Callan's voice was loud and obnoxious. "You look like a drowned rat."

"A beautiful one, though, no?" I laughed, standing on shaky legs wading through the water. I looked to Callan, who offered no hand in support, so I stepped over the fountain's stone edge with no assistance.

"You push your luck, sister." He glared at me with defiant eyes. His sword was drawn by his side.

"I was simply telling the truth. Rian is a snivelling coward." I refused to accept the blame here.

"Rian is to be my wife, sister. You have no right!" he roared at me.

"Tough luck for you," I sneered, fed up with this farce. "Your wife-to-be is a terrible person."

"Lynette! Stop your insults at once." Callan stepped towards me, his hand tightening on the hilt of his blade. I eyed it suspiciously but unafraid. He wouldn't hurt me. He couldn't; I was his sister.

"I pity your inability to see her true self, brother. She is worse than a larval worm," I spat, raising my hands to squeeze water out of my hair.

"Lynette, I said enough!" Callan charged forward, and suddenly pain bloomed from deep within my chest. We both paused, shocked. Slowly I looked down at the cause of my pain and saw his sword protruding from my chest.

"Cal—" I tried to speak, but blood filled my mouth, and my vision began to fade into shapes. The quiet breeze dulled as I felt my strength wane, unable to stand.

"Lynette!" Callan's panicked cry was the last thing I heard before darkness enveloped me.

I woke with a startle, clutching my chest. The dream this time had been vivid. Raising my hand to my forehead, I wiped the sweat away. I had been bold in my second life, often unafraid to speak harsh words, and arrogant with the people around me. In retrospect, I should have treated Rian Thornfax with a little more respect than I had, but my words were intentionally spiteful, and she responded in kind. I had been frustrated with my first life, wasting away locked in this manor, and I vented a lot of that frustration at high-society parties. I indulged in luxurious goods and alcohol and occasionally partook in illegal gambling. I was a perfect villainess in many eyes.

After reflecting on this in my third life, I didn't believe Callan had intended to kill me that night, but my repetitive actions of disdain towards his future wife with no care for his feelings had pushed his anger too far. It hadn't been the first time I had insulted his wife-to-be, but it was my last.

I often heard his last words calling my name in my dreams. His voice had been afraid, not the voice of someone with an intention to kill. He had always been a hothead, quick to act without thought to his actions.

Sitting up, I glanced down at the new mark on my right hand, the blood sign. Eduard had shown me how to hide my abilities as promised so others couldn't view them when I showed my sign. It was simple enough, a matter of actively concentrating with my mind and requesting that the skills be hidden.

"Sign," I murmured, holding my palm out with the back facing me. The glowingly familiar box popped up, its borders edged in red, framing the see-through centre. I had been surprised to learn, when finally viewing it for myself during Eduard's lesson, that I had unknowingly lied to Eduard yesterday. I did, in fact, have a skill hidden. I could only presume it was Vishka's doing when she melded with the blood sign.

Blood Sign			
General Information		**Progression**	
Name:	Lynette Heversham	**Core Innate Grade:**	0.02
Age:	21	**Core Condensation Grade:**	0.02
Rank:	Daughter of Viscount—Talbour	**Affinities:**	Unknown

Traits:	Beast Born (Hidden)		
Occupation:	Trainee of Zopan Empire Army		
Covenants:	Zopan Empire Army Blood Bond: *Guidance of Vishka (Hidden)*		
		Skills	
Aether:	0	Spirit:	1
Combative:	0		Beast Taming: 1 (Novice) (Hidden)
Body:	2	General:	1
	Poison Resistance: 10 (Initiate)		Social: −2 (Novice) (Hidden)
	Pain Resistance: 22 (Apprentice)		
Mind:	3		
	Research: 12 (Initiate)		
	Herbology: 57 (Adept)		
	Alchemy: 7 (Novice)		

I was surprised at the labelling system, not expecting such a detailed breakdown of skills. Eduard had explained that skills evolved in grade as they levelled. Eight classes ranged from the lowest, Novice, to the highest, Grand Master. Every time I met a level threshold, it would evolve into the next stage. The first was from Novice to Initiate. The next was Initiate, then Apprentice, Journeyman, Adept, Expert, Master, and finally Grand Master. The higher your level, the harder it was to grow, making Masters and Grand Masters in any skill incredibly rare.

It put into perspective my herbology level. It was Adept, the fifth stage out of eight. No wonder General Saika had been so eager to get me to sign a blood contract. He hadn't been kidding that reaching Adept took years. It was strange for someone my age to have such a high skill.

I sighed. Vishka's melding had pulled my past lives' experience into my blood sign. I couldn't think of any other explanation. I hadn't read one book on herbology in this life so far. There was nothing else it could be. It would somewhat explain my pain resistance, which was probably Garret's doing, putting up with his beatings for so long. I shivered thinking about those days.

The poison resistance could possibly be from the horrendous food I'd been eating growing up in this manor. I couldn't be certain; I had avoided eating it most of the time, so that made me question just how I had this skill. Maybe it had something to do with my first life and the disease that killed me. However, I'm pretty sure I possibly inhaled some toxic fumes once or twice when trying alchemy in my study in Garret's manor. The fact that I only had a Novice level in that skill despite my years of attempts to find a cure proved how difficult it was to learn without guidance.

My research skill must be attributed to my herbology training from the many books I read, trying to find new herbs to help with my disease.

Beast taming, though? That was an enigma, along with Beast Born. Vishka had hidden the skill, so it shouldn't be something I shared with anyone. Although I knew I had always had an understanding of kreshna; Callan and Eduard had always been embarrassed by that. Maybe this was why?

A soft knock on my door made me quickly close the blood sign.

"My lady? Are you awake?" Freda's voice hesitantly called out as she opened the door a crack.

"Come in, Freda," I replied, surprised she was even asking. Freda had never held back from walking in without approval before.

Her small frame stepped inside, holding the usual water basin.

"I have brought your morning water, my lady." She gently placed it on my desk.

"Thank you," I said apprehensively at her attitude. It was weird. When she remained standing nearby, it only felt stranger. Why hadn't she left yet?

"Um." She coughed into her hand awkwardly. "Is there anything I may help you with?" she asked, glancing around my room, raising my surprise further.

"No . . ." I said, a little dumbfounded. "I'm fine, thank you."

"Very well." She nodded. "One moment, my lady." She dipped out the door before quickly returning. This time, she held something wrapped in blue paper tied neatly with a dark blue ribbon.

"This is for you, my lady, from Lord Eduard." She placed it beside the water basin on my desk.

I started at the parcel, shocked.

"Eduard?" I asked, still unsure if I had heard correctly.

"Yes, my lady, for your . . . trip." She looked down, biting her cheek. "I have been informed that you are leaving." She shuffled on her feet as I stood up from the bed, my nightdress floating against my ankles.

"Yes, I will be leaving today to travel to the capital with the army," I said, my fingers glancing across the paper of the parcel. I could feel the shape of two boxes layered atop one another.

"I just . . ." She paused. "I wanted to wish you a safe trip, my lady."

I turned to face Freda as she struggled to look at me directly. "Thank you, Freda."

"Breakfast will be served in an hour." She dipped in a curtsy before leaving the room awkwardly to continue her duties.

After she closed the door, I watched it for a moment, still unsure of our interaction. However, my attention was quickly drawn back to the parcel.

Why had Eduard given me something? He didn't even bother buying me anything for any of my birthdays. Instead, he would just give me coins, so I could purchase something myself. That way, he didn't have to put any effort into the action.

Carefully I untied the ribbon releasing the delicate paper folded around the two boxes. The first box was smaller than the bottom one. Opening its lid, I sucked in my breath, unsure of what to expect.

Inside I found a neatly folded light blue cotton shirt. I lifted it; the cloth was thick and well-made. The stitching was tight, the sleeves cuffed at the wrists with silver thread, and a delicate stitched pattern of water lilies trimmed the neckline in the same silver as the cuffs. It was beautiful.

Beneath the shirt was a crinkle of paper. I pulled it out to find a second item. A pair of cotton canvas trousers in a deep black was hidden underneath. I held them against my waist and found that their length reached my ankles, just like my nightdress. The waist was a little wide, but they had loopholes for a belt. They shared the same silver threaded pattern of water lilies along the seam of a pocket on the right leg. They, like the shirt, were clearly of high quality, the choice of material cooling in the summer heat.

A little afraid of what the second, bigger box held, I gingerly lifted the lid. My eyes widening, I tugged out a tightly packed pair of boots. They were black like the trousers, the leather sturdy and cured with a crafted hand. Laces threaded up the centre of both, allowing an easier fit around my legs as they were knee-high boots. The soles were etched with grip and made for trekking undergrowth, not the dirt-trodden streets of a town.

I put down the items on my bed and stood back, inspecting them.

Why had Eduard gifted me with such expensive clothing? This kind of finery was beyond the scraggy burgundy shirt I had pulled out last night and more akin to something I might expect Rian Thornfax to wear. Not a disdained adopted daughter such as myself. I bought the only nice things I owned with Roger Heversham's money. Nobody ever gifted me such things.

What was he doing?

It was impossible to deny that they would be excellent for the march, especially the boots. I was a little reluctant to think of what I would do if I got them ruined during the trip. But it was likely to happen. Surely he must know that? For such expensive clothes to be wasted that way . . .

Shaking off this weird morning, I continued my routine, splashing my face with warm water.

Stripping out of my nightdress, I lightly touched the scar on my chest, the spot where Callan had stabbed me in my second life. It was an angry red line, a little jagged from his shaky arm. The blade had cut a little further down after the initial impact.

I had grown used to it in my third life, my excuse being that it was a childhood scar from before I was adopted when Garret had seen it. He couldn't exactly fact-check that, as no maid had ever helped me change in the Heversham house-hold since I arrived as a young girl. A solid lie I could explain away as having no memories of the incident in which I got it. I didn't have any memories of before I was adopted.

Rubbing my neck, I removed the strip of ripped cloth I had used to sleep in. I didn't think leaving my neck uncovered at any time was wise. Anyone could enter my room when I was sleeping and see the scar around my neck from my most recent death. I had no lie for that, not one that could be explained as it didn't exist a mere two days ago. Everyone had seen my neck daily, unlike my chest, which was always covered by garments. So I had to be very careful.

Conflicted, I eventually put on the clothes Eduard had gifted me. They were soft on my skin, comfortable, and a perfect fit, loose but not baggy. Grabbing a leather belt from my drawers, I added it to the trousers and tightened the laces on my knee-high boots.

Picking up the clothes I had gotten out last night, I put them in the rucksack I had prepared as spares. The woollen trousers would be useful if it got colder than planned. One of the maids had brought me a waterskin last night, so I made sure to tie that tightly to the side of the bag for easy access. After that, all I needed was food rations, which I would get from the kitchens before we left. There was always a supply of dried meat and rice I could use, maybe some cheeses and bread, but they wouldn't last for long.

Hauling my rucksack over my shoulder and grabbing my black cloak with my free hand, I left my room for morning breakfast.

Kara's pout and tear-filled eyes obstructed my vision as she clung to my shoulders fiercely. She blocked my path in the hallway towards the dining room, the anger and sadness of her quivering lip making me tense.

"How could you?" She trembled in her grip.

"Kara." I reached for one of her hands on my shoulders, but as I did so, she tightened her fingers, digging in.

"How could you, Lynette! How could you leave me!" Her voice was loud and piercing.

"I'm doing this for me, Kara. Please understand." I spoke calmly, hoping to calm her in turn. I had been nervous about what Kara's reaction might be. She had been happy for me when I left to marry Garret in my third life but had still made a fuss. Now that I was leaving for the army, and not for marriage, I wasn't sure how she would react this time.

"No!" she protested. "No." Her voice quietened as tears began to fall. "Wh-what i-if . . ." She couldn't finish her sentence as she began to hiccup with tears, but I knew what she was going to say.

What if I died?

"Kara." I cupped her chin and wiped a tear from her cheek. "Everything will be okay. I promise." I lifted her head to make sure she looked at me as she sniffled.

"You can't know that," she whispered, unconvinced. There was something I could tell her to convince her, but the thought made me uncomfortable.

"Eduard and Callan will be with me. They will keep me safe." I smiled through the lie; like heck they would.

"R-right." She loosened her grip on my shoulders and wiped her eyes with the backs of her hands. "Yes, our brothers will keep you safe." She seemed to cling to the idea as I'd hoped.

However, her tears quickly turned into a scowl. "I can't believe you did that to Garret."

"What did I do to him exactly?" I narrowed my eyes. Kara sadly was so spoilt she often only ever thought of romance.

"He wanted to marry you, Lynette! He must be heartbroken." She glumly sighed for him.

"Kara, I will not marry a man I have no love for." I bit my cheek, holding back what I wanted to say. She wouldn't understand. None of them would.

Kara covered her mouth in shock. "You don't? But at Sarah Gangley's, you danced together so well I thought you were smitten."

"I don't. I am instead doing what I want to do." I sighed, pulling her close. "Please understand that."

"All right," she mumbled against my chest, wrapping her arms around my waist. "Just come back," she whispered as I hugged her back.

"I will," I promised.

We stood together for some time. I thought she might know I probably wouldn't be coming back, not to this manor.

After we broke apart, Kara took my hand in hers and walked beside me to the dining room. I gave it a slight squeeze before we separated to sit at the table laid out for five. She chose to sit beside me this morning rather than in her usual spot beside Roger. It was nice.

It wasn't long before Roger arrived with Callan and Eduard. Roger greeted Kara with a smile, ignoring me, before sitting at the head of the table.

Callan didn't hesitate to glower at me, choosing to sit directly opposite before slouching in his seat, disapproval written all over his face. I rolled my eyes at his behaviour, turning away.

Eduard sat beside Roger as he always did; he glanced at the shirt I wore, and I couldn't stop the feeling of my cheeks reddening. He half smiled before focusing his attention back on Roger as they continued their conversation.

On cue, the servants immediately brought us all cups of tea and plates of steaming food. Freda approached as my servant, placing a plate on my setting; she smiled.

"It's a ham omelette," she whispered before pulling away to stand against the walls with the other servants.

Gingerly I lifted my knife and fork and cut a slice. Surprisingly, it was fluffy, cheesy, and edible. For the first time in this manor, I was being served a decent meal.

It must have been obvious as I didn't hesitate to devour it with gluttony.

Breakfast had been uneventful; Roger had spoken with both Callan and Eduard privately whilst I enjoyed my meal conversing with Kara. I encouraged her to continue her studies so she could work in the palace someday. She dreamed of meeting the empress and serving in the royal library.

I made sure to visit the kitchens when we were done and filled my rucksack with rations, a knife, and a simple metal cup. All vital when camping; I even found a spare flint strike that the cooks often used for making a fire. Then, happy that I had taken what I needed, I headed to the front of the manor to await Callan and Eduard.

I didn't have to wait long before Callan appeared. He wore a blue cotton shirt similar to mine and darkened brown trousers. The grey cloak of his station in the army flourished behind him. He had the same black brigand armour on his chest I had seen summoners wearing in the parade. From what I had put together, people wore a coloured cloak of the element they had an affinity with. However, anyone who was unable to summon an aether spirit wore a grey cloak with the colour of their element stitched on the hem. This was why Callan didn't have a blue cloak, as he couldn't summon an aether spirit yet. If the cloak was grey with a darker grey hem instead of a colour, their station was a foot guard, members who could not control aether.

"Tch." Callan frowned as he approached. "Typical."

"Excuse me?" I asked, unperturbed by his attitude.

"You know what." He folded his arms. "I had expected you to do *something* stupid whilst we were back, but you really know how to throw out expectations."

"What were your expectations exactly?"

"Oh, you know." He smirked. "Making a fool of yourself, wrecking something, causing a scene, that kind of thing."

"Ah. Well, I'm happy to have surprised you."

"Congratulations." He slowly clapped sarcastically. "I always knew you were a handful, but I didn't know you wanted to be demonic beast food."

"I won't be." I closed my hand into a fist, trying to convince myself. "I want to help. I can help."

"With your herbology?" he inquired. "You won't get a chance to use it if you don't survive."

"You almost sound worried that I won't."

"Don't worry. I'm not," he snipped as Eduard arrived beside Roger and Kara.

Like Callan and me, Eduard wore a similar blue shirt, his black trousers standing out against the dark blue brigand on his chest. Unlike Callan's, his cloak was a royal blue with silver buckles attached to the brigand armour. At his waist hung a jian safely tucked in its scabbard: a double-edged straight sword, the weapon of choice for the Heversham family. He passed another jian he was carrying in his hands to Callan, who took it happily.

"Lynette," Roger said, holding one out towards me.

"What's this?" I asked, surprised, hesitant to take it from him.

"Take it," he demanded, seeing my trepidation. "You are representing our household. It would be shameful if you did not leave with a weapon."

"Thank you." I took the jian, and the sudden weight made my arm drop. I quickly gripped it tighter. Callan snickered at me with a knowing look, his thoughts obvious at my frailty.

Not a good start. I could barely lift the thing.

"Is it heavy?" Kara asked.

"Yes," I said, not wanting to further divulge my weakness. I needed to consider strength training.

"It is made from the metal of a militon beast. It will be heavy," Eduard informed us as he tousled Kara's hair. A militon beast? Weren't those the demonic beasts commonly found in Ridge Pass? I thought I recalled reading that they had shells with metal studs.

"I have written a letter to the courts for your release from the blood contract. Eduard will present it when you get to the capital. I expect to see you return with Lord Garret at the next outing." Roger looked at me firmly.

"Callan," he called when I didn't respond, and instead glared at him. "You will train Lynette with the jian on the march. Make sure she can at least defend herself if there is an attack."

"What!"

"What?"

Both Callan and I exclaimed simultaneously.

"Father, I have responsibilities. I cannot train her as well," Callan objected, his voice raised at this command.

"Do not argue with me, Callan. Eduard will be preoccupied at the front of the march. You will have plenty of spare time in the evenings after your duties. You could do with the training yourself anyway." Roger stood his ground firmly, fully expecting Callan's objection.

"But—" Callan tried to speak, but one look from Eduard and he stopped. "Fine," Callan said sharply instead, turning his anger at the situation towards me.

I wasn't exactly happy about this either, but I couldn't find any reason to say no. I needed all the help I could get.

I had no idea how to use a jian.

CHAPTER TWELVE

Vishka's Guidance System
Eduard Heversham
Likeability: −17% (+2%)

Vishka's Guidance System
Callan Heversham
Likeability: −21% (−1%)

As the horse-drawn carriage moved onto a rougher road, I rocked a little in my seat. Eduard and Callan sat opposite, neither one looking too pleased. It had been a tearful goodbye for Kara, all her siblings leaving at once.

Roger had watched us go, holding Kara tight to settle her emotions. Eduard and Callan had both been troubled by leaving her after such a short visit, but it was the same every year since they each joined the army when they turned eighteen. The only difference this time was that I was leaving with them.

"Do you need to pick anything up before we leave?" Eduard broke our silence, directing the question to both Callan and me.

"Nah, Felicity is getting most of our stuff," Callan answered, leaning back in his seat.

"Felicity?" I asked curiously.

"A member of my squad." Callan rolled his eyes at me. "You may get one if you survive."

"Callan." Eduard scowled. "Enough."

"Whatever." Callan waved his hand in dismissal. "I'll teach her how to use a jian, but don't expect me to help with anything else."

"Callan, you will do what is required." Eduard's lip twitched. "You will be the closest to her."

"So what? She's a trainee now. We didn't get special treatment on the first march, nor should she."

"*We* had years of training prior, Callan. We didn't need support."

"She chose this knowing she had no training. So why should I suffer for it?"

"Because," Eduard said sternly, "Father has asked it of us."

I sat listening to them argue about me as though I weren't in front of them. It was irritating.

"I don't want Callan's help." I butted in, folding my arms. What use would help be from someone who didn't want to provide it?

"See?" Callan nodded at me.

"Lynette, to guarantee your safety, it's best that Callan assist you." Eduard sighed, frustrated with this conversation.

"I don't want his assistance. It would be unfair for the other trainees if no one else is provided with it. I will learn the jian only because Roger insisted." I shook my head at them both. Helping me would likely only make me stand out against the other trainees. Moreover, it could result in some bitter opinions towards me.

"Lynette, I must insist that y—" Eduard began.

"There you go, it's settled. I'll teach her the jian and nothing else." Callan cut Eduard off as the carriage pulled to a halt. "See you on the march." He pulled the door open forcefully, stepping out before Eduard could respond.

We both watched him enter the growing crowd of recruits, disappearing into the sea of coloured cloaks and raggedly dressed people.

"You know he's right," I said, watching the crowd and spotting a few faces I recognised.

"Right about what exactly?" Eduard raised an eyebrow.

"I shouldn't get special treatment." I stood up and took the first step out of the carriage. "I did choose this for myself. I accept the responsibility of that."

It didn't take me long to find the smaller group of recruits. They stood out from the crowd as no one had an official uniform yet, like me. Instead, we were all dressed in our own style of marching gear. Some people had leather gauntlets and chestplates, but they were not the black-dyed superior gear many of the fully trained members wore. Others wore poorly scraped-together cotton, strapping polished borrowed weapons to their belts. The disparity in gear between the nobles and commoners was extravagant.

It hadn't escaped me that the shirt I wore matched both Callan's and Eduard's, but it became even more strikingly obvious now that I was here. Did he gift me this clothing because it was our family's reputation to focus on water aether?

Standing there unsure where to place myself, I noticed several recruits approaching a brown-cloaked summoner. The summoner stood in front of a series of crates loaded onto a wagon. He handed out various items to the people who approached, logging it all on his clipboard. Moving over, I listened to their conversations and learned that many of the nobles were informing the supply staff about whom they wished to share a tent with. The commoners requested items they lacked and were informed of the repayment due when we reached the capital.

Before I knew it, I was in line, and it was my turn.

"Name?" the summoner asked with a pleasant smile.

"Lynette Heversham."

"All right, Lady Lynette, what can I do for you? Are you in need of any equipment?" he asked, the wrinkles around his eyes crinkling. "Anything you borrow will need to be returned or repaid when we reach the capital."

"I understand. I would like some armour, if possible, and a dagger."

"Is that all? We also offer spare clothing and food rations." He gestured to the crates stacked with goods.

"No, that should be fine. I have brought my own rations."

"Very well, hold on a moment." He looked me over, tapping his pen against his lips. "This should fit, I believe," he said, pulling out a very worn grey leather chestpiece. It was short and only covered my chest, leaving my waist uncovered.

"This is a short cuirass made from a stone vole beast. It's tough against piercing damage," he explained as I took the piece from him. "These are gauntlets made from the same vole." He handed me those as well.

"Now for a dagger . . ." he mumbled, searching through a crate of weapons. "Ah, this should do nicely." He pulled out a blade no longer than my hand. Its edge was serrated, the handle wrapped in blue leather. "This is a standard iron dagger. The hilt is wrapped in treated marsh snake skin. It should do for this trip."

"Thank you," I said, struggling to keep hold of it all.

"Now, your tentmate has already picked up your camping gear. Go find them to distribute the load and wait for the call to leave." He finished with a beam.

"Um . . . tentmate?" I wasn't planning on choosing anyone in particular. I was happy to have a stranger, in all honesty, even a commoner.

"Yes." The summoner smiled. "Miss Teresa Garpson requested you as a tentmate."

"Who?" I asked before realising I was furrowing my eyebrows.

The summoner chuckled. "The young lady standing over there." He pointed to my right towards a quieter part of the square. Following his direction, I saw a small girl with blond hair tied up in a tight ponytail. She wore a plain white cotton shirt and brown canvas trousers.

"Oh . . ." I said, surprised to see the quiet girl from the tent yesterday.

She requested to be my tentmate?

"Hurry along now. There's a queue," the summoner gently prompted me.

"Right, sorry, thank you." The words spilt out as I moved out of the way, readjusting the armour tucked in my arms.

Carefully balancing it, I walked towards Teresa. She noticed my approach quickly, her smile pleasant.

"Here, let me help you with those." She reached out and took the short cuirass from me, relieving me of my struggle.

"Thanks, um . . . Teresa, right?"

"Yeah, guess you heard I asked to be your tentmate," she said awkwardly, scratching the tip of her nose.

"I did. Why did you . . ." I paused as a slight pink hue formed on her cheeks.

"Well . . . it's hard to explain, but I like you." She chuckled nervously.

"But we've barely spoken." I was so confused. Nobody liked me.

"I know, but I saw what happened during orientation yesterday with that girl who was rude to you, and then that man who took you."

"Rian and Eduard?" My confusion only grew. Unfortunately, both of those interactions in the orientation tent were bad for me.

"Yeah." She scratched her nose again. "I sort of resonated with you and thought, well . . . sorry if I was being presumptuous, you're welcome to decline to be my tentmate. I'm just a commoner from Ingalham Town. I know nobles don't like associating with commoners, so I get that, but I also sense that you don't get along with many people here in Talbour, and I sort of thought you might be okay with being my tentmate. I don't know many people here. Of course, I know the other commoners who came with me from Ingalham for the sign-up, but I don't exactly get along with them, so I relate to you. Oh! I got your name yesterday when you were called up by—Eduard, did you say? He looked fairly upset with you, by the way. I hope everything is okay?" Words tumbled from Teresa so fast I barely blinked until she took a breath.

"Slow down." I laughed, surprised by the information she was spilling so fast. "You are from Ingalham Town? That must have been a long trip. You came with others?"

"Ah, sorry." Her hand covered her mouth. "Mother is always telling me I talk too much." She sighed, disgruntled.

"That's okay." I chuckled again. "So, Ingalham?"

"Ah, yes! I'm from Ingalham Town. It's a little strange here in comparison. There are lots of people. I travelled here with others from Ingalham by carts with some merchants for protection. We travel here yearly for the sign-up as the army doesn't come to us."

"That must have been a rough journey." I smiled, seeing the tension in her shoulders settle slightly.

"Oh, it was. I had to sit on the carts with my peers." She sighed dramatically. "It was exhausting."

"If you don't get along, I can understand how that must have been uncomfortable."

"It really was." She slumped. "That's why I resonated with you when I saw the looks the nobles from Talbour gave you." She scratched her nose again. That must have been something she did when she was unsure or nervous.

"I see. I must be honest, I am a little surprised." I shook my head, still processing this information. "But I would be happy to be your tentmate. I hadn't thought anyone would want to."

"So you don't mind that I'm a commoner?" Teresa brightened.

"Not at all." I waved my free hand. "I was adopted into nobility; status doesn't bother me like it does other nobles." At least it didn't anymore; I was driven in my second life to be accepted by my noble peers. Their disdain for my heritage was brunt and painful. I often looked down on commoners in the hopes that the other nobles would see me as one of their own. A bitter smile lifted my lips; I was foolish.

"That's great!" Teresa exclaimed, dropping my short cuirass and clutching my hand, her happiness seeping from her aura.

"Great?" I widened my eyes at her enthusiasm.

"Yes! We have even more in common than I thought." Her grin was so wide I could see most of her teeth.

"We do?"

"Yes." She nodded vigorously. "I normally hesitate to tell people this, but I think you will get it." She looked around us and then leaned into my ear, holding her hand over her mouth.

"I'm an illegitimate child of a noble," she whispered, surprising me yet again.

"You are?" Suddenly, what she had told me began to make sense. An illegitimate child with a commoner mother would be scorned by her peers. I had seen it before; it was no fault of the child, but commoners would see them as different from themselves. Nobles would see them as a dirty secret to hide.

"Yes, mother refuses to tell me who my father was, only that he's a noble from Ordil." She pulled away from me. "Oops, sorry!" she said, noticing my dropped short cuirass, picking it up quickly.

"I understand why you must not get along too well with the other commoners from Ingalham." I smiled.

"It's not been easy," she agreed. "Much like it probably hasn't been for you, right?"

"Right." I nodded with a sigh. "I'm glad to have met you, Teresa. I hope we can be good friends," I said, my stomach fluttering. I had never had a female friend before.

"Likewise." She grinned. "Now let me help you put these on!" She motioned to the short cuirass.

I tugged the shoulder strap of my new stone vole chest armour. Teresa helped me get it on with some grace and then showed me how to put on the matching gauntlets. They sat a little loose on my arms, so I had to pad them with some spare material from the supply cart. After seeing them, Teresa quickly went to get her own armour, and she now wore a similar design set. We then divided the tent supplies. Teresa had insisted on taking the tent itself, whereas I took the pegs, mallet, a strange metal pole, and a cooking set that had been provided. Finally, we each carried our own sleeping bag, a roughly sewn cocoon blanket tied to the top of our bags. It was a heavy load, and I could already feel my back straining.

"Are you worried?" Teresa asked me, tilting her head.

"A little." I bit the inside of my cheek. "I've never left Talbour before."

At least not since I was first brought here as a child.

"It is a little scary outside the walls. My stomach was in knots when I left Ingalham for the first time." Teresa looked over at the path leading out of the square. "There was a whole bunch of trees I had never seen before, and the ground was so rough that the carts jolted all the time. There were even some rocks so large you could fit a dozen people on them. I think they were called boulders." Teresa looked thoughtful. "The trees started to thin as we reached Talbour, though. The farther south we went from Ingalham, the more fields there were and less forest."

"I don't think I've ever seen a forest," I said, thinking back to all my lives. I hadn't seen much, having never left. Talbour had some patches of trees but nothing large enough to be called a forest.

"I will have to bring you to Ingalham, then." Teresa smiled. "Trees surround Ingalham, we have them in all of the streets. It's wonderful." She sighed. "I don't think there will be too many on the way to Zromore, as it's called the highland plains."

"I think you may be right. It's mostly open fields from what I know."

I wonder what that will look like.

"Zromore may have some. I heard they have the Haro Woods nearby," Teresa said as she tapped her chin.

"The capital has woods? I didn't know that."

"Yeah, not as good as Ingalham Woods, though." She smiled that toothy grin.

"Of course not." I chuckled.

"Hey, look!" Teresa pointed over to the sign-up stands. "Looks like they have finished up the morning recruitment. Maybe we will be setting off soon?"

"They have? Perhaps we should move to the—" I stopped, staring at the orange hair that bobbed with movement from the last table. His black cloak was decorated with a golden clasp, his trousers cut neat and adorned with leg braces matching the leather chestplate atop his burgundy shirt.

Garret.

"Lynette?" Teresa waved her hand in front of my face. "You stared off there for a moment." She tilted her head as I pulled my gaze away.

"Sorry, saw someone I would rather not." I pinched my fingers, trying to hold back my trembling.

"Oh, who?" Teresa started looking over.

"My to-be *fiancé*," I mumbled. "Not by choice."

"'Kay, so we stay away from him, yeah? Don't need someone you dislike getting near."

"Thanks." I smiled at her. I thought she might be the only person I had met who saw my discomfort so plainly.

"Anytime. I know all too well about wanting to avoid someone." Teresa wiggled her eyebrows, making me laugh.

"I guess you would," I said, feeling the trembling in my hands lessen. Was this what having a friend was?

"Let's move over there. Looks like that's where most of the trainees are gathering." Teresa motioned to a small spot outside the orientation tent. I nodded and followed her over.

So Garret had indeed decided to join the army earlier than in my previous lives. There was no other reason for it other than the change that I was here this time. Thinking about it, Roger had said I was to return with Garret. Perhaps he had instigated his sign-up this time.

That meant not only did I have Eduard and Callan to deal with, but also Garret Asher and, of course, Rian Thornfax, alongside all the others from Talbour who disliked me. It was somewhat comforting to know that people like Teresa, who had come from different towns, perhaps held no prejudice towards me. Not yet, anyway.

"Oi, you." Teresa and I paused as we reached the group of trainees. A young boy, maybe nineteen at a guess, approached us. He wore a torn, uncoloured cotton shirt and patched trousers tied with rope. From his phrasing to attract our attention, he was definitely not a noble.

"Reuben." Teresa rolled her eyes. "What do ya want?" Her articulation changed, and I was a little confused. She had spoken far more properly to me so far.

"Just wanted ta let tha girl know not ta bother with an outcast like you." The boy wiped his nose with the back of his hand. "Duty to inform her, ya know."

"Consider me warned." I frowned. Teresa really did have similarities to me.

"Oh, a noble, are ya?" The boy fumbled a bit but performed a messy bow. "Sorry, m'lady, didn' realise."

"Ya heard her, Reuben, now bugger off." Teresa narrowed her eyes, folding her arms in a humph.

"All right, all right." He held up his hands in defeat. "I get ya, Teresa, just doin' what I wa' asked by Tomin."

"Ugh, Tomin." Teresa huffed. "When ya gonna stop doin' whateva' he says, Reuben, ya better dan that."

Reuben shrugged. "Gotta do what I gotta do." He smirked before turning to me again. "M'lady." He bowed and then left us.

"What was that about?" I asked, raising an eyebrow.

"Sorry." Teresa scratched her nose in a blush. "I grew up with Reuben. He's from Ingalham, like me. He and a few of the other boys from my neighbourhood joined up. Reuben started following Tomin when we were about fourteen, and Tomin . . . well, we don't get on."

"I saw, but I was more surprised at how you talked," I said, making her blush further.

"Ah well . . . since you're a noble, I thought it best I speak with you the way Mother taught me," Teresa said with a meek smile.

"I will have to meet your mother." I said. "So I can tell her you spoke excellently."

"I would love the praise." She giggled.

We both waited quietly, chatting to one another about ourselves. I learned that Teresa grew up as an only child, raised by her mother alone. Her mother worked as a seamstress and had sometimes tailored items for nobility when they visited Ingalham, which was how she guessed she had met her mysterious father. There was, of course, a small pool of nobility in Ingalham, but as the town farthest north from Zromore, the capital, they had smaller trade coming in from other towns and instead specialised in exporting lumber from Ingalham Woods.

Talbour had a much larger trade system as a town at the centre of the landmass between Ingalham, Ordil, and Ridge Town. It was the first stop for all three before passing through to Zromore by land. Situated between two mountain ranges, it was protected and instead specialised in trade and food export because of this. Ingalham had a marquess, as all towns did, but only one viscount and two barons. Talbour, in comparison, had Marquess Rothstar, an earl, two viscounts, and several barons.

Teresa tried to describe the buildings to me and how they differed from those in Talbour, but it was hard to imagine commoner dwellings built into the trunks of trees by summoners who created the town many aeons ago. Apparently, it was a skill now lost to the empire, as the ability to manipulate plants was lost. This meant some new buildings looked like those that could be found in Talbour, built from brick and mortar, which were the nobles' and richer commoners' homes.

Teresa expressed her desire to one day rediscover the aether that built those homes. She wanted to be able to repair the homes of the commoners there, which were now patched up poorly from years of decay. She was fairly down at the prospects of that happening, knowing it was a slim reality considering it was lost so long ago and the countless people who had already tried and failed.

When she asked about me, I tried not to divulge too much about my life. I hadn't exactly been forthcoming so far. I explained to her about my adoption from Wayward Town to the east and how Cassandra had taken pity on a begging child despite my obvious Dramorian features. Then I told her of Cassandra's death. I didn't get into any details, but I did briefly mention how my status had created a divide between me and the other nobles. I then told her a summarised version of how Roger wanted me to marry Garret and my disagreement. I didn't tell her about my family life, only who they were, but she seemed happy with that, not pushing for more.

Our conversation ended as, around us, the supply carts began to pack up, summoners began to bark orders to one another, and the setup in the square became bustling. The last of the trainees gathered with our group, Garret amongst them, each with packs and tent equipment ready. Some looked scared, others determined.

"Trainees gather up." Nathaniel's voice spread out over us as he strode towards us. He was flanked by two other summoners, also wearing red cloaks like himself. I noticed, unlike yesterday, Nathaniel had a halberd strapped to his back; the staff was wrapped in a red leather skin, and the metal of the axe blade glinted beside the sharp spike mounted on top.

"I am Captain Hudson, your commanding officer for this march. You will do what I say when I say it. There will be no ifs, no buts. You do it." He slowly raked his eyes over the crowd to solidify his authority. "You will be placed in front of the back line of the march. This position is fairly safe, as trained summoners will cover your backs and fronts. Do *not* attempt to leave your position unless ordered to for your own safety," he said whilst one of the summoners beside him handed him a board.

"These are Lieutenants Sharpclaw and Cragborn. You will be divided into two groups of twenty, and they will be your team leaders." The two red-cloaked summoners stepped forward. Now that I got a better look, my eyes widened.

Lieutenant Sharpclaw was a very tall man, at a guess almost six feet; his shoulders were wide and his arms bulged with muscle, no fabric covering them. Two triangular ears poked through his shaggy brown hair, their dark hazel colour matching the furry tail that swished under his long cloak. He was a beast-kin. He folded his arms and stood straight with a no-nonsense attitude, his expression very serious.

Lieutenant Cragborn was a wiry man. His nose was crooked against a sharp narrow chin. He glanced across us all with scrutiny. What caught me were the bright red slits of his pupils, and two small spikes jutting out of his collarbone.

His ruby red hair was long, tied into a ponytail at the nape of his neck. It was such an unnatural colour I found myself staring at it. It was like the paint I sometimes saw women wear on their lips. He must be a daemon.

"When I call your name, move to the left," Nathaniel continued, clearing his throat. He began bellowing names at a fast pace. People started to scramble quickly when they heard theirs called, moving to the left as instructed. I heard Reuben and Tomin being called and looked to see if I could spot who Tomin was so I could recognise him in the future, but it was hard to figure out as so many people moved at once.

Eventually, Nathaniel finished the list without ever calling my or Teresa's name. "Those whose names I have called will be under the command of Lieutenant Sharpclaw." Sharpclaw nodded, happy with his group and moving to stand in front of them.

"Those whose name I didn't call, you will be under Lieutenant Cragborn." Cragborn gazed at us in silence, then proceeded to stand before us.

"Greetings." His voice was smooth, almost hypnotic.

I gulped, looking at the other twenty recruits in my group. They were mostly nobles, but there was the odd commoner like Teresa. Most of the commoners had been assigned to the left. I was in a group with Rian Thornfax and her followers, and worst of all, Garret Asher.

CHAPTER THIRTEEN

I grimaced at the smug smirk Garret sent me as our group followed Lieutenant Cragborn. Teresa noticed my reaction and swiftly moved us to the opposite side to avoid him. I thanked her and tried my best not to look his way again.

"Trainees," Lieutenant Cragborn's smooth voice began. "Your group has been assigned to me as recruits with core potentials. During this march, I will be evaluating your successes and failures alike. I hope none of you will be"—he paused—"disappointing."

Wait, but I didn't think I had core potential?

"Sir, what will you be evaluating exactly?" A noble I didn't recognise spoke out.

Lieutenant Cragborn sighed heavily. "Your basic ability to survive, for a start. The rest is up to me, don't question me again." He pressed his lips together tightly. "I expect you all to train, support your group, and listen to orders. Interpret that how you will."

"Tch, you expect us to be evaluated under conditions so vague?" the same noble argued, clearly not accustomed to having someone superior to him.

"Trainee Trigot, hold your tongue. Did I not just tell you all not to question me?" Lieutenant Cragborn glared at the young noble. The noble paled a little but nodded begrudgingly.

"Good," Lieutenant Cragborn said sharply. "We will be moving in five lines of four, a standard procession for a marching group of your size. I shall take the lead, and each group of four will take turns in where you are positioned within our formation. Each group of four will consist of two sets of tentmates. Choose your team between yourselves. I have no desire to be asked to assist in those decisions. Make your choice before we reach the gate," he finished, causing a flurry amongst us.

The gate was only a five-minute walk away.

"So we are together, then?" Teresa said, looking around for a potential pair for us to partner with.

"Yes, as tentmates, we need to find another pair, any ideas?" I asked, seeing pairs already forming groups of four.

"Not really," Teresa sighed. "It's mostly nobles, from what I can tell. I have no clue who anyone is." She slumped as our options were slimming faster and faster.

"I recognise some people, but they aren't exactly who I would want to pair with." I sighed, seeing Rian Thornfax and Lacey Weadall together. They were with Kit Balburn and another noble I didn't know.

"Maybe we should just wait to see who's left?" Teresa inquired.

"Perhaps. I don't think we are exactly the first choice for many people." I sighed, readjusting my backpack as we walked.

"Lady Lynette," a voice called, sending a chill through my bones. "You look lovely today." Garret's smile was insidious but probably flattering to anyone else's gaze. I gripped the straps of my backpack tighter for emotional support as my stomach tightened at his approach.

Gotta keep a calm attitude; this Garret hasn't done anything to me yet.

"Lord Garret." I forced myself to dip my head in a polite bow but nothing respectful.

"You must be Lady Lynette's tentmate." Garret looked Teresa over. "Pleasure to meet you, Miss . . . ?"

"Garpson," Teresa said, guarded after seeing my tense posture. "Teresa Garpson."

"The commoner from Ingalham? Lady Lynette, if you wish for a different tentmate, please do inform me. I will arrange for better company as soon as possible." Garret scoffed at Teresa, making her scowl.

"I am perfectly fine, Lord Garret. Thank you for your input," I mumbled, stepping closer to Teresa to try to prevent a possible retort. Garret had always been snobbish, even for a noble.

"Hmm, very well. I suppose I can stoop to teaming with a commoner if that is your wish, Lady Lynette. As your fiancé, I will grant you some leeway." He raised an eyebrow at Teresa's expression.

"With all due respect, Lord Garret, we have not agreed to be members of your group," I said, tightening my grip. *Nor have I ever agreed to be his fiancée, for that matter.*

"Nor is she your fiancée." Teresa growled what I was thinking. My eyes widened quickly, looking at Garret and the growing frown on his face.

"Stay out of this, commoner," he spat at Teresa, turning his attention back to me. "My lady, I do not believe you have much choice. In either matter, might I add." He smirked confidently. "Your options are already slim."

I blanched at his double meaning and attitude. He was right; most of the groups had already formed teams of four whilst we had been talking, and the gate was already in view. So we didn't have much time left to argue.

Panic began to set in. I felt my heart rate increase. No way . . . I couldn't cope with being on Garret's team for this journey. It would be about a month, maybe longer, until we reached the capital.

What could I do?

"All right, form five line teams of four. Your time is up," Lieutenant Cragborn announced as we approached the gateway separating Talbour from the world's dangers outside its walls.

"Excellent, the matter is settled," Garret sneered. "Lord Harold, you will be on my right, Lady Lynette will be on my left, and the commoner can stand beside her."

I stood frozen as Harold Eastmond approached to stand where instructed by Garret. He wore a fetching brown cloak and sported a tan-coloured armour set, two sai blades attached to his thighs. Their blades split into three. He glanced at me and Teresa and performed a respectful bow, placing his right fist on his chest.

"Ladies," Harold said solemnly, his dark brown cornrows neatly braided down to his shoulders.

"Hey," Teresa muttered, holding back her anger at our situation, reluctantly standing where Garret suggested on my left. "We can do this," she leaned in and whispered to me, grabbing my hand with a small squeeze.

"Right," I said, not convinced, my hand trembling in hers.

I felt sick.

The army quickly got into position. No fancy trumpets or drums were leading this time, as we weren't arriving for a celebration. We were leaving for battle-grounds. In front of us were at least a hundred or more troops, upon which approximately forty were foot guards, by my count. Grey cloaks, the foot guard, weren't at the front. They were situated in two groups of around twenty at the centre of the brigade near us. On the edges were the summoners, their cloaks a mix of colours in lines of four. Unlike the segmented colour split they had entering Talbour during the parade, it seemed each smaller group of four had a member of each affinity. I counted four separate groups of summoners on either side of the foot guards.

Behind us was a similar arrangement: twenty foot guards in the centre, four groups of summoners beside them, and a final segment of summoners behind them, bringing up the rear.

Then we, the trainees, were at the centre of this formation. Our two groups of twenty stood side by side, each with our lieutenants at the front. At our sides were the final two summoner groups, protecting us.

With such a defensive formation, it was hard to imagine how much danger we would be in. It was actually quite comforting to know that competent fighters surrounded us, and it settled my heart quite a bit. It wasn't great, however, that Callan was in one of the teams guarding the trainees.

His team all wore grey cloaks, their hems stitched with different colours. This showed that Callan was in a team of troops similar to himself. They had a strong core with an affirmed element each but couldn't yet summon an aether spirit. There was only one girl in his team. She wore a brown shirt matching the stitching on her grey cloak, her affinity earth. That must have been the Felicity that Callan had mentioned in the carriage.

I hadn't yet seen Eduard, but from our conversations, I presumed he was near the front, somewhere out of view.

"We leave when the gates open and the horn is blown," Lieutenant Cragborn informed us, standing in wait for the signal.

It wasn't much of a wait as shortly, the large stone gates of Talbour, taller than our highest building, slowly began to drag inwards. The stone scraped on the dirt, its creaking noise echoing throughout the vicinity. I could feel the ground vibrate a little at the weight of the stone.

The gate was never opened for merchants. Instead, a smaller door within the gate was used for everyday travellers. As a result, I had never seen the gate itself being opened before, and I marvelled at the scene. This was only done for the army.

A horn then sounded from the front, blown by one of the commanders perched on horses leading the brigade. The place where General Saika, Jared Baler, the hero of Ridge Pass, and likely Azriel Elkhart were.

"Forward!" Lieutenant Cragborn shouted, stepping into the march's pace. We all immediately followed suit. Ours was the third line of four in our group of twenty. It was a steady pace, a slow walk, and every step brought me closer to the large stone gates. Up close, I felt minuscule against them, like an ant looking up to a person.

As we passed, I held my breath. For the first time in all my lives, I was leaving Talbour, not as a child with little to no memory but as an adult fully aware of what was happening. I was leaving the safety of the walls of a town, stepping into the unknown, the dangers of demonic beasts and a wildness that plagued our population from living without such walls.

This was my first step forward to a different outcome. To survive.

The bright blue sky was vast as I left behind the gates of Talbour and proceeded into the unknown.

I won't die this time.

* * *

Grass, I had never seen so much grass before. Meadows of nothing but green stretched on for miles beyond what I was able to see. A few small encroachments dotted the meadows; they were walled off with stone, but I spotted a few house tops from behind them. They must be for the commoners who chose to live outside the walls. A myriad of squealing and a smell of faeces made my nose wrinkle as we passed the grounds used to breed subservient boar beasts and hens within those settlements. Hens were one of the few animals that couldn't use aether, so they were often a staple food source for both their eggs and meat.

The path we walked on was muddy, having already been trudged through by those in front. Dozens of footprints marred the ground as we left the small settlements and moved between two large fields, leaving Talbour behind. I glanced back and saw the two mountain ranges bordering either side of the town, hugging it in safety. The mountains soared high, taller than the gates we had left, but they weren't barren. They, too, were covered in green, a few trees dotting their peaks.

There was no water mass near Talbour. Our water was gathered from wells and the rains that frequented the area in spring. The ground soaked in the rains and held it for the summer months, making drought a concern, but it was rare and usually well prepared for. It was also why water summoners were well respected in Talbour. Roger Heversham had been called upon more than once when I was growing up to assist the local farmers who dared leave the walls to tend to the fields under the watch of Talbour's guards, fields we were now passing through.

A few farmers were tending the grain that grew, waving to us all as we passed them, their trained foot guards standing at the edge of the fields looking out for any dangers. I spotted a couple of the barons of Talbour amongst them, their status obvious from their clothes and the summoning cloaks they wore. With the army passing through, they too waved with a cheer, knowing that any demonic beasts we came across would be slaughtered, saving them the trouble.

Vishka's Guidance System
Congratulations! You have left Talbour
Quest Received
Reach the capital alive

Well, that was ominous.

My new quest from Vishka could have just been to reach the capital, couldn't it?

I sighed, tugging my backpack as we progressed farther and farther away from society and into the highland plains. A gnawing feeling began to resurface in my gut. Flicking my eyes left, I watched Garret grimace at the mud splattering his once pristine trousers. He seemed to be struggling with our change in environment and often leaned on Harold Eastmond for support. Harold didn't question it; he just carried on as though Garret hadn't leaned on him multiple times to wipe the mud off his clothes. Harold was turning out to be very patient, or was he apathetic? I wasn't sure. Either way, as both were baron heirs of the same rank, it wasn't something he should have to put up with.

Garret wasn't the only noble struggling. All around us, the trainees mumbled complaints and misgivings. But everyone kept moving, not wanting to be left behind.

Teresa seemed to be coping well. She didn't slow her pace or breathe heavily under the weight of her backpack. She seemed at home marching, carefully placing her steps and balancing her gear. She flashed me an encouraging smile, lifting my spirits a little bit.

"What do you think?" she asked me.

"About?"

"Being outside the walls; it's thrilling, isn't it?" She opened her arms wide, gesturing all around us. "It's so big outside the town walls!"

"It's definitely something." I watched a breeze blow, shaking the grains in synchronisation. "It makes me even more curious about what a forest looks like."

"It's completely different; you can see the sky in the plains, and it's like never-ending open freedom. In a forest, you're surrounded by trees. It is enclosing, and you can only catch glimpses of light through branches. It's a whole different experience. I can't wait to show you one day."

"What are you drivelling about?" Garret said, plucking off a speck of mud from his thigh.

"It is indeed interesting to have left the walls." Harold spoke without looking our way, his focus on the landscape around us.

"Sure, if you enjoy being worked like lowly commoners." Garret rolled his eyes. "This is demeaning. What happened to carriages? Even merchants use carts, but they have us walking like cattle."

"Lord Garret," I sighed. "The army is not a holiday. We are here to learn and train. There are no easy shortcuts."

"It is not a shortcut to give a noble what they deserve," Garret responded with a snap.

"This is how they weed out the weak," I mumbled, repeating what General Saika had said to me.

"What?" Garret frowned at me.

"Nothing," I said, turning away from him, but not before I saw Harold shaking his head.

"Gosh, he's annoying," Teresa whispered to me. "No wonder you don't want to marry him."

"That's not the worst of it," I whispered back.

We didn't speak again for some time. Instead, each of us concentrated on our momentum, steadying our breath and keeping pace with the large brigade for the journey ahead of us.

When the sky began to darken, I wasn't sure how many hours had already passed. No tower bell was out here to signify the times of day: morning, afternoon, evening, and dusk. It was disorienting. The bell had always been a part of life.

Not once had the landscape changed significantly around us. The only tell that we had travelled at all was the speck now in the distance that was Talbour and the mountains encasing it.

A horn suddenly blasted from the front, shocking many of us out of our trance.

"Halt!" Lieutenant Cragborn ordered as the march came to a standstill. It was hard to make my feet stop, and when I did, the weight on my back increased tenfold. My legs shook like jelly, and I struggled to keep standing, my exhaustion hitting me like I had been punched in the gut.

"We will be camping here for the night. Find a spot with your team but stay in the formation. No wandering out for privacy or any other such nonsense." Lieutenant Cragborn waved his hand, and those of us with some strength left immediately and rushed off to find the best spots.

"Come on. This looks like a good spot." Teresa pointed to a rather flat section of ground that was clear of debris.

"No, we will camp here." Garret slumped to the ground. "I'm not walking another step."

"But—" Teresa tried to argue, but I grabbed her arm and pulled her back.

"It's not worth it," I told her quietly.

"Fine, this will do. Let's get out the tent gear," Teresa grumbled.

I moved to take my backpack off. However, the moment the weight was released from my back, I suddenly felt myself falling forward.

Oh crap!

"Whoa there!" Teresa grabbed me, helping me sit down on the soft dirt. "I think today has worn you out, huh?" She smiled sympathetically. "Not used to physical activity?" she asked, not insultingly.

"No, I'm not." I rubbed my legs, trying to get the muscles to contract. I had not been training since childhood like many of the other nobles had. It had never been my future to join the army.

"You can say that again." Garret lay down on his back, having removed his own backpack. "This is nothing but torture; we are not accustomed to grunt work, unlike you commoners."

"Commoners don't go marching in the highland plains every day either, you know." Teresa bit the inside of her cheek, holding back what she really wanted to say as she pulled out the tent.

"Whatever, commoner." Garret waved her off, returning to staring at the evening sky.

"Why, you—" I could see that Teresa wanted to go over to him, but I grabbed her arm again and shook my head. She scowled but nodded, continuing to spread our tent out.

"Here, let me help," I said, pulling my backpack across the dirt to get the mallet and pegs.

We worked together to figure out the tent cloth they had given us; it was triangular, and we had been provided with a retractable pole to go with it. Teresa luckily had seen one before, so she knew we had to centre the pole in the middle of the tent cloth to raise it high, then use the pegs to secure the straps into the ground with the mallet. I struggled to put much strength into the mallet, but before I could succeed, Harold silently came over. Then, using his mallet, he secured the pegs for me.

Harold built his and Garret's tent alone without uttering a word of disapproval towards Garret, who remained lying on the ground. At one point, I thought he might have fallen asleep, but he called Harold to start a fire. That confirmed he was just fine letting someone else do all the work.

I really hated that man.

Gathering up some dry sticks from plant stems, we set up a makeshift fire inside a circle of rocks. As Teresa attempted to light the fire with the little tinder we had, I stood and wandered a little away towards the fields off our trodden path.

At least there is one thing I can help with.

Pollen made me sniffle my nose as I leaned down in the short grass to pluck a plant I recognised from the herbology books I had read. The flufftoru was white, soft, and fluffy like its name. It was growing consistently in the fields around us. I spotted a few summoners gathering it nearby. It was a common plant known for fire combustion and made great kindling on the road.

As I pulled another, the white fluff moulded around my fingers. I accidentally ripped the stem rather than its bud, pulling the whole plant out of the ground. The dirt dislodged, and I paused, my eyes widening at a dark orange splinter poking out of the earth.

Placing the flufftoru down, I dug my hands into the earth around the orange splinter, revealing an odd triangle-shaped lumpy plant. Its fluorescent orange was striking against the dull brown soil. I gently gripped the orange lump and yanked it, snapping it away from its tiny white roots.

I gingerly inspected the plant in my hands. It was a yanko plant. They were incredibly hard to find, as they grew under the soil sporadically. Too little or too much water would kill them, making them delicate plants to farm. It was an incredible antivenin when pulped.

I smiled at my new find, popping it into my backpack and carrying the flufftoru back to my group.

I showed Teresa the flufftoru, and she gleefully took it from me, getting our fire started at last. Teresa explained that she had often used flufftoru in Ingalham for the stove in her home when most of the bark was wet.

Teresa then brought some over to Harold as he was struggling to find something substantial to burn, unaware of the plants in the plains.

When we finally finished, all three of us seemed to deflate, letting the exhaustion overcome us. Garret sat up and pulled closer to the fire as we all got out our rations and replenished what we could of our energy.

"Gah, I can't wait until we're at foundation." Teresa winced, rubbing her feet.

"Foundation?" I asked, rubbing my own.

"Yeah, at foundation you can start to temper your body. Walks like this will mean nothing. I heard that some people can even move so fast that normal people like us can't see them."

"They can? I can't imagine that." I looked over to where Callan's group was. Neither Eduard nor Callan had shown me such power before.

"Yeah, I bet we're only walking at this pace for our benefit and the foot guards'." Teresa shrugged, biting on a piece of jerky.

"It is a difficult road to reach foundation," Harold said, staring at the fire. "First, you must complete condensation, the gathering stage."

"That's true. I heard you get a technique to start gathering once you reach the capital. I wonder if that's true," Teresa pondered.

"For commoners like you, perhaps," Garret smirked. "We noble houses have our techniques passed down to us from our forefathers. They are far superior to the standard drab you will get."

"Right." Teresa rolled her eyes. "Good for you."

"So you have started gathering?" I asked, trying to take away some tension between Teresa and Garret. I couldn't wait to get to the capital now, just to get him out of my presence. There was no way I was going to return with him, not if my life depended on it. I knew his darkness behind closed doors. I knew the man he was going to become. Right now, he was a smug child and nothing more, but I knew. I had experienced the pain his arrogance brought me.

"Of course, Lady Lynette, as you and Lord Harold surely have with your family techniques. It is allowed for us to do so a month prior to joining. Of course, I only started recently; I wasn't expecting to join this year," Garret said as he raised an eyebrow, a little surprised by my question. Harold nodded in confirmation, ever a man of few words.

So I was yet again deprived of something so basic for a noble by my family. No such family technique for gathering had been gifted to me. I sighed. Was it worth bringing up with Callan? Probably not. I wasn't sure I even wanted to use their technique anyway. I wondered if it was because they wanted to have my blood contract cancelled. I pursed my lips. They probably didn't think I would be staying, so they wouldn't bother to teach it to me.

"I have not started gathering," I informed them. "I do not yet have a technique, much like Miss Garpson."

"Really? That's unusual." Garret frowned. "Well, I guess you don't have a core, so what would be the point?" He nodded, seeming satisfied with that conclusion.

"Wait, you don't have a core?" Teresa asked, wide-eyed.

"It is weak, but I do have one." I smiled at her reassuringly.

"You do? That's excellent, Lady Lynette. Raise your core well, and our children will be guaranteed to have cores." Garret's input made me shiver. I hadn't revealed that information to please him.

"Lord Garret, you are engaged?" Harold Eastmond spoke, not with curiosity, from his tone. It was hard to gauge, in all honesty.

"Yes, it has been agreed with Viscount Heversham. However—" Garret looked at me unsatisfied. "Lady Lynette decided to join the army, so here I am to bring her back to Talbour safely first." His smirk made me cold.

"I have agreed to no such thing," I said numbly.

"Does that matter? You will be coming home with me once you are released from the blood contract. You don't belong here, Lady Lynette. You have already collapsed on our first day of a month-long march." Garret, like Roger, clearly didn't respect my opinion in this matter. What did I expect, exactly? He hadn't ever cared about my opinion in my third life either.

"You may say what you wish, Lord Garret, but I will not be returning to Talbour, not with you." My voice came out quiet, my throat tightening. I could feel the clamminess of my palms as I rubbed them against my trousers. I wanted to believe my own words so badly, but deep down, there was mistrust in myself, mistrust that what he said was the reality I would face in this life.

"A lady's choice is valued." Harold Eastmond nodded to me respectfully and side-glanced at Garret. His sincerity took me aback. Maybe not all nobles were pigs.

"Of course it is," Teresa vigorously agreed. "You will not be taking her anywhere, *Garret*," she snarled, dropping the honourific for a noble, a sign of respect used when conversing. It was only dropped as a sign of closeness for friends, family, and equals.

The insult wasn't taken well, as Garret sharply blazed in a fury. "I don't see what say you have in this, commoner worm. This is noble business. Agreements are made, and this one won't be broken, not by Lady Lynette or anyone," he firmly stated.

"We will see about that," Teresa huffed. "It may be fine in Talbour to force things your way, but in the capital, you will be the worm, I'm sure of it." She grinned at him, enjoying the anger on his face.

"Teresa . . ." I raised my hand to try to calm her, worried for her safety. Garret might only be a baron heir, but she was a commoner. He could have her killed if he wished, and there wouldn't be much she could do about it. Only commoners with rank were able to converse comfortably with nobles who deemed themselves superior to all commoners.

"In the capital, I will have your head for your insults," Garret said, as I had feared. I felt my heart pumping fast with my fear for Teresa.

"Oh, quiet, Asher, there's no honour throwing around authority for a commoner." Suddenly, Callan's voice sliced through the heated space, making us all pause.

"Lord Callan, I was merely warning this lowly girl of her status." Garret calmed his tone, jutting his chin in indignation.

"All I heard was you throwing weight around, which you don't have, Lord Garret." Callan sighed, bored. "Come, Lynette. We have training." He tilted his head to the left, his light brown hair hard to see in the firelight. "Let's get this over with."

"Right, can, um . . . Teresa come?" I asked, hesitant to leave her alone with Garret. As much as I doubted that Harold Eastmond would treat her with vindictiveness, I also doubted he would step in to defend her from Garret.

Callan heaved, aggravated by my request. "Fine," he said, "but she watches only." He turned and began to walk towards an open spot within the army camp.

I quickly scrambled up and jogged after him, Teresa following me closely.

Time to learn the jian.

CHAPTER FOURTEEN

Callan carved a sloppy circle into the dirt to indicate our training ground. His jian glinted, the steel mirroring the moonlight against his standard-issue black armour as he stood opposite me.

"Stay outside the circle, Miss Garpson." Callan lazily swung his jian in a movement I thought might have been a parry.

"Okay." Teresa sat down some distance outside the circle, the excitement in her eyes obvious; she was eager to see a real fight with swords, but I didn't think there would be much of one.

"All right, step one, Lynette, is stance." Callan sighed at my attempt to hold the jian that Roger had given me.

"Not like that, jeez." He shook his head and stomped over. "Like this." He grabbed my hands and moved them onto the hilt of the jian. "Open your legs. You need a solid foundation; otherwise, you lose balance."

I did as he instructed and found it somewhat easier to hold the jian, the weight lessening so it didn't pull my hands down. I still struggled to hold it upright, though, and Callan could tell from the look he gave me.

"The jian is all about flexibility. Its specialty is in stabbing and making precision cuts to strike your opponent. When paired with aether techniques, you can trip an opponent midmovement. Its double edge gives you more options than a claymore, but a claymore is far better for overhead attacks. Given your strength and height, I don't think a claymore would suit you anyway."

"Height matters?" I asked, getting a feel for the blade in my hands.

"Yes, if you are tall"—he paused—"and strong, your reach increases. A heavy weapon such as a claymore or halberd would be ideal. But a spear or lighter weapon would be better if you don't have strength. If you are short, a thick sabre or possibly hammers can be good for close range if you have the strength to wield them. However"—he scraped his jian against mine, making it tumble from my hands—"if you are both short and weak, like you are, swords or polearms are your best choice."

"So a jian is a good choice for me?" I asked, bending down to pick it up.

"Who knows." Callan shrugged. "A weapon calls to you or not; the jian has always called to a Heversham, but that may not be the case for you." He smirked, obviously insinuating that as an adopted daughter, I wouldn't share the power of the Heversham bloodline.

"A weapon calls to you?" I asked, ignoring his snide remark.

"Yes, like all things, weapons have aether imbued within them. It either resonates with yours or it doesn't." He rolled his eyes. "How do you not know this?"

"Because no one told me." I frowned at him. "Is there any point in learning a weapon before you have resonated with one?" Was I wasting my time here?

"Yes." He put his palm on his face, frustrated at me. "You won't resonate with a weapon until you can sense aether. That won't happen until you grow from gathering aether. This can take time. It's irresponsible to wait until you resonate to know how to defend yourself in a pinch."

"That makes sense," I replied. It would be dangerous to be defenceless for so long when training.

"Right. Now return to the stance I showed you; let's get on with this." Callan moved back a step and held his jian straight out with his right hand, his left stretched behind him.

I did as he said and returned to the stance I had before he knocked the jian out of my hand.

"Now, follow my movements," he instructed, and I quickly moved to copy him, holding my left hand out behind me.

He changed stance, pulling the jian back and his left hand forward, palm up; I followed, and then he moved the jian into a turn, his body flowing smoothly. I followed this dance with the sword, moving from one stance to another. My body didn't stretch as Callan's did, my joints didn't straighten half as well, and it was uncomfortable on my muscles as they strained. Some twinged that I had never used before, and before long, sweat coated my body as I tried to keep up with him. I was waning fast, but Callan continued unperturbed as the blade shook in my hand. My wrist was aching, it hurt immensely, and my chest was tightening as I tried to breathe.

A clang shattered the dance, my jian dropping from my hand as I fell to my knees. My body burned and my vision blurred as I tried to catch my breath.

"That's it?" Callan sheathed his jian, tutting, "You really are weak, aren't you?"

"She was already exhausted from the march." Teresa ran over and leaned down to me. She held my waterskin to my lips, and I willingly gulped down the refreshing liquid.

"I figured," Callan said with no sympathy.

"So why did you push her so much?" Teresa said accusingly.

"Because to grow, you need to push your limits. If you don't do that, you aren't worth a damn." Callan stared at her pointedly.

"Lynette, check your blood sign. Let's see if this resulted in anything," he continued as I managed to breathe normally again.

"All right, sign." I held my hand forward to check my details, and the red box appeared with the list of my skills and progression details.

Apart from one difference, my sign looked pretty much the same as it always had. "I gained a skill in stamina, level one, nothing else."

"That's normal, I guess. You haven't walked anywhere for this long before. Most people gain stamina on the march." Callan rubbed his chin. "A few more days of doing the stances, and you should pick up a skill with the jian; then you can practise on your own."

"Most commoners already have a stamina skill," Teresa mumbled, a little judgemental of nobles but not outwardly insulting us, just stating a fact.

"Obviously," Callan answered anyway. "You're commoners." He sighed, bored.

"I'll come to get you again tomorrow, be ready." He didn't wait for us to respond. Then, happy to be done with his task, Callan quickly left, heading towards his team's camp.

"Come on." Teresa helped me stand. "Let's get some sleep. It's going to be another long day tomorrow."

"Sounds like a good idea." I nodded, and we made our way to our tent.

Sleeping on the ground in a thin cocoon of material was an experience. I thanked Vishka for the warm weather in the highland plains; any colder and I was certain I would have been shivering. We marched all day from the moment dawn struck; my muscles protested with every step, but I forced myself to keep going. It was helpful to know I wasn't the only person struggling, as many trainees' paces slowed, and we were barked at more than once to speed up. Short breaks were allowed in the afternoon when the sun was highest in the sky. They were a welcome retreat from the pain enveloping my body. Garret continued to make jabs at Teresa and her commoner origins. I dreaded to think what he might have said if he knew she was an illegitimate noble child.

After we set up our camp in the evening, I would train with Callan, mirroring his movements to try to learn his dance with the jian. On the third day, when I hadn't gained a skill yet, he was so irritated that he allowed Teresa to join, hoping someone would get some value from his time. Unfortunately, she didn't have a jian to use, but she happily accepted following his movements alongside me even without one.

The constant exhaustion was taking its toll, especially with my lack of sleep and the extra training. The gap between my limited strength and that of the other trainees was growing wider. Each day, they seemed to grow more accustomed to our situation, their bodies fitter and healthier than my own. The landscape barely changed. Only the plants that grew became wilder as we left the carefully maintained fields of farmers. The dirt path we followed became more jagged, less trodden over time. We passed the carcasses of a few ratlike demonic beasts. They were the size of a large barrel, their chests torn open and cores removed. They had been killed by the summoners in the front of the brigade, so we had been surprised to see them as we hadn't known there had even been an attack.

We continued in this routine for almost a week before I felt a change. I changed my stance to the fourth movement of the flowing water method. Callan eventually told us this was the basics of the Heversham jian style; it consisted of seven movements designed to become the foundation for the weapons skills. It wasn't a highly guarded secret, so he wasn't breaking any rules showing Teresa, but the Heversham forefathers designed the next stage, so he wouldn't be showing her that.

As I finally got my arm straight correctly, I felt a tingle in my skin, and the fifth stance was more fluid than it had been before. It still wasn't perfect, but I understood the transition of the stance more than I had. Carefully I followed through the sixth, lowering my body towards a crouch, finding my balance a little more easily. Finally, in the seventh movement in an upward motion, I stood, moving the jian as gracefully as I was able, but it still wobbled in my grip.

"Better," Callan commented, sheathing his jian. "Did you get the skill finally?"

"Let me check; sign." I held my palm forward.

Blood Sign			
General Information		**Progression**	
Name:	Lynette Heversham	**Core Innate Grade:**	0.02
Age:	21	**Core Condensation Grade:**	0.02
Rank:	Daughter of Viscount—Talbour	**Affinities:**	Unknown
Traits:	Beast Born (Hidden)		
Occupation:	Trainee of Zopan Empire Army		
Covenants:	Zopan Empire Army Blood Bond: *Guidance of Vishka (Hidden)*		

Skills			
Aether:	0	**Spirit:**	1
Combative:	1		Beast Taming: 1 (Novice) (Hidden)
	Jian—Flowing Water: 1 (Novice)	**General:**	1
Body:	3		Social: −2 (Novice) (Hidden)
	Poison Resistance: 10 (Initiate)		
	Pain Resistance: 22 (Apprentice)		
	Stamina: 3 (Novice)		
Mind:	3		
	Research: 12 (Initiate)		
	Herbology: 57 (Adept)		
	Alchemy: 7 (Novice)		

My smile must have given it away, as he exhaled in relief.

"Finally, now I can practise what I want."

"Are we still meeting in the evenings?" I asked as Teresa congratulated me.

"Yes," he said, resigned. "But now I can leave you to it whilst I work on my own. We can't move on to the next stage until you get your skill to level ten. It is pointless unless you are barely competent at the basics."

"Oh, but I have only reached level three stamina in a week of marching. So I might not reach level ten before we reach the capital." I frowned. Was that a normal growth rate?

"Tough, it's not my fault you're not talented, sister," Callan gibed. "Even the commoner is better than you."

"That's unfair." Teresa pouted. "I'm used to physical exertion and grew up in Ingalham. I often had to climb trees and used to fight with sticks when I was a kid. I bet you did the same with them; what was his name again? Oh yeah, Eduard; you have a clear advantage, and so do I. I mean, I'm grateful you let me learn too, but come on, be more realistic and don't say she hasn't got talent, because maybe the jian isn't even her thing." She spoke so quickly I could see Callan straining to understand.

"It's all right, Teresa." I motioned for her to stand down. She really was fiery. "He's probably right. I'm not going to learn this any faster than the effort I put into it." If I were stronger and could hold the jian without struggling, maybe I could have advanced quicker. "I will just have to train harder."

"Do what you want. Just don't bother me until you reach level ten from now on." Callan dismissed us and turned his back. He didn't leave this time, though, and instead redrew his jian and began to practise a technique he hadn't shown us.

Teresa said she would warm up some rice and headed back towards our tent, but I held back a moment.

"What is it?" Callan asked when he noticed I was still there.

"I just wanted to say thanks." I awkwardly shuffled my feet. This was weird. "I know you didn't want to train me, but you did anyway when you easily could have lied about it." I felt uncomfortable saying this. I had thought about it for the past few days. There wasn't much else to do but think about things whilst marching.

Callan was definitely a hothead. He had been abrasive all of my lives, even killing me in my second. Yet he was up front with me, didn't lie about his feelings towards me, didn't lock me away for my behaviour like Eduard, and never hid from me and instead just told me his thoughts openly. Despite being disagreeable towards me, he was honest with me to a degree. There was only one occasion he had ever lied. That occasion spurned me with Eduard and Roger and was definitely a turning point in my life. But he was sixteen when that happened. Cassandra had just died, and I thought I understood now why he might have lied about that incident.

"Where is this coming from?" Callan stopped his practice and turned to face me.

"I just . . . I know I haven't been easy to deal with in the past." I looked at my feet. "I just wanted to tell you I appreciate it, your help, that is." I gulped as he stared at me in silence.

It was difficult admitting to him that I had been an unruly child. Not all of my tantrums were misguided, but many of them were probably overreactions. I definitely said and did things that unnecessarily escalated many situations that could have been avoided. If anything was going to change, I had to do it first.

"Get some sleep, Lynette," he said a little quietly.

I nodded. "All right, I'll see you tomorrow."

"Yes," he said as I turned to leave, the number above his head obscuring.

The next few days passed in a blur. I marched, trained, ate, and then slept. My muscles were growing more used to the walking and I found I had settled into the rhythm of my routine. Then, on the twelfth day of marching, rain fell.

Complaints and squelching of mud slowed our pace considerably as we continued forward. Glancing right, I could see Callan's group moving easily as he cast a shield above his team, blocking the water from reaching them. Above his head floated the familiar box I had become accustomed to.

Vishka's Guidance System
Callan Heversham
Likeability: −16% (+5%)

My gamble had paid off. I had been right to take the first step to improving our relationship. The last few days of training hadn't been as intense as they had been before; Callan had trained on his own as he said he would, but he sometimes would stop to point out my mistakes and even complimented Teresa on her second movement. He still got frustrated with us when we couldn't perfect a transition, but that was his nature. I knew it wasn't personal.

It didn't hurt me to admit I was jealous of his water aether right this moment either. My feet, for the most part, were protected by my boots, but my cloak and clothes were thoroughly soaked. Everything stuck to me like glue, and my backpack had absorbed just as much water with the increased weight dragging on my back.

The rain had intensified the march tenfold, and it was difficult to hear Lieutenant Cragborn over the roaring sound. One benefit, at least, was that it was an opportunity to refill our waterskins. Living off the water a summoner could produce was possible, but it didn't quench thirst as well as normal water.

"This is getting heavy," Teresa shouted to me, holding her hands on her head in an attempt to block the rain.

"Yeah, I don't know how much longer I can cope with this," I called back, worried. I had already struggled every day under normal conditions. My thighs were burning, and we hadn't reached midday yet.

"You think they will stop the march?" Teresa replied.

"I don't know. Maybe they are waiting to see if it will lighten."

"Doubtful." Garret grimaced, struggling with us. "This is probably nothing to them. They're trained, remember," he finished forcefully, pulling a foot out of a sloppy mud hole.

"Keep moving." Harold gripped his backpack tightly as it slouched down his back. I saw droplets dripping from it as the material couldn't hold any more water. "We're dragging behind."

Sure enough, the other teams of four were quite a bit ahead of us. We were at the back of the lines today in our rotation, and we were slacking. The foot soldiers and three groups of summoners bringing up the rear were closer than they had been before.

"Come on. We can do this!" Teresa tried to encourage us, but we were only as capable as our bodies allowed. The ground we walked on had already been trodden on by the hundred or so teams in front of us. It was retaining the rain so quickly that it had turned into sludge by the time we got there, and our feet stuck to it, making each step harder.

A horn suddenly blasted; its tone differed from usual, but everyone was still moving. Lieutenant Cragborn was shouting something, but I couldn't make it out.

"Can you hear what he's saying?" Garret asked, his pace slowing.

"No, but we haven't stopped like we usually do when a horn sounds," I said, doing my best to keep going.

"Didn't it sound different to you?" Teresa wiped her face but to little avail, as the rain quickly replaced what she had wiped away.

"Behind us!" Harold exclaimed, his pace suddenly picking up.

We all quickly looked back and paled, rushing to match Harold's speed.

The summoners bringing up the rear were engaging with dozens of snakelike demonic beasts.

My lungs protested, and my feet, I was pretty sure, were bleeding, but I didn't care. I ran.

Teresa, Garret, and Harold were with me as we did our best to reach the rest of our group ahead. They seemed so far away now that I was panicking. Together we rushed as the sounds of battle echoed in the rain behind us. I had grown lax. Days of marching with no dangers had made us grow comfortable and safe. I had forgotten just how dangerous the highland plains were.

I swivelled my head to check on us and froze, causing Teresa and Garret to stop as well.

"What is it?" Garret vigilantly looked around, shaking.

"Harold, where's Harold?" I cried, not thinking about honourifics in my panic.

"Harold?" Garret looked and realised he was missing. "Not my problem." He about-faced and continued to run on ahead towards the safety of our group.

"Coward!" Teresa hollered after him.

"Where did he go?" I swivelled back, looking for him. A mist had formed behind us whilst we had been running, likely from fire summoners using their aether in the rain.

"Over there!" Teresa pointed to a slumped figure in the mud a little ways back.

"Harold!" I shouted out, my heart hammering in my chest as I ran back to where we had come from.

"Lynette, wait!" Teresa called, but I couldn't stop. My body moved on its own as I ran towards him. I knew, logically speaking, I should have got the attention of a trained summoner, anyone who knew what they were doing. But I had faced death and lived it. I knew how painful, lonely, and fearful it was.

I couldn't stop if I wanted to.

"Harold!" I called again, sliding into the mud beside his prone body.

Grabbing his shoulders, I heaved. "Sorry, sorry, sorry," I chanted, pushing with all of my might to turn him over. He flipped onto his back with a plop, and I pressed my ear to his chest.

"He's breathing, thank Vishka," I exclaimed, checking his head next for any injuries. In no way was I a medical expert, but I could spot a head wound when I saw one. Thankfully there was nothing there.

"Did you trip? Come on, Harold, wake up." I slapped his cheek to try to startle him awake, but to no avail.

What had happened?

We were all running. If he had tripped, the mud was soft enough that he shouldn't have been knocked out. What was I missing?

"Lynette!" Teresa's voice grew closer, and I tried to figure it out. That was when I spotted it, the tear in his right trouser leg. Grabbing the material, I pulled the tear aside and to my horror, I saw two large incisions in his skin.

One of the demonic snakes had bitten him.

But when? None of them were close enough for us not to have noticed. Surely . . . we would have noticed?

Shit, is he dying? What do I do?

"Is he okay?" Teresa arrived panting, leaning her hands on her knees.

"I don't know. He was bitten by one of those things. I think he may be poisoned." I racked my brain for ideas about what I could do to help.

"He was? Does that mean there's one nearby?" Teresa quickly pulled out her dagger.

"Not sure, but take this." I unsheathed my jian and handed it to her.

"What? But you may need this."

"Not right now I don't. You are better at it than I am, anyway. Keep a lookout. I'm going to do something pretty crazy."

"Like what?" She eyed me, taking the jian and putting her dagger away.

"Like this," I said, pulling my backpack off my shoulders. I quickly rummaged through it, taking out the yanko plant I had found on the first day of our march. It wasn't as fresh as it had been. Its form was wrinkled, as I had not been able to dry it for storage as alchemists do.

I sucked in a breath and bit into the yanko. Its bitter taste made me want to spit it out immediately, but it needed to be pulped. I chewed, grimacing at its taste, then spat it into my hand.

"Lynette, what's that?" Teresa gripped my shoulder, pulling me back, revealing the bright orange mush in my hands.

"Yanko, it's antivenin," I shouted as the rain grew heavier.

"Does it work fast?" she said, afraid, her eyes darting around us.

"It will slow down the venom." I smiled nervously, slathering the pulp onto Harold's wound.

"All right." Teresa hesitantly acknowledged that we might have to wait.

I got back to work, pressing the pulp into Harold's leg, making sure to cover his wound fully. I had no idea how fast it worked. It wasn't a cure-all. Yanko could draw venom from the bloodstream, but I had never prepared or used it before. Chewing it was not the best way to pulp it.

But what choice did we have?

"I think that's all of it," I breathed, opening my mouth to catch some rainwater to rinse away the taste of the yanko.

"Let's hope so," Teresa said, looking directly ahead. "We have company," she whispered in fear as I heard a hiss glide through the rain.

I turned to find a large blue snake slithering towards us.

Its scales glittered in the rain, absorbing water. Its head was the size of a large hen, its body longer than five feet. It stopped a meter in front of us and raised its body onto its coiled tail. Opening its mouth, it revealed two very large, very intimidating fangs. Its forked tongue tasted the air as it trained its two beady yellow-patterned eyes on us.

"Oh crap."

CHAPTER FIFTEEN

The snake lunged, and we both screamed.

Teresa leapt left, narrowly avoiding it as it dived straight. The snake's tail coiled to indicate it was about to lunge again. She raised the jian and fumbled into the first stance of flowing water, trying to prepare, but the snake was faster. Its blue scales stood out against the green meadow despite the mud it slid through easily.

It flung itself towards Teresa, and she shrieked. Dropping her stance, she held the jian diagonally, bracing for the attack. Instead, the snake's fangs connected with the blade. Teresa struggled but held the snake back, centimetres from her chest. Her arms shook against its strength.

"Teresa!" I shouted in panic, seeing her struggling against it.

I had to do something but couldn't leave Harold like this. He was defenceless.

Teresa's foot slipped back as the snake pushed, its fangs growing closer to her chest. She couldn't hold the snake back for much longer.

Shit.

What could I do?

The snake's tail suddenly moved differently. I saw it stealthily curling towards Teresa's leg. The snake was going to trip her. She wouldn't be able to defend against it then.

Shit.

I scrambled into the mud, grabbed the dagger I'd borrowed from my boot, and ran towards the fight. Holding the dagger high with both hands for extra grip, I gritted my teeth and jumped onto its back, heaving the blade down with a sickening squelch. It resisted the leathery skin of the snake at first, but the blade didn't have much trouble piercing as it sank into muscle.

I shuddered at the sensation.

The snake hissed in pain, releasing its jaws from Teresa's jian and turning its attention to me. Its yellow eyes glared as it jolted its body in a fluid motion that threw me off. I tumbled, rolling into the mud, my head clashing with the ground numerous times before finally stopping.

Before I could react, the snake was already slithering towards me, its fangs headed for my prone body.

I felt an intense pain bloom in my right arm as I held it up to block my face.

Tingling shivered all over, mixing with the pain.

But I didn't have time to think about that.

The dagger I had used was still in my right hand. It had been pulled out with me when I had been thrown off. My hand had sealed around the hilt in fear as my pulse thumped in my ears.

Looking directly into the snake's face, its fangs plunging into my arm, I grabbed the dagger with my shaky left hand and stabbed at its head.

The blade struck into its eye.

The snake bucked in reaction, pulling its head up with my arm still encased in its fangs.

Then Teresa rammed its side with the jian.

I screeched as its fangs tore out of my arm, my blood coating its mouth. The snake hissed and wriggled around Teresa's blade; she pushed on the hilt of her jian, forcing it through the snake's flesh, striking the ground, and pinning it in place.

Not wanting to take chances, I rushed towards it and raised my dagger. Adrenaline carried my movements as I stabbed at its head repeatedly, blood splattering us, until finally it stopped moving.

Our chests were pumping as we stared at the dead demonic beast, our bodies shaking. I glanced at my arm. It was leaking blood from the two puncture holes.

"I think"—Teresa took a breath—"the others are coming." She finished nodding to the team of summoners running our way, Callan amongst them.

"Yeah." I mirrored her exhaustion as we spoke, gasping for air. I couldn't feel my arm anymore. "Finally." It was my last word before my vision darkened, my body growing numb.

"Lynette! Are you okay?" Teresa's voice was muffled, but I could still hear her. I couldn't feel much of anything anymore, but I was still aware of the sounds around me and the few blurry shapes I could see.

My vision shook, and I was pretty sure it was because Teresa was shaking me, my body limp to her touch. Was this what Harold was experiencing? Complete loss of control of your limbs with the awareness of it happening?

I would have shuddered if I could.

"Lynette!" A panicked cry whispered as brown fluff flopped above my head. It was odd, a little surreal. I was sure I'd seen that face before, those same blurry shapes of Callan looking down at me in my nightmares.

"Get her stabilised, soldier!" another voice called as the sounds of feet scuffled around me.

"Lynette, this will feel strange, bear with it." Callan's hands cupped my cheeks, a surge of warmth sinking into my skin. It was so startling I flinched. At least, I wanted to. Had I been that cold?

A heavy weight began to settle under my eyelids as they drooped, my mind growing fuzzy this time as sleep forced its way onto me.

Everything ached.

"Ow," I wheezed, finding it difficult to sit up. Above me was a bland beige fabric that wobbled in the wind. It looked patchy but also very high. I strained my neck to look around and saw that I was lying in a bedroll atop a sturdy rectangular mound of earth, and I wasn't alone. Beside me was a line of bedrolls, each with its own occupant as we littered the inside of a tent the length of a small house.

"You're awake?" I blinked to my side to see Zachary Weadall dressed in a tidy green cloak. It didn't have a speck of wear despite our journey.

"Somehow," I muttered. "Where am I?"

"Medical tent, we set it up after the attack. Unfortunately, too many were injured to keep going, so the march has been halted for a short time." Zachary reached out to me, and my reaction was to pull back.

"S-sorry," I stuttered. "Instinct." I tried to shrug it off, but Zachary gave me a look that made me redden.

"It's all right. I only want to check your vitals. You took a heavy dose of marsh snake venom." He held out his hand this time, and I meekly nodded, placing my own into his. He tightened his grip on my wrist with both hands, and the same pale green glow emitted from them as he had done at my assessment. Again, a tingling feeling buzzed in my skin as it darted around my body.

"Hmm, good." Zachary removed his hands as the light and tingling stopped. "You are recovering well. A bit of exercise now should eliminate the last of it from your system. Make sure to drink lots of water and eat plenty."

"Thanks," I said, rubbing my wrist. "What happened to . . ." I felt a lump in my throat. "Harold Eastmond, he was poisoned too."

Zachary smiled. "He's fine, thanks to you." He nodded to the opposite side of the tent. I followed his gaze and saw Harold fast asleep, his chest moving steadily. "Quick thinking using yanko pulp; marsh snake venom is deadly, even from a grade one. Luckily its venom is slow enough that you can extract it if you get there in enough time." Zachary grimaced. "Not everyone was so lucky." His eyes flickered to a section of the tent walled off by a sheet of material.

I felt bile rise in my throat.

"How many?" I whispered.

"Too many for such an attack." Zachary sounded pained. "The back team of summoners were ambushed, leaving many people open. The rain gave the beasts an advantage." His solemn words were enough for me to understand. The biggest loss had been commoners, people without cores or aether training to defend themselves against poison. People currently like the trainees.

"I commend what you did, Lady Lynette. But, as dangerous as it was, we might not be here right now without your poison resistance," Zachary said, the air heavy with the weight of his words.

Was it my own tragic irony that had saved me?

I wouldn't have poison resistance if I had not experienced my previous lives.

"Speaking of . . ." Zachary glanced around us. Most of the medical summoners—who wore brown cloaks, as earth summoners—were tending to other patients. "You never did get the chance to speak with me," he said, lowering his voice carefully, sitting on the earth mound that was my bed frame.

"No, sorry about that."

Zachary shook his head. "It couldn't have been helped. I know how Eduard can be."

"Demanding?" I said bitterly.

"Sometimes," Zachary said, a little uncomfortable. Eduard was his friend, after all.

"Why did you want to see me?" I asked, pinching my fingers.

"Let me be frank." Zachary's tone changed as he looked at me seriously, making me uneasy. "I'm worried about you," he said, causing my eyes to widen.

"What?" I stilled.

He sighed. "Lynette," he began, his drop of honourifics making me more nervous. "A girl raised in your environment should not have poison or pain resistance, nor should your body be as malnourished as it is."

"I don't know why—" My words stumbled, my hands shaking.

"When I used my aether to check your vitals at the assessment, it showed me just how frail you are. It doesn't add up. A viscount, not a pauper, raised you, and then there's your"—he paused, gauging my paling face—"your scars," he whispered as another summoner walked by.

"How do you know about those?" I whispered, clutching my shoulders tightly.

"I'm a medical officer. You were injured. I had to check that you weren't hurt anywhere other than your arm," he informed me, so matter-of-fact.

I felt my skin crawl.

Which scars did he see? My chest or my neck? I need to think carefully about this.

"I-I've had them since before I could remember." I meekly gave him the same excuse I gave Garret in my last life. Maybe he had only seen my chest scar. This was not the time or place to go talking about how I had died three times. He would mark me as crazy.

Zachary stared at me silently, not buying it.

"You told me you had your reasons for joining the army, Lynette. I won't pry, but I want you to know, if you need to, you can talk to me." His voice was kind, but I didn't feel comforted.

"It's all right, I'm fine, really, it's nothing to worry about." I forced a smile. "Did you . . . did you tell Eduard any of this?"

Zachary sighed. "No, I won't unless I'm asked." That possibility scared me, but I knew Eduard wouldn't ask. He was too prideful.

I remained in the medical tent for a few more hours. Someone had brought me a roasted snake on a stick to eat. It was palatable. One of the first things I did after my conversation with Zachary was to check the choker on my neck. The leather piece was still untouched, so he hadn't seen my neck scar. He likely had only seen the scar on my chest from Callan's sword.

It was unnerving knowing Zachary was suspicious of me. Was it even suspicion? He hadn't exactly said anything wrong. It was the opposite, in fact. He had recognised that my skills were unusual for the life I had led so far and broached that. When he saw my skills, Eduard had barely shown any interest in my poison or physical resistance. Did he not think them unusual as well?

I wasn't to leave until the poison had fully dissipated from my body, but my resistance meant I was the only one who had woken up. I could hear the patients' groans beside me as they fought against it. The earth summoners regularly checked them with their aether, giving them liquids ground from plants, medicines for antidotes.

I watched them work as they used earth to create the tools they needed and to find the plants required for their medicines. At one point, I even witnessed a man having his torn skin resewn. The earth summoner performing the miracle concentrated as tethers of brown light filtered from his fingers towards the wound. The tether dug into the skin and weaved the two pieces seamlessly, leaving no trace of a wound.

Watching them all had me wondering why a wind summoner like Zachary was working as a medical officer. Eduard had told me the army's medical staff was mostly earth summoners, as they healed with their aether. Could a wind summoner do the same?

"How are you feeling?" Zachary asked as I finished my snake skewer.

"Better," I said, feeling full after the chewy meat.

"Good, you should be able to leave soon. I've informed your escort." Zachary half smiled.

"Escort?"

"Someone who wouldn't stop nagging me." He rolled his eyes. "Teresa Garpson is very talkative."

I laughed. "Yes, she often has a lot to say."

"Indeed," he mused. "She seems like a good teammate."

"She is." I smiled. "Do you think Harold will wake up soon?"

"Maybe in a few hours. The yanko cleared out the majority of the poison, but there's still some lingering in his system. Rest is what he needs now."

"Let me know when he does wake up. I'm sure he will need an escort too." I chuckled, and Zachary nodded in mirth.

"Zachary." I sat up, and he looked at me, almost expectantly. "Um, this may be a strange question."

"Yes?"

"Why are you a medical officer?"

"Excuse me?" He raised an eyebrow. Maybe that was not the question he was expecting, or hoping for.

"Sorry! It's just . . . you're the only wind summoner here, so . . ." I paused as a look of understanding dawned on his face.

"Earth summoners make excellent medical officers because of the precision of control the element gives them." Zachary moved to sit beside me again, tapping a round silver medallion pinned to the collar of his cloak. "This is our profession badge," he said, and I looked at it more closely this time. An intricate realistic heart was sketched into the metal, resting within a pair of hands.

"Most summoners you see with one of these are earth summoners, but some of us take up the profession because there are things only we can do," Zachary continued. "As a wind summoner, I can control the flow of air in your lungs if they collapse. I can lift the injured without jolting them. I can also use air to seal off wounds from infection or extract harmful substances if something is inhaled. All of these things an earth summoner cannot do, but I also cannot stitch a wound back together, I cannot use my aether to pinpoint an infection, and I cannot create a comfortable location for the sick like an earth summoner can."

"So a profession is not limited to your affinity?"

"No, it is not, but everyone has a preference in how they use their power," he said, standing back up as voices I recognised were stopped outside the tent doorway. "Quite often, I find, the profession chooses you."

"Thanks," I said in appreciation for him taking the time to answer me. "I wonder what profession will choose me."

"Time will tell," Zachary answered, amused. "However, I think your escort may have arrived."

We both looked to the tent entrance, and sure enough, Teresa was marching towards us. Beside her was an unexpected accomplice as they argued incessantly.

"I said I would get her. I don't know why you have to come too," Teresa said, pouting.

"I'm her brother. I have more right to escort her than you do," Callan scoffed. He purposely increased his pace, knowing Teresa couldn't keep up.

"No fair!" Teresa moaned, lagging behind him.

"Lynette, how are you?" Callan asked me, rushing to my earthen bed.

"We weren't allowed to see you until you recovered," Teresa complained, scowling at Zachary.

"She's fine," Zachary interjected. "As I have told you many times, Miss Garpson."

"Thank you, Lord Zachary. Eduard and I are grateful." Callan closed his fist on the right side of his chest as he bowed. He was oddly calm. I was surprised he hadn't found something to be upset about yet.

"Yes, I'm sure." Zachary's tone made Callan raise his eyebrow, and I meekly looked away. I didn't know what Zachary presumed regarding my condition, but I was beginning to think he had come to his own conclusions.

I gave my thanks to the medical team, Zachary included, and left the medical tent with my two escorts on either side. Many of the people we passed in their beds looked to be recovering, their wounds healed and complexions brightening. The lucky ones.

As we reached the entrance, I saw that two foot guards were guarding the tent. Their spears were raised, poised for combat, ready to defend the injured should another demonic beast appear. They nodded to us as the sound of chattering and pots cooking surrounded me. The grounds we had stopped upon had become a bustle of soldiers who trained and relaxed in the crisp sun after heavy rains.

Laughter and jostling of young men caught my attention as they trained with their weapons, shared conversations around fires, and patrolled the perimeter. Several tents were the same size as the medical tent we had left. A familiar red tassel fluttered in the wind atop one of the smaller ones: General Saika's tent. Several guards stood outside it, and I might have glimpsed a group inside discussing something around a table.

No longer were we in uniform lines. Now the hundred or more soldiers had created a small canvas village in the open meadows.

I followed Teresa and Callan as they led me through the unfamiliar layout towards a small area where the trainees were. The two groups of twenty hadn't mingled, the nobles not wanting to be near the commoners, but they were side by side. All of them were resting their weary muscles, unused to the physical strains they had been through these past two weeks.

"Lady Lynette, you have recovered." Garret's sickening voice greeted us as he strode forward.

"Pfft," Teresa huffed. "No thanks to you, coward."

Garret glared at her. "I did what was best for my safety. You should have too, commoner."

"Do you annoy everyone?" Callan said, side-eyeing Teresa, making her frown.

"Callan?" I broached, sensing that maybe something had happened whilst I had been asleep.

"Lord Garret is right. You should never have gone running off on your own like that." Callan scowled at me, making me flinch. "Foolish." He suddenly lightly smacked me on the top of my head, his fingers gripping my hair as he turned my head to look at him directly.

"But Lord Harold—" I began.

"Doesn't matter." Callan narrowed his eyes. "If you had died, I would have had to deal with Father, idiot." His face softened ever so slightly. "Don't do that again."

"All right," I gulped as he released my head.

"Good. Take care of her." Callan threw something towards Teresa, and she deftly caught it. "My camp is over there. I'll see you for training."

I watched as he left towards his team's camp, a few meters away. The girl on his team, Felicity, spotted me looking and winked, causing me to blush and quickly look away, embarrassed.

Had Callan just lectured me? He never did that. Eduard did.

Vishka's Guidance System
Callan Heversham
Likeability: –9% (+7%)

CHAPTER SIXTEEN

My palms felt clammy under Lieutenant Cragborn's hardened gaze. His slitted red pupils sent shivers through my spine as he tapped the earthen table between us with his forefinger.

Not long after Callan had returned to his team, Teresa informed me of the latest news in the camp. It turned out she was pretty good at finding out the latest gossip. The heavy rains were the cause of the demonic beasts' attack. Furthermore, the marsh snakes that had attacked us did so in a swarm, which was highly unusual for their kind. This unusual behaviour was deduced from a nest some scouts found nearby afterwards. The broken eggshells there indicated that the rain had been the catalyst for their hatching, and the march had been passing by with unfortunate timing.

Because of this unusual behaviour, the summoners in the rear guard had been caught unprepared for such large numbers. Marsh snakes were deadly opponents in the rain, as high-level ones could camouflage in the water droplets. So they had snuck up undetected in large numbers. The weaker of their kind, unable to use this skill, held back at first and only approached during the midst of combat, causing more panic. It was one of the weaker ones that Teresa and I had encountered whilst defending Harold.

Our superiors lectured Teresa numerous times about our luck in this. Had it been one of the more skilled marsh snakes, we would not have seen it camouflaged and likely would have died before we knew what was happening. This was made more harrowing by the probability that Harold had been bitten by a camouflaged marsh snake, which was why we hadn't seen it occur. The two summoner teams that found us, one of them Callan's team, apparently detected it nearby and swiftly took care of it whilst those of us who were injured had been taken away.

Callan had put me to sleep through his aether manipulation. Teresa told me he had carried me to safety, with another team member collecting Harold. Her words describing how Callan would not part with me until a medical officer arrived made me feel strange. She was suggesting he had been protective of me and had been very crass to her about our actions. The object he had thrown to Teresa earlier had been an antivenin pill, a valuable and expensive item, per his words. He had offered it in trade to her during an argument whilst I slept, something about not relying on my poison resistance next time.

It was all very strange behaviour, in my opinion.

Callan had never shown much interest before in another individual. He always avoided the responsibility Roger had tried to place on him to the best of his ability. Eduard had reined him in many times because of his temper.

I had been called upon as Teresa had been informing me of this new information in her rushing speech. From Teresa's tense reaction and her retelling of being rebuked by our superiors, it appeared it was my time for stern words now that I was well enough to hear them.

"Trainee, I hate it when I am forced to reprimand my soldiers." Lieutenant Cragborn pursed his lips. His voice was as smooth as honey. I wondered if that was just him or if it was a trait of daemon.

"Apologies, sir," I said, standing straight, my hands folded behind my back inside his mediocre canvas tent. It was not as impressive as General Saika's tent, but it was much larger than the cramped low tents we trainees had. You could stand in his. In ours, we had to crawl.

"You put yourself and Miss Garpson at risk by running headfirst into danger like that. Despite my order to the group, you ignored it. I have been informed that my order was not heard because of the rain, but this is still defiance. From the actions of the others in your group, you should have determined that your team was to gather with them. Regardless, you abandoned your safety." The lieutenant narrowed his eyes, his finger still tapping in a slow rhythm.

"You do not have the luxury of abandoning your safety, Lady Lynette. You are currently a mortal. You have no training, fighting experience, or skills in using aether or a core capable of defending yourself. You are a baby in all senses of the word. Your first act should have been to seek help."

I bit my lip as his words rang true.

"However," he continued. "You did so to save your teammate's life. That is one small thing in your favour." He sighed, stopping his tapping. "In light of that fact, I have decided not to suggest we lower the evaluation score for you or Miss Garpson for disobeying orders, but you are both being strictly watched from now on."

"Yes, sir, I will seek an experienced summoner in the future." I saluted respectfully, feeling a little relieved. I had been worried that he might decide I wasn't worthy of joining the army. Maybe that had been my own insecurity, though. All too often, it had been easier for the people in my lives to abandon and shun me.

"You will be placed at the front with me in the future, so such a thing should not be required," he stated, a little angry. "I do not enjoy unruly trainees' relatives nagging me, nor Captain Hudson. It is a waste of my time."

"S-sorry, sir," I said, feeling my cheeks redden. I wanted to say it wouldn't happen again, but I had no control over my brothers' actions, even less so for Nate. I was surprised to hear his name mentioned alongside them at all.

Just what had they said to the lieutenant?

My brothers were probably only worried about Roger's wrath if I died. After all, it would be a shame if he couldn't keep his promise of my betrothal to another noble.

"As you should be," the lieutenant said coldly. "Don't let it happen again. Now go. I have work that actually matters." He shooed me away.

I couldn't have left fast enough.

A few hours passed before I was notified that Harold Eastmond had awoken. Teresa and I, and sadly Garret, went to the medical tent to fetch him. Harold was unusually quiet. He wouldn't—or couldn't, perhaps—look at me properly. A man of few words, he was strangely even quieter. He took in our new small canvas village with a curious gaze, much as I had done, listening to Garret prattle about unimportant things.

As night fell, I sat around the fire to eat some poorly cooked rice and snake meat. There had been plenty to go around after the attack. Teresa had decided to train by borrowing my jian. She had already reached level seven in the flowing water skill and was improving at a quick pace.

Soft thuds beside me indicated someone had sat down on the ground next to me. I glanced right and saw Harold solemnly eating a snake skewer. His legs were crossed neatly, the tear in his trousers revealing a patch of smooth dark skin. Like my arm, all signs of injury had disappeared thanks to the handiwork of the earth summoners of the medical profession. It was as though we had never been injured. Such power was incredible. Too often, I had seen commoners suffering from broken limbs and lesions in Talbour. It made me uncomfortable knowing how easily we had received such treatment when many would beg for it.

"Lady Lynette." Harold spoke low as he gazed into the fire. "I understand I owe you my life."

"Uh," I stammered. "Please don't think much of it. I only did what I wanted to."

"On the contrary." Harold shook his head. "You honoured me, Lady Lynette, and for that"—he turned and bowed his head deeply, making me blush—"I offer you my sincere thanks and gratitude. If you ever require my aid, please ask."

"R-right, I will." I wanted to say he didn't need to do such a thing, but from his posture and the tense hardening of his jaw, I could see that this wasn't easy for him. Telling him I didn't want to burden him with owing me his aid would have likely been insulting.

"What are you two talking about?" Garret sat down opposite us with a small bowl of rice. He narrowed his eyes at my expression, catching that I had been blushing. "You know she is my fiancée, Lord Harold?" he said accusingly.

"It doesn't concern you, Lord Garret," Harold said with a heavy sigh.

"Oh? I think the opposite. Anything involving Lady Lynette concerns me. I am her fiancé, and it is my duty to ensure that she stays in line with her propriety," Garret sneered, and I gripped my metal cup of boiled water tighter.

Propriety? Was he really suggesting I already belonged to him?

"I will be training with my sai blades with Miss Garpson." Harold stood, not wanting to be a part of this. "Lady Lynette, Lord Garret." He bowed to us and left, looking back at me as he did so. I saw the unspoken suggestion that I could call him if required.

"Lord Garret." I pressed my lips tightly now that we were alone. "I am not yours to accuse of such things."

"You *are* mine, Lady Lynette. The faster you accept that, the happier you will be." Garret smiled sickeningly.

"Then you will be waiting a long time, Lord Garret," I growled. "I have no interest in you."

"So you prefer unknown men from lowly taverns? If that is your type, I can become a dishevelled man for you. Just ask," he said with a grin, slurping on his watery rice.

"There is nothing you could do that would make me accept you, Lord Garret." I grimaced. So he knew of my scandal, but it did not seem to have deterred him as much as I had hoped.

"I think you will find there is much I can do. I am far better than any scum that may have seduced you. But don't worry; I will erase their experience from you with my own soon enough." His determination sent shivers down my spine.

"You keep referring to him as scum." I smirked, realising something. "You have no idea who it is, do you?"

"I know all I need to." Garret scowled. "You are a commoner adopted into nobility. The fact that I even show a shred of interest in you should be exhilarating enough. Your resistance is quite preposterous, though I suppose that is expected. You are the Crazy Cerue Lady, after all."

"Then why do you show such interest in me? I do not believe I have insinuated that I have feelings for you," I said, trying to recall the ball at which we first danced. It had been so long ago.

"You are a deadly rose, Lady Lynette—beautiful, but your thorns are sharp. As a man who appreciates luxury, I enjoy the challenge of getting what I want. A complacent woman such as your sister is boring. She has no appreciation for the life she has, whereas you?" He paused to watch my reaction. "You will appreciate what I can offer you, a woman with no prospects. I can give you a life of comfort. You will never have to fear living as a commoner again."

"So, you want me because you believe I will be grateful?" I asked, to confirm that I had understood. Garret truly was an egotistical, selfish man.

"Precisely." He grinned happily. "Your beauty is, of course, also appealing. You are a rare treasure in Zopan," he said, referring to my Dramorian features. My hair colouring and skin tone were indeed rare in Zopan. I was also a trophy he wished to acquire.

"I find your reasoning flawed, Lord Garret." I put down my cup and stood so I could glare down at him.

"You are presuming I have no other options but to marry you, so I am not forced into the life of a commoner or the shame of living as a burden on my family as an unmarried woman into old age."

"What other options do you have?" He raised an eyebrow smugly.

"My options?" I tutted. "They are quite simple," I said, causing him to frown. "I become a commoner, or I succeed in my training and open my choices for marriage to anyone but you."

"Tch," Garret retorted. "You barely have a core. Those choices will not improve."

"Then I will gladly become a commoner," I declared, earning a spiteful glare. Garret opened his mouth to respond but closed it as we both spotted Callan making his way over for my scheduled training session.

As Callan stood watching, I stumbled through the fifth stance of flowing water with my jian. He pointed out my mistakes and quickly moved my arms into the correct positions with his hands. Teresa and Harold were nearby, both working on their own practice as they lightly sparred. Teresa was using her dagger against Harold's two sai blades; she was much slower to react than Harold, but her speed in avoiding his attacks was improving.

"You keep messing this up," Callan chided me, lifting my arm higher.

"Sorry, it's difficult to raise," I said, my arm shaking, the weight of the jian pulling it down again. "I don't think I'm any good with it," I sighed, trying to move into the sixth stance.

"Probably," Callan agreed.

"Honestly, I may be better training with my dagger," I said, dropping the jian for a third time as it clattered onto the ground.

"Did you get a skill with it?" Callan asked, picking it up for me as I slumped in defeat.

"Yes, I think I got it when I killed the marsh snake," I said, holding my palm forward. "Show skills."

Blood Sign			
Skills			
Aether:	0	**Spirit:**	1
Combative:	2		Beast Taming: 1 (Novice) (Hidden)
	Jian—Flowing Water: 2 (Novice)	**General:**	1
	Dagger Strike: 3 (Novice)		Social: −2 (Novice) (Hidden)
Body:	3		
	Poison Resistance: 15 (Initiate)		
	Pain Resistance: 23 (Apprentice)		
	Stamina: 4 (Novice)		
Mind:	3		
	Research: 12 (Initiate)		
	Herbology: 57 (Adept)		
	Alchemy: 7 (Novice)		

Surprisingly, I had gained a few levels with the dagger in my onetime use of it during the fight. With no prior training, I was shocked to see it at level three in comparison to the jian, which was still only level two despite my many nights of training with it. My poison resistance had also grown by five levels from the attack, alongside my pain resistance and stamina growing by one.

Callan looked over my sign, interested, his eyebrows scrunched, and he flicked his attention to me for a moment before waving his hand to let me know I could put my palm down. I realised this was the first time he had actually seen my skills. I hadn't shown them to him before.

"You may be right, but you can expect your levels to increase much faster during a fight than they would in training. That's why those two are sparring." He nodded to Teresa and Harold.

"So if I had used the jian instead of my dagger, I could have grown my level faster?"

"Yes, so don't give it away next time." He tutted at me. "That's why the commoner gained so many levels in it."

"Understood," I sighed, knowing I would probably do the same again. "So should I spar as well?"

"No, until you get the basics, you could hurt someone. Those two are well enough trained with their weapons that they won't do that." So Teresa also had competence with the dagger she was using? I was a little jealous of her speed in gaining skills.

"So I just need to keep practising." I sighed, moving to take the jian from Callan. He handed it to me but looked thoughtful.

"Yes, I want to keep practising the flowing water stances as we have been, but you are horrendous with it." He rubbed his chin, debating something with himself. "I guess it wouldn't hurt," he muttered more to himself than to me.

"Callan?" I asked curiously.

"Sheathe it and get your dagger out. I can use this to practise myself." He stepped back from me, and I quickly did as he instructed, seeing as he wasn't going to explain.

He stood some distance away, then raised his arms and closed his eyes in concentration. Suddenly water droplets began to condense in the space between us. The droplets' numbers increased faster and faster until an odd blob formed, wiggling, unable to stay stationary. The blob of water bent and grew taller as it absorbed more water droplets. It continued to grow until a figure my size stood wavering on its feet.

I stared at it, jaw open, as the strange creature slowly began to step towards me.

"Fight it!" Callan ordered as he held his arms straight and pinched his features, trying to keep control of the water.

"R-right," I stammered, grabbing my dagger and running to it, ready to attack.

I sliced at its jellylike arm, my dagger moving through the water with ease, splitting its arm in two. But it quickly strung strands of water from the two separated limbs and reconnected them. Turning, I angled for its legs, this time my dagger moving through the water, sending it toppling to the ground as it lost its balance. The water blob re-formed its legs and crawled towards me, which was creepy. I continued to charge and stab at it, with it healing itself repeatedly.

We continued like this for a while until the blob suddenly fell apart, the water sloshing into the ground as Callan breathed heavily, leaning on his knees for support. I grabbed my waist, feeling a tight stitch from my running, my dagger shaking in my hand as my body tried to keep up with the intense exercise I had performed.

"So?" Callan shouted from a distance as he got back his breath.

"Sign," I muttered, and saw the familiar box appear. There it was, my dagger strike skill; it had risen from level three to level five, and my stamina had also pleasantly increased to level five.

"I gained two levels," I said, pleased that my hunch had been right. The dagger was a far better weapon than the jian. I simply had no affinity for the weapon.

"All right, we will do this every evening as well as your flowing water stances." Callan strode over, wiping sweat from his brow.

"What was that? What you created?" I asked.

"A water clone; it is meant to look exactly like the person I want it to, but I'm not that good with it yet." He shrugged. "So this is great training for me too."

"That's good, then. I don't want to distract you from your own training." I smiled, and oddly he reciprocated with his own.

"Oh, you will be helping lots, got to get something out of this." He grinned a little maniacally, and I felt my stomach flip. Was he going to work me to the bone?

CHAPTER SEVENTEEN

The canvas village remained in place for the next five days. With not much else to do, Callan had me training nonstop. I had wanted to protest more than once, but I knew training was my best option for surviving the rest of the trip to Zromore, the capital. As each day passed, my ability to pinpoint the best spots to strike with my dagger improved, and my handling of the weapon increased. I grew more adept at moving to avoid the strikes his water clones would launch, their arms elongating into whips. As I improved, so did his water clones. They began to take on a more humanlike appearance in the shell of water. Eerily they looked more like Callan every day, down to the small dimple on his left temple and the scar on his right hand.

I dodged a whip as it struck to my left. Rolling, I quickly slashed out as it came back, cutting its arm neatly in two. I learned it could not reattach its limbs if I severed them completely. Instead, they had to be regrown anew, which was a much longer process. Now that it was one arm down, I launched myself forward and stabbed at the water clone's chest, ripping the blade down much as Callan had done to me in my second life.

The clone popped as it disintegrated in a slosh.

"Not bad. You need to get better at getting behind your opponent. It will make it more difficult for them to attack you." Callan gave me pointers as he shook out his arms. He no longer had to hold them out straight to control the clone.

"I need to increase my speed to do that." I sighed, readjusting the loosened tie in my hair, letting it fall around my shoulders.

"You need better stamina to do that," Callan said as he drew his jian. "I will be training with my team now, so I expect you to keep this up." He patted my head and lightly rustled my hair. "Good job." He smiled, and I nodded, happy to be praised.

Ever since the marsh snake attack, Callan had been unusually sociable with me. We often ended our training with him patting my head. The more I put into my training, the more his likeability for me increased. It had steadily been increasing day by day.

Vishka's Guidance System
Callan Heversham
Likeability: −4% (+5%)

I smiled at the new number. It was so close to 0%. I was finally near a fresh start with him. My life of demands and spoilt tantrums, which had caused his low opinion of me, was slowly washing away with our improved interactions. I felt a little warm and fuzzy knowing I was so close, ever hopeful that the scenario of my second life was growing further away from recurring.

Rubbing my legs for circulation, I took a deep breath and began to run lightly at a steady pace around the training circle we had created. Alongside our battle training, with the lack of marching, my stamina growth had stagnated, so I had taken to running daily to try to keep it level. My muscles twinged less and less each day as I did so, and I found that I could keep going longer, achieving more laps. I was steadily increasing my body's strength bit by bit, but malnourishment was still a large issue. With only scraps of dried meat and rice left, the camp was running out of viable food options after our week stationed here. Some of the summoners had formed hunting groups, and we occasionally were lucky to get the leftovers from demonic beasts, but it wasn't much. As trainees, we only got what was left after the trained soldiers took their share.

Teresa and Harold had created a regular sparring session. Despite Callan's protests, I lent Teresa my jian when she asked, and she had also improved considerably in using it. Now she was skilled enough with it to spar with Harold instead of using her dagger. I watched as they fought nearby during my run. They sparred with a skill I could only hope to achieve one day. Harold was incredible with his sai blades. Having had training with them since childhood, he often used trickery and feints to surprise Teresa, who was honest and straightforward with her attacks. She was not as good as Harold, but her speed and fluidity with the jian were obvious as she dodged Harold's swipes and returned with her own, having skidded behind him.

Garret eventually decided to train as well. He slighted our efforts for the first two days, claiming it was pointless for me to even try, as my future was to marry him and merely manage his household. Callan had quickly aggravated Garret, though, advising him to mind his own business in the politest way he was capable of. I smiled, remembering Garret's face during that conversation. He had not been pleased but could not argue against the son of a viscount.

As the rest of the trainees also began to train with their teams, Garret caved and also began to practise with his sabre. As much as I hated to admit it, he was also very skilled. Like Harold and most of the nobles, he had been taught his weapon since childhood. Its handle was heavy, and he specialised in frontal overhead strikes with strength I could only imagine having. Rian Thornfax and Kit Balburn often sparred with him. Their familiarity with each other's abilities showed that they had often sparred together in childhood.

"Lynette?" An unfamiliar voice grabbed my attention, so I slowed my pace to a stop.

"That's not her, idiot," Another person spoke, and the sound of a slap on a shoulder followed. "Why would she be here of all places?" I turned around to see a man with tawny hair roll his eyes.

"Hugh? Jacob?" I said, unsure myself, and they both froze midstep.

"You see! It is Lynette!" Hugh joyfully cheered, running over to me, his arms filled to the brim with scrolls.

"Well, I'll be damned!" Jacob rubbed his tawny hair, surprised, following his fellow foot soldier.

"You joined the army?" Hugh said; his eyes were wide, and his brown beard cracked with small spots of mud stuck to the fuzz.

"Yeah." I meekly nodded. "I joined the morning after our card game." I smiled, remembering how Hugh had passed out from alcohol during our game in the tavern.

"You could have told us! Jeez, we're always looking for card players." Hugh laughed, nearly dropping his scrolls.

"I think she has been a bit preoccupied for card games, Hugh." Jacob shook his head in mirth.

"Does Nate know?" Hugh asked with a glint in his eye.

"Um, yes, he does," I answered, feeling shy from the look he gave me.

"Hmmm, then you absolutely must join our next card game." He grinned mischievously.

"Ignore him." Jacob swatted Hugh on the head. "He just wants someone to beat Nate again."

"But he *always* wins," Hugh moaned, making me laugh.

"Who are you two?" An arrogant pest interrupted us. Garret quickly stomped over to us, placing his hands on his hips as he glared at Hugh and Jacob. "What are you doing talking to foot guards? Is one commoner not bad enough, Lady Lynette?"

"Excuse me?" Jacob stepped back with a frown.

"Lord Garret, you are being rude," I commented, stepping away from him myself. These last few days, Garret had been watching me like a hawk, inserting himself into my business wherever possible. After my declaration that I would rather become a commoner than marry him, he had grown very tense.

"Rude? I can say what I want to a commoner. No noble is a grey cloak." Garret snickered, stepping closer to me again in unwanted protectiveness.

"Lady Lynette? Lynette, are you a noble?" Hugh asked quietly. I could see the shock in his expression. I knew that expression all too well; it reminded me of the look people had given me in the past.

I wonder if they will think differently of me now?

"Yes, my full name is Lynette Heversham. I'm the daughter of Viscount Heversham of Talbour," I informed them, as I knew Garret would have if I didn't.

"The Crazy Cerue Lady?" Jacob scrunched his eyebrows. "But you're not at all as horrible as the rumours say."

"Ah, well." I coughed into my hand and looked away, embarrassed. So there were rumours about me outside Talbour?

Gosh, had I been that awful?

"Rumours can't always be trusted," I said, knowing that these particular rumours were probably true. I had been a very difficult person in my youth.

"As your fiancé, I will make sure such rumours are squashed." Garret, once again, stated that unneeded bit of information. He had been announcing it to anyone who asked, despite my denials. It was incredibly irritating.

"Fiancé?" Jacob shared a puzzled look with Hugh, who shrugged. They both then looked at me expectantly.

"I am not his fiancée," I grumbled. "Lord Garret believes otherwise."

"It has been agreed with Viscount Heversham. Stop pretending already, Lady Lynette." Garret scowled at me, frustrated that I still hadn't conformed to his wishes.

"That is good to hear, Lady Lynette." Jacob bowed his head to me with a smirk towards Garret. "I am sure Lord Nathaniel would not have been pleased to learn of such a thing."

"Indeed." Hugh caught on and mirrored Jacob's attitude. "Lord Nathaniel would have been rather upset."

"Lord Nathaniel? As in Captain Hudson? Why would he care?" Garret asked defensively.

I saw what they were doing, and as petty as it was, I took the opportunity. "Please give Lord Nathaniel my greetings, Jacob, Hugh. I have missed him these past weeks, as he has been occupied with his duties."

"Of course, Lady Lynette, he will be happy to hear from you. After all, you are so close." Jacob smiled innocently as Garret paled.

"Quite," I said, enjoying the look on Garret's face as he realised just who I had spent the night with, sullying my reputation.

Garret's clinginess to me subsided after my conversation with Hugh and Jacob. Instead of following me around announcing our engagement to all who would listen, he now sat far away from me, offering me the occasional glare. I had thought my scandal had not been a success in deterring him, but it turned out, by the luck of Vishka, Nathaniel Hudson had been an excellent choice. Once Garret realised that I had spent my evening with another noble, and not a commoner, his arrogance had deflated.

"How is it that this is black on the outside but barely cooked?" Teresa sat beside me, prodding a charred piece of meat in her metal dish.

"Beats me. Mine isn't much better." I showed her my attempt at cooking the demonic beast we had been given, which looked similar to hers. Our breakfast was pitiful.

"I can't wait to get to the capital." Teresa sighed. "Maybe then we can at least get something that won't poison us." She grimaced, took a bite gingerly, shrugged, and then continued to eat it.

"It's at least better than the rice." I was growing weary of the lack of protein in our food.

"I heard we may be moving out soon. The higher-ups finally got a plan together or something," Teresa stated, hopeful.

"Have the injured all recovered?"

"Most of them," she said with an upset undertone. Not all of them had made it.

Suddenly a horn blasted throughout the canvas village. We all stilled, unsure if this was a horn to announce danger.

"Listen up, trainees!" Lieutenant Cragborn's voice hollered over our group's small camping area. "Pack up. We leave in an hour. Anything not packed will be left behind."

Teresa and I looked at one another. We quickly shovelled our charred meat into our mouths and got up to put our things away in our backpacks.

We all rushed. Soldiers from all directions were running to pack up their things. Tents were pulled down, fires stamped out, and earthen creations destroyed. I didn't think I had ever seen such fast movement before as the entire brigade cleared away the canvas village.

Ahead of us, soldiers regrouped into their formations, having cleared away faster than we trainees had. Lieutenant Cragborn lorded it over us as we scrambled and barked at those who were too slow or commanded others to leave items that had been found during our respite.

Eventually, our team stood in front of our group of twenty; Lieutenant

Cragborn stood directly in front of us. As he had told me, we were going to remain at the front so he could keep an eye on us. The rear guard followed behind us as the last of our group assembled. I spotted Hugh and Jacob amongst the foot guards, and they flashed me a smile. I returned it, but a gnawing feeling sank into my gut, seeing the lower numbers of their troop compared to before.

The horn blasted again, and we were off.

We marched consistently until late in the afternoon, with no break this time. Lieutenant Cragborn instructed us as we marched that there was going to be a break soon. It turned out our delay and the reason for the canvas village had not been just for the injured. On our planned route to the capital, a scouting party had returned with the information that a grade seven demonic beast had set up its nest directly in our path. The snakes we had fought had only been grade one, so hearing that such a powerful beast was blocking our path was terrifying.

The generals had been discussing what to do about it for the past week as they waited for the injured to recover. A plan had apparently been put together, so we continued our march. Our next break was to coincide with the generals' attack on the beast.

"Halt!" Lieutenant Cragborn called as the soldiers in front also slowed to a stop. "All right, this is our break. We could move again at any moment, so stay prepared and keep vigilant." He turned and headed towards Lieutenant Sharpclaw as they quietly discussed matters not for our ears.

"Scary, isn't it," Teresa whispered, her hand clutching her dagger. "A grade seven is no joke."

"We should be safe here." I tried to comfort her. "We are surrounded by summoners, and the action is up front this time."

"It would be wise to remain on guard." Harold pulled out his waterskin. "A grade seven is incredibly rare. It is extremely unlucky that we have come across one at all."

"This whole march has been unlucky," Garret grumbled.

"At least we are closer to the summoners this time." Teresa nodded to Callan's team on our left and another ahead of us.

"Right," I agreed, pulling out my own waterskin and basking in the relief the water gave me. I had tried to limit what I used, as I hadn't had a chance to ask Callan to refill it this morning.

As we waited, Teresa and I sat to rub our feet whilst we could, and I spotted a few others doing the same. Rian Thornfax was one of them; we hadn't spoken much during this whole trip. She had avoided me as much as I had avoided her, and that had been best for us both.

"Sign." I called up my skills to check them over, hoping to have gained some more stamina.

Blood Sign			
General Information		**Progression**	
Name:	Lynette Heversham	**Core Innate Grade:**	0.02
Age:	21	**Core Condensation Grade:**	0.02
Rank:	Daughter of Viscount—Talbour	**Affinities:**	Unknown
Traits:	Beast Born (Hidden)		
Occupation:	Trainee of Zopan Empire Army		
Covenants:	Zopan Empire Army Blood Bond: *Guidance of Vishka (Hidden)*		
Skills			
Aether:	0	**Spirit:**	1
Combative:	2		Beast Taming: 1 (Novice) (Hidden)
	Jian—Flowing Water: 4 (Novice)	**General:**	1
	Dagger Strike: 8 (Novice)		Social: −2 (Novice) (Hidden)
Body:	3		
	Poison Resistance: 15 (Initiate)		
	Pain Resistance: 23 (Apprentice)		
	Stamina: 7 (Novice)		
Mind:	3		
	Research: 12 (Initiate)		
	Herbology: 57 (Adept)		
	Alchemy: 7 (Novice)		

I hadn't raised my stamina any higher than it had been yesterday. I closed the box, biting the inside of my cheek. How difficult was it to raise my levels for body and combative? I had trained so much, but they had barely moved overall. At least my dagger skill was increasing at a steady pace.

As I sat rubbing my feet, a vibration in the ground and an echoing roar froze all of us. All chatter paused as the roar enveloped our brigade.

"It's beginning! Get ready to move!" Lieutenant Cragborn rushed back to us. We all stood quickly, putting our boots back on as the ground rumbled.

"Just what is the grade seven?" Rian asked, unease lacing her voice.

"A horned baildon," Lieutenant Cragborn answered, looking ahead.

"A what?" I asked with unease, seeing the fear on the nobles' faces.

"It's like a kreshna," Harold whispered, his hand shaking ever so slightly on his sai blades. "Except a hundred times larger, and they control earth."

"Earth? So the ground shaking . . ."

"Yes, they burrow in the ground to make their nests and ambush anything that passes atop them. Their skin is as dense as rock, and they can swim through the ground like you or I can in water."

My face paled as I joined the others in comprehension of their fear. "How terrifying," I squeaked, just trying to imagine such a thing. I didn't feel so safe anymore.

We all jolted, tense, as a figure came running towards us. It was oddly familiar. As it grew closer, I saw a flash of blue in the late-afternoon sun, and familiar silver eyes pierced my way.

Eduard.

He stopped with ease, showing no exhaustion.

"Captain Heversham." Lieutenant Cragborn greeted him with a salute. "What news?"

"The generals have begun the attack. I will be relaying any orders from here. For now, you are to remain stationary with the trainees." Eduard glanced at me before swiftly moving to inform Lieutenant Sharpclaw and the other summoners. I watched him as he approached Callan's team and saw him harden his expression. Eduard then spoke with Callan separately for a moment before moving on again. Callan's team immediately left their spot and came closer to us. All of them had drawn their weapons.

I couldn't take my eyes off Eduard. It was so strange. There was no number floating above his head.

"Stay close to us. There's a chance the baildon could try to escape this way," a young man from Callan's team with a neatly trimmed brown beard informed us all.

"Of course, corporal Cavendish," Lieutenant Cragborn answered, drawing his weapon, a hulking spear.

We all drew our weapons at this new information, mumbles of panic echoing through the group. I dreaded thinking about what the commoner group might be feeling right now.

"Captain Hudson is preparing a defence." Eduard reappeared, the air above his head still devoid of a floating number; I tried squinting at him to see if I was unable to see it for some reason, but it just wasn't there.

"Why is he different?" I mumbled, trying to focus on this rather than a possible impending attack. Anything to shift my mind from my encroaching fear.

"Water clone," Callan whispered, suddenly beside me. "He's very good at them. I'm surprised you noticed."

"A water clone? But he's conversing with the lieutenants." Callan's clone had no thoughts or any signs of intelligence. Plus, they were obvious water images. They did not appear as flesh and blood like the Eduard here.

"He can split his consciousness between them." Callan explained. "That's why he's at the front of the march."

"It's incredible." I studied the clone further. I probably wouldn't have noticed anything different if it hadn't been for the lack of a number over the water clone's head.

"I'll get there with mine eventually." Callan frowned, seeming a little upset at my praise of Eduard's skill.

Our attention was drawn to the front of the brigade as a sudden flash of lightning pierced the sky. A loud boom followed the crackle as it intensified.

"Lord Azriel." Callan watched with us all.

"He uses lightning . . ." I mumbled, watching the flash of repeated sparks littering the sky.

"He is god-blessed, a member of royalty, and a poor match for a horned baildon." Callan frowned, raising his jian. "If he has gotten involved, things can't be good."

It was as though Callan's words had drawn the calamity.

The ground under our feet began to shake uncontrollably. Several trainees fell over, unable to keep their balance, myself amongst them.

Callan grabbed my arm, his grip tight and forceful, before throwing me to his right.

"Dodge!" he screamed as the ground around us began to split apart. A horn the size of my whole body protruded from the spot where I had been standing. I froze, wide-eyed; I could have been skewered just now.

Trainees and summoners scrambled out of the way as the earth was ruptured. A hulking mass forced its way up, shovelling dirt sideways as a bleeding and charred demonic beast emerged. As Harold had described, it did indeed look similar to a kreshna, with two large curled horns beside floppy ears on its head. Its snout was like that of a kreshna bull. Its legs and torso were made of muscle coated in dozens of spiked scales. A row of horns lined its back down to its short tail.

The beast was humongous.

Earth summoners rushed over and raised columns of earth to keep the soil it was shovelling from burying the trainees and foot guards nearby. A huge pile was coming my way, and I quickly rolled as fast as I could towards one of the blockades. In my escape, the hilt of my jian rammed into my stomach, winding me.

Orders for each team were interlocked with one another. I struggled to hear Lieutenant Cragborn over the shouting but saw that he had gathered a group of trainees who had escaped the ambush.

I pushed myself up and ran past summoners who were shooting fire, water, wind, and earth at the horned baildon. The creature didn't even flinch at the firepower being directed towards it and instead swiped its clawed hand in a circular motion.

Directly in my path.

Earth washed like a wave where its claw directed, swallowing the summoners and many of the foot guards, billowing towards me.

Sliding, I leapt to get out of its way, landing flat on my front as the earth wave avoided me by inches.

"Lynette!" Rian Thornfax grabbed my wrist and hauled me up, and we shared a look of panic.

"This way," I huffed, trying to get oxygen back into my begging muscles. We ran together as summoners sprouted from the earth that had just swallowed them, whips of fire launched at the beast, wrapping around its feet, toppling it over. It crashed into the ground with a wallop, causing Rian and me to stumble, but we kept going.

Nathaniel Hudson flew through the air as he slammed his flaming halberd into the side of the horned baildon. On impact, the flames seared and sharpened, splintering in all directions into the beast's gut. It screeched in pain and rocked its body in our direction again, rolling away from the flames.

We had nowhere we could go.

There was no way we could outrun it.

Its body loomed above us.

I felt Rian shaking as she gripped my hand, and I squeezed it back, understanding her fear.

We continued to run, afraid of what was inevitable.

I saw Callan and Eduard's water clone running towards us, but it was too late.

We couldn't get away in time.

That was when the ground opened up beneath us as we fell, tumbling down a tunnel into darkness.

CHAPTER EIGHTEEN

Something blurred my vision. I tried to wave it away, but my hand wafted straight through it.

Vishka's Guidance System
Quest Received!
Obtain the knowledge of Albus

I blinked at the box in my face as it refused to let me sleep. Then a groan beside me told me I wasn't alone, and that was when I remembered the horned baildon. With a start, I sat up, my head ringing, making me clutch it with a moan.

Rian lay beside me, facing similar disgruntlement as she rubbed her temples. Our legs were tangled together in the dirt cavern we had fallen into. We carefully separated, both of us aching from the fall. I was bleeding from my forehead, judging by the blood on my hand.

"Where are we?" Rian grumbled, clutching her bleeding arm gingerly.

"Looks like a cavern," I said, pulling myself up onto my feet by grabbing a stalagmite sticking out of the hard stone floor. Water dripped onto my cheek from a stalactite above; the shock of the cold droplet made me flinch. I raised my head to find the culprit and sucked in a breath.

Small black bodies nestled between the stalactites. The smell of stagnant water and animal musk filled my nose. Our only light was a small beam from a hole in the ceiling, the tunnel we had fallen into during the horned baildon's attack.

"I don't think we're alone," I whispered, pointing to the black bodies above.

Rian saw them and held a finger to her lips. "Craven bats," she said, answering my thoughts as she silently stood. So, more demonic beasts, I guessed from her nervousness. They shuffled slightly, and we stilled until they settled again.

We had been lucky they hadn't woken up when we fell.

We looked around very slowly, stepping carefully on the stone floor to try to prevent any echo we might create. The cave we had fallen into was cramped; one side was a dead end, but the opposite had a narrow but long corridor. We had no other option but to follow it. Unfortunately, neither of us had the skills or ability to get back up through the tunnel. It was too high up.

I used the bumpy stone of the walls to support my feet as a sharp jarring pain began to spike in my right thigh. I must have landed on it when we fell. Rian protected her arm as she took the lead in the narrow corridor. We were both injured and alone in an unfamiliar place.

My unease increased.

If the craven bats attacked us in such a narrow place, I doubted we would be able to defend ourselves.

Silently, we walked the length of the cave, ever mindful of the craven bats above. They did not lessen in number as we proceeded, which only worried me more. As we walked farther away from the tunnel we had fallen through, the light decreased. Soon we were in darkness, and I had to use my hands to feel my way forward. It was difficult, and I tripped a few times, stubbing my feet on rocks that I couldn't see. We hitched our breaths every time we made a noise, but thankfully, the craven bats did not respond.

It felt as though we walked in silence for hours before a small strange blue light filtered ahead of us. We rushed towards it, the claustrophobia of being unable to see making us a little desperate. As we reached the light, we were welcomed by a bizarre blue glow from thousands of small mushrooms that lined the walls. Rian and I hesitantly approached them, but when they didn't seem to release anything at our approach, we deemed it safe to keep going. As we continued on our path, avoiding touching the mushrooms, the corridor grew wider until, finally, the cave opened up and we could stand side by side.

Navigating around a large broken boulder, we gasped at the scene before us, basking in the light of thousands of mushrooms.

Inside this underground cave were the ruins of a temple.

It was hard to think of it as anything else. Broken statues of the gods encircled a dried-up fountain at the centre of the cavern. Crumbled pillars of stone hinted at an archway once existing; the runes carved into the stone were faded and brittle. I saw Vishka's statue, placed not at the edge of the circle of gods like it was in modern temples but at the forefront of them all.

"What is this place?" Rian whispered in awe, gently tracing a rune with her fingers as we approached the fading archway.

"It looks incredibly old," I replied, stepping past the temple entrance and making my way towards Vishka's statue, staring at the worn features of her bandaged eyes. "The arrangement of the gods is different here than the temple in Talbour."

"You've been to the temple?" Rian said, surprised.

"Once. Just before we left." I lightly touched Vishka's hand and felt the stone threaten to crumble, so I quickly pulled away.

"Maybe this place is from before the age of Carosel?" Rian pulled out a scroll and began to trace some of the runes from the archway. "I have never seen these runes before."

"The age of Carosel? You think it could be that old?" I asked, leaving Vishka's statue to explore further.

"It's possible. These runes aren't in any of my textbooks. So it would make sense that this temple could be from the beginning of the Zopan Empire." Rian studied them carefully, tracing copies onto her scraps of rolled paper.

"Do you believe in that bedtime story? About Carosel, the gods chosen, clearing the land of demonic beasts?" I asked, remembering the stories Cassandra often read to me as a child.

"One person killing a plague of demonic beasts across an entire land?" Rian stopped her tracing and looked at me pointedly. "No. I do not believe such fairy tales. It's just a story to glorify the royal family's first descendant."

"Probably." I sighed. It was a little unbelievable; the deadlands were just as dangerous as the story describes Zopan once being. It took yearly trips to cull the demonic beasts there to keep Zopan safe, and there were no signs of their numbers permanently diminishing.

"What about the idea of being god-blessed? The story said Carosel gathered the others like them, united the five tribes, and created safe havens for the people. Do you think that's exaggerated?"

"Pfft." Rian shook her head at me. "What are you going to ask next? Do I believe in the gods? I never took you to be so pious, Lady Lynette."

"Is it a crime to be curious?" I scowled at her response. I wasn't pious, at least not until Vishka responded.

"No. I do not believe that. Carosel could not have united all of the five tribes. The war of Hirsch would not have happened if that were the case. The Jagged West would have been a part of the empire since the beginning. It just sounds better to say they did."

"What about the god-blessed?" I asked, interested to learn more about Rian's thoughts. She so openly dismissed the tale all children were taught. If I were a judgemental, pious person, I could have been offended by her distrust of a god-chosen.

"The god-blessed are just people born lucky to have unique aether. It's a shame we don't know more about them or why they can use unique aether."

"Yeah." I sighed; it would be pretty cool to use lightning aether. "I wonder what types of aether used to exist. Teresa told me about her town being built from an old plant aether that no longer exists."

"A lot of that knowledge was lost during the Hirsch war. It is a shame," Rian replied.

"I wonder why this temple hasn't been found before," I said absently as I bent down to the floor, inspecting one of the glowing mushrooms that grew on the temple's rotting walls. They clustered together tightly in pockets all around. A weird purple moss dotted between them stood out against the pale luminescent blue of the mushroom heads.

"I wouldn't know." Rian's pencil scratched loudly in the chamber.

"I think these are angel shrooms," I said, pulling out my dagger and covering my hand with the cloth of my dirtied black cloak. I lightly wrapped my hand around a cluster, being careful not to touch it with my bare skin, and cut it with my dagger.

"And?" Rian said impatiently.

"Don't touch it. If it is angel shroom, it can paralyse you for four hours."

"That's likely why there aren't any craven bats in here, then," Rian said, coming over. "Why are you touching it if it's so dangerous?"

"I'm not." I raised my clothed hand. "It only affects you if it touches your skin."

"So why are you gathering it?"

"It's rare. It may be useful," I said, ripping a section of my cloak with my dagger and creating a small bag from the cloth by tying the ends. Carefully I placed the angel shroom inside and went to gather some more. In truth, I had never actually seen angel shroom in person before. I had only read about it in books, so I wasn't completely sure that this is what this was. Many aether plants looked similar; it was unique markings and identifying what grew nearby them that allowed confident identifications.

"How do you know about this stuff?" Rian raised an eyebrow quizzically, watching me work.

"Herbology skill, Adept," I answered, seeing the shock on her face.

"*You*, the Crazy Cerue Lady, are Adept in herbology?" Rian clearly didn't believe me.

Typical. She did always think the worst of me.

"Yes," I said, a little snippy. "Do you find that hard to believe?"

"Incredibly so." Rian sighed reluctantly. "But I will trust you. We only have each other here, and I have nothing to lose."

So now you want to trust me? When there isn't anyone else to protect you?

"True enough." I bit my cheek, filling my cloth bag to the brim. I placed it in my backpack before ripping another section of cloth from my cloak to make a second bag. This time I filled it with the strange purple moss. I wasn't sure what the moss was. It could have been one of three I knew of. It was difficult to identify something you had never seen before.

"What's that?" Rian's question pulled me out of my gathering task. She was looking at a small glinting piece of metal on a pedestal at the back of the temple.

I finished stuffing my cloth bag with the purple moss and stood beside Rian as we tried to figure out what it was. The metal was shaped peculiarly. It had many pointed angles and resembled a star. It was solid black, similar to the onyx stones that had once lived in my bracelet. A series of runes were etched into the pedestal around it. It looked ominous.

"Try picking it up," I hinted, looking at Rian.

"You pick it up," she replied, crossing her arms.

"You found it, so you should pick it up." I took a step back.

"You're the one who wants it. You should pick it up." Rian stepped back farther than I had.

We stared at each other.

Laughter broke our silence in this oddly serene moment.

"Seems we both don't dare go near that thing." Rian smiled, readjusting her twin serrated sabres.

"Probably best we leave it alone," I agreed too soon.

Vishka's Guidance System
Pick up the memory shard

Ah, crap.

Seriously, Vishka? Do you want me to get this thing? It seriously screams trap. Those runes surrounding it could do anything. I mentally chided Vishka and her demands.

"Okay, I'll get it," I sighed, trudging towards the ominous memory shard. Vishka was leading me to a path of survival for this life; whatever this thing was, if she said I should pick up it, it was probably important.

"You're seriously picking that thing up?" Rian tried to stop me as I outstretched my hand.

"Yeah, it seems too valuable to just leave here," I lied. I couldn't say it was because Vishka told me.

"No, stop!" Rian pulled me back away from it, looking at me gloomily.

"I'll get it," she said, swiftly turning towards it. "If either of us has a chance of understanding what those runes do, it's me. I'm the best choice." Rian hesitantly approached the black star.

"Lady Rian, let me do it," I said, but Rian had already reached for it. Suddenly a force erupted from the pedestal, flinging Rian across the temple; she crashed with a thud into one of the walls.

"Rian!" I ran over to her limp body. She was crumpled in a heap. I gently shifted her body and quickly pulled off my cloak, scrunching it into a makeshift pillow for her head.

She was knocked out cold.

My heart quickened as I checked for her vitals; they were there, just barely. The blow to her head on the stone wall must have knocked her out. I felt a growing bump at the back of her head. Taking off my backpack, I rummaged through it until I found the willowspire I had purchased back at the market in Talbour. Its long green stems fell into my hands. Grabbing two loose stones nearby, I did my best to grind the willowspire into a paste. Without a proper mortar and pestle, it would have to do. Using my metal camping cup, I poured in some of the remains of my water and mixed it with the pulped willowspire.

Gently lifting Rian's head, I poured the mixture into her mouth and was relieved that she was able to swallow it. That should help with her inflammation. Hopefully, it wouldn't be too long until she woke.

I leaned against the wall beside her, glaring at the memory shard. If I went to get that thing, the same would likely happen to me. The runes must be a defence preventing anyone from taking it. So how the heck was I supposed to get it?

I was puzzled about this conundrum for some time until I heard Rian stir.

"Lynette?" She groggily awoke, shifting her body.

"I'm here." I nudged her boot with my foot, and she turned to see me sitting beside her.

"Ow." Rian hissed, sitting up and rubbing the back of her head. "Did that thing chuck me?" she asked, glaring at it too.

"Yeah, pretty badly. I gave you some willowspire to help with the swelling, but I think you will live." I smirked, and she looked at me grumpily.

"*Live* is an overstatement. My head is screaming." She winced.

"It should settle down soon, hopefully. I have a little willowspire left if it gets worse," I said, shuffling to help her stand.

"Thanks, I may take you up on that." Rian sighed. "You still want that thing?"

"Yes." I shook my head, not really wanting it. "Got any ideas?"

"No, it's obviously a defence rune structure from that force it emanated. I'm surprised it still had so much power left, considering its age." Rian frowned. "Runes decay with time, and so does the power inscribed with them; these must have been a lot more powerful when they were first made."

"You know a lot about runes?" I asked, slowly edging my way closer to the memory shard.

"Yeah, my family are rune experts. Did you not know that?"

"Not really." I shrugged, stepping closer. I hadn't come up with anything to get past the runes, but one wild idea struck me. Vishka wouldn't intentionally put me in harm's way. She was acting as my guidance system so I could actually survive this life, unlike my last three. Maybe, just maybe, Vishka had done something to me that would allow me to get past them. She had before when I got my blood sign.

I wouldn't know unless I tried.

At least now Rian was awake; if I got chucked she could watch over me.

"Have you been living under a rock? Hey, wait, what are you doing?" Rian saw me getting closer to the memory shard. "Are you crazy? You saw what just happened!" she hollered, trying to pull me back again, but I was faster.

My hand stretched out and touched the memory shard, and everything went blank.

CHAPTER NINETEEN

A pure black empty space that seemed to stretch for all eternity was all I saw. There was no discernible ground on which I stood, but each step created a shimmering ripple throughout the darkness.

I heard a light scratching sound somewhere in the vast emptiness, and with nowhere else to go, I headed towards it. I wasn't sure what had happened. One moment I had been in the cave with Rian at the ruins of a temple. The next, I was here in this strange place. What was most eerie was my trepidation. It almost felt familiar, like I had walked in this darkness before but had no memory of it.

As I neared the scratching sound, a small orb of light floated into existence. It definitely had not been there moments ago. Approaching the orb, I felt a sense of self. It was warm, understanding, and inviting. Something within me leaned forward, driving me to hold it.

"Welcome."

I spun around to see the source of the mysterious voice, but no one was there.

"Hello?" I called, my anxiety heightened.

"Child of Vishka." A man appeared amidst the nothingness. His body was ethereal. I could see no perceptible features, just a shadow in the darkness. "Why do you seek me?"

"Um, who are you?" I asked, my voice hesitant in the presence of the creepy being. In a way, he was similar to Callan's water clones. His body blended and shifted in the shadows of this place as he seemed to ponder my question.

"I am the memory of Albus," he said, his voice wavering as his shadow flickered.

"Albus?" I tried to think where I had heard that name and why it bothered me when he said it.

"Yes, Albus" was all he offered in return, only confusing me more.

"Wait," I mumbled, more to myself, "didn't Vishka give me a quest to find the knowledge of Albus?" A memory surfaced of a box that had appeared when I fell down the tunnel with Rian.

"Then, you seek the knowledge of Albus?" he asked, as though he had been expecting my request.

"I—I guess I do," I said, unsure myself. Just what was this knowledge?

"Very well. You meet the requirements for Albus's teachings."

Suddenly his shadow zoomed forward, floating at high speed, the space moving around him.

"Ugh—" I stepped back on instinct at his sudden closeness.

"For me to share this knowledge, you must adhere to an agreement, child of Vishka."

"L-Lynette, my name is Lynette."

Why is he calling me the child of Vishka?

"Do you accept?"

"What—what I am accepting?" I asked. His faceless gaze peered into my soul as he silently evaluated me. It felt invasive. The hairs on my arms stood up, facing his intimidating presence.

"A trade," he finally said, not elaborating.

"A trade? A trade for what?" I asked, a sense of dread sinking into my skin.

"I will one day ask something of you. You cannot refuse," he answered, his voice low and ominous. Something deep inside triggered my fear.

Something I could not refuse?

What did he want from me?

My hands shook as he stood, silently awaiting my reply. Was Vishka's quest really worth the gravity of this shadow's trade?

"I—I accept," I whispered, my blood draining from my face.

I had to believe in Vishka. What other choice did I have?

"The contract is complete," Albus said.

Suddenly the darkness warped, the orb of light moving with us. I felt as though I were falling, and I tried to hold in a scream as nausea threatened in the pit of my stomach.

The warping stopped, and we were now somewhere that looked exactly like where we had been, but it was different somehow. This space felt just as familiar as the orb had been to me. Darkness still surrounded us, but now the orb floated in the centre of the space as it bobbed.

"Your core is very small." Albus inspected the tiny orb, poking it, and as he did so, I felt a shudder in my skin.

"That's my core?"

"Yes, we are in your mindscape. I see you have experienced death from this darkness," he said, making me gape.

"Wh-what are you talking about? I have no idea what you mean," I said shakily, awkwardly laughing.

"You cannot hide your thoughts in your mindscape, child of Vishka. Do not worry. Now that you have absorbed my memory shard, I can only converse with you." He stopped poking the orb, my core.

"All right," I said hesitantly, unsure what else I could say if this shadow knew my thoughts. I looked around a little closer now that I knew this was my mindscape. It explained why I had felt a sense of familiarity here. It was me. This place was the inner workings of my core, the very centre of my being, and it was empty.

"What are you?" I asked, gazing at my tiny core and studying the glow it emitted. It was unnerving looking at him and his strangeness.

"I am the memory of Albus," he repeated, not really answering my question.

"Yes, but what is that exactly?"

He straightened, holding his hands behind his back. "I am the remnants of a man called Albus, stored in a memory stone. The stone was a mere shard, not as powerful as the ones you used to cheat death, so I am a fragment of the man he was," he answered, but his words only raised more questions.

"Wait a minute." I held up my hands. "The stones that were on my bracelet were memory stones?"

"Yes," he said, his featureless face looking at me. "Very powerful ones. Suitable for the child of Vishka."

"Wha—but—what?" My words tumbled out as the shock of this information flooded my brain. I had known that the bracelet and its stones had something to do with me coming back to relive my life. Vishka had confirmed it, but she hadn't really explained how.

"If I returned from death using a memory stone, why are you different?" I asked, my mind reeling. Why was he different? Why had I returned, and did that mean anyone with a memory stone could return from death? How did you use a memory stone? Had I done something to trigger my own regressions? Why was he calling me the child of Vishka? Was it because I had a guidance system from her?

Would I . . . would I become like him?

"My stone was created by Albus. It was never intended to allow him to return from death once more, but to store his memories for the future of Teralia."

"He created your memory stone? But wait, Teralia, what is Teralia?" Again, even more questions than answers from this man.

"Yes. Like you, Albus was gifted three memory stones from the gods. However, he decided his knowledge was worth more to the future generation, to the next child of the gods. So he shattered his final stone to create me, a memory to guide the future of Teralia, the kingdom."

"There is no kingdom of Teralia," I mumbled as this information sank in. I had succeeded in picking up this memory shard because, as he put it, I was a child of Vishka. The runes around the pedestal must have been to prevent anyone who did not qualify from gaining this knowledge of Albus.

I winced. Maybe Rian wouldn't have gotten hurt if I had attempted to pick up the memory shard first.

Wait a minute, did he just say he was a memory of another child of the gods?

"Oh? What is it called now?" Albus asked. His tone changed for the first time in our conversation. He sounded surprised, no longer speaking in the droning tone he had been using as though he were talking to a child.

"I do not know if it is the kingdom you knew, but we are in the Zopan Empire."

"I see." He turned and looked at the floor in thought. "I suppose much time has passed, then." He sighed heavily, returning his attention to me.

"Enough with our history lesson. Your core is too weak to support me for such conversations. However, despite its small size, I am thankful that you have come to me before beginning to gather. This will make what I can teach you unpolluted by whatever teachings exist in your time."

"Support you?" I asked as he circled my core, studying it.

"Yes, you do not have enough aether for me to stay here long." I believe he would have frowned if he had the features to do so.

"So you can stay longer if I grow my core?" I asked.

Did I really want him to stay around longer?

"Yes, now listen to what I have to teach you. The first thing you must do is learn how to gather aether. This is no simple task. The stronger you grow, the better techniques you will need. However, for a core of this size, you must not use a technique that is too taxing, as it could break you. I believe the best technique for you to use would be this." Shadow Albus flicked his hand, and a scroll appeared. It floated across to me, and I plucked it from the air in my mindscape.

"'One with all'?" I read the technique's name in my hands, my first time holding such a scroll. I had seen them in the past but had not really understood what they were, having no knowledge of what was required to be a summoner, aether or otherwise. I had thought of scrolls as text documents I was not allowed to access. Eduard had always forbidden me from reading the ones in the manor's library. On the other hand, Garret did not have any to store, at least not anywhere I knew about.

"Correct. Now absorb it," Albus insisted rather urgently.

"How do I do that?" I asked, causing him to make an annoyed sound.

"So many questions," he muttered. "Will it so. Here, in your mindscape, you control the space. Will for the knowledge on that scroll to be absorbed. Quickly."

"Y-yes." I straightened at his snippy tone and closed my eyes tightly. He said I had to will it to be absorbed, right? Okay, I could do this.

Absorb, absorb, absorb.

The feeling of the parchment in my hands began to lighten. I opened my eyes and watched it burn from the bottom up, fragmenting into the vast space. My mind throbbed as images instantly flashed behind my eyes. I saw runes, so many runes. I saw how to build them in my mindscape. How to surround my core with the runes in interlocking patterns, how these runes would suck aether from the world into my core.

"Build your runes, now, whilst I am here to correct them," Albus insisted.

I nodded, the knowledge of how to do so flooding my mind. I walked up to my core and cupped it in my hands. Strands of aether leaked from the orb connecting with the skin on my palms, and I quickly redirected it into the vast, empty space surrounding my core. The aether strands glowed a pale white as they rose above and began to weave into the symbol of a rune. I knew from the scroll that I could create only one rune right now, but with time I could create more.

The rune formed as I directed the aether into a spiral shape. I carefully pulled a strand to weave it through each circle but cried out in pain when it touched another strand.

"Again," Albus pressed as the rune fell apart.

I repeated this process four times until finally the rune formed and stabilised in my mindscape. I looked at it and watched as it hung above my core. Faint motes of aether filtered through the centre of the rune directly into the tiny orb from the vast darkness. The orb pulsed as it drew it in greedily. I wished I could say I felt stronger, my body revitalised, but I didn't feel any difference at all.

"Well done, leave this rune running, do not turn it off, and your core will grow steadily. You will know when you can add another."

"I don't feel any different." I pursed my lips, a little disappointed.

"Patience." Albus sighed. "My time is up. I will see you when I am replenished." His shadow vanished in a puff, leaving me alone in my mindscape.

Just how did I leave this place?

I opened my eyes, returning to the temple hidden in the cave. My hand was still outstretched as it had been when I grabbed the memory shard. Except this time, the shard was no longer there.

Vishka's Guidance System
Quest Update
Congratulations! You have obtained the knowledge of Albus
Use this knowledge wisely

I dropped my arm and quickly stepped away from the pedestal. As I did so, a column of energy dropped, and I baulked.

"Finally," Rian exclaimed as she ran over and grasped my shoulders. "You are a crazy bitch; do you know that?" She glared at me. "What the heck made you do that?"

"I figured why not try again." I looked away from her intense gaze back to the pedestal, which now stood empty.

"You're crazy," Rian said, chiding me. "You stood there frozen like a ghost for hours. That thing raised a shield, so I couldn't get to you. Do you know how worried I have been?"

"Hours? But I was only gone for a short while . . ." It hadn't felt like hours in my mindscape, maybe one hour at most.

"No, you were frozen for hours." She scowled. "What happened? What was that thing?" she inquired, seeing that it was no longer on the pedestal.

I hesitated. Was this something I should be honest about? I quickly decided against complete honesty. This was Rian Thornfax. Omitted truths it was.

"I was in my mindscape. That thing sucked me into it," I said, and she looked at me, surprised.

"Why would it do that?"

"I don't know, but I hadn't ever been in my mindscape before, so I didn't know how to get out." I rubbed my ear, a little embarrassed. I had, in fact, been stuck in there for a while before I realised, I could will myself to leave like I had willed myself to absorb the scroll Albus had given me.

"You didn't know how to leave, seriously?" Rian rested a hand on her hip as she looked at me with doubt.

"N-no, I figured it out eventually." I laughed, trying to shake off the tension.

"I can't believe I was out here pacing over you being stuck in your mindscape." She huffed, shaking her head. "Is that really all that happened?"

"Y-yes," I said, but my voice wasn't very convincing. Rian's expression proved that.

"Come on, I found a room at the back of the ruins we can rest in whilst you were *occupied*." She narrowed her eyes at me, her suspicion burning in her gaze.

I nodded and followed her to a small hole in the wall near the pedestal. We ducked and crawled through it into a room carved into the temple's stone. Rotting wood showed signs of a desk having been here once, a broken bedframe and scraps of cloth black from mould. There were some angel shrooms but not as many as there were outside the room.

Rian settled down in one of the empty corners, using her brown cloak to soften the ground a little, her backpack as a pillow. I took the opposite corner, seeing my cloak already placed there, and slumped to the ground, my body protesting. Now that we had stopped moving and there was a moment of quiet, all of today's exhaustion, fear, tension, and anxiety cascaded over me.

"So," Rian said, picking at some jerky she had saved. "Any ideas on how to get out of here?"

"Not really, unless we can find a miracle." I sighed, finding a scrap of meat I had cooked yesterday. It probably wasn't the best, but I had poison resistance; it should be fine.

"Miracle indeed." Rian leaned her head on the back of the wall. "They have probably left, you know."

"What?"

"The brigade; they probably think we're dead."

"Maybe," I said, for the first time realising that possibility.

"Wouldn't you? With a horned baildon, even if we had just fallen into a ditch, it would have still crushed us or suffocated us under the earth with its abilities. They definitely think we're dead."

"The army waits for no one weak enough not to survive," I said, echoing General Saika's words.

"Unfortunately for us." Rian finished her jerky and began to untie the loosened braids of her fluffy brown hair. "Why did the Crazy Cerue Lady join the army, anyway?"

"Me?" I shrugged. "I wanted to get away from things."

"Things? Like what? I thought you lived a life of luxury," she sneered. "You love to flaunt your fancy things."

"Maybe once upon a time." I half smiled. "Not so much lately."

"I don't get it." Rian sat up, her braids now fully undone, so her wild hair framed her face. "What changed for you? You used to be so . . ."

"Abrasive?" I finished her sentence, and she dubiously nodded. "I just . . . I just realised I wanted something else, something more. I don't want to be a trophy for some noble to parade around at social functions. I actually want to, well, do something with my life for once." I finished curling my legs up close to my chest.

Rian looked at me silently as she contemplated a response.

"Is this to do with Garret Asher?"

"Would you want to marry him?" I asked, raising an eyebrow and causing her to smile.

"He is a pompous ass, isn't he. You know, he told me he was your fiancé a dozen or so times." Rian rolled her eyes. "The man is irritating to a fault."

"I'm glad you understand." I exhaled a little in relief that I didn't have to convince her of his character. "So why did you join?"

"Oh, that's . . ." Rian looked away, debating something, and then sighed. "Here." She unsheathed one of her serrated sabres and handed it over to me.

I raised an eyebrow. Rian waved it at me again impatiently, so I took it, tensing my arm muscles for the weight. When she let go, I was shocked to find that the blade was light, so light I had no trouble lifting it. The hilt, wrapped in a sable green leather, felt cool in my hands. Bringing it close, I could see a series of runes etched into the metal. The patterns were delicate as the runes blended together at the base of the weapon.

"It's so light," I marvelled, handing it back to her.

"It was a gift from Vayan. All Thornfaxes join the army. It is a tradition, no matter our gender." Rian returned the serrated blade back to her scabbard, a strained look on her face.

"Your sister?"

"Yes, she is an enchanter, a prodigy." Rian pulled a face of irritance. "Albertine assisted in making the blades. Vayan enchanted them." I recalled that they were both older than Rian. She was the youngest of three siblings.

"My father expects me to become like them. A summoner of prestige to bring honour to the family. So they made me these blades to ensure that I had the best." She clamped her jaw.

Rian then closed her eyes and took a deep breath. "They expect me to surpass Vayan. She surpassed Albertine, so I have to be better than Vayan."

"Didn't you say Vayan was a prodigy?" I asked, remembering that Vayan was the second oldest.

"I did," Rian sneered.

"That's a lot of pressure to live up to," I said, seeing the emotion in her eyes.

"It is," she affirmed.

"What would you want to do? If you weren't enchanting." I leaned my head on my knees as Rian looked at me. She copied my stance, cuddling her own legs close as she thought about my question.

"Clothes," she said, surprising me.

"Clothes? You want to be a seamstress?" I couldn't hide my surprise, which made Rian smile gingerly.

"Yeah," she sighed. "I would love to make clothes."

CHAPTER TWENTY

Music chimed in the foyer as guests danced merrily, enjoying the evening's amusements. I sat alone by a table near the balcony, sipping my flute of champagne, glaring at Rian Thornfax.

Rian stood surrounded by handsome bachelors, all eager for her attention. She bragged of her life as a summoner in training, of the adventure she had seen. They fawned over her, rapt with her words as she described a life I could never have.

Envy rose in the pit of my chest.

I fluttered my fan to hide my snarl as she headed towards my table. I stuck out my leg and grinned as she tripped, her blue dress pooling around her.

"Rian! Are you all right?" A young noble infatuated with her offered to help her stand. She took his hand, embarrassed, turning her eyes towards me.

"Cerue," she said mockingly. "What do you think you are doing?"

"My, oh my." My green eyes flashed, my mouth hidden as I gently tapped my lips with my fan. "What ever do you mean, Lady Rian?"

"You did that on purpose," Rian said accusingly, and rightly so.

"Are you suggesting I intentionally caused you to step on your dress?" I feigned shock. "However could I do such a thing?"

"You tripped me! Don't pretend otherwise, Cerue," she roared, causing guests nearby to look at her, displeased.

"Lady Rian, I honestly do not know why you accuse me so. It is unbecoming." I lowered my fan just enough for her to see my smirk. "I am offended you would think such a thing of me."

Rian snapped, grabbing a flute. She moved to throw it, but a firm hand snatched her wrist.

"Lady Rian, I think that is enough." Callan tugged her away, angrily flashing me a look. "I think you should leave now, sister."

"If I must." I rose from my seat, my own anger flaring. But of course he would come to her rescue, not mine.

I stared at the stone ceiling above as a spider ran away into a hole. Without the morning light, I was unsure what time it was, or if it was even morning. Looking over, I saw that Rian wasn't in her bedroll. I was alone in this cramped, aging room. Sitting up, I absently rubbed the bracelet on my wrist.

So much had happened yesterday that I hadn't really had a chance to digest it all. Albus, just what was he? He had described himself as a fragmented memory of the real Albus, a man who had once lived in a place called Teralia. He had died and returned like me.

I wasn't the only living person to have experienced death. That knowledge alone was comforting. I wasn't unique. We had both been gifted memory stones. I had always wondered why I could not remember where my bracelet came from. If the gods gifted it, perhaps that was the reason. Maybe I was not supposed to have known.

But why did they gift it to me?

What did Albus want from me?

I sighed, tugging my legs from my bedroll, and stood to stretch my limbs. Then, peeking through the hole into the temple, I saw Rian. She held her twin sabres leaning forward on her right leg; swiftly, she changed position as she practised her weapon form. Her frizzy brown hair had been neatly rebraided, keeping her eyes clear as she concentrated.

I leaned on the wall and watched her. I had always been envious of Rian Thornfax in my last three lives. She was popular, intelligent, and well liked by the people around her. She had everything I had craved, and my envy came out in ugly bouts. I had been nasty to her. I knew that. However, seeing her upset often cheered me up, even if only for the briefest moments.

I had nightmares as a child after the incident with the rocks she had pelted me with. My confinement afterwards and the distrust it caused in my family seeded my hatred. But we had been children. It was easy to forget that children could often do things without understanding the consequences.

In all fairness, Rian had never hurt me in such a way again. In fact, I remembered receiving a box from her shortly after. She had sent me an apology, likely out of guilt for lying about what had happened.

I smiled, thinking of the stuffed rabbit she had gifted me. It had been my first gift after Cassandra had died. My only gift. The rabbit had been poorly stitched, so I had thought it was a gift she hadn't cared about, something she had given me out of obligation for her actions. Its poor quality and tattered workmanship had made me think she was just insulting me further.

Now?

I had been petty.

If I had accepted her apology, things might have been different. Maybe we could have even been friends. But instead, it was difficult to let go of my anger and frustration. I ended up taking out a lot of anger with my family on her. Maybe if I had known then what I'd learned yesterday, I might not have been so hasty in my actions towards her.

"Having fun watching?" Rian called as she swiped her blades in the glow of the angel shrooms. She winced a little from the movement, her arm shaky from her injury during our fall into this cavern.

"A little." I smirked. "What form are you practising?" I asked, seeing her skill with her blades.

"It's called the soaring tempest." Rian spun and swung the blades in a jolted movement. "Albertine taught me."

"I'm envious," I admitted, drawing my jian. "I'm hopeless with the flowing water method." I began the first movement, inspired to practise by Rian's dedication.

"Don't be," Rian sighed, completing her final stance. "My father didn't give me a choice but to learn." She sheathed her blades and wiped the sweat from her forehead. "You're lucky you could enjoy being a child."

"Right . . ." I said grimly. My childhood had not been enjoyable.

"Hey, I, um . . ." I started to say, a little fidgety leaning into the second movement. "I never thanked you for the stuffed rabbit you gave me when we were kids."

"Oh—" Rian paused, surprised. "That." She scrunched her eyes, scratching her head awkwardly. "That's okay. You don't need to thank me, it wasn't a great gift." She looked at me hesitantly.

"Did you . . . make it yourself?" I asked with a small smile, my inclination guiding me.

Rian's face turned beetroot red. "Yeah," she whispered, embarrassed. "Sorry, it was bad."

"No." I shook my head. "I'm sorry I didn't realise sooner."

She frowned, looking away. "I should never have treated you like that back then." Her voice was laced with guilt. "I'm sorry for being so . . . small-minded."

I stumbled a little and silently took in her words. No one had ever apologised to me before.

"Thanks, I appreciate it."

I continued to practise for a while whilst Rian rested nearby. I tripped on the fourth movement, my thigh not quite recovered, and lost my balance, breaking apart the movement. I tried it again, and after a few more times, I finally completed all seven movements. A familiar tingling echoed in my body as I did so. I was beginning to recognise the feeling more now. I seemed to feel it when my understanding of something improved and my level grew.

Holding my palm forward, I called, "Sign."

Blood Sign			
General Information		**Progression**	
Name:	Lynette Heversham	**Core Innate Grade:**	0.02
Age:	21	**Core Condensation Grade:**	0.02
Rank:	Daughter of Viscount—Talbour	**Affinities:**	Unknown
Traits:	Beast Born (Hidden)		
Occupation:	Trainee of Zopan Empire Army		
Covenants:	Zopan Empire Army Blood Bond: *Guidance of Vishka (Hidden): Knowledge of Albus*		
Skills			
Aether:	1	**Spirit:**	1
	One with All—Gathering: 1 (Novice)		Beast Taming: 1 (Novice) (Hidden)
Combative:	2	**General:**	1
	Jian—Flowing Water: 5 (Novice)		Social: −2 (Novice) (Hidden)
	Dagger Strike: 8 (Novice)		
Body:	3		
	Poison Resistance: 15 (Initiate)		
	Pain Resistance: 23 (Apprentice)		
	Stamina: 8 (Novice)		
Mind:	3		
	Research: 12 (Initiate)		
	Herbology: 57 (Adept)		
	Alchemy: 7 (Novice)		

I studied my improvements and was surprised to see that my social level had increased. I hadn't been expecting that. I also had not been expecting to see a new covenant. I hadn't signed a blood contract with Albus. Our agreement had been more permanent than I thought. I quickly decided to will that covenant hidden. Probably best I kept that a secret. I didn't really want to start explaining about memory stones and how they were gifted by the gods. That would raise even more questions and probably cement my nickname as the Crazy Cerue Lady even further.

My jian skill had increased but only by one level. At least it was improving.

"Do you use 'Sign' every time to check your skills?" Rian asked me as I lowered my palm.

"Is there another way?"

"Yeah, just say 'Sign update.' You will only see the changes," Rian informed me with a shrug. I thanked her and noted that for the next time I felt that strange tingle.

"I think we should look around, try to see if this cave goes anywhere else." Rian pulled up from her resting stance, wiping some grime from the back of her trousers.

"I don't think we have any other options," I agreed.

We split up and began to search the temple and the caves surrounding it. There were a few offshoot tunnels, but they weren't long, and we could see that they were dead ends without walking far. More craven bats were snuggling in each of them. I headed back to the temple to try to find another way whilst Rian explored the runes etched on the walls.

I rubbed my hands against the brittle stone, trying to feel for any structural weakness. I didn't have much success. There was no opening I could find. Our situation trapped here was looking grim. We only had a day's worth of food rations left, and I had no more water. We couldn't survive long down here.

Going back the way we had come wasn't an option. Neither of us could reach the tunnel in the cave ceiling we had fallen from.

Heading back into the old room we had slept in, I slumped on the ground where my bedroll lay. I looked around the room. Judging from the remains of the furniture here, it might have been a living space for a monk. Maybe it was where Albus had lived.

Standing, I walked to the broken desk and tried to open a drawer. The wood creaked, and with a harder tug, it stubbornly opened. It was empty. I slammed it shut again with a frown.

Just what were we meant to do?

If this was where Albus had lived, would his memory know?

Did I want to talk to that creepy man again?

I sighed heavily. We were out of options.

Closing my eyes, I centred my breathing, trying to enter my mindscape. I didn't know how long I stood there before I felt a sinking familiarity. Then I opened my eyes and stood in the vast, empty space, my tiny core floating at the centre of the darkness. My rune was still working, slowly pulling aether from the outside world. They were the only source of light in this space.

"Albus?" I called, and received no response.

"Albus, do you know a way out of this temple, out from this cave?" I asked again into the silence.

I waited, but no reply came. Sighing, I hovered my hand above my core, feeling its warmth. It was a strange thing, this tiny orb. Its centre glowed gently, a swirling mass of cloudy liquid. It looked similar to the evaluation globe I had used during the test to join the army.

"Desk." Suddenly Albus's voice echoed, jolting me from my core.

"Desk?" I quickly responded, confused. I had already checked there.

"Behind it." Albus's voice quietened with each word, his presence disappearing. He sounded strained, as though talking took a lot of energy. That was when I remembered he had told me he needed to replenish. Perhaps he wasn't able to respond to me at the moment.

"Thank you!" I called, willing myself to leave my mindscape.

I returned to the room and quickly grabbed the corner of the rotting desk. I tried to shift it, but the wood had a solid line of mould clinging to the wall it rested against.

"Rian!" I shouted as I tried to move the desk, my grip slipping.

"What?" she said as she appeared, ducking under the hole into the room.

"Help me move this. I think something is behind it," I said, and Rian raised an eyebrow questioningly.

"Why do you think that?" she asked, approaching the opposite end of the desk.

"Just help me move it," I sighed, making her roll her eyes.

"Fine, on three." She counted, and we lifted together. Unfortunately, the wooden legs broke as we did, and the desk crashed to the floor in a cloud of dust enveloping us. We coughed, waving it away as it settled around us. As it did so, I saw nothing special on the wall where the desk had been. I frowned, disappointed.

"Wait . . ." Rian narrowed her eyes. "Do you feel that?" she asked, leaning her head against the wall and tapping it. Her eyes widened as she stepped back with a smile.

"What?" I asked, hope rising.

"There's a breeze, and it sounds hollow. I think this may be our way out," she explained, rummaging in her backpack, still on the floor. "Hold this." She handed me a bottle of ink. It was bright red. I almost mistook it for blood. Next she took out a metal pen. It was thin with a pointed nib.

"What are you doing?" I asked, watching her take the bottle back and dip her pen in the red ink. She raised her hand to the wall and began to draw a series of runes. She was careful and delicate with her work.

"It's a rune to break this down. I'm not very good at them yet, though, so it may explode." Rian sent me a sheepish look.

"I-I'll pack up our stuff," I said nervously.

What kind of explosion is she talking about?

Quickly I rolled up our bedrolls and stuffed them back into the ties on our backpacks. Next, I put my cloak back on and made sure to stand far back from the wall Rian was enchanting.

"Shit," she blurted out, jumping back. "Cover!"

She didn't need to tell me twice.

We both scrambled out of the hole in the wall as the red runes began to glow. The light grew brighter and brighter. Suddenly a bang shattered the quiet, a rush of stone collapsing as the small room fell apart. We sheltered our eyes, ducking behind one of the gods' statues as stone chunks flew out towards us in sharp shards and billowing dust.

CHAPTER TWENTY-ONE

The place where Vishka's statue had once stood now had a headless figure, her hands broken. Rian and I gingerly poked our heads around the statue's body to look at the destruction her rune had caused. Somehow, the pedestal that Albus's memory stone had been on was still intact. Chucks of rock were scattered around it. The room that had been behind the pedestal was in pieces. Losing the back wall had shattered its integrity, bringing the whole thing tumbling down.

We carefully threaded through the minefield of stones towards the area we had blown up. Where the small room had once stood now loomed a cavern. A soft wind fluttered on my skin, a smell of dampness and moss filling my nose. The air didn't smell stale. I grinned. If the air wasn't stale, this tunnel could lead outside.

"I think we may need some of these glowing mushrooms," Rian said, noting the cave's darkness.

"Good idea." I took off my backpack and rummaged for the small cloth bag I had made for them. Being cautious, I opened the top of the bag to allow their glow to act as a light source for us.

"Let's hope this gets us out of here," I mumbled as we stepped into the darkness.

Rian silently drew both of the sabres and looked up. Craven bats occupied the rafters of this tunnel as well. We weren't surprised to see them. Luckily, navigating the stalactites with the mushrooms was more manageable. So we didn't cause as much noise as we had when we fell down here. Slowly we made our way forward, using the wall for support as we still had our injuries.

We stopped when we came to a crossroads. The cave split into two separate paths. Each looked as dark as the other, no sign of which might lead us out.

"Got a coin we can flip?" Rian asked, lowering her blades.

"No, but we can always backtrack," I said, unsure of which direction to take.

"Want to go this way? The other smells a little bit like rotten eggs. It could be sulphur." Rian wrinkled her nose at the right path. Its deeper darkness loomed as it ran steeply downwards.

"Sure," I sighed, lifting my dagger high. "Left it is, then." I did not really like the idea of going down farther in this cave.

So, we headed down the left path, keeping vigilant. The cave structure didn't change much as we did. Stalagmites still dripped water; the walls slimy to the touch. I noticed that the craven bats' numbers were decreasing. Maybe they were close by? Hidden by darkness our mushrooms couldn't show? I tightened the grip on my dagger.

A smell of faeces and rot struck the air.

It was worrying.

With a lack of craven bats, we shouldn't be smelling their acid excrement so strongly.

A drop of water fell onto my cheek as we reached a turn in the tunnel. Something snapped under my foot, and my throat closed.

I knew where the bats had gone.

The bones my foot had crushed were small, and a skull nearby indicated I had stood on the remains of a craven bat.

Raising the mushrooms for a better view, Rian and I stilled. Fear crawled into us as we saw the boneyard we had entered. Hundreds of bones littered the floor. Some were half decomposing, worms infesting the dead.

We had entered something's nest.

Slowly, we backed away, looking at one another in fright. We should have taken the path to the right.

Rian suddenly held in a squeal as she stepped on another bone, and the sickening crunch echoed down the long tunnel. We both waited, our breaths the only sound.

A terrifying roar reverberated down the tunnel directly behind us. Rian and I spun towards the path we'd just walked. Had we passed it? Or had it been watching us?

Maybe we had been correct in not taking the path to the right.

A second roar sounded, much closer now.

"Run!" Rian cried, running directly into the boneyard.

We sprinted with all our might across the treacherous bone-littered floor. The air was rank, and I couldn't get enough into my lungs. My adrenaline spiked as my thigh protested.

It ached from our fall in here. I misstepped on a half-shattered skull and saw Rian pulling up ahead. Every step threatened a broken ankle in this darkness.

We turned as the cave grew narrower and high-pitched screeches came down from above. Craven bats fell from the ceiling in swarms.

Rian slashed at the bats in her path, and they fell, torn apart. "Shit, they're freaking everywhere!"

The winged hairless creatures outstretched their tiny claws to my face, trying to find purchase. I stabbed one that tried to put out my eye, but another was already in my hair, and a third was trying to rip my ear. They were all around me, a living veil as I tried to follow Rian.

"Faster, come on!" Rian called back, her voice an echo away from me.

One tried to bite my cheek. The bat screeched in pain as I grabbed its wing and pulled it, tearing it away. I blocked my face with my arm as another dived at me. I could barely see.

More came.

My hair was tugged, torn by their claws as I stabbed them. They were quick, agile creatures avoiding my attacks, their red eyes piercing. One bit into my right shoulder as it landed. I screamed at the shock, grabbing its head to yank it away from my body.

The roar that was chasing us angrily answered my scream. I could hear its footsteps crushing bones now. It had entered the boneyard.

"You okay?" Rian hollered as she came back for me, beating the bats away with her sabre. Before I could thank her, she spun and dodged another as it swooped overhead.

"Keep moving. It's closer!" I yelled as Rian's breath came short; her footing as unsteady as mine.

Ahead the cave narrowed further. We parried and dodged as many bats as possible, but they peppered us with small teeth and claws.

I listened to the footfalls behind us and could hear the panting of the beast, its wet breath working like a bellows.

Ahead I could see a small stream of light.

"There!" I pointed.

"Let's hurry. I think it's nearly on us," Rian said as a deafening roar approached.

The craven bats swarming us changed their actions. First, they flew away from our path, scrambling. Then, afraid, they rushed into the rafters of the cave ceiling. Some were tearing apart their own dead as they hauled bodies with them.

A pounding so close made goose bumps rise on my skin, and a warm wind blew at my back. Daringly, I turned my head to look as I kept running and instantly regretted it.

A canine-like demonic beast trained its glowing yellow eyes on us. Its mouth hung open, spit connecting its serrated teeth as it hunted us. It was larger than a horse and could likely crush me in one swoop of its claw. Its dark blue skin blended into the darkness as its clawed feet dug into the stone to gain traction. It weaved across the cave terrain, jumping onto the wall, running and snapping at a stray craven bat that had failed to escape. The beast swallowed the bat in one chomp.

My heart threatened to leave my chest, it was pumping so fast. Rian had blood trickling down her face, her left arm shaking as she struggled to keep hold of her sabre.

We kept running.

It came towards us with the force of an avalanche.

Its claws ripped through my cloak, shredding it into tatters as I leapt away.

The beast circled in front of us across the stone walls, blocking our path.

"We have to fight." Rian looked at me, and I understood from her eyes how much trouble we were in.

"All right," I agreed, my nerves wavering as the beast's teeth glinted hungrily.

Raising her blades, Rian nodded, and I dashed right.

The canine beast leapt forward as I did, and it landed where I had been moments before. I dropped the angel shrooms and readied my jian in my right hand, my dagger in my left.

I have not trained enough for this!

The beast swivelled its head and rushed towards us.

Rian tried to block its claws, crossing her blades and losing one in the encounter. I saw my chance and ducked, taking the fourth stance of flowing water to plunge towards the beast. I aimed for its legs, but the swing went awry and bounced off its thick hide. Its focus shifted and it rushed me.

As I backpedalled, its muzzle rammed into me, and I went flying. The stone floor caught me, crushing the air out of my lungs.

"Lynette!" Rian cried.

Panic flooded me as its meat grinder of jagged teeth came for my face. I tried to get away, but I was too slow. I looked into its jaws as they stretched impossibly wide, and I knew death was coming.

Its jaws clamped onto my shoulder. My bones snapped, and my vision fled as pain filled every corner of my mind. I could hear myself screaming as it pulled back, trying to rip the flesh off my bones.

"Get away from her!" Rian charged with her remaining blade. She slung it at the beast's neck. The blade sliced into its hardened skin.

But it wasn't enough.

The beast released my shoulder, and I fell to the ground in a lump. I cradled the ruin of my mangled arm close. It hurt. By the gods, it hurt so much.

The beast turned its attention to Rian and snarled. Rian snarled back, her courage overwhelming.

She raised her right blade high, then attacked. They clashed together as the canine beast snapped at her head. She danced around it, narrowly avoiding its claws, then whipped her blade upwards. It cut into the dog beast's chest, ripping through its muscle.

The beast howled and then rammed its head into her. Its two horns pushed her to the ground. Rian rolled right, slipping past the beast's paws as it tried to pin her down.

Rian's screaming pierced my fog of pain, and I looked to see her limping where its claws had drenched her thigh in blood.

She was losing.

We were dying.

We were as good as dead.

Rian continued to battle it, but its hide was too thick, its strength too monstrous.

I clutched my shoulder, blood coating my hand. Crawling, I pulled my limp arm with me, an idea forming. I couldn't help in this state. The muscle in my shoulder was severed.

There was only one thing I could do.

I grabbed the bag of angel shrooms.

"Rian! Bring it here!" I gasped, the pain intensifying from my movement.

Rian circled the beast as best she could and ran to me, her blade poised back. The beast dug its claws into the stone and ran up the wall after her. It scaled alongside as she ran and pounced.

"Duck!" I shouted, and Rian skidded, lowering her body. The beast had already leapt and couldn't stop its momentum as it passed her and headed for me.

I threw the bag of angel shrooms at it.

Some mushrooms scattered in the air. The cloth bag must have felt like something living because it gobbled it up.

Rian grabbed my leg and slid me across the stone floor as the beast crashed.

Its movement slowed as it stalked us, and I stumbled back.

It came at us both, and I felt a laugh bubble up inside me. Was this how my fourth life would end?

Its jaws came closer, determined to end us.

Then it dropped to its side. Its body shook, twitching and convulsing.

Rian immediately ran to it and stabbed it directly in its heart.

The dog beast wailed, its throat crackling from its paralysis.

It moved no more.

CHAPTER TWENTY-TWO

O w," I complained as Rian tied scraps of my cloak around my shoulder and chest.

"Sorry, bandages aren't my thing." She lightened her touch, dabbing some of the blood from my arm. The blue shirt Eduard had given me was ruined. The sleeves were torn, holes dotting my chest from the craven bats. My cloak only reached my waist, the ends shredded.

Rian looked similar. We were both scratched, with minor bite marks puncturing our skin. We remained vigilant of the craven bats still in the rafters. They watched us with their beady eyes, but they kept their distance after we took down the canine beast.

"There, that's the best I can do." Rian sighed glumly, pulling away as I tested my new arm sling. The muscles in my shoulder had been torn. My right arm was no longer functional. Not without extreme pain. I didn't know if I would have kept conscious during the initial bite without my pain resistance skill.

"Thanks. Are you okay?" I asked, seeing the tear in Rian's left leg from the beast. Her blood had dried and flaked on the material of her trousers.

"I'll be fine. It didn't get too deep." She winced as she walked over to the canine beast's body. It lay on the cold stone floor, its eyes void of life. "I'm going to get its core. Do you want to get the craven bats?"

"Ugh, sure. I just dig them out, right?" I gingerly took my dagger with my working left hand and picked up one of the bats' bodies. It was weird using my left hand like this; I had to adjust my grip.

"Yeah, should be in their chest." Rian stabbed into the canine beast's carcass and began to dig.

I grimaced, holding the bat. Its hairless body felt cold. I had never touched anything dead before. I placed it on the ground and sank my dagger into its dead flesh. The sensation was weird as its body squelched when I ripped my dagger down until I felt something hard resist the blade. Biting my lip to hold back my nausea, I put my dagger aside and stuck my hand into the wound, grabbing the hard round object in its chest. With a yank, I removed the small core of the craven bat.

The object in my hand was a dark green. It throbbed with energy the moment it touched my skin. Aether swirled in its centre, and it felt warm, unlike the body I had pulled it from.

"Wind core." Rian glanced over my shoulder. "Most craven bats will have them."

"They didn't use wind aether, though?" I asked, picking up another to repeat the process.

"They weren't at a high enough level to do so. We got lucky this thing"—Rian kicked the dog beast—"didn't have a chance to use its water aether." She held out a much larger dark blue core.

"It was more than luck," I sighed, my shoulder throbbing. "It was a miracle."

"No, it was your insight about those mushrooms that saved us." Rian carefully picked up the mushrooms scattered on the floor as I stabbed another craven bat.

"I didn't think we would use them so soon," I said, pulling out a fourth wind core and adding it to my backpack.

"I doubt this will be the only demonic beast we encounter," Rian mumbled, handing me the mushrooms she'd placed in another cloth bag made from the remains of my cloak. She then began helping with the rest of the craven bats. "We should probably devise some tactics for the next one we encounter. Especially now that you can't use that arm."

"Right, I won't be able to help much, so you will have to do most of the fighting." I frowned. I was already weak to begin with. Now I was pretty much useless.

"Well, let's get out of here first, and we can discuss our options on the way?"

"Sure." I nodded, and we quickly finished up with the remaining craven bats. We ended up with twelve small wind cores and one medium water core. Rian kept the water core, and we split the wind cores between us. I had no idea how to use them, but I remembered that Eduard had said beast cores were useful for summoners.

We cut some of the canine beast meat for our rations, as we didn't know when we would come across more food. I didn't like the idea of eating it, but as Rian put it, it couldn't be that bad. The marsh snake beast meat was edible, so in theory, this should be too.

Leaning on each other, we finally headed for the light at the end of the cave.

* * *

We shielded our eyes as we approached the light. After being in the cave's darkness for so long, they hurt from the intensity. Unfortunately, the source was from a gap up a short incline. I found it challenging to keep a grip with just one hand, and Rian struggled to push up the slope with her leg. Nevertheless, we climbed, helping each other where we could, and squeezed through the gap ungracefully.

Finally, we were out.

The plains of the highlands stretched far out, the meadows gently swaying in the fresh wind. The air was clean, and I took a deep breath of relief. The sky was bright, and there was nothing around that I would classify as dangerous.

It was just us.

No sign of the army brigade.

"They left, then," I grumbled. I had thought they might have, but it was depressing to see our theory confirmed.

"As I thought they would. Come on. Maybe they left a trail we can follow." Rian grabbed my good hand and dragged me forward from my stupor.

"Are we even close to where they were?" I had no clue where we were.

Did Rian know?

"No idea, but if we walk in the opposite direction from the tunnel, we might find something." Rian drew one of her blades, her eyes darting around us, looking for danger.

I hadn't thought of that. Retracing our steps above land could get us back to where we fell.

Nodding, I shifted my backpack and kept up with her pace. It was easier now that she was limping every other step.

We walked for some time as the sun beamed down on us. Without the brigade surrounding us, the plains felt empty. I hadn't realised how accustomed I had grown to the noise of others marching beside me. Without them, I felt exposed. A bird's cry in the sky made me jump as I became anxious from the quiet. I worried that we could be ambushed at any moment. After that, it became difficult to think of anything else.

In an attempt to divert my anxiety, I held my palm forward as we walked.

"Sign update," I called, and a list of shortened information appeared.

Blood Sign Updates:

Jian—Flowing Water: 6 (Novice) +1

Dagger Strike: 10 (Initiate) +2

Pain Resistance: 25 (Apprentice) +2

Stamina: 11 (Initiate) +3

The shortened information made it much easier to check my skills. The added note of how much they had improved was also helpful. I was happy to see that my dagger strike and stamina skills had evolved to Initiate grade. That could be why I didn't feel as exhausted walking as I had when first starting the march. My body was slowly getting better accustomed to strenuous activity.

Soon the sky began to darken, and we slowed our pace. We agreed it was too dangerous to walk at night, so we set up a makeshift camp. Unfortunately, neither of us had a tent. Both of our marching partners had them. So we laid our bedrolls directly on the ground, the night sky sparkling above.

We managed a small fire and attempted to cook the canine beast meat. Rian saw me turning it on a stick and rolled her eyes, grabbing it from me before I could finish. She sprinkled a powder onto it and then set it beside hers after piercing it with holes. I watched it cook and couldn't quite figure out why she had been mad at my cooking. However, when I bit into the cooked meat, my eyes widened as the flesh melted in my mouth with a pleasant taste of pepper and salt.

"This is good!" I exclaimed, my ravenous stomach begging for more.

"Why do you sound surprised?" Rian laughed, biting into her own.

"I—I just, I didn't know you could cook." I meekly blushed, devouring the meat.

"It's nothing, just a skill I picked up." She shrugged, smiling, clearly happy about the compliment.

"Do you think you could teach me? Whatever I cook turns black," I asked, eager to learn. If I could cook like this, I wouldn't have to rely on others to make my food for me.

"Sure, I don't think I could stand by whilst you burn perfectly good food anyway." Rian grinned and proceeded to show me her techniques.

Apparently, piercing the meat allowed the heat to cook through it better, and adding spices improved the flavour considerably. I attempted to cook a few small chunks on my own, but they still burned, and I pouted in frustration. Rian explained that I wasn't turning them enough, so I tried again with a few more small pieces when a tingle sizzled in my body.

"Sign update," I called excitedly, and a box appeared.

Blood Sign Updates:
New Skill Gained
General: Cooking: 1 (Novice)

"You got the skill?" Rian asked, enjoying my enthusiasm.

"Yes! I can't wait to show Teresa. She is just as bad as I am." I popped the small chunk I had cooked into my mouth. It wasn't as good as Rian's, but it wasn't burnt.

"She's that commoner you are teamed with?"

"Yes." I nodded. "She's from Ingalham."

"Oh, that wooded town? She must have travelled here with Lord Caspian Landrick." Rian cleaned her metal skewer and placed it back into her backpack.

"Landrick? You mean the Marquess of Ingalham?"

"Yeah, his son joined up this year with us. He's in my team, he seems okay. A little standoffish."

He must the noble I hadn't recognised in their team.

"Sounds familiar," I teased, and Rian scowled.

"I am not standoffish." She folded her arms with a glare.

"Sure, and I'm not a Crazy Cerue Lady." I raised my eyebrow. We looked at each other before smiling.

"Maybe I could stand to loosen up a little." Rian slouched, leaning back on her bedroll to stare up at the sky.

"Maybe, but then I would have to start acting sensible," I responded, leaning my head in my good hand as I lay in my own bedroll.

"True, that may be difficult for you," she said, teasing me back, and we laughed.

"I never did ask you," Rian continued, a little hesitant. "Why did you . . . why did you do that?" She paused, seeing my confusion. "The um, night with a man in a tavern, of all places," she clarified.

"Oh, simple answer?" I asked, and she nodded.

"I wanted to annul my engagement with Garret Asher. Didn't do much good, though."

"You ruined your reputation just to cancel an engagement?" Rian's voice rose in surprise. "Why don't you just refuse?"

"I did," I sighed. "My father thinks marriage to Garret is the best choice for me." I looked up at the sky as the stars watched us. It was a beautiful night. "He wouldn't listen."

"I'm sorry," Rian quietly responded, her face frowning. "I understand. I can't refuse my father either."

"I know." I smiled sullenly, remembering that Rian wanted to be a seamstress, not a summoner.

"Maybe when we get to the capital, you could be a seamstress as a hobby?"

"Perhaps." She fidgeted in her bedroll. "Do you know what you want to do? As a profession?"

"No clue," I sighed. "I still need to learn what my options are or what I'm good at. General Saika said I could join the medical research team with my herbology skills."

"He doesn't give recommendations often. Albertine works under him."

"Oh? What does Albertine do?"

"She chose the warrior profession against Father's will. He wants all of us to be enchanters." Rian raised one of her blades high as she inspected the runes etched onto the metal.

"I see. I think Eduard is in some clerical role. He doesn't tell me much."

"Callan?"

"I'm not sure. He never told me, but from his personality . . . I would guess he wants to be a warrior." I had theorised as much from his station guarding us trainees.

"Makes sense, he is . . ."

"A hothead?" I finished her sentence as she grinned, nodding.

"Yes, a hothead."

"Do you talk much? With Callan, I mean?" I asked, knowing that they were engaged in my second life. In my first and my third life, they hadn't gotten engaged. I never understood why, as I was primarily trapped in either Heversham Manor or Garret's mansion. It had bothered me. I had wondered if it was my antagonistic actions towards Rian in my second life that had made the difference. That and the fact that Callan had perished in my third life during an excursion into the deadlands.

"Not really." Rian shrugged. "He only ever interacted with me when we . . . argued." She sheepishly looked away, confirming my suspicion.

So I had been their catalyst.

We talked into the night, discussing cooking techniques, nobles we both disliked such as Garret, and ideas for what the canine beast might have been. We distracted ourselves from our situation as we did so, taking comfort in each other's presence. We came up with a battle plan should we be attacked again. Eventually, we took turns sleeping so one of us could guard against demonic beasts.

Then morning came.

CHAPTER TWENTY-THREE

Rian and I ran through the grass in the morning sun. The rigid green spines reached our waists as we tried to keep our balance traversing the terrain. Our path to finding the brigade's trail had led us directly into an overgrown meadow. It screamed danger as we could not see the creatures that might lurk within. So, we decided to run.

Walking would have given any beasts more time to reach us. We made noise as the reeds snapped in our way. Rian slashed with her sabres, creating a pathway as we rushed. There hadn't been a way around the field. It had stretched so far, we could not see where it began. We had no choice but to keep going forward, to go through it.

I saw some reeds shake to my left and readied my dagger.

"Left!" I called, and Rian changed our direction.

The reeds grew denser as we moved to the right, away from the shaking reeds. They scratched against my arms as seeds scattered with our disruption. I sneezed as some fell into my face, my arms now bare since my shirt was ruined. Only my grey gauntlets provided protection.

The reeds shook, and a clicking noise alerted us to something ahead. Rian slowed as she readied her sabres and bent her knees. Reeds parted, and a demonic rat beast jumped out. Its two large teeth were hurrying towards us. I swiftly slid beside Rian and lowered my stance to the beast's height, stabbing at its head as it aimed for our legs. My distraction was enough for Rian to swipe her blades down into its torso, killing the small rat beast.

We didn't stay to gather its core. We kept running.

More reeds shook as the creatures followed.

Two beasts sprang into our path of destroyed reeds and nipped at our heels. I kicked one and threw an angel shroom at the other. It fell, twitching in a strangled cry. The beast I had kicked changed its target, jumping onto its friend to devour it.

We continued.

Last night we had decided I would do my best to distract whilst Rian would land the killing blows. Unfortunately, I couldn't wield my jian, not correctly, because I was primarily right-handed and could not lift it alone with my left. My dagger skill, however, gave me the same talent with either hand now that it was initiated. So using all we had, I did my best to keep the beasts away. This allowed Rian to focus on our direction and to tackle any that got too close.

The plan was working so far.

An echo of clicking hummed from all around us. The reeds shook, and the earth under our feet vibrated. I tried to keep my footing steady, but a rock caught my toe, and I slipped as Rian continued to run.

"Shit," I cursed, scrambling to pull up with my good arm. As I did, I saw five of the furry beasts hurry towards me through the gaps in the reeds.

They pounced as I rolled, crushing more reeds.

Two tried to burrow into my chest as they dug at my leather cuirass. A third bit at my arm, taking a chunk of my sling as the others ran our way. I panicked and stabbed at one as it neared my throat, my blade slicing into its eye.

Then Rian was there. She bashed one with the hilt of her blade, knocking it off me. I elbowed the one at my left arm and kicked at the one at my feet. Rian grabbed my biceps and heaved me to my feet, dragging me along as we ran into the overgrowth.

She had already sawn many reeds as we ran on a clear path. Rian sliced a rat as it jumped out at us, and I cringed as one tried to bite my ankle. Suddenly, a thundering of feet ahead surrounded our senses alongside a pungent smell of musk as the rat beasts chased us.

The ground shook harder, small rocks bobbing in the dirt as we avoided another rat beast.

I screamed in shock as the head of an ox beast burst through the reeds. It collided with a rat beast and stamped it, raising its head to bellow in victory. Unexpectedly dozens of ox beasts sprang through the reeds in a stampede, rushing by us. They battered the rats with their horns and swatted them with their tails.

"What the hell?" Rian stopped and stared as the beasts ignored us.

"Kreshna," I breathed in awe. "Wild kreshna."

Rian held her blades high as she twitched anxiously at the kreshna surrounding us. Wild kreshna were just like any other demonic beast, but they were subservient. That meant they did not attack out of feral instinct. Instead, they only attacked when threatened or in defence of their young.

I placed my hand on Rian's and lowered her arm slowly.

"Don't." I shook my head. "If they feel threatened, they could attack us."

"What? How do you know that?" she said agitatedly, her body buzzing with adrenaline.

"Just trust me, okay? I know kreshna," I said, rolling my eyes at her stubbornness.

The kreshna slowed their attack as the rats scampered away into the reeds. The bull snorted, stamping his foot three times, and the others responded in kind. Their tense muscles loosened as the hulking bodies regrouped and calmed down.

"See?" I pointed to the bull as he lowered his head and began to graze on the rigid reeds of grass. "If we stay calm, they won't bother us." I sheathed my dagger and rubbed the spot on my right arm where a rat beast had tried to bite me. It had only gotten the material of my makeshift sling, though.

"All right, I'll trust you." Rian lowered her blades slowly and sheathed them. "How do you know about kreshna?"

"I like them." I shrugged. "I didn't get to use horse-drawn carriages, so I took an interest in them."

"Why didn't you use horse-drawn carriages? You're a noble." Rian frowned.

"Not a blood-born noble." I smiled, and she furrowed her eyebrows.

"Right, sorry. I forgot," Rian sighed. "I never considered that before. I suppose Viscount Heversham wouldn't have let you. He is an advocate for the noble privilege."

"Very much so," I confirmed. Roger Heversham had always believed noble blood was worth more than that of a commoner. He would never have accepted me as his daughter if it weren't for Cassandra, who had brought me into the family. He was very devoted to his wife.

"That couldn't have been easy for you. Knowing he thought less of you." Rian stepped closer to me as a kreshna snorted nearby.

"It—it wasn't," I said, the words alien. I had never openly admitted to hating my life with the viscount. It was strange, admitting it now to Rian Thornfax, the woman I once considered my social rival.

Roger's hatred for commoner blood had been what caused the majority of my treatment from the servants in the household. They looked at me with the same disdain he showed, following his example. My tantrums and social embarrassment had only solidified that. I was a plague on the household the servants held dear. So they had felt no social demand to treat me as they should have for my station. Why should they, when my own family treated me so? No one would reprimand them.

"I think I understand why you wanted to join the army now." Rian's expression gave me pause. "Why you wanted to do something else with your life."

"Just from kreshna?" I asked, raising my eyebrow.

"I catch on quick enough." She smiled, bumping my good shoulder.

"Right, you were always *witty*." I exaggerated the word, and she shook her head at me.

"Witty enough to deal with you, maybe."

"That's all the wit one needs," I joked, and she laughed playfully before her expression turned serious. "I really am sorry, you know, for what I did to you. You didn't deserve that, when we were kids."

I openly stared at Rian, taken aback.

"It's—let's put it behind us," I said, awkwardly pinching my fingers.

Maybe I can change my relationship with Rian after all.

"I'd like that," Rian said with such a gentle smile it made me blush. "All right, so what are we doing about this?" She waved at the herd of kreshna surrounding us. We were, in all senses of the word, trapped by them.

"You may not like it, but I do have an idea," I said, and she narrowed her eyes.

"Just what do you want to do exactly?"

"Something crazy." I grinned, and she moaned.

"*Lynette*," Rian whisper-shouted as I crouched in the reeds. "Are you sure about this?" She tucked beside me as we hid from the kreshna.

"Pretty sure," I lied. I wasn't sure in the slightest.

I had always had a connection with kreshna, but the ones I'd met were already trained and bred in captivity. They were in no way the same as a wild kreshna. However, something had been bothering me since I got my blood sign. It never made sense why the captive kreshna responded to me so differently than others. They were stubborn, abrasive creatures who needed wrangling by strong, stable hands. They were not beasts that could be ridden. Yet I had ridden them multiple times.

"Just . . ." I paused, trying to think of a way to do this. "Stay here, okay? I will call for help if I need it," I said, and Rian bit her cheek.

"Don't get yourself killed. This is really stupid," Rian tutted, gripping the hilt of her blades.

"Maybe, but I want to try," I said, and she glared.

"I'll be here," she said resignedly.

"Thanks." I squeezed her shoulder to reassure her that everything would be okay. But I had no idea how this would go.

Carefully, I split apart the reeds and stepped closer to the bull kreshna as he grazed. The wind blew onto me, so I was downwind, which was good as I was fairly sure I stank. I hadn't bathed since we left Talbour; light water splashes from water summoners was not the same as a good bath. I was also now covered in dried blood and mud. I probably stank worse than the kreshna.

Stepping lightly, I avoided a stone in my path and crept to the beast. His snout blew hot air, separating the reeds as he prodded forward, grazing. Slowly, I reached out my palm, keeping my body void of hostility.

The beast stomped its foot at my approach, and I held back from going any farther.

"Shhh." I made a soothing sound to calm his agitation. His floppy ears flapped as his brown eyes watched me. "There, there." I held my palm forward again, but he wafted his head, threatening me with his two curved horns.

I stepped back as he stamped his foot again. He snorted at me, his breath flickering my hair around my neck.

"I mean no harm," I said quietly. "We need your help." I didn't know why, but somehow, it felt right that I should bow. It was as though the knowledge of what to do had always existed in my mind. I bowed my head and bent my knees to keep myself low before him. The bull's head felt closer as his breath shifted. I felt his rough snout nuzzle the top of my head as he inspected me. I stayed there, not moving.

One wrong move, and this bull could kill me.

He could ram his horns into my chest.

I held my breath.

The sensation of his touch lifted away, and I dared to raise my head ever so slightly. He stood before me, watching patiently.

I raised my palm forward again, my hand shaking.

He met my palm with his snout.

I stilled a little in relief, a little in disbelief.

Steadily, I rose from my crouched position, keeping my hand on his snout, gently rubbing it. He nuzzled me back and nodded his head, whipping a fly with his tail.

"Lynette?" Rian whispered from her hiding position in the reeds.

"It's all right," I replied, being careful not to shout. "Stand slowly, and come over."

"This is crazy," she whispered, rising from the reeds. The bull jolted a little at her appearance, but I quickly patted his snout.

"She's a friend. Please, will you help us?" I asked again, and the bull stamped its foot. It swished its head, and suddenly it bellowed into the sky.

I jumped back, and Rian tightened her grip on her blades as the other kreshna ran towards us, enclosing us tightly. They all bellowed into the sky in unison, even the young ones.

A tingling buzzed in my skin as the bull approached me again. He turned his body and bucked his head back before lowering his legs to lie on the ground.

Rian and I glanced at one another, and she shook her head in incredulity.

"I can't believe you did it." She stared in dumb shock at the bull as he bobbed his head again impatiently.

"Neither can I." I advanced to the bull and held on to one of his horns.

"What do you mean, neither can you? I thought you said you knew this would work!" Rian exclaimed, following my lead.

"I lied." I shrugged, using the horns of the bull as support to lift my legs around his torso.

"I can't believe you did that." Rian scowled, gingerly taking my hand as I lifted her up onto the beast. She quickly grabbed my waist, her arms holding tight.

"We could have died," she said, pouting, but her stiff posture told me she was nervous.

"Then it's a good thing we didn't." I gently squeezed my legs, and the bull lifted our bodies, leaning into his stride as he stood. I quickly gripped the raised scales at the base of his neck.

"Now what?" Rian tightened her grip some more.

"Now we ride."

CHAPTER TWENTY-FOUR

I shifted a little as the ridge of the kreshna's back began digging into my rear. I had made the right choice in approaching the bull of the herd. I hadn't known I could tame the wild kreshna, but my inclination had been correct. The beast-taming skill Vishka had hidden was definitely what made this possible.

Because I had tamed the bull, the rest of the herd followed us. Their numbers kept the demonic rat beasts at bay, and they acted as our guard as we rode through the reeds.

It was nice to rest for once.

My body was battered and bruised, and from the soft slump on the back of my shoulder, Rian was also exhausted. Her chest moved steadily against my back as she slept, leaning on me. I held her hands around my waist to keep her secure so she wouldn't fall off.

Shifting to hold Rian's hands with my left hand, I gingerly raised my injured right. "Sign update."

Blood Sign Updates:
Dagger Strike: 12 (Initiate) +2
Stamina: 12 (Initiate) +1
Beast Taming: 3 (Novice) +2

The confirmation of my theory gave me confidence. My beast-taming skill had indeed been what had allowed me to tame the wild kreshna bull. So why had Vishka hidden it? Was it connected to my beast-born trait? I had no idea what that even meant for me.

I sighed, lowering my hand as it began to hurt.

What did any of this mean?

So much had happened in this life that I had never experienced before. It was baffling how much I had missed. My memories were often fuzzy on details, but I remembered enough of what mattered. Yet I had never come across anything like beast-born. There was much I still had to learn about Zopan and what being a child of Vishka meant.

That was what Albus had called me.

Vishka had told me she couldn't tell me why I had been reborn back in the temple of Talbour. But somehow, I knew it couldn't have been for no reason. Why else would the gods have gifted me memory stones? Was there something I was supposed to do? Was her guidance leading me to something I didn't want? All I wanted to do was survive.

I sighed, my mind reeling as I tried to reason with this.

We rode through the reeds in peace, the kreshna pausing to graze every other hour. Our pace was twice as fast as it would have been if Rian and I had walked. I gently woke Rian on the third hour to stretch our legs as the kreshna grazed. We still had to try to find the brigade. I had no idea how to look for them. I hoped she did.

Rian used a round device from her pocket. A needle in the centre spun, indicating our direction. I recognised it as a compass. I had seen them in the stalls of Talbour's market and on the pocket of Eduard's jacket from time to time. She told me that we needed to be heading south, as the capital was south of the highland plains. So we rubbed our sore rears and got back on the kreshna bull I had decided to name Kuru.

We continued until darkness stained the sky and the kreshna settled. They grouped in pairs, snuggling against one another as they bedded down for the night. Their young nestled between their parents after a short time of play. They had tried to approach us, but a swift bump from their mothers dragged them away. Kreshna were very protective of their young; we were still a threat.

Rian tried to make a fire, but I quickly stopped her. The flames could be dangerous in the reeds, and we didn't know how the kreshna would react. So we ate cold cuts left over from the night before, and I shared Rian's water as mine was still empty. We took turns on watch, and I finally got some sleep. My body was aching for the rest.

I awoke once at the sound of feet to find the bull, Kuru, watching us, guarding his herd. He didn't bother us after that, but it showed me he was still anxious about us. Finally, morning came, and we packed up to pursue the brigade.

"I don't get it." Rian frowned, tapping her compass. "We should be close by now. We were only a few days behind. At this pace, we should be catching up."

"I think we just need to get out of these reeds first." I sighed, getting sick of seeing them, quite frankly. We had been travelling with the kreshna for the past six days. My shoulder had grown numb, or I had gotten accustomed to the pain, I wasn't sure. I knew I was feeling sluggish regardless. We had rationed our water and food supply and Rian had ran out of water yesterday. Neither of us had outspoken it, but we were both afraid. If we didn't find the brigade, there was a chance we could starve. Not to mention, if I went without treatment for much longer my wound and Rian's would fester.

I couldn't see the end of these reeds. We had been foolish to think we could run through them. Without the kreshna, I was confident we would have perished alone in them. I was hoping we were maybe just not high enough to see the edge of the green stems.

A small hope.

It was getting so bad I was starting to miss Talbour.

I shivered internally at the thought.

"We could maybe follow their trail if we could see it." Rian slumped against me, her twin blades clattering against her thighs.

"Maybe," I said, though my hope was dwindling. Would their footprints still be on the ground after so long? I didn't know.

A bellow suddenly split the reeds. The kreshna halted, responding.

Kuru stomped and charged. I slipped at the sudden jolt of his legs and grabbed his horns to lift my body back into place. Rian yelped as she clung to my waist and tightened her grip.

"What's happening?" Rian panicked as we sped through the reeds. They snapped at us, whipping against our skin, red lines forming on our arms.

"I think one of the females was attacked," I theorised as we came close to one of the small kreshna. She was thrashing her hind legs, kicking at something we could not see, hidden in the reeds. The female bellowed again as a flash of fire erupted from her side.

Kuru's muscles throbbed as he ran careening into the fray in a burst. The earth lifted at his feet as he jumped, swallowing the flames whole.

The faces of four soldiers stared up at Kuru.

We stared back.

Then Kuru charged.

The soldiers scattered as Kuru lowered his head, his horns aiming for an older man wielding a sabre. The man dashed, sinking into the earth with each step as he fell into the soil, his brown cloak flowing behind him.

A second man raised a lance, coating it with flames. He darted towards us, and I could feel the heat of his flames as they licked at Kuru.

Kuru slammed up a shield of earth, blocking his attack.

A third swung a flail on a chain as he chased after the female. Water was scissored in slashes with every spin towards her, and her cry of pain rang horribly in my ears. Blood streamed down her flank as she limped to get away. But the water summoner didn't stop, his water blades cutting into her deeper.

"*Stop!*" Rian cried as I held on to Kuru. He stamped the ground, and the earth rose in columns around the female, creating a cage to protect her. I pulled his horns back in an attempt to make him leave, but Kuru refused, his eyes focusing on the fire summoner.

The fire summoner readied his weapon in a twirl, creating a fire vortex.

Kuru charged at him.

Earth flowed from his feet and clung to his face and armour as he crashed into the shield of fire. The flames stretched around Kuru as he pushed against the fire summoner's lance. I could see the strain on the summoner's face as he slid backwards. His feet slipped, and Kuru bucked his head, breaking the shield and directly impacting the chest of the summoner. He flew through the reeds, and I held my breath, but the earth summoner suddenly rose from the ground to catch him.

"Kuru, stop, please," I begged, glancing to my left to see the water summoner swinging his flail towards us.

"Please, run away." I felt my voice catch, and Rian squeezed me as tears threatened to fall. I didn't want this. This wasn't how this was supposed to go.

Abruptly an arrow shot into the sky, and it split into dozens of copies shining green against the sun.

I swiftly lifted my arms to shield my face, and Rian grabbed me, pulling me into her as we braced for the impact.

Kuru reared, and I felt myself slip.

Rian and I tumbled as we lost our balance, crashing into a tangled mess.

A rumble deafened us as earth rose in a dome of protection above the three of us.

The arrows pounded into the dome, their tips sinking through the brown, crumbling soil. We looked up, amazed at the power Kuru had. He was a powerful kreshna.

"Run, Kuru, please." I tried again to convince him, and he paused to study me.

I reached out to him but suddenly felt my body sinking. A hand snatched out from the ground around my mouth, dragging me down. My heart hammered, and I frantically tried to pull the hand away. But my body was already waist-deep. Rian struggled similarly against the earth summoner as he dragged us into the depths of the earth with him.

I coughed soil up out of my mouth as we were thrown out of the ground. Leaning on my good hand and knees, I couldn't take in the air fast enough after that suffocating experience. Rian fell onto her back as she gasped, her body trembling in shock.

The earth summoner appeared behind us, rising from the ground slowly, like he was a freaking daisy, his piercing brown eyes glaring at us.

"Who are you?" he demanded with an accent I couldn't place.

"Trainees," I croaked out, wiping the spit from my mouth.

"Sure, and I'm a tragot beast," he spat sarcastically. "What in Urish's name are you doing here?"

"We got separated, you ass." Rian scowled, finding her voice as she righted herself. "Urish has nothing to do with it." She glared at him.

Urish was the god of justice and exchange; was this earth summoner suggesting we were outlaws?

"Urish," he growled threateningly, drawing a short sword, "has everything to do with it."

"Vernan, lower your sword." The water summoner dragged the limping fire summoner through the reeds towards us. "They aren't a threat."

"We don't know that. They could be bandits." Vernan narrowed his eyes at us.

"I don't think a pair of girls in that bad shape would be bandits, Vernan." A man I hadn't seen leaned his arm on his hip. He carried a carved wooden bow on his back and a quiver of feathered arrows. He swished his green embroidered cloak and leaned down to our level.

"But he does raise a good point. What are you doing here?" he asked, rubbing his long, pointed ginger beard.

"Like I said." Rian bit her cheek in frustration. "We got separated from the brigade. We're trainees."

"I don't know many trainees who can ride kreshna." The wind summoner raised an eyebrow.

I blanched at his gaze. What should I say here? Should I keep my beast-taming a secret?

"Well . . . we do." Rian spoke before I could, struggling to stand. To our surprise, the wind summoner helped her. Why did she not say anything?

Rian glanced at me and meekly smiled. Was she keeping my secret?

"All right, say I believe you. Just how have you two survived out here?" the wind summoner asked.

"We haven't," I sighed, cradling my right arm. It was pulsing in pain. I had landed on it when Kuru had thrown us off his back.

"We got by," Rian interjected.

"You look like a wreck." The water summoner shook his head as he took something out of his pocket and shoved it into the fire summoner's mouth. The fire summoner swallowed it and immediately belched, his eyes flying open. He quickly stuck out his tongue and scratched at it, trying to get the taste off.

"Ugh, damn it, Frank, you know I hate that stuff." He made a yuck noise and drowned it away with water from his waterskin. I gulped, seeing the water trickle down his stubbled brown chin.

I hadn't drunk that much water in days.

The water summoner laughed. "Then don't get yourself thrown off next time, Deacon."

"Whatever." The fire summoner looked away from Frank, displeased. "If it weren't for those two distracting me, it wouldn't have happened."

"Suuuure, that must be it." Frank smirked at him, and Deacon punched him in the shoulder.

"Shut it," he snarled, standing up and shoving Frank away.

"The kreshna, did you . . . did you kill them?" I whispered. I didn't know how long we were in the ground when Vernan pulled us in.

Kuru . . . was he still . . . I clenched my teeth, not wanting to think.

"No." Deacon clicked his tongue. "Couldn't exactly finish the job with you there."

I smiled as relief filled my heart. I would have felt guilty for so long if he had been killed by the soldiers he was helping us find.

"Don't look so happy. They were our meal for the next few days," Vernan said, tightening the grip on his sword.

Frank laughed at his friend and smoothed down his dark blue cloak. "I guess we should figure out what to do with you two, then."

"I say we leave them." Vernan gave us a dirty look. "I don't trust a word they say."

"The feeling is mutual." Rian folded her arms and tapped her foot. Vernan jutted his chin and began to step towards her, but the wind summoner grabbed the back of his brown cloak, pulling him back.

"Enough, Vernan, we aren't leaving them. That would be irresponsible."

"Arjun is right." Frank nodded. "If they are trainees, the duke's heir will want to see them."

"Duke?"

"Duke?"

Rian and I spoke, both knitting our features.

"Lord Azriel." Deacon spun his lance, sweeping his hand across its widened metal.

I gripped Rian as she helped me stand. My hands shook a little, so I quickly took a deep breath.

"All right, let's go, then," I said, moving forward, determined to get back to safety.

To meet the man who had killed me.

CHAPTER TWENTY-FIVE

The group of summoners who stumbled upon us were savage in this landscape. They ran without strain through the rigid reeds, only stopping for Rian and me to catch up. Before we knew there was danger, they had slaughtered the rat beasts that tried to pounce on us.

I had tried to look back to see if Kuru had truly moved on with his herd, but there was no sight of them. Vernan had brought us far away from our initial encounter when he captured us. He swiftly sank into the ground as we moved, reappearing beside us occasionally to breathe before disappearing again. His ability to flow through the land was incredible, as much as I hated complimenting him. He moved through the earth much like the horned baildon had. He was nimble and quick to spot danger, alerting the others before anything got too close.

Deacon steamrolled ahead, leading us; his lance was always poised for defence, and he tensed, prepared when Vernan announced a demonic beast closing in on us. He stopped, bracing his weapon as a lithe demonic beast of medium size sprang from the reeds. Its four tiny legs and elongated snout pummelled into Deacon's lance, but he shook it off, unafraid. Blocking its attacks, he held it from reaching us.

Frank stepped in and swung his flail. Water streamed from his rotation, slicing into the torso of the demonic beast, its blood splattering into Deacon's defensive fire, sizzling away. Frank then grabbed the chain and lowered his flail to slam it directly onto the beast's head, smashing its skull with a crack.

Their attacks were coordinated, precise, and well trained. Arjun guarded our rear; his bow hitched with an arrow as Deacon ripped a brown core from the beast's chest. We barely waited as they gathered the remains of their kills before we were pushed to run again.

Watching them work was amazing; I had never seen such skill before. They didn't waste energy dodging or stumbling like Rian and me. They truly were summoners powerful enough to traverse the highlands alone. Not once did I see them pause to catch their breath from exhaustion. What level of cultivation had they reached? Were they at the foundation stage, or had they climbed to core solidification? What grade were their cores to use aether so easily? Questions burdened my mind as I ran, the pain of my arm spiking with every jolt of my feet on the uneven ground.

I tried to keep my pain from showing, but I couldn't stop the pang of my cheeks, gritting my teeth when I stumbled on a dip. When I glanced at Rian beside me, her expression was stern as she held on to her thigh with one of her hands. She actively pulled her leg forward to keep it going as we tried to keep up with the summoners. She was struggling but didn't voice a complaint.

Deacon slowed, holding his hand up, and we halted, our chests heaving. My vision was blurry as I sucked in as much air as possible, trying to replenish what my muscles craved. My mouth was dry, and I couldn't generate any saliva to soften the cracked taste of my lips. I could feel my body was reaching its limit.

"I have alerted those on guard." Vernan popped up out of the ground, his hands held behind his back as his brown cloak billowed in the wind. "I recommended we take them into custody."

"They aren't going anywhere, Vernan." Frank rolled his eyes, stepping up beside us, his flail hanging over his shoulder. "Let me have that." He held out his hand, gesturing to my water flask tied to the side of my backpack. I gingerly unfastened it and passed it over to him.

Frank took it and popped the lid off; raising his hand over it, he concentrated, and water began to drip from his fingers into the flask.

"Th-thank you." I eagerly accepted it back and immediately drank the refreshing liquid as it soothed my mouth, hydrating my body. "I never knew water could taste so good." I sighed in satisfaction, wiping my chin as it dribbled from the flask.

Frank chuckled with a smile. "The highlands is no place to be without a water summoner."

"Yes, yes, we get it, you're amazing." Deacon shook his head, leaning his hand on his hip. "Now, can we go already, or do we need to carry them?"

"Sorry about him; when he hasn't eaten, he gets cranky," Frank mused, knowing full well that Deacon's scowl was directed his way.

"I get cranky?" Deacon stormed. "Don't even start with that nonsense." He raised his finger, pointing at Frank accusingly. "You moan like a baby if you don't get your bloody walnuts."

"Walnuts are an important fibre, Deacon. Nothing beats them." Frank shrugged, winking at me.

"Walnuts are disgusting." Deacon pursed his lips, his agitation growing.

"Enough, both of you," Arjun sighed, pulling his hand through his short ginger hair. "We can discuss the importance of walnuts later. These girls need medical attention."

"Hmph." Vernan grunted. "They need detaining."

"Vernan, not now." Arjun slumped his shoulders. "The brigade is up ahead; it's not far. Do you think you can make it?" he asked us, concerned by our shaking limbs.

"We're fine." Rian straightened and adjusted her backpack in determination.

"If it's not far, I think we can manage." I tried to smile, but it didn't feel genuine. From Arjun's look, I didn't think he believed we were as fine as Rian claimed.

"We will keep our pace slow," Arjun decided, causing Deacon and Vernan to shoot us an irritated look.

"Fine." Deacon spun and shifted his lance from hand to hand. "May as well gather if we're walking," he mumbled.

"Good idea." Frank grinned, pulling up beside Deacon to match his pace.

"Bugger off." Deacon tried to push him, but Frank didn't budge, continuing to smile as he annoyed his friend. They took the lead as they squabbled, and Arjun stayed with us as we followed. Vernan disappeared into the ground and continued to scout for us.

"Lynette," Rian whispered as we avoided a section of turned-up soil. "Are you okay?" she asked, seeing my grimacing face.

"I think the bone in my shoulder has moved." I held my arm for support as the pain throbbed intensely from my broken shoulder. It had begun to numb until we had fallen from Kuru; the impact must have aggravated my collarbone. It felt out of alignment compared to before.

"Do you need me to retighten the sling?" she asked.

"No, I don't think it will make much of a difference." I sighed. "Hopefully, a medic summoner can fix it." I tried to stay positive. I had seen their work when I was in their tent; they had easily fixed broken bones and mended torn skin. Surely they would be able to fix my shoulder too.

"All right," she said as we fell behind Deacon and Frank. "Do you mind . . . if I lean on you?"

I saw her flinch, gripping her leg tighter as some dried blood on her wound cracked. "Sure." I changed position so she was on my left, and we linked our arms around our shoulders to support one another. Together, we walked, both of us avoiding Arjun's gaze as he frowned at us. It went unspoken, but I knew neither of us wanted to return to the brigade being carried. The mere thought sent goose bumps down my skin. That scenario would be far too embarrassing.

* * *

The noise of chattering, pans clanking, and swords clashing alerted us to the brigade. Rian and I looked at each other, our grip tightening as the sound of safety in these treacherous highlands was upon us. We quickened our pace as the reeds became sparse, and the sight of a meadow filtered through the gaps. We pushed through the last reeds, revealing the view of gathered soldiers, their coloured cloaks dotting the landscape.

The light was beginning to dim, so they were settling for the evening. A few canvas tents had been raised as groups patrolled the outskirts of the brigade formation. Fires were lit, and the smell of freshly cooked food wafted to our noses as our stomachs rumbled in anticipation.

"We made it." I exhaled, crumbling to the floor, my legs giving way. They had been burning for so long. My chest muscles relaxed as my breathing hitched through my pain; I hadn't realised how tight from the tension I was.

"Yes. Now you can be questioned." Vernan smirked at us, his head popping from the ground. "I will go inform Lord Azriel." He nodded to Arjun and sank back in.

"What's his problem?" Rian muttered.

"He's a follower of Urish." Arjun offered his hand to me, and I took it as he pulled me back up to my feet. "Don't take it personally; he treats everyone as suspicious." He sighed.

"He's rude." Rian crossed her arms. "If he's so devoted to Urish, he should join the temple."

"Ha." Deacon grinned at Rian. "The temple wouldn't have him. He's far too shifty for the likes of those pompous pricks."

"Deacon." Arjun frowned. "You shouldn't insult the gods' guardians."

"Who cares? Not like they can do anything," Deacon scoffed. "Bunch of wimps."

"'Wimps' is not the word I would use." Frank smiled. "Soft, maybe."

I raised my eyebrow at their words. Only those who couldn't successfully master aether became monks. But some became guardians, those gifted with strong cores who willingly chose to join the temples.

"Frank," Arjun groaned. "Don't encourage him."

"What?" Frank batted his eyes innocently. "It's a fair observation."

"Stop it, both of you." Arjun wrapped his arm around my waist, and I stiffened at the unexpected gesture. "Come on; Lord Azriel will be waiting." He forcefully pulled me forward. I didn't have the strength to push him away, and he knew it. I could barely walk; I was so exhausted.

Resigned, I accepted his help as we headed towards the camp. It was better than being carried, at least. Frank tried to offer Rian the same, but she waved his help away stubbornly and limped behind us. I could see the strain on her face and wished she had accepted, but she was too prideful.

As we approached the edge of the camp, I noticed we were at the front of the brigade. The equipment and tents were cleaner and sturdier and generally looked more expensive. The summoners had golden thread embroidery in their high-necked cloaks and clasps of metal, each with delicate carvings pinned to them.

Some were sparring. Their speed as their weapons clashed was too fast for my eyes to follow, the sound echoing throughout the camp. Aether sizzled from their bodies as they fought in a blur of movement. One of the summoners had entrenched his body in an armour of hardened earth, much as Kuru had done. He laughed at his opponent, who swung a single sabre at his chest, the blade clanking away, defeated.

His opponent, eager to try again, coated his blade in a film of aether with his hand. Air whipped at my hair as he did, and I could see stray leaves flying around him. He sprang forward and swung his sabre again but did not hit him. Instead, the wind rushed forward with his blow, slicing into the earthen armour, leaving a scar. The earth summoner raised his eyebrows, then laughed again, encouraging the wind summoner to keep going.

Their skills were on another level from the measly practise I had been doing. Would I ever be able to have power like that?

Arjun took me past the sparring and farther into the camp. Summoners were gathered around fires here, resting after the day's march. They all looked up at our approach, curious, but did not interact.

Their personal tents were three times as large as ours. Each tent had an emblem on the front of the flap, symbolising their team's profession. Many of them had a symbol of two sabres crossing, and a few had the medical profession sign of a heart within a pair of hands. One I had not seen before was also quite frequent; it looked like a gavel at the centre of a laurel wreath. The wreath reminded me of what Urish's statue often wore, a symbol of his faith. Maybe that sign had something to do with him.

"Team five reporting," Arjun said as we approached the camp's centre. We stood before a large cream canvas tent; a deep purple ribbon blew in the wind atop it, and golden embroidery decorated the canvas. Two older men watched us sternly, their golden spears tall beside them. They crossed the spears in front of the tent flap and scrutinised us. Those spears; I had seen them on the day of my execution. These men were guards of the crown, of royal blood.

"Lord Vernan Argole informed us," a guard with greying hair said to Arjun. "Are these the bandits?"

"They aren't bandits," Arjun replied, irritated. "They said they got separated from the trainees."

"I see. His grace will want to see them." The older guard nodded to his younger companion. The younger guard pulled his spear back and saluted before opening the tent to go inside.

"You may leave them here. We will deal with them." The older guard stood his spear up straight and stared at Rian and me. I felt tiny under his gaze, a lump forming in my throat.

Arjun nodded and gave both us a pat on our backs as he stepped back with Frank and Deacon. "See you again sometime, trainees."

"Perhaps." Rian raised her head with a small scowl as she spotted Vernan popping up from the ground beside them. Frank gave an amused nod as he saluted to us before happily pushing Deacon away to follow Arjun and Vernan, leaving us alone waiting with the guard of this tent.

The flap opened, and the younger guard returned, signalling to the older one.

"Go in; his grace will speak with you now." The older guard didn't leave room for us to object.

Rian gripped my hand, and I held my breath at the darkness behind the cream tent flap.

CHAPTER TWENTY-SIX

The inside of Lord Azriel's tent was immaculate. The floor was smoothed without a bump, by earth summoners, probably. A rack of sabres was neatly placed to the left, their metal glinting under a large floating aether light hung at the centre. The light illuminated the space we could see so clearly.

The back of the tent was cordoned off by a rattan divider hiding what was beyond. In front of us was a desk made of earth and wood. The wood was melded into the solid earth so hardened it could have been stone. Papers littered the table beside a large skin map; on the map were small wooden figurines placed in various places. I didn't know what their purpose was, nor how the summoners had travelled with all this equipment when we struggled with just our backpacks.

I stilled, and Rian squeezed my hand as iridescent purple eyes followed us into the tent. Lord Azriel sat behind his desk, his hands folded as he leaned his elbows on the stone hearth. I found myself gulping at his stare as it pierced us.

All we could see of his face were those purple eyes.

His mask was different to the one I had seen at my execution. Metal covered his chin up to his nose; rivets bolted to connect the top helm on his nose bridge. A gap separated the two pieces for his eyes to inspect us. Part of his cheeks showed through the gap as two large pieces layered at the sides of his eyes, ending in a point above his forehead. It didn't have the same horns as in my last life; maybe he would get that mask later.

What drew my attention, however, and made my mouth gape was the floating box hovering above the head of Lord Azriel.

Vishka's Guidance System
Azriel Kamil Elkhart
Likeability: ???

He had a likeability meter! Seriously? But I had never met this man; I had no history with him for this to make sense. I was not acquainted with Azriel in any of my lives, unless you counted chopping my head off. So was that why he counted? Because he had been someone who had killed me once?

Vishka, please, this has to be a mistake.

A thump in my side made me close my mouth as Rian nudged me. She cleared her throat and saluted Lord Azriel, leaning down onto one knee with difficulty. I shook myself out of my haze and copied her etiquette, keeping myself balanced as I rested my left hand on my right shoulder. Unfortunately, it hurt, so I didn't perform the action as gracefully as I had intended. I hoped it didn't come across as rude, as you were supposed to salute with your right, but I had no way of doing that with my injury.

"Rise." Azriel's voice was slightly muffled behind his metal mask, but its deep tone was strong enough to bypass it.

"Who are you?" he asked as we struggled to get back up.

"I am Lady Rian Thornfax, daughter of Earl Thornfax of Talbour." Rian introduced herself with such elegance I would have found it difficult to believe she was in pain right now.

"I am Lady Lynette Heversham, daughter of Viscount Heversham of Talbour." I widened my eyes as the question marks of Azriel's likeability meter suddenly blurred. He narrowed his gaze to me, but I couldn't tell what that might be for. It was impossible to read him in that mask.

"Heversham?" he said, his tone hinting at surprise. "I did not think the Heversham's had a daughter who wished to join the army."

"My sister, Kara, indeed does not wish to join the army." My voice wavered; how did he know such detail about my family?

"And you desire differently?" He leaned forward, his eyes flicking over my sling and the blood on Rian's leg.

"Captain Cavendish," Azriel called before I could respond. The tent flap opened, and the older guard who had spoken to us on our arrival appeared.

"Yes, your grace." The guard saluted and lowered to one knee as we had done.

"Bring one of the Thornfax's here to identify this girl," he ordered, and the guard stood, bowing his head, leaving us as quickly as he had arrived. I saw Rian tense at his command.

"Just how did you get separated from the trainees?" Azriel asked, his voice curious. The deep purple cloak he wore gently slipped off his shoulder as he moved his calloused hands. Purple was the signature of royalty, so I wasn't surprised to see that his cloak mirrored that. Azriel was the lightning dragon, the second cousin of the empress. His stature and prowess as a summoner were well known.

"The horned baildon," Rian answered. Because she was the daughter of an earl, etiquette decreed that she speak rather than I unless I was addressed directly.

"We were ambushed by it during the attack, your grace. We were caught trying to avoid it and fell down a cavern that opened after it dislodged the earth," Rian explained.

"A cavern?" Azriel's eyes glittered with interest. "There is no such cavern I know of on this route."

"I suspect it has been buried for some time." Rian dipped her head. "It likely would not have been discovered without the horned baildon."

"I see; I will have to investigate it when we return to that point." He nodded in thought.

Rian hesitated before continuing. "There were remains of a temple in the cavern, your grace; runes were carved into the stone of its walls I had never seen before."

"Intriguing. Did you record any of them?"

"Yes, your grace, I made etches of them on some of my scrolls." Rian glanced at me and bit her lip. "There was also . . ." She paused, and I felt my pulse rocket. Was she going to tell him about the memory stone?

"There was also a strange demonic beast in the cavern," she finished, and my heart calmed down.

"What did it look like?" Azriel asked, glancing at me as well. It seemed he had caught Rian's hesitation.

"It was a large beast with canine-like features that survived by eating craven bats. It had a water core and was a difficult foe. We were lucky to beat it."

"Ah, that sounds like an agiluf. Indeed, you were very lucky to survive it." Azriel leaned back in his wooden chair. "How did you get here from the cavern?"

"We found a route in the cavern that led outside. Then we traced our way back on the surface until we came across the tall reeds blocking our path."

"The prairie expanse," Azriel informed us.

"Yes, your grace. We traversed the prairie expanse until we encountered a group of summoners."

"Whilst riding a kreshna?" Azriel raised his eyebrow, and we both stilled. Vernan must have given him that bit of information.

"Yes, your grace." Rian shifted her stance nervously.

"I am curious how you managed that feat. It takes trained stable hands to settle and train a domestic kreshna to pull a carriage, let alone ride a wild one." The tone of his voice changed as he viewed us with suspicion. "How did you do that?"

Rian opened her mouth and then closed it as she tried to think of something to say. I watched her panic and sighed. I couldn't ask her to hide this; it was my action that was raising his suspicion.

"Your grace, may I speak?" I asked, and he turned his attention to me.

"You may."

"I have experience with kreshna and used that knowledge to our advantage in a bad situation. You may check with my brothers to clarify this, but I have ridden kreshna since I was a child."

Azriel's surprise, expressed in his body language at my words, made me hold back my urge to flee. He looked at me with a gaze that made me squirm, and the silence that followed only made me more anxious. The numbers in his box blurred even faster.

"Your grace." Captain Cavendish interrupted us, saving me from Azriel's response. "Lady Albertine Thornfax is here," he called from behind the tent flap.

Azriel pulled his eyes away from me. "Allow her in."

The tent flap flew open, and a woman of medium height with brown braided hair and features similar to Rian's urgently rushed into the tent. She made to run towards Rian but stopped herself and quickly saluted, lowering herself to one knee; her cloak was deep green.

"Your grace, this girl is my sister Rian. I can confirm her identity." She fidgeted in her position.

"Very well, you may leave. I know all I need to from her."

"Thank you, your grace!" Albertine brightened quickly, standing and enveloping Rian in her embrace. Rian moaned with a heavy sigh and patted Albertine's back. "I'm so glad you're okay!" Albertine hugged her harder. "We thought you were dead!" She pulled back and cupped Rian's face in her hands. "You look terrible. Did you eat enough? Did you have water? My gosh, you must be exhausted. Come on. I'll get Imran to heal you up in no time."

"Sister, please, stop fussing." Rian rolled her eyes and meekly looked away from Azriel's amused glance.

"I'll stop once Imran has healed you." Albertine took Rian's hand and turned to face Lord Azriel.

"If you will excuse us." Albertine bowed. She placed her hand on Rian's head and made her bow alongside her, so I followed suit and saluted.

Azriel waved his hand towards us. "You are excused."

We stood to leave, my heart settling and the pain in my shoulder throbbing in anticipation of being healed.

"Not you, Lady Lynette. I have more questions." Azriel's voice at my back sent dread into the pit of my stomach. Rian flashed me a look of concern, but she couldn't say anything. We had no choice but to follow Azriel Elkhart's commands. He was the son of the duke of the Frozen South; his status was higher than ours.

Rian mouthed to me that she would be outside as Albertine led her away from the tent.

Leaving me alone with Azriel Elkhart.

I held in my sigh and turned back to face him. His eyes didn't hold the same amusement they had for Albertine's care for her sister.

I pinched my fingers, standing before Azriel Elkhart and his stern gaze. He tapped his finger on the stone desk, leaning his head on his hand. The box above his head still hadn't settled on a number, as it blurred consistently.

It was nerve-racking to stand before him.

Lord Azriel Elkhart, I knew from my past lives that he would ascend to the title of duke in a couple of years when his father stepped down. However, his imposing nature was enough to remind me. He had enough authority, as the heir, to sentence me for any misdoings.

"What do you wish to ask of me?" I hesitantly dipped my head in a small bow.

"You said you have ridden kreshna since childhood," Azriel stated. "How?" he demanded.

"I cannot explain, your grace." I really couldn't; I had no idea why I had the beast-taming skill and Vishka wanted me to hide it. "All I know is since I was young, I have understood them."

"You realise that is a non-answer?" Azriel's tone made me cringe.

"I apologise; I cannot answer what I do not understand myself." I felt my nails bite into the palm of my hand. I could tell Azriel about my skill, but then I would have to admit I had hidden it. That would likely spark a whole new round of questions.

"Then we should seek to understand," he said, and I knew if I could see his mouth, he would have been frowning.

"Yes, your grace." I pressed my lips together.

"As you suggested, I will discuss this information with your brothers. I believe Lord Eduard Heversham is nearby," Azriel mused, and a sense of dread trickled in my skin.

"Your grace?" I asked, and he paused. "May I request you do not summon my brother at this moment? I am injured and wish to deal with my health first."

"Surely that is more reason for me to summon him?" Azriel asked, perplexed.

"I do not wish to worry him," I lied. I frankly did not want to deal with his lectures.

"Very well. However, someone must identify you." Azriel's tone indicated he didn't trust my words.

Albertine had identified Rian, but she had not acknowledged who I was. I doubt she would know; we hadn't interacted much in my life. I only knew of her from occasional glances at social events in Talbour. She likely did not share any interest in me.

Right now, I was an enigma.

A woman who claims to ride kreshna from childhood must be strange and suspicious. From Azriel's earlier statement about not knowing of a daughter of the Heversham's who wished to join the army, he was probably even warier of me.

"May I make a request?" I asked, and he narrowed his eyes. The purple was so strange as it shifted under the mage light.

"Very well." He lowered his hand and straightened in his seat. The tent canvas wobbled in a gust of wind, but I didn't feel its chill reach me. I tried to think of who would be willing to come and get me. Maybe Teresa? No, she was a commoner and a trainee. She would not be trustworthy enough. It probably should be someone Azriel was acquainted with.

"Captain Hudson and I are familiar, your grace." I bit my lip. Nathaniel was my best choice.

"Lord Nathaniel?" Azriel stiffened, and his eyes suddenly glared at me. "How do you know Lord Nathaniel?" he asked quickly.

"W-we met in Talbour." I stumbled over my words from his reaction. The numbers in his box shifted faster and darkened.

Vishka's Guidance System
Azriel Kamil Elkhart
Likeability: –35%

I struggled not to exclaim out loud at the number that now showed.

It was a minus figure? How? What did I do wrong?

This is insane, Vishka!

I hadn't said anything insulting that could justify that figure! But wait . . . was it when I mentioned Nathaniel?

"I see, so you are the one." Azriel's voice changed dramatically from suspicious to hostile. His body language scared me, as he no longer appeared relaxed but on edge. Almost as though he was waiting to grab one of the sabres hanging nearby.

"Y-your grace?" I stuttered at this change.

"What are your intentions towards Lord Nathaniel?" he asked with no hesitation.

"M-my intentions?" My mouth gaped. Wait, was he talking about my scandal? Had it spread so far that even Azriel had heard of it?

The box blurred again, and I withheld a scream.

Vishka's Guidance System
Azriel Kamil Elkhart
Likeability: –39% (–4%)

"I will not ask again," Azriel commanded, and I gulped at this turn of events.

"I hold no intentions, your grace," I spluttered, my chest tightening with anxiety. Minus fifty percent was the number I risked death with; it was only eleven numbers away!

"No intentions? Then just what is your relationship?" he asked, and the box blurred again.

Vishka's Guidance System
Azriel Kamil Elkhart
Likeability: −45% (−6%)

Oh crap. Now it was only five percent away from my possible death.

"W-we are friends, your grace, nothing more." I rushed to kneel, holding my head down before him. This was crazy, even by my standards.

Was I going to die here over my scandal?

His silence made sweat drip down the back of my neck under my choker, where my scar was. I dared to look up and saw that the box numbers were blurring again as he watched me stoically.

"Friends?" he tutted, finally relaxing a little. "I will confirm this."

"Y-yes, your grace." I nodded, my body shaking.

"Captain Cavendish," Azriel called, and the older guard entered the tent. He looked at my prostrated pose and raised an eyebrow at Azriel.

"Bring Captain Hudson, please." Azriel leaned his head into his hands, his purple eyes not moving from my form.

"Yes, your grace." Lord Cavendish left.

The silence between us was agonising as we waited.

I kept kneeling for some time as we waited for Lord Nathaniel. Azriel watched me like a hawk; I swore he could see the tremor in my hands as my anxiety spiked. His numbers remained blurred as they recalculated.

I had no idea why he was so upset with me over this scandal. He must think that I had actually slept with Nathaniel instead of the ruse that it was. But why did that bother him so much?

Did he . . . like Nathaniel?

"Your grace, Captain Hudson has arrived," Captain Cavendish announced, and my body jumped from the surprise after our silence.

"Bring him in," Azriel said, his voice deep.

The flap burst open, and red filled my vision as Nathaniel flourished his cloak on entry. He paused and looked at me, his honey-blond hair loosely falling into his hazel eyes. I meekly smiled, my shoulder pulsing in pain and my mental fortitude thinning.

"What are you doing, Azriel?" Nathaniel gasped and immediately leaned down to me. His rough hands gently touched my shoulders. He quickly pulled away when he saw the pain from his touch on my right shoulder. "Are you all right, Lynette?"

"I-I'm okay," I croaked, feeling my chest swell and tears threatening to fall. This was all too much. I just wanted to rest.

"I had questions." Azriel shrugged as Nathaniel threw him a dirty look. I was shocked he was so brazen with him.

"Could they not have waited? You are too much sometimes." Nathaniel shook his head in exasperation.

"So, she is your friend, then?" Azriel ignored Nathaniel's complaints.

"Yes, Lynette is the lady from Talbour." Nathaniel helped me stand, his hand supporting me on the small of my back.

"And she is aware of your preferences?"

"For goodness' sake, Azriel." Nathaniel rolled his eyes. "Lady Lynette is not after my hand. She is not at all like the noble ladies we know in the capital."

"Your hand?" I squeaked, trying to keep track of their conversation. Did Azriel think I wanted to marry Nathaniel?

"She is an engaged woman, Nathaniel; her actions do not give me confidence." Azriel leaned his head on his hand again, his body posture returning to one without hostility.

"I think that was the point," Nathaniel sighed.

"I'm not willingly engaged," I mumbled, rather annoyed. How had that information reached Lord Azriel's ears? How far had it spread already? The more people believed it, the harder it would be to break it fully.

"Oh? Lord Eduard Heversham says otherwise, Lady Lynette."

"With all due respect, your grace, Eduard has no say in my marriage." I tightened my palms as my breathing began to quicken. What was Eduard doing? Why would he talk about my marriage with Azriel Elkhart? Or was that not the case at all? Of course, as the son of a duke, Azriel would want to be informed of social gossip.

"Azriel, I told you the circumstances." Nathaniel jutted his chin out.

"Whether that is true or not, she claims to be able to ride kreshna," Azriel said accusingly.

"You can ride kreshna?" Nathaniel looked at me, surprised.

"Yes," I sighed, leaning into Nathaniel's arm as the weight of my own legs began to become heavy.

"That's impressive; you will have to show me." Nathaniel grinned, gracefully accepting my weight. Azriel looked at our closeness with suspicion.

"Yes. Lady Lynette will demonstrate this when we reach the capital."

"I will?" I blinked in a stupor. Eduard and Callan had always wanted me to

keep quiet about riding kreshna; it was taboo. So why was Lord Azriel so interested in this?

"If you are telling the truth, what better way to prove it than to demonstrate?"
Azriel picked up a pen from his desk and began to write something on a scroll.

"Azriel." Nathaniel tightened his grip on my waist. "I'm sure Lady Lynette is
being truthful."

"We shall see."

"I will gladly do as you ask, your grace." I attempted to bow, but Nathaniel
pulled me back. I looked at him questioningly, but he shook his head.

"I have nothing to hide from you," I finished, hoping that he wouldn't see
through my lie.

"There you have it; now, let me take her to a medic." Nathaniel gently began
to lead me to the tent opening.

"Very well." Azriel scribbled, then stopped. "Lady Lynette, I will send for you
when we reach the capital."

"Y-yes, your grace," I answered, but my skin itched. I wanted nothing more
than to never see this man again. The numbers in his box had not yet settled,
and I feared how easily they changed. He was a man quick to dislike me. I had
no idea of his temperament, but I did not want to risk my life trying to figure
that out.

"Don't worry, I'll make sure I'm the one who gets you." Nathaniel smiled at
me so warmly. His kindness was truly soothing.

"Nathaniel." Azriel stopped his writing and glared at him.

"Azriel, you are scaring Lady Lynette." Nathaniel stood his ground. I couldn't
decide if he was brave or uncaring of breaking etiquette with Lord Azriel.

"Fine. But I do not approve," Azriel said, relenting with a heavy sigh.

"I'll add that to the list." Nathaniel rolled his eyes again. "Come, Lady
Lynette; I know a good medic." Nathaniel moved to take me away from this
anxiety nightmare.

I glanced back at Azriel and saw the box over his head settle.

Vishka's Guidance System
Azriel Kamil Elkhart
Likeability: −30% (+15%)

CHAPTER TWENTY-SEVEN

The sky had darkened considerably whilst I was in Azriel Elkhart's tent. Leaving the stuffy enclosed space was refreshing as the cold evening air tickled my skin. Nathaniel guided me through the blanket of soldiers gathering in their tents. The pain in my shoulder had begun to numb. My nerves had worsened, or I was just growing more accustomed to it.

"Just what happened? I thought you were dead," Nate asked me, his voice lowered as we weaved through a set of fires.

"Not quite," I sighed. "We fell into a cavern."

"A cavern? Ouch, that must have been a shock."

"Not as much as the agiluf," I muttered, carefully avoiding a group of grey-cloaked soldiers as they drank something that did not smell like water. They stumbled a little, and their faces were red. Were they drinking alcohol? I wrinkled my nose; they must feel competent to be willing to get drunk out here in the highlands.

"An agiluf? Did you survive one of those at your level? Colour me impressed, Lynette." Nate gently tugged me to the left, and we walked away from the centre of the crowded tents.

"It was pure luck; I'm fairly sure we would have died without the angel shrooms we found."

"Angel shrooms?"

"They paralyse anything they touch for hours." I smiled, and Nate raised an eyebrow.

"Maybe I should get some of those."

"I'd be happy to give you one." I laughed, but the action sent a jolt of pain through my body. I guessed I wasn't as numb to it as I had thought.

"Easy, we're not far from a medic." Nate frowned as he patted my back comfortingly.

"I hope so," I sighed. "I don't know how much longer I can stay awake," I said, feeling the exhaustion of the past few days. It felt like I hadn't slept well in months, rather than a few days.

"I'll get you there, don't worry." Nate adjusted my backpack. He had taken it from me when we left Azriel's tent. "I'm sorry about Azriel. He should have known better than to keep you in this state."

"Don't be, he was just checking that Lady Rian and I were genuine." I tried to be optimistic. But, honestly, I did feel he was unreasonable. I had no idea what made him so angry with me.

"Don't pander to him, Lynette. He doesn't deserve it." Nate shook his head at me. "He shouldn't have treated you that way."

"Are you . . . are you close?" I asked, my curiosity burning. Nate had spoken to Azriel so openly; he had even addressed him directly without honorifics.

"We grew up together." Nate looked away from me and sighed. "He can be a little protective of me because of some things that happened in the capital," he said with a half smile.

I got the sense there was more to this than he was saying.

"You don't need to tell me. I understand." I squeezed his hand, which was wrapped around my waist. I knew all too well about not wanting to discuss personal pain.

Nate shot me a grin that I was growing more familiar with. It was always charming. I considered him my friend, but in reality, I barely knew Nate. He was just a man who had shown me kindness. There was much regarding him I had no right to inquire about.

"You don't." Nate shook his head. "But thank you for the sentiment." I could see his eyes darken as he checked my steps on the uneven ground. Something was on his mind.

"I didn't think you would be coming to the capital when I agreed to participate in your scandal." He sighed and looked at me with a bit of sadness. "There are probably some things I will have to tell you now that you are. However, that can wait. First, we need to get you healed."

Nate took me up to a group of four personal tents. I was surprised to see that he had brought me to a team's camp, not the medical tent I had woken up in before. Maybe it hadn't been set up?

These tents were arranged neatly in a circle, and a glowing fire lit the darkness. Its shadows flickered on the canvas and the faces of two summoners. They both paused what they were doing at our approach, and I widened my eyes as I recognised one of them.

Zachary Weadall paled when he saw me leaning in Nate's embrace. He dropped his metal plate and fumbled to stand ungracefully from the earthen seat he had been using.

"Lynette! Is that you?" Zachary rushed over to us, and his hand instantly began to glow the green I had seen him use before. He took my hand, and I felt the tingling of his aether as it seeped through my system, inspecting my health.

"How are you alive?" Zachary furrowed his eyes in concentration, gripping my hand tighter.

"She fell into a cavern with Lady Rian Thornfax." Nate took me to the earthen chair Zachary had jumped up from. Zachary followed along, never releasing my hand as I gratefully accepted the offer to sit.

"How bad is it?" A man I did not know bent over me. His brown hair was slicked back smoothly, showing off his rather large forehead. He wore the black armour of the army over a dirtied brown shirt and simple brown trousers. His belt had rolls of bandages attached and bottles tied with string.

"Her clavicle and humerus are fractured, the muscles have been shredded, and the ligaments need mending." Zachary released my hand and then placed his own against my forehead. I tried to move back at his closeness; I could feel his breath on my chin and see the flecks of darker blue in his iris.

"She has a fever and likely has an infection on top of that. She is also severely dehydrated."

"Right, I'll start with her bones," the man replied, pulling off my sling. When he reached for my cloak clasp, I instinctively grabbed it to prevent him.

"Lynette." Zachary spoke gently, his eyes creasing in worry. "We need to see your injury; we can't heal you with your gear on."

"I—um, b-but," I stammered, gripping my clasp tighter. Did Zachary seriously want me to undress in front of these people? Out in the open like this? I knew Zachary had seen me, he'd said so himself, but at least I was unconscious for that. To do so knowingly in front of three others . . . Nate was here! I didn't want anyone else to see my scars. I couldn't; it was too embarrassing.

"It's all right; we only need to see your shoulder." Zachary smiled calmly, cupping my hand and grasping my clasp. "It's all right, I promise," he repeated soothingly, with a voice that hinted he often had to calm people down like this.

"All right," I gulped. They shouldn't see my chest scar if it was only my shoulder. Right?

Zachary slowly pried my hand away from my clasp and undid it himself. My tattered cloak fell down my back in a crumple. He then unfastened the shoulder straps of my short cuirass and helped me pull it off. That action was inscrutably painful as my arm did not want to lift how we needed it to. Left in only my ripped sleeveless blue shirt, I felt my cheeks heat. The material on my chest was thankfully still intact, thanks to my cuirass, but my stomach was littered with holes from the craven bats' bites.

"I just need to pull this down. Is that okay?" Zachary was being cautious with me as he hovered his hands over the scrap of material, now acting as a strap on my shoulder. I eventually nodded, my feet fidgeting as he softly pulled the strap down to expose my collarbone.

The gentleman I did not know quickly pressed his hands against my skin; I yelped as the pain from his heavy-handed touch sent a shock wave through my arm.

"Sorry, I know it hurts, but this shouldn't take too long." The man furrowed his eyebrows as brown aether strings zipped from his fingers. My skin tightened as the aether pierced it, and I could feel it wriggling through my muscles like a worm. I didn't want to look; I knew my bone was exposed, and my muscle was torn and flapped from the agiluf's teeth. Seeing it again would make me sick.

I heard a crunch and shut my eyes, biting my lip, but I couldn't stop my scream. Pain flooded me. My bones were being dragged back into place inch by inch, and every tiny movement was intolerable.

Zachary cupped my face as I began to sweat and shake, forcing me to look at him.

"Bite this." He shoved his hand into my mouth the moment I took a breath. I tried to push him away, but he stubbornly grabbed my hand and held it out.

I couldn't take it; the pain was too much.

My mouth clamped, biting into Zachary's hand.

I expected my teeth to squelch into his flesh, but instead, it felt like I was biting a soft branch. My eyes watered, but Zachary didn't express anything, only concern as he watched the earth summoner work. Was he so strong that my teeth couldn't even make him bleed? No wonder he used his hand instead of an actual branch.

I struggled this way as the earth summoner knitted my bones back into place. He then shifted his focus to my muscles. I felt a tugging sensation invade my skin as it was sewn together with his aether.

Thankfully, fixing my muscles was faster than fixing my bones. Finally, his aether withdrew, leaving my shoulder swollen and red. Zachary removed his hand from my mouth, and I took a deep breath as the pain subsided into tenderness.

"That's all I can manage." The earth summoner collapsed to the ground, his breathing ragged. He wiped the sweat from his brow, and I saw his hands shake.

"Thank you." I bowed my head to him, my own hands shaking from the onslaught of pain. "Thank you for healing me."

"No problem, it's what we do." The man smiled up at me, then took a swig from his waterskin. "Can't believe that used up my aether storage; you had so many fractured bones."

"How do you feel?" Nate asked as I pulled my strap back up onto my shoulder. He had been watching from a few steps away. I had noticed him hovering closer every time I screamed.

"Better." I stretched my right arm and moved it in a circle. "It's still tender, but I can move it again."

"Sorry, we don't have any herbs left to reduce swelling." Zachary frowned as he picked up my cuirass.

"That's okay; I have some. I will brew a tea with them later." I smiled, and Zachary looked at me with a smirk.

"Of course you do; I don't know why I didn't think you would."

"Willowspire is always useful." I blushed, taking my cuirass back from him.

"Indeed." Zachary smiled as he poured water into his metal cup. "Here, drink this, you need to get rehydrated, and we need to monitor your fever."

"You said she had an infection?" Nate sat on an earthen chair beside me, glancing at me with a look I could only describe as apprehension.

"It's likely she does, but I can't pinpoint one if there is. Unfortunately, we can't heal infections with aether. So she will need to be watched in case her temperature spikes." Zachary pulled the earth summoner up from the floor.

"Just how did you get so injured?" the earth summoner asked, and Zachary looked at me, just as curious.

"An agiluf," I sighed, sipping my water. The flames of the fire were beginning to warm me against the night's chilled air.

"Blimey, it must have tried to tear your arm off." The man raised his hand, and brown aether flickered; he frowned and more forcefully flexed his fingers. Aether streamed this time into the ground, and earth rose on command. It spilt out like a mole beast digging, and then the soil bundled together and moulded into a chair. The man slumped into it with a sigh. "Just need to recuperate, and then I can make you one, Zachary."

"I'm fine, Brendan." Zachary chose to stand near me. "Don't wear yourself out and just gather what you need."

"Rightio." Brendan saluted playfully. He then sat forward in his chair and closed his eyes. Leaning his elbows on his knees, he formed a circle with each of his hands, bringing them to his chest. His body grew very still, and I watched, waiting for something to happen, but nothing did. He remained motionless in that position.

"You won't be able to sense the aether he's gathering until you grow." Nate leaned his head on his hand, amused by my confusion.

"You can sense aether, then?"

"It is a part of the world. Eventually, you will be able to feel it." Nate smiled. "You will learn once we reach the capital. Lieutenant Cragborn will tell you all about it."

"That cranky man? He's teaching the aether course again?" Zachary raised an eyebrow.

"He's very good at it." Nate shrugged. "He prefers teaching to excursions."

"That's because he can spend time with his books." Zachary sighed. "Good luck with that one, Lynette."

"I'm starting to think I should be worried." I set my empty cup down and raised my hands towards the fire. Nate and Zachary laughed at my expression as they shared a look that only made me more nervous.

How cranky could Lieutenant Cragborn get?

"Lynette," a voice whispered with emotion, making me freeze.

A figure stood on the other side of the fire; his dark brown hair faded into the night, but the flames revealed his steel grey eyes as they stared at me.

"E-Eduard," I squeaked.

CHAPTER TWENTY-EIGHT

Vishka's Guidance System
Eduard Heversham
Likeability: −14% (+3%)

Eduard's form beyond the fire was surreal. His blue high-necked cloak blended into the night, and his pale skin stood out. He lifted his arm to reach out, then halted and dropped it. His gaze made my stomach flip, and I curled my fingers into a fist.

I hadn't seen Eduard since our carriage ride from the manor in Talbour. He had been at the front of the brigade for our journey, which, I guessed, was where I was now. I felt Zachary's hand on my shoulder and flinched at his touch.

"Eduard, Lynette has just received treatment," Zachary said.

"I know. I heard her screams." Eduard's jaw clenched. "What happened?"

Had I been screaming that loudly?

"She was bitten by an agiluf." Nate smiled. "I took care of her; it's the least I could do after Lynette requested me."

I shot Nate a panicked glance as he impishly grinned. Why did he have to tell Eduard that? I flicked my attention back to Eduard and saw him balling his fists as he glared at Nate. The number in his box changed.

Vishka's Guidance System
Eduard Heversham
Likeability: −20% (−6%)

"Why was I not informed that she had returned?" Eduard spoke in a strained voice; I could tell he wanted to say something else but refrained from doing so.

"Beats me." Nate shrugged. "She was in too bad shape for me to send a message."

Eduard grimaced for a moment, his shoulders back. "When will she be returning to the group of trainees?"

"She has a temperature, and I'm worried she may have an infection. So I want to keep her here to monitor her." Zachary squeezed my shoulder and smiled. "So not until I'm satisfied she has recovered."

"I see. I will monitor her tonight. You should take some rest, Zachary." Eduard stepped around the fire and towards our group. "You do not need to be here, Lord Nathaniel." He narrowed his eyes at Nate.

"I am here because I was asked to be." Nate smirked, and I so desperately wanted to shrink away.

"Your presence is no longer required." Eduard stood at his full height, looming over Zachary. The hairs on the back of my neck stood on end at the tension in his body.

"Oh? I think that is up to *Lynette*." Nate purposely exaggerated my name to show our closeness. He stood and touched my other shoulder to solidify our relationship. Eduard's look could have killed a smaller man.

"I think it's best I stay as a medic," Zachary chimed in, with a smile that was no longer kind.

I was surrounded.

All three of them shared competing scrunched faces above me as I shrank in my seat. I was suddenly very envious of Brendan sitting alone without a care in the world as he silently gathered.

Just how did this keep happening to me?

I wanted a peaceful night's rest, that was all. Not more anxiety; Azriel had been enough for one day.

"I feel fine, honestly. I will go back to my gro—" I tried to stand, but both Zachary and Nate pushed me back down in unison with their hands on my shoulders.

"No."

"No!"

"No."

All three of them swivelled their heads to me, and I gulped.

"I am her brother, so I shall stay. Zachary, I will call you if you are needed." Eduard glowered.

"You may not know when I am needed. You cannot check her health with aether as I can." Zachary patted my shoulder.

"I am responsible as her captain, so I shall stay." Nate butted in, his hand tightening on my shoulder.

I wanted to bury my head in my hands.

Vishka, how do I get out of this mess?

"Can't a guy gather in peace?" Brendan opened his eyes, and we all stilled. "Why don't you just ask Lady Lynette who she would prefer." He sighed, stretching his arms above his head.

No, no, no, no. Don't do this to me, Brendan!

The two I didn't choose might be upset; I didn't want to get in the middle of their argument!

"Splendid idea." Nate smirked confidently.

"I can accept that." Zachary nodded respectfully.

"Very well." Eduard tightened his lips.

They all looked at me expectantly. Each one of them had confidence that I did not. Oh, what should I do? My eyes flitted between them as they loomed above me.

"U-um," I said, and they all leaned closer.

"E-Eduard," I gulped, watching the box above his head.

I had no choice.

I would have preferred Nate or Zachary, but I couldn't risk that number dropping any lower. He was already upset that I had requested Nate instead of him. It fell so quickly the moment Nate told him. I dreaded how upset he would be if I chose someone else now.

Vishka's Guidance System
Eduard Heversham
Likeability: −15% (+5%)

"Are you sure, Lynette?" Nate pouted and leaned down to my level.

"Y-yes." I forced a smile. "Eduard is my brother; I shouldn't bother you or Zachary any longer than I need to."

"It wouldn't be a bother." Zachary frowned. "It is my job as a medic."

"The matter is settled. Both of you agreed to accept her choice." Eduard raised his chin and straightened. "You can leave now, Lord Nathaniel."

"Fine." Nate sighed and stood up. "I will just be over there if you need me, Lynette." Nate pointed to the centre of the camp we had walked through. "My tent is the one with a burnt doorway."

"Burnt?"

"Yes." He grinned, and fire flashed from his fingers. "I get carried away sometimes."

"She won't need you." Eduard glared.

"You can't decide that." Nate raised an eyebrow, which infuriated Eduard even more. He rolled his eyes at Eduard's reaction and tucked his hands into the pockets of his trousers. "Call me any time you need to." Nate winked, and I blushed from his candour.

"Th-thank you," I muttered under Eduard's gaze.

"I will be in my tent, then." Zachary sighed, releasing my shoulder.

"Keep an eye on her temperature, Eduard, and make sure to drink that willowspire, Lynette," Zachary instructed us, and I nodded.

"I will. Thank you for your help, Lord Zachary."

"Zachary, Lynette, you can just call me Zachary by now." He smiled, and Eduard frowned, moving to sit in the chair Nate had vacated. Nate shook his head at him as he did so.

"R-right." I smiled. "Thank you, Zachary."

"All right, then, time to get some kip." Brendan yawned and opened one of the tent flaps. "See you in the morn, gents."

"Yes." Zachary glanced at me, hesitating for a moment. "Wake me if you need me."

"I will." Eduard nodded and then proceeded to scowl at Nate. "Why are you still here?"

"Just making sure." Nate lifted his brow, then lowered it again to infuriate Eduard.

"Nathaniel," Eduard snapped.

"I'm going," Nate sighed, relenting. "Get some rest, Lynette, you need it." He rubbed the top of my head gently and then left the camp, raising his hand into the air as he did so. A flame sprang from his fingers to guide his way through the night.

I fidgeted in my seat, grinding the willowspire in a mortar and pestle that Zachary had left me. It was much easier than when I had been crushing it with rocks for Rian. I gently tapped the plant with the pestle, echoing into the night. Then, switching my technique as the plant began to split, I rotated the pestle to mash the leaves. Finally, I added some water and continued to grind it until it became a paste. I could drink it diluted with water, but from the tenderness in my shoulder, it would be better if I spread it onto a piece of gauze. Willowspire worked best as a tea for stomachaches or headaches. I didn't have any gauze to use for Rian, so tea was my best option then. However, it would work significantly better for reducing inflammation on physical injuries when used as a poultice.

I picked up the gauze from Zachary's supply and spread it along the material, ensuring that it was even.

"Aren't you supposed to drink that?" Eduard asked. He had been watching me silently as I worked. His eyes followed my every movement, and frankly, it made me uncomfortable knowing he was inspecting me.

"It works better as a poultice." I hesitantly raised the gauze to my shoulder.

Eduard pondered my words, but from his expression, he did not appear to counter my decision. Shifting in my seat, I turned away from him and lowered the strap on my shoulder to place the gauze. Getting it to sit right was awkward, but I managed it after some struggle. The cold mush felt soothing on my skin, like stepping into a cold bath on a hot summer's day.

"Why didn't you request me?"

I froze at Eduard's question. Then, pulling my shoulder strap back slowly, I nervously turned back in my seat to see him staring at me directly. His expression was strange, anguished almost, but I could see the familiar anger reflecting from his steel eyes.

"I—I . . ." I tried to find the right thing to say, anything that wouldn't upset him. Eduard was prideful; he must have seen my choice of Nate over my family as dishonourable.

"I didn't want you to have to clean up after my mess again," I finally said. But, in truth, I did not want him to lecture me about my behaviour. He always had something to complain about; I was an embarrassment to him.

Eduard frowned at my response, and his numbers blurred. I pinched my fingers to distract myself from looking.

"Dying and then surviving is not something so trivial," he said, raising his hand towards me. I flinched as he came closer, his knuckles brushing against my cheek.

"I didn't want to believe it when Callan told me you had disappeared." He tightened his lips and pulled his hand away. "You were reckless."

"It's not like I chose to fall." I pulled back and brought my knees up on the chair. "I couldn't have gotten away if I tried."

"You should have tried harder."

"Ha." I laughed with grit. "That wouldn't have mattered. The baildon would have swallowed me into the earth regardless of how fast I ran."

Eduard looked down at his hands as he linked them together, watching the fire.

"What about when the marsh snakes attacked? You should have gone to the safety of your group, but instead, you stupidly ran out alone."

"I did that to help Lord Harold Eastmond." I pursed my lips.

"His welfare is not your concern."

"I couldn't just go to safety whilst someone else was in danger, Eduard."

"I told you that joining the army would be dangerous."

"I know," I said, hugging my knees closer. Resting my head against them, I rubbed my eyes as they began to feel heavy.

Did Eduard genuinely believe I should have prioritised my own life when someone else could have died?

I knew that this march was to weed out the weak; General Saika had said that much. However, I couldn't, wouldn't, stand by whilst someone died in front of me. My heart couldn't take that. They wouldn't come back, not like I did.

"Has Callan been training you?" Eduard said.

"Yes, I'm not very good with a jian."

"Of course, you won't be. You have never trained with a weapon." Eduard leaned back and pointedly looked at me. "Practise."

"I have been," I sighed.

"Hm." Eduard made a noise of disapproval. "It doesn't matter. I will have your blood bond revoked when we reach the capital."

"I don't want it revoked." I frowned.

"Lynette, if anything, this trip has proved you can't survive being a soldier. You have nearly perished twice."

"I will learn."

"You will fail. Your core is too small."

"It will grow."

"It won't." Eduard set his jaw as I argued with him.

I knew my chances were slim; I knew my core was small. But seeing the strength of the summoners on this march . . . I had grown hopeful. Was it so bad to want to be more than I was? To be like Arjun and his team when they found Rian and me? They were so powerful, they didn't have to be afraid of the demonic beasts that attacked us. I couldn't envision them struggling against someone like Garret.

There had to be a reason Vishka had wanted me to have Albus, to make use of his knowledge. He had given me a technique for gathering; it was more hope than my family had ever given me for my independence.

I had to grow stronger. I wanted to be able to allow someone to bite my hand with no pain like Zachary had. I wanted to be able to survive against a demonic beast without relying on someone else. If I were a summoner, I wouldn't have to be afraid anymore.

"I don't think it will be approved," I finally said after some silence between us.

"Why?" Eduard narrowed his eyes, his body tensing.

"Lord Azriel Elkhart has asked me to demonstrate riding a kreshna."

"What?" Eduard said coldly, his gaze flaming with rage. "Why would he do that? What did you do?"

"I rode a wild kreshna through the prairie expanse."

"Lynette! How many times have I told you, kreshna are dangerous beasts that should not be ridden." Eduard's nostrils flared. "Reckless." He clicked his jaw, flexing his fists. "I will deal with the Lord Azriel." He breathed deeply. "Come, you should sleep. You are exhausted."

"Fine," I sighed. I was finding it harder to keep my eyes open, so sleep did not sound so bad.

"You will share my tent." Eduard reached down to grab my backpack and the attached bedroll.

"Y-your tent?" I perked up a bit, my eyes widening. He wanted me to sleep in his tent? Seriously? But he always chose to avoid me; he never wanted to be close to me.

"Yes. I won't have you sleeping outside." Eduard held out his hand to me; I looked at it and debated. I would have preferred to sleep outside rather than share his tent . . .

"Lynette." Eduard scowled impatiently.

"All right." I reluctantly took his hand. It was much larger than my own; his fingers clasped around easily, his skin rough against mine which was smooth. Would my hands become rough like his if I trained more?

Eduard tugged me to my feet and then led me to one of the tents in the circle.

"Wait." I paused at the tent's entrance.

"What?" Eduard lifted the flap and unfurled my bedroll next to his own. The tent was larger than the one I'd shared with Teresa. With Teresa, we were so close that I often woke up with her legs sprawled over me. However, this tent had considerably more room for space between our bedrolls.

"This is your camp?" I asked, surprised. I thought he had only come here because of my screams.

Eduard's mouth lifted into a small smile. "Yes, this is my camp. Zachary Weadall, Brendan Duane, Lorand Stobel, and I travel together."

"Lorand?"

"He's on patrol tonight." Eduard held open the tent flap and gestured for me to go in.

I bit my lip and entered his tent, glancing at the box before he closed the flap behind us.

Vishka's Guidance System
Eduard Heversham
Likeability: −12% (+3%)

CHAPTER TWENTY-NINE

Chaos splintered around me as I stood at the centre of our dining room. The table had been shoved from its position, its cloth strewn, and cutlery thrown on the floor. Food dripped from the edge of the polished wood table. Angry and fearful glares stared at me from hollow husks.

My hand tightened around a shard of pottery that had once been my plate. I looked at it as blood began to seep down my wrist from the wound it had caused in my palm. My hands were small, smaller than I remembered.

"What is the meaning of this?" Roger Heversham stamped his cane as he entered the destroyed room. His expression was one of hostile fury.

"Correcting their mistake," I spat at one of the maids huddling in the corner of the room, afraid. They had tried to feed me spoilt food again. It was insulting; I was a lady of this house; they should not treat me this way.

"Lynette." Roger gritted his teeth. "Apologise."

"What?" I narrowed my eyes. "Why should I apologise to a servant who gave me spoilt food?"

"Your delusions are impeccable." Roger raised his cane towards me. His water snake slithered from its handle and dropped to the floor. I gripped the shard harder as it came closer, rising on its tail to extend its tongue. Like its master, the snake had an edge of irateness.

"Apologise," Roger stated with a tone that didn't accept anything else.

"No." I tried to hold back the lump in my throat as the snake glared.

"Father," a boy's voice called from the hallway. Eduard entered the room, his hands behind his back as he took in the mess I had made. He was shorter, his features more like those of a boy than the man he was now.

"I will deal with her, Father." Eduard scowled at me.

"Very well. Make sure she understands this is not acceptable." Roger sighed with a look of disappointment.

"Yes, Father." Eduard strode towards me.

I stepped back, but he quickly grabbed my wrist, blood sticking to his fingers. He lowered his gaze to the shard and forcefully pulled my fingers apart. The shard fell to the floor as I tried to rip my wrist from his grip.

"Foolish," Eduard chided me. "Your hand could scar."

"I don't care," I muttered, looking away from him.

"Stupid girl," he growled, tugging me forward. I couldn't resist his strength as he dragged me out of the room past Father.

I pushed and smacked his arm with my free hand, but no matter how hard I tried, I could not break free. Instead, Eduard yanked me relentlessly up the manor's staircase and down the desolate hallway of paintings until we reached my room.

Wrenching my door open, he brought me inside and deposited me on my bed. I crossed my arms and flexed my bleeding hand as he released me.

"You will stay here until you learn that disrespecting the servants like that is wrong." Eduard glowered, his hand on my doorframe. He watched me flex my hand with a small grimace before closing his eyes with a heavy sigh.

"You must learn to be a noble, Lynette. You are no longer a street beggar."

"Then why do they feed me spoilt food?" I shouted, rising to my feet, my hands clenched at my sides.

"Stop it!" Eduard growled. "They would never do such a thing."

"B-but they did!" I felt my tears welling up; why did no one believe me? "Cassandra would believe me." I hiccuped, rubbing my small hands across my eyes.

Eduard's eyes steeled as he cracked his jaw. "Mother isn't here anymore." He slammed the door, leaving me alone to my sorrow.

My body seized as I tried to turn in my bedroll. It felt heavy, like a weight was holding down my limbs. I blinked open my eyes and held in a shriek at Eduard's face looking down on me. His hands squeezed my arms as his eyes searched my face, concerned.

This was not how I thought I would wake up today.

"E-Eduard?" I said, unsure what he was doing over me like this.

"You were crying." Eduard released me and leaned back, giving me room to pull myself up and rub my eyes. I was surprised to see that he was fully dressed; his high-necked cloak was without a crease, and his dark blue armour was without a speck of dirt. Had Eduard been awake for some time already?

"I was? It must have been a dream." I hesitantly inched away from him.

"What was your dream?"

"Oh, um, I don't remember," I lied. I remembered it vividly. I hadn't thought about that day in a long time. It was the first time Eduard had locked me in my room for my behaviour. The first of many after Cassandra. I hadn't complained about the food again after that.

Why was I dreaming of my childhood? Usually it was memories of my past lives.

"Lynette." Eduard raised one of his eyebrows. "You are not good at lying."

Heat rushed to my cheeks. Was I that bad?

No, he probably just thinks I am always lying.

"I—I should change." I tried to bypass the subject. I did not want to talk to Eduard about my dream.

"Hm." Eduard frowned, displeased. He opened his mouth to say something, then closed it again firmly. "I will be outside." Eduard stood and opened the tent flap, pausing momentarily. He looked back at me and pulled his eyebrows before finally leaving.

I released the breath I had been holding.

What would Eduard have said if I had told him I had been crying because of his actions?

I pinched at the hem of my blue shirt, the first present he had ever given me. Unfortunately, it was ruined; there was no point in clinging to it anymore. Pulling my backpack over, I shuffled its contents around until I found the spare burgundy cotton shirt I had packed. It was inferior to what Eduard had given me, but it was better than a torn, holey mess. I pulled off the blue shirt, then checked the gauze on my shoulder, peeling it away. The poultice had soaked into my skin, and the redness had faded. I rolled my shoulder, happy that it no longer felt as tender.

After putting on my new shirt, I attempted to get my short cuirass back on. The grey leather was scratched and worn at the centre from the rat beasts. Holes pierced through it against my right shoulder where the agiluf's teeth had tried to rip the flesh off my bones. My matching gauntlets sat nicely against the fabric of my new shirt. However, they were still loose on my arms. I restuffed the gap with the spare material I had left. My boots were caked in mud; they had dried in the heat of the fire last night. The mud crinkled away as I bent the leather before pulling them up to my shins.

Finally, I debated if it was worth using my cloak. It was torn and no longer reached my knees; the fabric was shredded to my waist. I decided to keep it; it would be useful if it rained again. Attaching it around my shoulders with the clasp, I readied myself at the tent opening.

Hesitatingly I lifted my hand, then dropped it again.

Was Eduard going to ask about my dream again?

I pressed my lips and took a deep breath, ripping the tent open.

Bright light attacked my eyes; I raised my hand to shield them. The area outside Eduard's tent was quiet, empty. I looked around and finally spotted him a short distance away, talking to a man with fluffy brown hair. The man had a spear strapped to his back; his eyes were sunken, surrounded by dark circles. His posture was slouched in comparison to Eduard's upright stance.

"Lynette." A kind voice alerted me to another presence.

"Zachary." I smiled as the blond of his hair glinted in the sunlight. "How did you sleep?" I moved to the fire pit, its embers still burning from last night.

"Very well, thank you." He smiled back. "How are you feeling?" He held out his hand in a gesture I recognised. I placed my hand in his, and his fingers glowed green, his aether tingling my skin.

"I don't think I have a fever anymore." My skin did not feel as warm as it had last night.

"No, you seem to have recovered." Zachary dropped my hand gently. "That's good; the swelling in your shoulder has calmed down too," he said, and I noticed how he seemed to ease a little.

Had Zachary been worried about me?

I smiled; he really was an interesting man. I had found Zachary difficult in Talbour; he often talked to me with disapproval. My actions in society were loud and, quite frankly, obnoxious at times. There were many cases when I could have solved an issue with my words, not my actions. Maybe if I had, Roger would have believed me about the spoilt food.

"Does this mean I can go back to the trainees?" I asked, hopeful. I wanted to check on Rian; she had been hurt, and she hadn't been waiting outside Azriel's tent as she had promised.

Zachary paused. "I don't know."

"What do you mean?" I furrowed my brow, confused. I was healed; I had no reason to stay at the front of the brigade longer. I should surely return to my group.

Zachary glanced towards Eduard. "Lord Azriel has made it very clear you are to return the capital safely."

"What? Did he? When?"

"This morning." Zachary gave me a look of pity. "He is very interested in your claim of riding wild kreshna."

"How do you . . ."

"Gossip travels." Zachary smiled apologetically. "Eduard was not . . . happy about it."

"I see." I slumped my shoulders and slouched into one of the earthen chairs. Zachary handed me a cup of water and joined me in the other chair.

"I didn't know you could ride kreshna." Zachary raised an eyebrow inquisitively.

I half smiled. "It's not something I thought was worth sharing."

"Eduard told you not to, then," Zachary said with a knowing tone.

"Yes," I sighed, drinking my water as it refreshed my body.

"He likely didn't want this happening."

"Lord Azriel's interest?" I asked, a little puzzled by what he meant.

"Amongst others." Zachary leaned forward and lowered his tone; his expression tightened. "Lynette, no one can ride kreshna. The fact that a young girl like you can is strange." He reached out and held my hand. I felt the warmth of his skin, surprised I didn't flinch from his touch. "Promise me you will be careful."

His gaze made my stomach crumple. "I will be careful."

I knew that riding kreshna was unusual; I had thought Eduard and Callan were making me hide it because they were embarrassed by me. Had I been wrong? Had I maybe . . . not understood just how strange it was? Were they actually . . . trying to protect me by making me hide it?

"Lynette." I jumped at Eduard's voice as he approached us with the man he had been conversing with.

"Hey there." The man waved sluggishly and yawned. "Lady Lynette, right?"

"Ugh, yes." I blinked at the man as he scratched his beard.

"This is Lord Stobel," Eduard said, introducing the fire summoner. This must be Lorand, the man who was on patrol last night. No wonder he seemed exhausted.

"A pleasure to meet you." I bowed my head slightly as I did not know his rank. The man yawned again, covering his mouth.

"Sure. Zachary, can you give me a boost?"

"Yes, you need it." Zachary grinned and pushed up out of his seat. He walked over to Lorand and held his hands out towards him. I watched as Zachary's hand glowed green and aether strands as fine as silk sprouted from his fingertips. The aether sank into Lorand's face, and as it did so, Lorand's sunken eyes began to perk, his skin brightened, and his posture straightened.

"Perfect." Lorand smiled, rolling his shoulders.

"What did you do?" I asked, amazed at how different Lorand was now. He no longer had sluggish movement; all signs of his tiredness had vanished.

"Aether transference," Eduard answered. "We take turns on patrol on the night shift and share our aether in the morning to revitalise our stamina."

"It allows us to safely keep watch whilst travelling in the day," Zachary added. "It's something all summoners must learn how to do."

"Is this something Lieutenant Cragborn teaches?"

"Yes." Eduard narrowed his eyes towards me. "The summoners' class is not something you will need to take."

I frowned but didn't respond to his statement. If we had been alone, I might have said something I would have regretted.

A noise behind us made us all turn as one of the tents collapsed. Brendan waved, a tent pole in his hand as he shoved the end to compact it. "Best we get cleared up; we will be setting off soon."

"Yes. You need to return to your group, Lynette." Eduard raised his hand, and water droplets began to form in the space between us. They formed faster and thicker, grouping together into a blob. The blob bent and shifted; legs and then arms formed and finally a head. Then, with a pop, the water shifted its colours and changed from its watery hue into a solid form.

A second Eduard stood, his arms folded behind his back.

"My clone will escort you."

"What about . . ." I glanced at Zachary. "Lord Azriel . . ." I paused as Eduard's face darkened.

"I have spoken with him. He has permitted you to return."

"All right." I hesitantly stood up. "Let me get my backpack." I quickly returned to the tent and collected my belongings.

CHAPTER THIRTY

The tents were brought down, and fires were kicked out promptly. The speed at which the professional summoners worked overshadowed all of the trainees. I tugged my backpack, getting used to my shoulder again, watching in admiration. The soldiers showed their experience and were deft as the night setup was stuffed into bags or hauled onto carts. Foot guards sharpened their weapons with whetstones and picked out rocks from the soles of their boots.

Eduard's clone walked with me, silently leading me through the brigade. I flicked my eyes towards the water clone and bit my lip.

"So," I began. "Do you . . . Um, how does this work?"

"How does what work?" Fake Eduard raised an eyebrow.

"You are, um, a clone? Do you have Eduard's thoughts?"

"I copy my conscious mind when creating a clone. When the clone has ceased, everything it learns or has done returns to my main body." The clone spoke as though he were the real Eduard; it was unsettling.

"So Eduard will remember our conversation when you . . . cease?"

"My clone's memories become my memories."

"You know it's weird that you talk like you are Eduard."

"I *am* Eduard." The clone raised its eyebrows, confused by my statement.

Okay then, so the clone didn't know he was a clone.

I rubbed my arm suddenly, feeling strange being next to this thing. If it weren't for the lack of a box above his head, I might have been torn on whether he was the real Eduard and the clone had instead stayed behind.

"All right, well, *Eduard*, may I suggest that when you create a clone, you give it the semblance of knowing it is a clone?" I said pointedly. If this conversation returned to Eduard's mind, hopefully, he would take my suggestion on board.

"I do not see how that matters," Fake Eduard said. "My clones are useful to allow me to be in several places simultaneously. If they knew they were clones, they would not perform as I would."

"Right . . ." That wasn't my point, though. I was more concerned about how creepy this was for anyone interacting with Fake Eduard. Did he say *several?* Did that mean there were more Eduards around the brigade? I shuddered at the thought.

"Why do you need so many clones?"

Fake Eduard glanced at me, his lips tightening into a line. "It is useful."

"Useful how?"

Fake Eduard frowned at me but seemed to be considering something. "I am in the administration profession. My role is to assist with the infrastructure of the army. Being in several places is a skill highly valued for that role."

"I see," I said, and he didn't respond. So Eduard was in administration? It was the first time he'd told me that in all of my four lives. He never did like to speak about his life in the capital, unlike Callan, who loved to brag about his exploits.

"So, do you help send messages to the other teams?"

"I do. I help link information and ensure that the generals are informed of anything important through descriptive reports. The administration profession allows the army to keep intact without error; we ensure that procedures are implemented and maintain stability."

How very much like Eduard. The profession suited him.

"Don't you tire of filling out paperwork all day? It must be a little boring."

"Stability is not boring, Lynette." Fake Eduard raised an eyebrow at me. "Without structure, there is chaos."

"You mean like me?" I said with a coy smirk. Eduard had called me chaotic more than once.

"If you were not so insistent on going out of your way to make a scene at every outing, but instead behaved, then maybe I would not call you chaotic."

"Perhaps." There was some truth to his words. "You know, 'Crazy Cerue Lady' is growing on me."

Fake Eduard stopped walking beside me and glared.

"That is not a name you should be proud of."

"It fits me, though, doesn't it?" I stopped as well, turning to face him. I suppose being called that was another thing Eduard hated about me. It was not a name that brought the Hevershams pride.

Fake Eduard's gaze locked with mine, and then his expression began to strangely soften. "Is that why you were crying?"

I was taken aback by his question.

"No, that isn't why."

"Then why?" Fake Eduard stepped forward, but I instinctively stepped back as he did so, making him frown.

"I have no reason to tell you." I began to anxiously flick my thumbnail against my forefinger. I couldn't tell him about my dream. He wouldn't accept his actions being the reason. Even if this was just a clone of Eduard, I didn't trust his judgement enough to openly share my feelings with him. He wouldn't believe what I said anyway.

His upper lip lifted as his eyebrow twitched at my answer. "Very well."

We walked silently after that.

The brigade began to grow more lively as summoners and foot guards roused. We passed an area with a growing populace as a couple of water summoners started refilling waterskins for others. A line of foot guards had queued and were chatting whilst waiting for their refills.

"Lynette." Fake Eduard slowed his pace, pressed his lips together, and unfolded his hands from behind his back. "I—" He paused, seeing my hesitation. "Walk faster; we will be setting off soon." He quickly turned and continued to stride forward.

I stayed where I was, unsure what had just happened.

What did Fake Eduard want to say to me? Why did he withhold it?

Fake Eduard stopped walking ahead and turned around to face me again. He raised his eyebrow expectantly. "Lynette?"

I shook out of my surprise and quickened my pace to catch up with him. I frowned. Was it just me, or was his clone less uptight?

"I informed Callan and your group of your return this morning. They should be expecting you, so we can't delay."

"Oh, do you know if Lady Rian Thornfax is back with her group?"

"I did not ask." Fake Eduard's strides slowed a little as he saw me lag behind. "I expect she has recovered if she requested her sister when you arrived." He pinched his lips together, narrowing his eyes. I flinched and looked away. But, of course, even his clone would still be unhappy that I had requested Nate over my family.

"That's good; I was worried about her." I sighed, stepping into a sloppy piece of mud. It squelched on my boot, and I had to pull my leg to get it unstuck again.

"I did not think you would be."

"Why would I not be worried?"

"I am well aware you and Lady Rian do not get along," Fake Eduard said.

"Ah." I rubbed the back of my neck awkwardly. "She's not as terrible as I thought."

"Does that mean you will finally stop your pointless squabbling?" Fake

Eduard asked as we reached the middle of the brigade. I could see in the distance a lack of brightly coloured cloaks. Instead, the people gathering together wore weathered outfits as they scrambled to pack away their things.

"I only argued with her because . . ." I wanted to say because she had shown me such disdain. Because I had not been able to accept that she had made a mistake; because I had embraced my jealousy. We were both unforgiving of each other equally.

"It does not matter," Fake Eduard said. "The fact that you finally realise you were uncouth is enough."

"Of course," I sighed, rolling my eyes. Uncouth? My manners were appropriate for someone who had been insulted, but Eduard never listened when I explained why I acted in such ways. There was no point in arguing with him. I had done so many times in the past.

We slowed our pace as we came closer to the trainees. Fake Eduard stopped as Lieutenant Cragborn spotted us. The lieutenant's red eyes and long hair stood out against the trainees. He motioned to Fake Eduard and began to make his way over to us.

"Lynette," Fake Eduard said quietly as we waited for the lieutenant to meet us. "I am glad you came back."

I stilled as he spoke words I had never imagined I would hear from him.

Fake Eduard smirked at me as I stared at him incredulously.

"Survive to the capital." His words were garbled as his solid form began to shimmer. The colour drained and returned to a watery blue before sloshing into the ground.

Lieutenant Cragborn's eyes felt like he was sharpening a blade as he jutted his chin. I stood with him where Eduard's clone had once been, still a little shell-shocked by what he had said. The real Eduard would never have said such a thing. Perhaps his clones were not as identical to Eduard as he had suggested. My face heated; now the real Eduard would know of our conversation since his clone had ceased.

"Lady Lynette, were you injured in the head, or are you ignoring me?" Lieutenant Cragborn scowled, tapping his foot.

"Uh, sorry, Lieutenant." I meekly smiled. "I am listening."

"Good. I want you to return to your group, but you are to stay within sight of me at all times," he said, irritated. "I don't know what you did with a kreshna, but it has been made *very* clear to me you are not to perish."

"Oh, sorry." I could sense that this was a burden the lieutenant did not want responsibility for.

"Indeed." His brows knitted. "If a demonic beast attacks, you are to stay within five steps of me. If we are separated, you need to find me. Understood?"

"Understood." I saluted.

"Good. Now go find your team." He jutted his head in their direction. I didn't wait for any more orders and left him.

As I arrived at the group of trainees, many didn't pay me much notice at first, but the nobles I recognised stopped what they were doing, their eyes widening at my return. The whispering that followed ricocheted as more and more of the trainees were prodded by their friends, who were pointing at me. I swallowed the lump that suddenly formed in my throat. Then, dipping my head as though it would hide me, I rushed past them.

"Lynette!" Someone squealed as arms enveloped my body. My hugger shifted me from side to side in her embrace.

"Teresa." I smiled as she pulled back, beaming.

"I can't believe you are alive! Your older brother sent his clone thing and told us this morning; I thought he was telling us some sort of sick joke. But no! It's real! You are alive and here! Oh my gosh, I've never been so relieved. You have to tell me everything that happened; I want details! Your brother said you were hurt? Are you okay now? I saw Lady Rian earlier, but she wouldn't tell me a thing; she even told me to get lost. Can you believe that? So rude." Teresa's words overpowered my mind as I tried to process everything she was saying.

"I'm fine." I patted her with a chuckle. Her blond hair swished, tied into a high ponytail, and she crinkled her blue eyes with a smile.

"Lord Zachary Weadall and Lord Brendan Duane used their abilities to heal me."

"So you were hurt that bad?" Teresa pouted and began to check me over, brushing down my arms and feeling my forehead like a mother hen.

"I'm fine now." I grinned, taking her hand away from my head. "A lot happened."

"You have to tell me!" Teresa linked her arm to mine and led me towards the rest of our group.

I began to talk about the cave and the agiluf as we took our short walk. I didn't have a chance to get into the rest as we reached our destination.

Harold stood waiting. His back straightened, looking at nothing in particular. His hair was no longer as neat as it had been; some of the tight cornrows had loosened. His beard had grown a little longer, and he had a giant tear in his cloak, splitting it from the bottom up to his waist.

Garret was beside him. His arms crossed as he chatted to Harold. Garret's black cloak was dirty, and his clothes were caked in dried mud. His red hair was out of place, and a thick red line now stretched across his cheek.

I took another look at Teresa and noticed she had a rip in the hem of her shirt, and one of her boots was hastily tied on with some string wrapped around her ankle, a tear running up the seam.

"Lady Lynette." Harold nodded in greeting. "I am glad to see you are well."

"Yes, it was excellent news that you survived, Lady Lynette. I was distraught by your loss." Garret made a face of sorrow to show concern. I did not care for it.

"I'm sure." I rolled my eyes towards Garret.

"Did something happen whilst I was gone? Why do you have a scar on your cheek, Lord Garret?" Surely a medic summoner could have healed it? They hadn't left a trace of a wound when they healed me.

"You could say that," Teresa sighed. "After the baildon, we were pretty shaken up; you weren't the only person who died that day." She grimaced.

"Oh," I said, pinching my fingers. "Who?" I asked quietly.

"A summoner and a noble trainee," Harold answered, tightening his grip on one of his sai blades.

"One of the commoner trainees, too," Teresa added.

"I'm sorry," I whispered, wrapping my arm around Teresa's shoulders to try to comfort her. I could only hope no one she knew from Ingalham had been the person that died.

"Lord Trigot perished." Garret fumbled with his sabre. I remembered Lord Trigot was the trainee who had questioned Lieutenant Cragborn about his evaluation methods when we were selecting our groups.

"I see; I did not know him," I said, tightening my arm around Teresa. I could have been amongst those; I was amongst those who died for others. However, they would not be coming back like I did.

"My scar is because the medics did not have enough aether left to fully heal me." Garret ground his teeth. "My injury was not as *important* as others," he said with disdain.

"It wasn't," Teresa said, eyeing Garret with hostility. "After the baildon, a pack of rat demonic beasts came out of the prairie expanse. They were a pain to deal with; it got overwhelming, but the summoners took care of them in no time."

"*They* were ruthless ugly things. They dared to scratch my face." Garret glared at Teresa.

"Well, they tore my boot apart; I got over it. So should you," Teresa spat.

"My face is more important than a commoner's boots."

"Your face looks better with the makeover." Teresa smirked. Garret seethed, opening his mouth to argue, but Harold interrupted.

"They tore my cloak." Harold frowned, looking at it longingly.

"Mine got ruined too." I showed Harold the tattered remains of my cloak. He looked at me with such sympathy.

"I am very sorry, Lady Lynette," Harold sighed sadly.

I had to cover my mouth to hide my small smile at his despondence. He seemed very upset about his ruined clothing. But I could also tell from the twitch of his mouth that he just didn't want to hear Garret and Teresa argue.

A horn blasted into the air, and we paused our conversation. I caught Lieutenant Cragborn pointing at me with his finger, then down at the ground in front of him. I got the message, and we all moved over to the front of the trainees as we readied for the march.

CHAPTER THIRTY-ONE

Lieutenant Cragborn was true to his word and kept glancing back at us as we marched. I found that my breathing had improved considerably with my increase in stamina. I did not tire as quickly as I had previously, and my muscles did not burn as they once had.

However, the sun was particularly high, and the warmth of its rays made me sweat. The ground was growing less muddy and more rocky. I had to be careful of where I walked to prevent my foot from slipping on the uneven footing.

The prairie expanse thinned as we walked alongside it. Its reeds grew shorter until, eventually, we passed them and returned to a landscape of meadows.

I informed Teresa of what had happened to Rian and me as we marched. Teresa asked many questions, and Harold was also interested, especially in the agiluf and how we defeated it. Garret had demanded I give him the angel shrooms and beast cores as my fiancé; something about what I have should be his. This nonsense was quickly shut down by both Harold and Teresa. Garret had moped about civility for a while but eventually relented against our hard gazes.

He was too cowardly to fight against us all.

Soon the afternoon loomed, and we slowed for our break. We did not set up fires and instead settled on the rocky ground chewing on cold rations. I was excited to show Teresa my cooking skill in the evening, if there was anything for us to cook, that was. By disrupting the hunt of the kreshna, Rian and I had deprived the brigade of much-needed meat.

Knowing this, I felt a small amount of guilt.

However, I still wouldn't have chosen differently. Kuru had helped us; it would have been wrong for me to have helped the summoners of team five in their attack.

I caught Rian's eye as the trainees tucked into their rations. She sat some distance away with her group: Lacey Weadall, Kit Balburn, and the noble I did not know. He must be Lord Caspian Landrick, the son of the Marquess of Ingalham that Rian had mentioned.

Rian smiled at me and mouthed that she would speak to me later; I nodded and continued my conversation with Teresa.

Teresa told me of how horrible it had been without me; she had butted heads with Garret and his stuck-up attitude towards commoners. Harold did not intervene and only provided distractions from time to time. She had struggled, and I could see how emotionally drained she was. My death must have been a shock alongside the terror of the horned baildon attack.

Whilst we ate, my eyes wandered to the summoners nearby. Callan had not approached me yet; he had stayed with his group. However, I noticed he was acting more sternly than usual. His attention was focused on the land around us, and he often seemed to be fidgeting, keeping his jian drawn at all times. His body language suggested he was on edge, and I frowned as I saw an argument brewing between him and his teammates, judging by the looks on their faces.

After our break was over, we set off again for the second half of our march for the day. The smell in the air changed as we progressed. It was something I had not experienced before. It reminded me of salt, and the wind began to pick up considerably as my hair whooshed around me. Teresa handed me one of her spare hair ties, and I fastened my hair into a poorly made bun to keep it out of my face. I had lost my own in the prairie expanse.

The salt smell grew stronger as the march angled right. Large stones and hills became a struggle to climb, and my muscles soon found their familiar ache again. In front of us, I could see the brigade slowing as we stepped ever higher up the hill we were traversing. Every breath burned my lungs as I found it harder to get oxygen the higher we went.

Sounds I did not recognise—heavy, loud throbs—thumped repetitively across the landscape. I gripped my backpack tighter. Was that the sound of a demonic beast? Its noise was so loud it could be as terrifying as the horned baildon. Why had they not sounded an alarm?

Finally, the horn sounded for the end of the day's march. I relaxed my shoulders to catch my breath, trying to suck in as much air as I could. Harold dropped his backpack and immediately began to set up his tent, not wanting to lose momentum before resting. Teresa followed suit and quickly pulled out our tent. I wiped my brow of sweat and helped her set it up, then proceeded to start a fire.

As I got the flames to burn the flufftoru, I heard the noise of someone approaching. Lifting my head, I saw Callan as he entered our camp for the night.

His brown hair was a mess, his hands had blisters from training, and his grey eyes looked down at me with an emotion I could not place.

"Hi, Callan." I meekly waved to him.

Was he mad at me?

"Lynette." Callan held out his hand and gestured for me to take it. I looked at his box and gulped. Placing my hand in his, I allowed him to pull me up from the fire I had been crouching upon. "Come with me." He tugged my hand, leading me away from the camp.

I looked back to Teresa for guidance; she had been around Callan whilst I was away, but she just shrugged, having no clue what Callan wanted.

"What? Are we training?" I tried to slow him down. I wasn't up for training tonight; I still felt exhausted after the past few days and was looking forward to getting an early night.

"No, we're not training," Callan said as he continued to lead me through the camps that were being set up.

Vishka's Guidance System
Callan Heversham
Likeability: 5% (+9%)

Callan took me higher up the hill past the brigade and towards where the sound of throbs was loudest. I panicked a little, looking back at Teresa, but she was already occupied talking with Harold. Why did Callan want to bring me closer to those scary sounds?

"Where are we going?" I asked hesitantly as he continued to drag me farther away from the brigade towards where the hill met the sky.

I could not see beyond its edge, which was unnerving.

"To show you something," Callan answered without looking at me as we reached the top. I paused as he stopped at the edge of the cliff, the smell of salt thick in the air.

"Come here." Callan loosened his grip on my hand and gently tried to pull me towards him.

My feet did not want to move, so I firmly stood still.

"Wh-what is it?"

Was he going to push me off? Was that why he seemed so angsty today? Was he upset I didn't die?

"Just come here," Callan said, irritated at my refusal. He lightly pulled with more strength this time, and my feet budged against my will into the place he wanted.

I gasped at the top of the cliff.

I had never seen anything like it. A vast stretch of deep blue water disappeared into the horizon. Turquoise glinted on its surface as waves pushed against the bottom of the cliff we stood atop. White foam gathered as the waves bellowed below. Seabirds swooped, skimming the surface with fish hanging from their beaks.

"It's beautiful," I breathed, gazing at the scene and realising it must be the ocean. I had heard stories about its grandeur, how there was no end to its vastness, but I did not think I would ever see it.

"I thought you would like it." Callan smiled, satisfied. "See over there?" He pointed into the distance over to the right of the cliffs, where they bent around the ocean. I had to squint to make it out, but I saw what looked like stone walls. They were small to me, but I knew that from this distance, it meant they were incredibly large. Two large towers planted on the ground reached into the sky as the cliff sloped to meet the ocean on its beach. I saw small vessels bobbing in the ocean near a structure that led out from the walls.

"Is that . . . ?"

"Yes, that's Zromore, the capital." Callan confirmed my suspicion.

"Does that mean we are close? Is the march over?" I asked, a little excited.

"A week or so yet, but we are close." Callan smirked at my enthusiasm.

"I have to show Teresa and Rian!" I turned to go back for them, but Callan quickly grabbed my hand, holding me back.

"Lynette," Callan said in a pained voice. I turned back and saw him looking at me in a way that made my stomach flutter. "I'm sorry," he whispered, frowning. "I'm sorry I couldn't save you back then."

"Callan." I relaxed in his grip. "It wasn't your fault. There was nothing that you could have done."

"I could have gotten to you faster."

"You would just have ended up hurt." I smiled. "The fact that you care is enough for me."

It was more than anything he had ever shown me in the past. Callan often got angry, he often said things to purposely push people, and he was quick to make judgements. But he never shunned me like Eduard did when I had an outburst in public. He had always been up front with me about his thoughts on my behaviour. However, he had never been friendly enough to show a single hint that he cared.

Callan frowned. "That is not the point."

"Isn't it? It's not like you directly got me killed; you didn't stab me with your sword." I smiled hesitantly, rubbing my chest where the scar remained from that very act.

"I would never do such a thing." Callan scowled.

"Wouldn't you?" I couldn't help it; I knew those were words I shouldn't say, but they tumbled out before I could stop them.

"Lynette." Callan dropped my hand. "That isn't funny."

"Is it not? But you found it fun to tell Roger I stole Mother's necklace, didn't you?"

"Lynette, what does that have to do with anything?" Callan raised his voice as he glared.

Vishka's Guidance System
Callan Heversham
Likeability: –8% (–13%)

I glanced at the box as the amount it had risen drastically fell.

"It has everything to do with my life." I could feel my face contorting into a malicious look.

What am I doing? Why can't I stop?

"Are you seriously spouting such nonsense?" Callan growled, his number blurring again.

"Of course." I smirked. "It was that day I first received rotten food. It was that very day that Roger lost his respect for me. It was that very day that my truths became dirt. It was that very day that I learned I could not trust you."

Callan paled as he looked at me wide-eyed. His body stilled as he opened his mouth like a fish.

"Lynette . . . I—I didn't realise . . ." Callan paused as he took in my expression.

"No. I suppose you didn't." I smiled viciously. My emotions about my mistreatment balled up inside me as I saw his pained eyes. I could see his regret, his anguish at learning the truth of his actions.

But I did not care. Not at this moment.

"Lynette." Callan croaked a little as he swallowed. "I'm, I'm so sorry."

"Yes. Well. It is enough for me to know you cared about my life at least once." I abruptly turned away from him, afraid he would see the tears in my eyes.

Haven't I cried enough today?

"Lynette!" Callan called as I walked away down the hill.

I had never confronted Callan in any of my lives; I had always been too afraid.

This time, I could not have stopped my bubbling emotions as they erupted out of the cage I had hidden them within.

My feet carried me faster down the hill as I wiped my wet cheeks with the back of my hand. I did not dare to look back at Callan as he called after me. His voice drifted against the wind the farther away I walked until it faded against the roar of the ocean waves.

My chest stung, my stomach clenching in a knotted mess.

I had not intended to have that conversation.

Not now, not here.

It was like I had vomited the words up uncontrollably. I hadn't been able to stop once I started.

Callan had been trying to do something nice, an act within itself foreign to me. He had shown me the ocean, something I had never thought I would see. Why? Why did he suddenly care enough to do something like that? Why did he not ever show such effort in my previous lives?

Why now?

I clenched my fists as my heart quickened.

What made him suddenly show any semblance of care? Did it really take my supposed death for him to notice me? Or was it just his guilt over seeing me "die" that made him care?

I reached our makeshift camp and immediately headed for my tent. My stride must have been strange as Teresa frowned up at me from her seat near the fire. I flashed her a weak smile before ripping the tent flap open to hide away.

I did not want to deal with anyone.

I wanted to be alone.

I sat on the hard stone ground beneath the thin material of the tent floor and hugged my legs close. I hadn't checked Callan's meter before I left. It had probably dropped even further than it had during our conversation.

I sighed and tucked my head into my knees, strands of black hair that had escaped from its tie tickling my face. That day, if Callan hadn't told Roger Heversham that blatant lie about Cassandra's necklace, I might have had a different life. Roger might have trusted my words more. But, instead, I was branded a liar.

The ball in my throat that I had held back released its grip. I quietly allowed my tears to soak into the material of my trousers as I muffled my sobs.

I sat waving my legs, watching the chess game on the table before me. A gentle hand rustled my hair, and I looked up at a woman's smile, her pale grey eyes glistening.

"Now, Callan, are you trying to lose?" she said, tucking her hand around my waist as I sat on her lap. Her ash blond hair, neatly contained in a decorated hair net, did not move as she shook her head at the young boy across from us.

"I'm trying not to! You are just too good at this game, Mother." Callan scrunched up his face as he pondered his next move.

"Oh? Is it not that you want to let me win?" Cassandra teased with amusement. "What would you suggest he should do, Lynette?"

"Me?" I asked, blinking in surprise.

"Yes, my dear, what would you do?"

"I doubt she can beat you," Callan grumbled, crossing his arms as he bit the inside of his cheek.

I looked at the chessboard and contemplated what Cassandra had taught me about the game. It was a game of wit and cunning, she had told me. The goal was to predict your opponent's moves and outmanoeuvre them to capture their king.

I puzzled over the board, then hesitantly raised my arm towards the rook. "I would move this here." I shuffled the piece across the board.

"Well done, Lynette! You have blocked my attempt to steal his queen." Cassandra beamed at me, making me blush at her compliment. I turned to Callan, excited to be able to help my brother, but paused as he glared at the rook, rubbing his chin.

"I could have done that," he said with a huff. "Still didn't take your king, though."

"I have no doubt." Cassandra chuckled. "You are both excellent, as expected of my children." She shifted her legs and removed her hand from my waist as she reached for her neck.

"As a reward, I want you to have this, Lynette." Cassandra unclasped her necklace and pushed it into my hands.

"Mother!" Callan protested. "That is your favourite necklace."

"Yes, and now it shall be Lynette's." Cassandra's gaze made me clutch it tightly. I had never received jewellery before. Cassandra had saved me from starvation; she had clothed me and given me a home and a family. I looked up at the object of my affection and felt warm.

"Are you sure, Mother? You have already given me so much," I said hesitantly, opening my hand to give it back. I did not want to take more from her. This surely should not be mine but Kara's.

"It is yours now, dear." She wrapped my hand back around it.

"Why does she get your necklace?" Callan muttered as his image blurred.

The room changed, and Cassandra and Callan faded away, the study warping in my vision.

My purple walls encased me as I sat alone on the four-poster bed of my room. Unable to touch the floor, my feet hung limply as I clutched a necklace in my small hands.

Cassandra's necklace.

It felt cold in my hands, the delicate metal worn from age. It was all I had left of her. Kara would inherit her dresses and other valuable jewellery. Eduard and Callan inherited her jians and a ring each for their future brides.

I tucked it to my chest, wrapping my hand around the emerald setting. Cassandra's final gift to me before she left on her trip, before she died.

"Where is it?" a voice boomed, jolting me as the door to my room was thrown open. Roger stood in the doorframe as he looked around.

"Father?" I asked, standing up, keeping Cassandra's keepsake close.

"Where is it, Lynette?" Roger's hands shook as he rushed to my dressing table, picking up my jewellery box.

"Where is what, Father?" I asked again as he emptied its contents and began

to rifle through the few belongings I had. Finally, he picked up the bracelet I had brought with me, glancing at its black onyx gems before putting it back down.

"Cassandra's necklace, Lynette; I can't find it." Roger slumped to his knees as his voice shook. My chest clamped as I saw his distress, his sadness.

"I—I have it, Father." I gingerly walked over to him and opened my hands to show him Cassandra's necklace. Roger's eyes watered as he reached out for it, gently taking it from me as he studied it, relieved.

"I thought I had lost it," he breathed, stroking the emerald longingly.

"Mother gave it to me before . . ." I couldn't finish my words as his sadness ignited my own grief.

"She did?" Roger glumly answered, reluctantly offering it back.

"No." A voice at the door made us both look at Callan with similar frowns.

"What do you mean, no?" Roger tensed, pulling back his hand, his grip tightening on the necklace.

"Mother did not give Lynette her necklace." Callan directed his grey eyes away from me as I froze at his words.

"Callan—" I exclaimed in shock. "But you were there!" I did not understand why he was saying this.

"Lynette, is this true? Did you take Cassandra's necklace from her room?" Roger's voice hardened as he stood, his tall frame towering above mine.

"It's not true! I swear Mother gifted it to me!" My heart raced in panic.

"Then why does Callan say otherwise?" Roger looked at us both, his brows drawing a line.

"I—I don't know! Mother gave it to me when we were playing chess!" I could feel wetness crawling down my cheeks as my vision blurred.

"Callan?" Roger looked at his son, knowing he and Cassandra often played together.

"I do not know what she is talking about." Callan pinched his lips together.

Roger's glare pierced my small body as he lifted the necklace and placed it into his pocket. "Lying and theft are not condoned in this house, Lynette." His voice held such anger that I shook, stepping back from the man and rage I had never seen before.

"I will forgive this transgression once, Lynette. Do not lie to me again." He narrowed his eyes.

"But—but—that's—that's not true!" I stumbled on my words as I reached out after his back.

"Come, Callan." Roger stormed past my brother and into the hallway.

"Callan!" I pleaded to the boy in my doorframe, his light brown hair cut short, but received only a look of conflict as he closed my door.

Leaving me alone, without my only keepsake.

CHAPTER THIRTY-TWO

I awoke with Teresa's legs sprawled out over mine in our tent. A faint smile graced my lips as she responded with a snort to my movement. It had become a familiar sight to wake up like this over the past few weeks. Teresa had a habit of moving in her sleep, and with such a small tent she often ended up like this. Carefully, I extricated myself from her and slipped out of my bedroll.

The sun peeked through the tent's fabric, casting a warm glow inside. I stretched my limbs, feeling the soreness from yesterday's emotional turmoil and physical exertion. It had been a restless night, burdened by the weight of my past. Seeing Cassandra again, even if only in my dreams, was difficult.

As I made my way towards the tent entrance, I hesitated, glancing back at Teresa, still lost in slumber. She had become a comforting presence in my life, offering solace and understanding when I needed it the most. Last night, she had found me in my misery, without questioning me, simply embracing me as we fell asleep together. I silently appreciated her friendship, feeling warmth in my heart before finally stepping outside.

The camp was awakening, with scattered voices and the aroma of breakfast permeating the air. I took a deep breath, attempting to clear my mind and find a sense of calm amidst the chaos that plagued me. I needed to gather my thoughts and find a way to move forward from the events of yesterday. I should have known better than to let my emotions get the best of me.

I walked towards the communal fire, which was currently unoccupied, unlike some of the others. A group of trainees had gathered nearby, exchanging morning greetings and sipping mugs of hot tea. I found a spot by our fire and sat down, relishing the coolness of the morning air against my skin.

Harold and Garret had yet to awaken, their tent filled with the familiar sound of Garret's snores. I pursed my lips as his guttural noise reminded me of our past together. I often lost rest when he stayed in my room during my marriage. I hoped Harold was a heavy sleeper.

I picked up my abandoned metal cup from the ground, which I had left there the previous night when Callan came to fetch me. I placed a pot over the fire and poured in some water to boil.

Returning to my spot, I gazed into the flickering flames, their dance captivating me as I lost myself in contemplation.

Memories and unanswered questions swirled in my mind, tormenting me. How had things come to this? How had my relationship with Callan become so strained, burdened with resentment and mistrust? I still couldn't understand why he had lied that day. I couldn't recall what I might have done as a child to provoke such a response from him.

Prior to Cassandra's death, I had always believed we were growing closer as siblings.

What had I missed? Or was it simply my childhood naïveté?

Lost in these thoughts, I let my gaze wander to the cliff concealing the ocean. The rhythmic crashing of the waves against the shore seemed to echo the turmoil within me. I wondered if the answers to my questions lay hidden somewhere, much like the ocean behind the cliff.

A yawn broke through my reverie, and I turned to find Teresa sitting beside me, a concerned expression etched on her face. She placed a gentle hand on my shoulder, offering support. I appreciated her presence.

"How are you feeling?" she whispered, her voice soft. "We didn't really talk last night."

"I'm all right." I forced a smile as my thoughts continued to swirl. "At least, I will be."

"Did you have a fight with Callan?"

"Yes," I sighed. "It was unexpected."

"I'm sorry." Teresa squeezed my shoulder, her blue eyes meeting mine. "I often have arguments with my mother; it's never easy when it's family."

"Thanks," I muttered, my lip twitching numbly. I highly doubted her arguments with her mother were anything like my family's conflicts. Her mother loved her.

"If there's anything I can do, just ask." Teresa nudged her shoulder against mine with a cheery smile. "I don't want you to be trapped in your thoughts alone. That's not good for anyone." Her eyes flickered for a moment, a hint of strain evident. "I know what that can do to a person."

"Your father?" I inquired.

"Yeah." Teresa slumped. "It's hard to just let go, you know?"

"I understand," I replied, leaning my head against hers as she tucked her chin close. Teresa must have had as many burning questions about her father as I did about Callan's actions.

We sat together in comfortable silence, waiting for the water to boil. Then, as it started to bubble, a soft thud made us look up to see our visitor.

"Look at you two getting cosy." Rian raised an eyebrow, her hands on her hips. Her brown hair was neatly braided, and her limp was no longer apparent. Though her trousers were still ripped, I could see that her leg injury had healed.

"It's called friendship." Teresa rolled her eyes. "What brings you here? Don't you have noble stuff to attend to?"

"Noble stuff? Really?" Rian shook her head. "I came to check on Lynette." She picked up our boiling pot and poured herself some water before offering it to us. We extended our cups, and she filled them before sitting down next to me.

"How are you?" Rian blew on the steam billowing from her cup, adding a sprinkle of tea leaves into the brew and swishing it around.

"Recovered and back to my normal self," I replied, mixing in some of my own tea and offering some to Teresa, knowing she had run out.

"That's a relief." Rian sipped her tea. "Sorry, I wasn't there when Lord Azriel released you. Albertine wouldn't let me wait." She frowned. "She fusses too much."

"It's all right, Rian," I reassured her, taking a sip of the warm tea. "I appreciate your concern, but I understand that Lady Albertine was just looking out for you."

Rian nodded with a grateful smile. "She has always been like that, a bit overprotective. I swear getting her to go back to her own team was a nightmare."

Teresa spoke up, her voice filled with curiosity. "So, how did your encounter with the Lord Azriel go? Did he say anything significant?"

I hesitated for a moment, contemplating how much to share. Rian and Teresa were my friends, and that in itself was new territory for me. I hadn't told Teresa about Kuru yet; after Zachary's warning, I had been unsure about mentioning it.

"It was a conversation regarding my ability to ride kreshna," I began, choosing my words carefully. "Lord Azriel wants me to demonstrate when we reach the capital."

"You can ride kreshna?" Teresa's eyes widened in excitement as Rian drew her eyebrows together.

"It was an interesting experience, to say the least," Rian said.

"Wait, you rode one too?" Teresa exclaimed, looking between us. "No fair!"

"A horse is far more comfortable." Rian absently rubbed her lower back, making me smile.

"Certainly, I imagine a horse is faster, too." I chuckled, knowing Rian was probably thinking about how the grooves on a kreshna's back made for a sore rear.

"Can I ride one too?" Teresa eagerly looked at me, and I felt a small pang at her excitement.

"I don't know. Rian could because I was there with her." I patted Teresa's knees, and her eyes dimmed.

"About that," Rian began, her voice cautious. "It's why I wanted to see you last night, Lynette, but you were already asleep when I came."

"Ah, sorry, I retired early." I meekly tucked a strand of hair behind my ear. I had forgotten she had wanted to speak with me.

"I told you Lynette was tired," Teresa mumbled, looking away from Rian.

"Yes, I know," Rian sighed, looking around us before huddling a little closer and lowering her voice.

"I have never heard of anyone being able to ride a kreshna before," Rian said, her expression serious. "Subservient demonic beasts can be domesticated enough for us to use them as labour. But it is unusual that you were able to get one to trust you enough to let you ride it, especially a wild kreshna." Rian pressed her lips together. "Lynette, what you did has never happened in any recorded book. Demonic beasts have never been tamed to the point that they allow a rider. People have attempted to have the small, cute ones as pets, but it never works out. They are wild, dangerous creatures made of condensed aether."

Rian's words resonated with me as I tightened my grip around my metal cup.

"You know, now that I think about it, my uncle is a stable hand. He has a scar on his right arm from a kreshna," Teresa mused. "He always told me to stay away from them without proper training or something. Even the domesticated ones can be dangerous."

"Yes." Rian nodded. "That's why nobles don't use them, as we have the luxury of using horses."

"Am I that strange?" I asked, my voice a little hollow. I thought maybe my beast-taming skill was just rare, but if what Rian said was true, then it might not exist in any records. Why did I have such an ability? Just who . . . what was I?

Rian's gaze softened as she looked at me, understanding evident in her eyes. She reached out and gently squeezed my hand.

"Lynette, you're not strange," Rian reassured me. "You're unique, but you have to be careful because of that. We don't know the full extent of your abilities or their meaning, but it doesn't make you any less than who you are."

Teresa nodded, her expression filled with empathy. "Rian is right. You must have a special connection with kreshna, and it's incredible. It's something to be proud of."

"It doesn't change that fact you are still the Crazy Cerue Lady." Rian smirked playfully, nudging my shoulder, making me smile.

"No, I guess not." I laughed, leaning back on my hands.

I took a deep breath, absorbing their words of support and encouragement.

Their unwavering belief in me warmed my heart and helped ease some of the self-doubt creeping within me.

"Thank you, both of you," I said. "I'm still trying to understand it all, but having you by my side means a lot."

Rian smiled, her eyes slanting. "We'll figure it out together, Lynette. You're not alone in this."

Teresa nodded enthusiastically. "Absolutely! We're your friends, and we'll support you no matter what."

Feeling their unwavering kindness, I couldn't help but smile back at them. The weight of uncertainty lifted slightly, knowing that I had friends who accepted me for who I was, strange abilities and all. It was something I had never had.

"Thank you," I repeated, my voice filled with sincerity. "I'm grateful to have both of you in my life." I really meant it. As much as Rian and I might have been at odds in the past, I had never had anyone I considered myself close to in my life.

Who knew it would only take surviving the highlands together to patch our fractured relationship?

Rian raised her cup, and Teresa and I followed suit, clinking our cups together in a silent toast. As we sipped our tea, a sense of camaraderie enveloped us, strengthening our bond.

At that moment, I realised that despite the challenges and mysteries Vishka had placed on me, I wasn't alone. With Rian and Teresa by my side, maybe I wouldn't have to face this life suffering alone.

Together, maybe I could survive this life. I had always been alone in my past lives; maybe that was where I was going wrong. I took another sip of my tea, savouring the warmth that spread through me, both from the drink and from the budding friendship that surrounded me.

CHAPTER THIRTY-THREE

Rian stayed with us as we cooked our breakfast. She surprised Teresa and me with some of the meat she had saved from the agiluf. Teresa's joy over being able to eat meat that wasn't charred was obvious as I excitedly showed her my new cooking skill. Rian taught Teresa as she had done for me, and we both congratulated her when Teresa gleefully pumped the air at gaining the skill for herself.

The smell of our cooking drew Harold and Garret from their slumber, and they joined us around the fire and partook in some of the shared offerings. As the sun rose higher in the sky, Rian eventually left our group to rejoin her own as the camp began to pull down their tents.

Harold helped Teresa and me as we doused the fire and packed away our things, preparing for our daily march. Garret didn't really say much to us, choosing to avoid us for the most part as he packed. I did notice his occasional glare towards Teresa, however, and reminded myself to keep an eye on that. Garret was a man who held grudges, and I feared that his conflict with Teresa might worsen.

"Since when did you and Lady Rian become close?" Teresa asked as she stuffed the metal cooking pot into my backpack. "I thought you didn't get along, you know, from her comments to you back in Talbour."

"Oh," I said, a little taken aback. "It sort of just happened." I smiled, adjusting the straps on my shoulders.

"That's great." Teresa grinned. "I wish that would happen to me with the others from Ingalham." She sighed dramatically as she stepped beside me. "Lady Rian seems nice."

"They will come around." I patted her back reassuringly. "How could they not once you show them how great you are?"

"Oh, they don't know what they're missing." Teresa wiggled her eyebrows, and we both burst out into laughter as we fell into position for the march.

Harold stood on my right and Teresa on my left as we lined up at the front. Garret shuffled in beside Harold as the other trainees began to line up behind us. I flashed Rian a smile as she stood behind me with Lacey Weadall and Kit Balburn, along with their fourth member, Lord Caspian. The second group of trainees mirrored our lineup as the commoners without cores stumbled into place. They looked ragged compared to our group, their skin rough and eyes filled with a determination I hadn't seen in many of the nobles. They must have struggled on this march; unlike many of the nobles here, I doubted they would have had much prior training, much like me.

Lieutenant Cragborn was over to our left, a little distance away with Lieutenant Sharpclaw. They were discussing something, and from the look of Lieutenant Cragborn's features, it was a serious conversation.

A small bump on my side brought my attention to Teresa as she nodded to something over my shoulder. I turned and immediately grimaced as my eyes met Callan's staring at me.

He stood with his group, but he ignored them as they prepared for their guard of us trainees. A mixture of emotions played across his face—regret, hesitation, and perhaps a hint of longing. I blinked, my breath catching in my throat as I saw the box above his head.

Vishka's Guidance System
Callan Heversham
Likeability: 10% (+18%)

I quickly broke away from his gaze, pinching my lips together. I did not want to talk to him, not yet. It didn't matter if his opinion of me had improved. I had pushed back my pain from his betrayal in every life, swallowing it deep down into a pit of acceptance and resentment. I had wanted to pretend it had never happened; I had wanted to forget about my bitterness over losing Cassandra's keepsake. It was all I could do, as no one had ever believed the truth of the matter. It had become pointless to address it, especially when I only saw Callan for a few weeks a year.

Yet trying to ignore it for so long had only hurt me more.

I wasn't ready to forgive him. I didn't know if I even could. It was plenty that he no longer hated me enough for my life to be at risk.

"Trainees." Lieutenant Cragborn approached, commanding our attention. We all straightened our posture and saluted with our fists over our chests.

"Lieutenant," we all called in unison, greeting him as he stood in front of us, his red eyes roaming across our formation.

"Today, it is our turn to install the deterrent device. I assume you know what that is?" he said, and many people nodded, but a few looked puzzled. I felt my fingers curl around my backpack strap; I had heard of those. They were designed to repel demonic beasts.

"What do they teach youth these days?" the lieutenant muttered quietly so only those close to him could hear. "As part of the yearly expedition to the dead-lands, it is the army's duty to maintain the deterrent devices that keep these paths safe for merchants and travellers. In our journey, we have come across demonic beasts purely because these devices have been drained since our last visit. Each section of our brigade takes turns refuelling the devices as we march. Now it is our turn," he explained in a bored tone. "Lieutenant Sharpclaw has the device. I want you all to watch as part of your education as trainees. Come." He swiftly turned and headed towards Lieutenant Sharpclaw, and we followed.

The muscular beast-kin stood at the centre of the two trainee groups, hold-ing a large metallic contraption. The device looked like a combination of a vase and an intricate sculpture. Metal tubes extended from it, and a dull, pale white glow emanated from the centre.

"Trainees, gather around!" Lieutenant Cragborn called out, his voice resonat-ing with authority. We formed a semicircle around Lieutenant Sharpclaw, our eyes fixed on the device.

"This is the deterrent device," Lieutenant Sharpclaw began, his voice sharp and authoritative as one of his brown furry ears twitched. "It harnesses the power of aether to create a barrier that repels demonic beasts. As we march, summoners are responsible for refuelling these devices, ensuring the safety of the path."

"Don't demonic beasts consume aether?" a commoner asked from the second group as he leaned closer to get a better look.

"Yes," Lieutenant Sharpclaw answered. "Demonic beasts consume the aether of other living creatures. However, when aether has left the vessel of our cores, it cannot be consumed, but it can be harnessed," he explained. "Summoners chan-nel their aether through their cores, which can then be used to generate powerful attacks or, in this case, fuel the deterrent device, reinforcing the barrier it creates and ensuring its effectiveness."

"How does it work?" the same commoner asked with bright eyes as he looked towards Lieutenant Sharpclaw with reverence. The commoner's scraggy grey tail swished under his black cloak, and a small smile broke on my face. This young boy clearly idolised Lieutenant Sharpclaw, a fellow beast-kin.

"This particular deterrent device creates a focused barrier of aether at a dis-tance of about two hundred and forty-five thousand feet. The barrier blocks demonic beasts by sending out a charge that repels them. As the aether is drained, the barrier size diminishes, as this one has. Currently, this device is only able to deter a demonic beast from five feet."

The commoner gasped as his eyes widened. The barrier right now would barely reach past Lieutenant Sharpclaw. No wonder we had come across a grade-seven demonic beast if the deterrent devices were that weak.

Was this normal to let them drain so much?

"Unfortunately, because of a unprecedented delay in the deadlands, our scheduled return has caused them to diminish to this state. Teams are assigned to refuel them most of the year, so usually they are not so depleted by the time the brigade gets to them." Lieutenant Cragborn answered my thoughts as a look of hesitation crossed many of the trainees' faces.

"With our delay, it was too dangerous to send a team alone to refuel them after the capital received word." Lieutenant Sharpclaw rubbed his growing stubble with a hand that had sharpened nails.

Coming across the grade-seven beast would have certainly been too much for one team of four to handle.

"Now observe closely," Lieutenant Cragborn interjected, his voice cutting through the murmurs. "Summoners, step forward and demonstrate the refuelling process."

I stilled as Callan's group moved to the forefront. His grey eyes caught me for a moment before he refocused on the deterrent device. His team surrounded the device as Lieutenant Sharpclaw placed it on the ground and stepped away. With practised precision, they raised their hands above the device and took deep breaths, centring their bodies to a calm stillness.

Felicity, the earth summoner on Callan's team, then moved her hands, controlling the ground to rise beneath the device, lifting it to waist height. The fire summoner—Corporal Cavendish, I had heard Lieutenant Cragborn call him— then hardened his expression and flexed his fingers.

I wonder if he is related to Captain Cavendish who I met at Azriel's tent?

"Together." Corporal Cavendish nodded to his team, and they leaned back on their left legs, extending their right hands towards the device.

All of their hands began to glow the colour of their affinity. Aether strands leaked from the skin on their palms, drifting towards the device. The pale white centre of the device flashed suddenly, and I had to shield my eyes. The trainees mumbled in shock, blinking away the disorientation; my eyes widened at the four summoners around the device.

The aether from the summoners was being sucked rapidly from them. Callan's expression strained as the flow of aether increased from his palm, and his arm began to shake. The wind summoner began to sweat, his light blond hair tied at the nape of his neck. Felicity adjusted her position as she fell forward a little, and Corporal Cavendish stared at the device as he fiercely concentrated.

The pale glow at the centre of the device brightened as more aether was sucked in. The light thrummed as it expanded, filling the diameter of the device until it flashed again. I squinted at the brightness, afraid of missing anything if I looked away again.

All four of the summoners dropped their hands, their breath heavy as their shoulders heaved, stepping away from the device. Strained, Felicity pulled her arm back and, in a quick motion, lowered the ground pillar, dragging the device deep beneath the earth and burying it.

"That, trainees, was aether transference. One of the first skills I will be teaching those of you with the talent to become summoners." Lieutenant Cragborn scanned our group with a thin lip.

"Remember, trainees, this is an essential part of a summoner's duty," Lieutenant Sharpclaw said, walking over to Callan's group. "The upkeep of the deterrent devices is crucial for maintaining the safety of Zopan and protecting those who travel through these lands." Callan's group lined up in front of the lieutenant.

Lieutenant Sharpclaw raised his hands, and they glowed red, his aether forming into strands and spreading out onto Callan's group, sinking into their skin as he replenished them. It was the same as when Zachary had restored Lorand when I had stayed with Eduard's camp.

"As you progress in your training, you will learn more about the intricacies of aether manipulation and how to wield its power effectively," Lieutenant Cragborn elaborated. "If you do not master this skill, you are unqualified to become summoners."

I heard a few of the trainees gulp around me.

So did those who couldn't master the skill end up becoming monks at temples?

I looked at Teresa and grimaced as she paled, sharing my trepidation. My core was almost nonexistent; I could only produce one mote of aether. There was no way I could produce what was needed for maintaining a deterrent device. The gathering technique Albus had given me hadn't improved my ability as I had hoped.

"Now come. We should be arriving at the capital in just over a week. Then we can begin your training." Lieutenant Cragborn directed us back to our position within the brigade as we awaited the horn to signal the march.

We all quickly stood a little taller, a sense of responsibility settling upon my shoulders. The realisation of what it meant to become a summoner weighed on my mind. It was more than just gaining strength to protect myself. If I followed this path, I would be held liable as a safeguard for the Zopan Empire and its people. I would have a duty to follow that was greater than my own survival.

I had always known that the army was the safeguard of Zopan. I had been warned as much by General Saika that we could not refuse if called upon. I thought that just meant engaging with demonic beasts. Clearly, there was more responsibility than I knew.

My life as a civilian had never borne such weight.

The horn blasted from the front of the brigade, and Lieutenant Cragborn commanded us to move. We trainees moved forward; my steps were filled with determination, and a newfound appreciation for summoners settled in my heart.

CHAPTER THIRTY-FOUR

After the deterrent device demonstration, the march did not seem as difficult. We marched for a week and a day into a changing landscape. We rose higher as the ground rounded from the flat highlands. The air was thinner, and I found myself gasping for heavier breaths to replenish my oxygen. Garret stumbled on a jutted rock, cursing as Harold helped him back to his feet, keeping him in line with our team. After our scheduled rest for lunch, we slowed our pace as the climb became more straining on our thighs.

Eventually, we reached the peak separating the highlands landscape from the view of the capital. We all paused as the city came into view; it was still far away, but we could see the grand stone walls blockading the structures within.

Two large towers loomed on either side of a narrow strip of land surrounded by water. To the right of the towers was the vast ocean, its waves thumping against the cliffs and dripping onto beaches of yellow sand at the base. Teresa gasped as she saw the sparkle of the waves in the afternoon sun. She grabbed my hand and excitedly pointed to a boat bobbing on its surface.

On the left of the towers was more water. This stretch of blue was still and calm as it basked in the sun, gently reflecting a gleam of turquoise. It was Oran Lake; I had read about it in books, but I had never imagined it being so large. I could not see the other side of it.

As we stood there, admiring the breathtaking view, Lieutenant Cragborn snapped at us for stopping. Reluctantly, we tore our gaze away from the captivating sight and resumed our trek towards the capital. We quickly continued behind the lieutenant as the path led us downhill, winding through large rocks and pebbled ground. The air grew cooler as we descended, providing some relief from the sun's heat. I almost slipped at the angle at which we walked, grabbing Teresa for support as she helped me past a rather tricky dip in the ground.

The scent of the ocean mingled with a smell of manure as we neared the edges of a stretch of farmland at the base of the cliff. As in Talbour, farms sprouted in well-maintained fields outside the capital's walls. Golden heads of wheat gently swayed in the wind, and green leaves fanned in rows of vegetables on neighbouring fields. I could see small cottages in the distance and blobs of movement in the fields as farmers tended to their crops.

Teresa and I walked side by side, occasionally exchanging words in hushed tones. I could tell she was still captivated by the view of the capital and the vastness of Oran Lake. I shared in her awe, but my mind was also filled with thoughts of Callan. His presence to our left stirred up conflicting emotions within me, and I couldn't shake the feeling of uncertainty.

Throughout our march, I felt his burning gaze at the back of my head. It was difficult not to look his way, and I had been tempted too many times. I had actively avoided him since our last conversation, choosing the safety of my tent when I saw him approach. So far, my hiding method had been successful.

We halted at the foot of the cliff as the brigade began to fan out at the edge of the farmlands. The horn blasted as the last of the summoners in the rear guard descended, signalling the end of the day's journey. As per our routine, we quickly set up camp at our designated spot for trainees. Tents were erected, and we hurriedly organised for the night, gathering flufftoru for the fire and laying out our bedrolls. The fatigue of the day's march weighed heavily on our bodies. However, our increase in stamina released much of the exhaustion we had experienced when we first began the march. Teresa and Harold were still perky with energy and eager to continue training.

Settling on a spot near the fire alone, choosing to rest instead, I held up my palm. "Sign."

Blood Sign			
General Information		**Progression**	
Name:	Lynette Heversham	**Core Innate Grade:**	0.02
Age:	21	**Core Condensation Grade:**	0.02
Rank:	Daughter of Viscount—Talbour	**Affinities:**	Unknown
Traits:	Beast Born (Hidden)		
Occupation:	Trainee of Zopan Empire Army		

Covenants:	Zopan Empire Army Blood Bond: *Guidance of Vishka (Hidden):* Knowledge of Albus		
Skills			
Aether:	1	**Spirit:**	1
	One with All—Gathering: 1 (Novice)		Beast Taming: 3 (Novice) (Hidden)
Combative:	2	**General:**	1
	Jian—Flowing Water: 6 (Novice)		Social: 1 (Novice) (Hidden)
	Dagger Strike: 12 (Initiate)		Cooking: 2 (Novice)
Body:	3		
	Poison Resistance: 15 (Initiate)		
	Pain Resistance: 25 (Apprentice)		
	Stamina: 14 (Initiate)		
Mind:	3		
	Research: 12 (Initiate)		
	Herbology: 57 (Adept)		
	Alchemy: 7 (Novice)		

I was pleasantly surprised that my social skill had increased. Maybe it had done so during my conversation with Rian and Teresa this morning. I smiled, turning the spoon in the pot above the fire, preventing the rice from sticking to the metal. I was improving my skills, albeit slowly.

"You gained the cooking skill, I see, Lady Lynette." Garret approached, standing opposite me against the fire, instantly making my smile drop.

"Yes, Lady Rian was kind enough to teach me," I replied, rolling my eyes at his twitching smirk. Teresa had been the one cooking since the deterrent device as I was often in our tent instead.

"Hmm, I will have to thank her. A wife who can cook is welcome in my household." He stared at me with an expression that made me flinch. His eyes sharpened as he moved past the flames gracefully, his hands behind his back, towards me. "We will be reaching the capital soon," Garret said, sitting beside me.

"Yes. I am very much looking forward to civilisation," I said, inching away from him. I was excited to finally having a bath.

"As am I. Your blood contract can be revoked, and I can take you home to Talbour. Now that the deterrent devices have been refuelled, our journey shall be pleasant in comparison to this farce of a march." Garret ignored my intention to increase my distance from him and instead closed the gap between us. I frowned at his hands as he rested them on his knees.

"I find myself repeating these words, Lord Garret. I will not marry you, or be returning to Talbour."

"Then I shall repeat my own words back to you." Garret snatched my wrist, and I felt my heart quicken as he dragged me close. My skin crawled like a thousand ants were running up my arms at his touch.

"You are mine," Garret sneered in a hushed tone. His breath blew against my cheek as he leaned towards my ear.

I tried to pull away from Garret's grasp, my heart pounding in my chest as visions of his beatings flooded my mind. My chest tightened as I tried to hide my quickening breath, but the tremble of my hand was impossible to stop.

No, I need to keep calm.

"I am no one's," I said, my voice hitching slightly. "I have made my intentions clear, and I will not be forced into a marriage or taken back to Talbour against my will."

"Oh? You forget, Lady Lynette. You have no control over that decision." Garret's grip on my wrist tightened, his fingers digging into my skin. A sharp pain shot through my arm. I winced but refused to let him see the extent of my discomfort. "Don't think that Lord Nathaniel will protect you. What does the son of a marquess care about a girl like you? You are nothing, just a girl he used and threw away. You are far better off with me. I am offering you a life of luxury, and you dare to reject it?"

I tried to steady myself, but my stomach flipped at his words as fear surged throughout me. So I had created a scandal with the son of a marquess?

No wonder Nathaniel had told me that things might be complicated now that I was coming to the capital.

"Why do you care?" I swallowed my hasty reply. "Why do you try to force my hand like this?"

"Because I always get what I want," Garret spat, his eyes burning with a mixture of arrogance and frustration.

I remembered his beatings, his obsession with gaining power that did not belong to a baron. Garret had always been a man who tried to appear more than he was. He relished having others to tower over, and he despised his lack of superiority in noble society. Fear mingled with anger within me as I looked into his brown eyes in defiance.

I will not go through life with this man, not again.

"Your obsession with control is your own downfall, Lord Garret," I said through gritted teeth, trying to maintain my composure. "You may think you hold power over me because of an agreement with Viscount Heversham, but I will not surrender my freedom so easily. Your promises of luxury mean nothing to me when they come at the cost of having a man like you by my side."

Garret's face twisted with rage, his grip on my wrist growing even tighter. He grabbed my other hand, which was pushing against him. "You are mistaken, Lady Lynette. You belong to me, and I will ensure that you realise that."

A surge of desperation and panic rose within me as I recognised the look in his eyes. It was the same expression Garret wore when he was more than willing to force his way with me. I doubted he would do something like that here, but knowing that was his intention was enough.

My eyes darted across the camp towards Teresa, but she was far away, too far to take notice, as she was embroiled with Harold in their training. I tried to find Rian, but I could not see her camp; there was only one person I could think of who might be close enough. My panic led me towards Callan's team; they were a distance away, but I could see that they were chatting around their fire.

Of course, Callan's back was to us.

"Cal—" I tried to call, but Garret slammed his hand over my mouth, pulling my head down so the action was hidden between our huddled bodies. A surge of adrenaline coursed through my veins as fear exploded, fuelling my actions as I fought against his hold, desperately trying to break free.

He was too strong; he always had been.

With all of the strength I could muster, I bit down on Garret's hand, hoping to startle him enough to release me. He yelped in surprise but did not pull his hand away, glaring at me.

"Lady Lynette." He bared his teeth at me, keeping up his hushed tone. "Face your circumstances. You have no choice but to be mine. Your little stunt with Lord Nathaniel has not deterred me or your father. Your betrothal has already been agreed upon. Accept that, and I will treat you as a loving husband."

Loving husband, my ass.

His words rang hollow in my ears. I had already been down this road before, hoping for a loving and respectful marriage, only to be met with pain and abuse.

I refused to let my third life repeat itself.

With renewed determination, I glared at Garret, trying to pull his hand away from my mouth with the one he'd released, my nails digging into his skin, but he only tightened his grip on my wrist.

"Stop that," he gritted out. "I do not want to hurt you, Lady Lynette. There is no point in struggling like this. No one will believe you if you tell them." Garret grinned manically. "Who would believe the Crazy Cerue Lady over a trusted noble like me?"

His words made me pause my struggle.

Was he right?

My stomach numbed as I realised he probably was. Maybe Teresa and Rian would believe me, but the people who mattered, my brothers and Roger, they definitely wouldn't. They had never trusted me. They hadn't in my third life when I had tried to tell them what sort of man Garret Asher was.

I felt my strength wane.

Was I truly trapped in this marriage again?

"Good." Garret's grin widened as tears welled up in my eyes, and my struggle weakened. "Accept that you are mine." He revelled in his perceived victory, loosening his grip on my wrist.

No.

I refuse to marry this man.

Gathering all of my courage, I stomped hard on Garret's foot and bit harder into his hand. The pain rippled through my own foot as my teeth sank into his skin, but it was a small price to pay. Garret yelped but did not release me.

In desperation, I shifted my weight and lunged forward, catching him off guard. We tumbled, and he released his grasp on me. With a surge of energy, I stumbled away from him, gasping for breath.

"You underestimate me, Lord Garret." I shook, my legs carrying me away from him. "I may not have the support of my family or their trust, but I will not allow myself to be yours. I would rather die." I spat on the ground, clearing my mouth of Garret's blood.

Why not die again? It would be better than living with him.

Garret's nostrils flared as he glared at me with a mixture of anger and disbelief, clutching his injured hand and nursing his bruised foot. I could see the fury burning in his eyes, but I refused to back down.

"You will regret defying me, Lady Lynette," he growled, rising to stand.

"What's going on here?"

Startled, we both stilled, turning towards the source of the voice.

Callan stood a few paces away. His eyes narrowed with concern, and confusion was etched on his face. Relief washed over me, something I had never experienced when Callan appeared. Without a word, I threw myself towards him.

"Lady Lynette attacked me." Garret's voice rang out, and I froze.

The weight of the accusation hung in the air, threatening to crush me as Callan hardened his expression and glared.

CHAPTER THIRTY-FIVE

Callan's gaze shifted between Garret and me, a mix of surprise and anger. He narrowed his eyes as he took in my dishevelled hair and Garret's prone form nursing his injured hand.

Callan clenched the hilt of his jian as he stepped towards us.

"Callan, I can explain!" I stuttered as fear etched onto my heart. The box above his head blurred as Callan raised his hand to stop me from coming closer to him. He shot me a look with his grey eyes, and I pressed my lips together tightly.

"Lynette attacked you?" Callan's voice held a hint of scepticism as he focused his attention on Garret.

Garret nodded, his eyes fixed on me as he pushed up onto his feet. "Yes, Lady Lynette lunged at me out of nowhere. I was merely trying to get to know her better, as my fiancée."

I opened my mouth to speak, to defend myself against Garret's false claims, but the words caught in my throat. Callan met my eyes; uncertainty was evident in his gaze, and I slumped my shoulders.

The realisation struck me with a heavy blow—Garret was right.

Who would believe me over a trusted noble like him?

As far as anyone knew, Garret was a man of standing, with no rumours or unsightly behaviour in his past, unlike me. He knew well to keep his darkness hidden behind closed doors. The odds were stacked against me, and my own history further worked against my credibility. People believed I had attacked Rian as a child with a dagger, set fire to a commoner's stall, and engaged in questionable behaviour during social events. Of course, Callan wouldn't believe me over Garret.

Why would he?

Callan surveyed Garret, his grip on his jian tightening. He seemed to be assessing the situation, trying to make sense of the conflict before him. I could see the battle raging within him, torn between his trust in me and the doubts planted by Garret's words.

Garret took advantage of the silence and stepped closer to Callan, a self-assured smile on his face. "Lord Callan, I assure you, Lady Lynette is not men-tally secure at the moment. She's been playing a game with us all, manipulating situations for reasons I cannot fathom, even going so far as to involve Lord Nathaniel. I never expected her to resort to violence. I was merely trying to understand her better."

Callan's gaze hardened as Garret continued to weave his tale of deception. The doubt in his eyes seemed to grow, and I could sense his internal struggle intensifying.

Maybe he would believe me?

I mustered the courage to speak, my voice trembling with a mix of fear and desperation. "Callan, please, you have to believe me. Garret is twisting the truth to suit his own agenda. I would never attack him without reason."

Vishka's Guidance System
Callan Heversham
Likeability: 8% (−2%)

Callan's jaw tightened, his grip on his jian never wavering. Flashes of my second death coursed through my mind as I fixed my gaze on his hand holding the weapon.

Callan turned his attention back to me, his piercing eyes scrutinising my vulnerability.

"Lord Garret, on behalf of my sister, I apologise for any discomfort you may have experienced." Callan spoke through gritted teeth.

"Cal—" I tried to intervene, but Callan's glare silenced me.

"I implore you to forgive her on this occasion," Callan continued as Garret smirked at me, satisfied.

Callan's words pierced my heart like a dagger.

I couldn't believe what I was hearing.

How could he side with Garret, someone he barely knew, over his own sister? The pain and betrayal cut deep, and I struggled to hold back tears of frustration.

"Callan, you can't be serious," I pleaded, my voice trembling. Why had I even hoped he might believe me?

Of course, he wouldn't.

Garret, revelling in his victory, stepped even closer to Callan, a smug expression plastered across his face. "Lord Callan, your forgiveness and understanding are truly admirable. I am confident that once we are married, Lady Lynette will come to see the error of her ways and embrace her role as my wife."

Callan scrunched up his face, tightening his grip further on his jian. "If you will excuse me, Lord Garret, I will speak to Lynette regarding her behaviour."

"Of course, Lord Callan." Garret grinned. "Please do make sure she is well. I fear I may have hurt her when defending myself."

Callan's eyebrow twitched as he strode towards me. "Lynette, come with me," he muttered, grabbing my forearm.

I felt numb as Callan dragged me away from the camp into the darkness. I watched his back silently as he took me away from the brigade towards a small clearing empty of people.

What was Callan going to do?

What more was there to say to me?

He must have thought I was deplorable for attacking Garret. I was surprised he had kept so calm all this time.

Callan stopped when we reached a raised ridge of earth beside one of the wheat fields, releasing my arm. He turned towards me, his face filled with rage and a mix of other emotions.

I prepared myself for his anger.

"Lynette, why did you admit to attacking him?" Callan shouted, his voice filled with a mixture of frustration and disappointment. His words hit me like a slap, and I stumbled backwards at the intensity of his reaction.

"I . . . I didn't," I stammered, my voice barely a whisper.

"Yes, you did." Callan's features softened for a moment. "You said you wouldn't attack him without reason. In other words, you did attack him." He sighed, shaking his head.

"I was trying to defend myself! To tell you the truth, but you wouldn't listen!" I widened my eyes as Callan angrily huffed.

"I would have listened. Why do you think I came over?" Callan raised his hands, frustrated.

"Then why did you take Garret's side?" I clenched my fists as confusion swirled in my mind.

"Because," Callan began, looking at me hesitantly. "I did not want the situation to worsen. If Garret took it any further, then it would be his word over yours, and . . ." He paused, hesitantly glancing away. "You haven't exactly got a good track record."

"So what, you think I did attack him?" I crossed my arms over my chest, taking another step away from him. Of course, he would think that.

"That's not what I said." Callan frowned, his lips thinning as he looked at me, conflicted. "You know as well as I do there is no evidence for either side. I wanted to defuse the situation without risking you going to trial for attacking another noble. Lynette, will you tell me what happened?"

"What?"

Was he seriously asking me for my side of the event?

"Just tell me what happened. I want to hear your side." Callan looked uncomfortable as he shifted on his feet. "I want to listen."

I stared at Callan, a little shocked.

He wanted to listen to my side?

But Callan never cared for anything I had to say. He always assumed he knew the reasons for my actions and reacted based on his quick judgements. Not to mention . . . no one had ever asked me that before.

A lump suddenly formed in my throat. Tears welled up in my eyes as a mix of relief and disbelief washed over me. I had grown so accustomed to being dismissed by Callan, by everyone, that the idea of him actually wanting to hear my side of the story felt foreign, surreal.

Callan reached out towards me as I wiped away a stray tear, and I didn't flinch as he rested his hand on my shoulder, gently squeezing it.

"I know there is a lot I have to make up for, but—but let me try," Callan said with pursed lips.

I took a deep breath and tried to compose the swirl of emotions in the pit of my stomach.

"All right," I whispered, a faint thread of trust etching into my heart.

I might as well tell the truth.

What was there to lose at this point?

I explained how Garret had approached me, his attitude and actions towards me, my struggle to free myself from his grip, and my fear of his aggressive words. Callan's expression grew furious as I spoke, his grip on my shoulder tightening.

"That little son of—" Callan snarled as I finished. His reaction made my chest harden.

"Y-you believe me?" I asked, hesitant, and he released his hand. His eyes softened as he looked at me, his anger giving way to concern.

"Yes, Lynette, I want to believe you," Callan said earnestly. "I won't make the mistake of not trusting you again."

New tears swelled as he spoke.

Was this really happening?

"Why?" I asked, my disbelief still ricocheting through me.

Why was Callan like this?

Why did he believe me now of all times?

Callan stilled at my question. He reached for my hand, and I gingerly let him take it as his fingers inspected the growing bruise on my wrist.

"I didn't know what my lie about Mother's necklace did to you." His eyebrows drew close as his voice lowered.

"Why did you do it?" I whispered, wanting to know his reasoning more than anything. It had plagued me for three lifetimes. Maybe now, I could finally get answers.

"I—" Callan faltered as he looked up from my wrist, capturing my gaze in his grey eyes. "I was never happy Mother gave you her necklace. When I saw how grief-stricken Father was at her passing"—Callan sighed as his fingers moved from my wrist to my palm—"I wanted to lessen his grief, perhaps even mine."

His words hung heavy in the air as I struggled to process the weight of his confession.

Callan's actions had been the catalyst for my pain and suffering all these years, and yet here he was, admitting he had lied. It was a moment of vulnerability I had never witnessed from him before.

It was also oddly satisfying, hearing him finally admit it.

"I didn't consider what accusing you of stealing it would do," Callan continued, his voice tinged with regret. "I thought I was protecting Father. He would have given you something else of Mother's anyway. So what did it matter if you didn't have her necklace?" Callan laughed cynically and shook his head. "If I hadn't seen your plate before we left Talbour, I probably wouldn't have believed you on the cliff." He twitched his lip.

Right, he likely would have thought I was being dramatic.

"What you said—" Callan paused, his hand tightening for a moment around my wrist. "It was foolish of me to think that accusing you would have any positive outcome. I was clouded by my own selfishness and jealousy, and I didn't consider the consequences of my actions. I'm sorry, Lynette. I truly am." Callan's voice held a mix of remorse and sincerity.

"Just how much have I missed of your words? How many things have been the truth that I perceived as false?" His eyes hardened, never breaking from mine as his own frustration leaked out. "I've questioned many things since our conversation."

I stood there, still processing his words, my hand in his. It was a lot to take in, but a part of me wanted to believe that he was genuine and truly regretted his past actions.

Was this the same Callan who had killed me? Or was he a different version from the ones in my other lives?

No, regardless, his actions as a boy were the same in all my lives.

"Callan, I . . . I appreciate your honesty," I finally managed to say, my voice fractured. "But it doesn't change the fact that your actions caused me immense pain and suffering. I've carried that burden for so long."

He nodded, his gaze downcast. "I know I can't undo the past, Lynette. But I want to make amends. I want to be a better brother to you. I want to earn your forgiveness." He sighed, his hand shaking a little in mine.

Tears continued to stream down my face as I looked at him, my heart torn between the lingering hurt and the flicker of hope that maybe, just maybe, things could change between us.

"I don't know if I can forgive you yet, Callan," I admitted, my voice choked with emotion. "I never did receive anything else of Cassandra's." I smiled meekly as Callan's eyes widened.

"What? But surely Father gave you something?"

"No, Roger didn't give me anything. He said I didn't deserve it after . . ." I left the words unsaid as Callan's expression changed to disbelief.

"Lynette, I . . ." He pulled me forward, his hand tightening around mine. My body fell into his as he wrapped his arms around me in an awkward embrace. I stilled at the action; not once had Callan ever embraced me.

For a moment, I hesitated, unsure of how to respond. Having Callan's arms around me, offering comfort and support, felt strange. But deep down, I yearned for that connection with my brother, for the bond that had been strained and broken for so long. I had always yearned for it.

But I can't forgive him yet. My heart won't let me.

Slowly, I relaxed into his embrace, allowing myself to feel the warmth and security it offered. The tears continued flowing down my cheeks as I let out a sob, releasing the pent-up emotions that had weighed me down for three lifetimes. Callan held me tightly, his grip strong yet gentle, as if afraid to break me further. So we stood there, his arms wrapped around me as my own hung limp.

"I'm sorry, Lynette," Callan whispered into my ear. "I'm sorry for everything I've put you through. I never should have doubted you in the past."

His words pierced my chest, and I could feel their sincerity. It was a step forward, a step towards healing the wounds that had festered between us for so long, but the anger and pain still lingered in my heart.

"I want to believe you, Callan," I murmured against his shoulder. "But it will take time. I need time to heal and process everything."

"I understand," Callan replied, his voice filled with understanding but also a strain I wasn't familiar with. "I will give you all the time you need. Just know that I will make it up to you."

Did he truly understand?

As we stood there, holding on to each other, I couldn't help but feel a glimmer of hope. Hope that maybe our fractured relationship could be repaired. It wouldn't be easy, and the scars would always remain. I didn't know if I could ever forgive him because of his words alone. However, perhaps we could find a way to move forward, to rebuild the bond that had been shattered one day.

> **Vishka's Guidance System**
> Callan Heversham
> Likeability: 12% (+4%)

CHAPTER THIRTY-SIX

Callan escorted me back to my camp when Teresa and Harold returned. He hadn't wanted to risk leaving me alone with Garret and even went as far as to swear he would make sure I wasn't alone with him again. It was a nice sentiment, but I didn't know how he could keep that promise. Callan couldn't be aware of my situation at all times.

I wasn't ready to forgive him yet, or to place my trust in him.

I couldn't erase everything that had happened between us so easily. The scar on my chest wouldn't let me forget how fickle his emotions could be.

Thankfully, Teresa was tired when I returned, so we decided to retire early for the night, which allowed me to avoid the smirk on Garret's face as he watched me. His irritating expression made me want to punch him as he watched us eat rice around the fire. Instead, I held back from saying anything to Garret, letting him think Callan had scolded me.

Callan had been right.

As much as I hated to admit it, attacking another noble outside of a duel was a punishable offense. If Garret wanted to, he could easily accuse me of attacking him, and the likelihood of my side being believed against his was slim. Without a witness, it was possible I would be framed in a trial again.

Sleep did not come easy as I lay in the tent beside Teresa. She grumbled as she shuffled, trying to find comfort on the bumpy ground. I watched her nose twitch as she dreamed peacefully; we would likely reach Zromore, the capital, tomorrow. It would be the end of this march.

I sighed, shifting my gaze to the fabric of our tent, blocking the stars from view. The darkness mirrored the conflict in my heart. The night was quiet, interrupted only by Garret's snores from nearby.

As I stared above, my thoughts wandered to the uncertainties that awaited in Zromore. The capital was a mysterious place to me; I wondered if it was anything like Talbour. I knew it was where the politics of Zopan was centred, where Roger, my brothers, and even Kara had gone in the past. Roger had always said the capital was where nobles made alliances with other houses and where social etiquette was followed strictly, and it was the centre of power for the empire. It was where the empress resided, where summoners trained. It was also where I would truly learn what it meant to be a soldier in the Zopan Army.

I sighed. I couldn't shake the nagging feeling that Garret would not let things rest. He had always been one to hold grudges, and the incident today had surely fuelled his desire for control. He wasn't going to accept my refusal to marry him. Even my scandal with Lord Nathaniel hadn't stopped him. I needed to remain cautious of him and try to avoid him as best as possible.

Callan's change in attitude added another layer of complexity. His words of remorse and his promise to be a better brother seemed genuine, but they puzzled me. It was hard to trust him after the pain he had caused in the past. He had lied so easily once; I couldn't be sure he wouldn't do so again.

I couldn't heedlessly rely on him, not yet.

Callan was too volatile; our past had taught me that much. Even if he did want to help with my problem with Garret, there wasn't much he could do. Callan had no authority over my marriage. Only Roger could make that decision, but first and foremost, I had to prevent my blood contract from being annulled.

Eduard would likely present Roger's letter for annulment quickly. He had made it clear he didn't think I was suitable for the army.

Preventing the annulment had to be my priority; Vishka wanted me on this path.

I didn't know if I was suitable for training or even battle, but at least being a soldier would grant me some independence from my family's control of my life. Besides, I was surprised to find myself envious of summoners. I wanted to be like them. For the first time in a long time, I actually wanted to do something with my life, however short it might be once my disease resurfaced.

I rolled to my side, attempting to find a more comfortable position in the tent. With a heavy sigh, I closed my eyes, hoping that slumber would eventually find me.

We marched in even rows through the farmland of Zromore. The rhythmic sound of our footsteps resonated through the air as we moved in unison. The landscape stretched out before us, painted in shades of green and gold, with the fertile fields of wheat swaying gently in the breeze.

As we pressed forward, the towering gates of the capital came closer into view, standing tall and imposing. They dwarfed Talbour's like a horse standing beside a child; my eyes widened at the sight. Their grandeur hinted at the city's significance beyond, where power and influence converged. Each step brought us closer, and anticipation coursed through the trainees like an electric current as whispers murmured amongst those of us seeing it for first time.

It's larger than I ever imagined it would be.

The transition from farmland to the Oran Lake marked a subtle shift in the scenery. The golden waves of wheat fields gradually receded, unveiling the glistening expanse of the lake. Its calm waters mirrored the sky above, creating a serene tableau amidst the approaching urban life.

The shimmering presence of Oran Lake offered a brief respite from the march, a momentary escape from the uncertainties that plagued my thoughts. I spotted a small cluster of bodies by the lake's edge, their brown fur and slender forms scurrying into the water at our approach. If I had to guess, the aquatic creatures looked like otter demonic beasts.

My attention was sharply drawn back to our imminent arrival at the capital as those who lived outside the walls stopped their work and waved to us. I saw some leading boar beasts by ropes tied around their necks; others had woven baskets filled to the brim with harvests. They all looked happy to see us, their hands caked in dirt and their clothes patched.

With every step the gates grew larger still. I sucked in a breath and tried to ready myself, both physically and mentally, for what lay ahead—the challenges, the opportunities, and the nobility within the walls of Zromore, the heart of political power in Zopan. Teresa thrummed with energy as she excitedly gazed at the gates in awe. Harold subtly smiled beside me as Garret breathed a heavy sigh of relief.

As we marched onwards, anticipation mingled with apprehension, forming a heady blend of emotions inside me.

This is it, isn't it? I have actually made it to the capital, despite being as weak as I am.

A horn blasted, and Lieutenant Cragborn raised his hand for us to slow to a stop as we reached the entrance to Zromore. He turned to face us, his voice cutting through the air, demanding our focus.

"All right, ready up," the lieutenant shouted, and a wave of anticipation rippled through our ranks. "In a moment, we will be entering Zromore. For many of you, this will be your first time at the capital," he continued. "As per tradition, the citizens will greet our return with a parade, much as Talbour does."

Teresa couldn't contain her excitement, her grin beaming. "How thrilling! I've never been in a parade before," she exclaimed, her enthusiasm palpable.

Lieutenant Cragborn's glare silenced her immediately. "Quiet!" he barked, and Teresa shrank back, holding my hand.

"As I was saying . . ." Lieutenant Cragborn narrowed his eyes, ensuring discipline amongst the trainees. "The brigade will reorganise for the parade into formations by affinity. Meanwhile, the capital will send out the instrumental guard for our entrance. As trainees, you will be stationed behind the foot guard. I expect you all to be on your best behaviour, remain in your rows, and greet the citizens as future upstanding members of the army. Understood?"

"Yes, sir!" We saluted in unison, our voices filled with excitement.

"Good. Now follow me to your positions," Lieutenant Cragborn commanded, and we fell into line behind him, marching with purpose towards our designated places. My stomach fluttered with nerves as we prepared to make our grand entrance with the brigade.

The brigade quickly fell apart from our former formation. Rank was mixed as summoners gathered with their matching affinities. The first squad was formed of fire summoners, the second squad was earth summoners, the third was the water summoners, and the fourth was the wind summoners. Behind them formed a foot guard unit, albeit a bit smaller than the group we had left Talbour with. Finally, at the very back, were we trainees. I tried to see if I could spot Eduard or Callan, but the many bodies of the wind summoners and foot guards in front of me blocked any chance of that happening.

Maybe it was for the best that I couldn't see them.

I felt a small tap on the back of my shoulder and turned to find Rian leaning towards me.

"Hey, are you nervous?" Rian asked in a hushed tone as we stood waiting for the signal for the parade to begin.

"A little. Is it that obvious?" I smiled hesitantly, clutching my backpack tightly.

"A little." Rian smiled. "Don't worry too much; I doubt anyone will pay much attention to us."

"You think?" Teresa whispered, glancing towards Harold, who appeared calm and composed compared to us. His focus was fixed on Lieutenant Cragborn's back.

"Would you care much about a bunch of trainees compared to the summoners?" Rian raised an eyebrow at Teresa.

Teresa blinked, considering Rian's words. "Well, I suppose you have a point," she muttered reluctantly.

"We're just here to show that the army is training new recruits for the future. Our role is more symbolic than anything else." Rian shrugged rather calmly.

"I-I'm still nervous." A quiet voice to Rian's left made me shift my gaze. Lacey Weadall meekly stepped closer to Rian, her blue gaze shaking as she tucked some of her auburn hair behind her ear.

A snort on Rian's right made me frown. "Listen to Lady Rian, Lady Lacey. If you can't handle a parade, then how can you handle being a summoner? You can't even hold a weapon without flinching." Kit Balburn rolled his light brown eyes as he tucked his shirt neatly around his plump belly.

"I—I want to be a researcher," Lacey whispered in response to Kit's comment, her voice barely audible. Her hands trembled slightly, betraying her nervousness.

Rian's expression softened, and she placed a reassuring hand on Lacey's shoulder. "There's nothing wrong with wanting to pursue a different path, Lacey. Not everyone has to be a front-line summoner. Research is crucial to advancing our understanding of aether and its applications."

Teresa nodded, offering Lacey a comforting smile. "Exactly! Each of us has our own strengths. Whether you're on the front line or behind the scenes, every role contributes."

Lacey's eyes brightened a little at their supportive words. "Thank you," she whispered, her voice filled with gratitude. I smiled towards Rian and Teresa; I really had found some good friends.

"Of course you would say that, Lady Rian; your aim is to become an enchanter." Kit sighed. "True power comes from the front lines. You will have to learn to fight to pass the first evaluation. It's an essential part of being in the army. You can't hide from it."

"It is a requirement," Harold said, nodding at Kit's words. "All trainees must learn to fight."

Lacey paled. "I—I will do my best," she said without confidence.

"I await the day you successfully defend yourself in battle." Garret snickered as he tried to flatten some of his unkempt ginger hair.

I saw Rian's grip tightening on Lacey's shoulder as she shot Garret and Kit a disapproving look. I also glared at Garret as he spoke with that sickening voice of his.

"That's enough, Lord Garret." I narrowed my eyes at his frowning face. "You too, Lord Kit. Everyone here will go through the necessary training to defend themselves. Lady Lacey has plenty of time to learn."

Why are they being so demeaning?

"Lady Lynette, what pray tell will you contribute? Some herbs? Your core is pitiful. The army doesn't need a Crazy Cerue Lady to ruin their reputation," Kit Balburn snarled defensively.

"I wouldn't worry, Lord Kit; Lady Lynette will be returning with me to Talbour at the next outing." Garret smirked at me.

"I still do not understand why you want to marry her." Kit sighed. "Far better women don't cause such drama out there."

My patience wore thin at Garret's and Kit's remarks.

"If you truly do not want to see how I got my reputation, I suggest you stop being so narrow-minded, Lord Kit," I retorted, feeling my emotions stir. How long would I have to put up with such prejudice from the nobles of Talbour? "I would be happy to demonstrate what some herbs can do, if you like? Perhaps I could introduce you to one of my angel shrooms?"

Rian's lips upturned at my comment. "Oh, I don't think he deserves that, Lynette."

"I beg to differ," Teresa huffed. "Can I be the one to do it?" She eagerly looked at my backpack, where the paralysis mushroom resided.

The tension in the air grew thicker as Teresa's suggestion hung between us. Garret and Kit exchanged wary glances, realising the threat of my words. Lacey, who had been quiet throughout the exchange, seemed taken aback by the sudden turn of events. Lord Caspian, the son of the Marquess of Ingalham, watched us all with a thoughtful expression. It was the first time I had properly looked at him up close. I noticed his eyes flick towards Teresa in uncertainty.

Did they know each other?

Before anyone could react further, a voice boomed from behind us, cutting through the mounting hostility.

"That is enough!" Lieutenant Cragborn's stern command echoed, capturing everyone's attention.

We all stilled and quickly turned to face the lieutenant, straightening our postures. Lieutenant Cragborn, a tall and imposing figure with bright red hair, made his way towards us, his expression a mixture of disappointment and disapproval.

"Lady Lynette, it is not becoming of a trainee to engage in quarrels with fellow recruits," Lieutenant Cragborn said, reprimanding me firmly. "Your duty is to represent the army and uphold its values, not to indulge in personal disputes."

I lowered my gaze, biting my lip to stop myself from saying something I would regret. Whilst Garret and Kit had provoked me with their derogatory comments, I had indeed allowed my emotions to dictate my response.

"I apologise, Lieutenant," I said, my voice strained. "I allowed myself to be carried away. It won't happen again." At least I would try not to, as long as I could avoid Garret.

Lieutenant Cragborn's stern expression softened slightly. "See that it doesn't," he replied. "The army is a team, and unity is paramount. Respect for one another is vital for our success."

Then he turned his gaze towards Garret and Kit, narrowing his slit pupils. "As for both of you, Lord Kit and Lord Garret, I expect better behaviour from nobles who are heirs to their houses and represent the highest ideals of our society. Making disparaging remarks and belittling fellow trainees are not befitting of your station. You will show respect and support for your comrades or face the consequences."

Garret and Kit exchanged glances once again, their smirks replaced by uneasy expressions. They nodded in acknowledgement. However, their glares towards me as soon as the lieutenant looked away were hard to miss.

"All right, stay in line, trainees." Lieutenant Cragborn raised his voice so all of the trainees could hear him. "The parade is beginning," he announced as the drums began to beat.

The large gates of solid metal creaked open, the sound reverberating through the chatter of the trainees. The ground beneath my feet vibrated, sending a wobble through my legs. Delicate images carved into the towering structure cast shadows on the ground as the great hunk of metal they decorated slowly eased open. Then, in time with the beating drums, the brigade stepped through to the capital beyond.

Our group followed Lieutenant Cragborn's lead. Beside us, in the same formation, was Lieutenant Sharpclaw with his group of commoners and future foot guards. With every step forward, I could hear a roar growing louder from beyond the gates.

My stomach began to churn as my nervousness began to mix with adrenaline at the sound intensifying with every step. I had never heard anything like it. It was both daunting and exhilarating, sending a shiver down my spine. The beating drums changed pace as the front of the brigade entered the capital, matching the rhythm of our marching and amplifying the energy that greeted us.

Teresa fidgeted beside me as we finally approached the gates. The intricate carvings etched into the towering metal structure came into view. The images depicted fierce battles between demonic beasts and powerful summoners, capturing the essence of the ongoing struggle against the encroaching dangers of Zopan and the stories of war I had read about. The level of detail was astonishing; every stroke of the artist's hand conveyed the struggle and raw power of the confrontations.

But as the gates rose higher as we drew closer, the carvings became less discernible. The sheer scale of the structure made it impossible to fully appreciate the artistry that went into its creation. Yet even from my limited vantage point, I could sense the immense skill and dedication that had been poured into crafting such a masterpiece.

The roar grew louder, its vibrations thrumming in my ears. I wanted to cover them. It was so fierce, but that would be disrespectful to the people of Zromore. Beside me, Teresa's eyes darted back and forth, trying to take in the grandeur of the carvings amidst the chaotic flurry of movement. I could tell that the sight and sound overwhelmed her, just as it did me.

As we crossed the threshold of the imposing gates, the scene that unfolded before us was nothing short of awe-inspiring. The capital, a sprawling city with magnificent architecture and bustling streets, lay spread out in all its splendour.

Streets teemed with people greeting us, their faces filled with excitement and joy as they watched our procession. The cheers and applause of the crowd blended with the roaring chants that seemed to echo from every corner of the city and into my body. Banners bearing the black and yellow emblem of Zopan fluttered in the wind, adding vibrant splashes of colour to the scene. Flowers were thrown from windows as people dangled from the ledges of tall pristine buildings lining our path.

Zromore was nothing like Talbour.

The people here appeared well cared for, their attire clean and their expressions joyful. I couldn't see any children begging for scraps. Or maybe they were hidden?

It contrasted starkly with the struggles and hardships I had often witnessed in Talbour. The sheer number of people gathered in one place was awe-inspiring, and perhaps unsettling. I couldn't help but feel some trepidation at their eager gazes, making my steps stiffen. However, Teresa nudged me forward, ensuring that I kept pace with them.

I had never seen so many people in one place.

As we marched forward, the foot guards ahead of us leading the way, the crowd's energy surged. They cheered and waved, their enthusiasm contagious as many trainees enjoyed the attention. I spotted some green summoned wind spirits diving into the crowd as the birdlike forms performed acrobatics, eliciting more cheers.

I glanced around, taking in the sights and sounds. The buildings stood close together with multiple levels from light grey stone. They formed neat rows creating the path we were currently following. For some, the bottom level showcased shops, their wares displayed behind glass, under wooden signs with pictograms. Not all commoners could read, so I wasn't surprised to see them.

In the distance, the terrain of the city rose over higher ground from the disjointed rooftops. A wall encircled the inside, blocking any detailed view beyond it, splitting the city. However, above the wall a familiar steeple of white hinted at the Grand Temple of the capital.

Could I really do this? Could I truly become a summoner?

The parade continued, each step bringing us deeper into the heart of the capital. The cheers grew louder, the chants more fervent, as the excitement reached its peak. The presence of the crowd was electrifying. I could feel the hairs on my arms rising from the experience, though I was growing more uncomfortable by the second from the immense attention.

Amidst the waving streams of fabric, I caught glimpses of a market behind the crowd. Stalls similar to Talbour's lined the narrow streets separating the buildings. Except here they seemed to multiply in number. The market was packed with people as they browsed a variety of goods, food, and trinkets. The smell of something delicious wafted over, making my mouth water as I saw some of the citizens holding sticks of steaming meatballs, tempting my taste buds with their savoury scent.

My eyes widened when I spotted something far more interesting as we passed another street. This street was littered with raw vegetable stalls, and at the end of it stood a cart filled to the brim with a green lump that split into three brown stems.

Jabascus root!

My heart skipped a beat at the sight. So the capital had jabascus root! My excitement tingled beneath my skin. I had to remember where we were so I could come back to get some before they packed the market away. The market could only be temporary for the parade, much like Talbour's festival.

I quickly glanced at the buildings to try to pinpoint something to help me find my way back. However, the uniformity of the architecture made it challenging to choose a specific landmark. They all looked the same to me.

I frowned as we moved farther away and I desperately tried to find something. A clang took my attention to my left, and I smiled as I saw something different. There it was: a building with an open front, unlike the others. It looked like a large workshop of some sort as sparks flared inside against large metal anvils. That would have to do as a landmark until I learned the layout of the capital.

The streets paved with large cobbles hardened beneath our feet as we neared a stone archway dividing the city. As we passed under its dome, the crowd began to thin and was replaced by people dressed in fine clothing. Their gazes upon us felt scrutinising, and I gulped as I recognised those eyes of judgement and inspection.

We had passed the commoners' section of the capital. Now we were entering the nobles' plateau. The buildings here were not so tall and thin, packed into neat rows. Instead, the streets opened up, replaced by small pockets of greenery situated between wide, immense structures. Each had a blockade of fencing surrounding it, hiding its gardens from view. These were the manors of low-ranking nobles.

As we traversed, I saw the crowd begin to fill out again, though their cheers were not as overwhelming. The brigade began to slow, and ahead, I saw the formation begin to change.

The summoners began to move, stepping out of the straight line we had been in. Instead, the groups of summoner affinities separated into a horizontal formation, the fire summoners forming a squadron on the far right, followed by the earth, water, and wind summoners.

Lieutenant Cragborn veered left, and we followed, separating from our formation to move to the left of the foot guards as they came to a standstill. I looked at Teresa, confused, and she shrugged, unsure herself as we repositioned at the far end in a large open area of stone.

When we came to a stop, I couldn't stop my breath from catching now that we could see in front of us. Before us was a golden gate attached to pristine white walls as they surrounded a building in the distance. Its majestic steeples fluctuated in height, its length longer than any building I had ever seen as golden windows reflected the sun's rays.

The empress's castle, it had to be.

Before the gates, platforms stood draped in purple fabric. A canopy of wood and fabric atop them shielded its occupants as they sat on thrones decorated in golden lace. Two flags of Zopan hung at its base, fluttering proudly and gently in the wind, bearing the emblem of two dragons connecting their claws.

We stood there, awaiting further instructions as the crowd's cheers diminished to a hushed anticipation. I glanced at Teresa, her uneasy expression mirroring my feelings. Finally, we all stilled as a figure on the throne stood up under the shaded canopy.

"All hail the empress!" a voice boomed from the grandstand.

"Hail the empress!" Suddenly the voices of the crowd and the army chanted repetitively. I quickly followed suit, joining in the chant, holding my fist to my chest in salute as Lieutenant Cragborn did, watching his movements.

The figure raised her hand, and we all silenced as she stepped into the light. It was difficult to see her so far to the left. However, I could see her Draygon stark white hair contrasted against the dark purple of her elegant ruched gown. Jewels sewn into her skirts and the centre of her bodice glinted in the sun. Her hair was pinned delicately with pearls as her aged, weathered expression roamed over us. The empress, Zirianna Ragon, was just as rumours described. An intimidating woman of power and authority, her presence commanding respect and awe.

I felt my body go cold as I stared at her.

My hands began to tremble as my breath locked.

Vishka's Guidance System
Zirianna Everglade Ragon
Likeability: ???

CHAPTER THIRTY-SEVEN

The empress's piercing gaze swept over the assembled brigade, and a shiver ran down my spine. Her presence alone exuded authority and power, and I couldn't shake the feeling of insignificance in her presence. Her ethereal purple eyes seemed to linger on us trainees for a moment; I automatically straightened with a gulp, but she quickly turned away from us.

A lone soldier stood forward from our formation, his dark purple cloak flourishing behind him. Azriel Elkhart bowed.

"Your Majesty, the Imperial Brigade stands before you, ready to serve and protect the Zopan Empire with utmost dedication and loyalty." Azriel's voice echoed as he remained bowing to his second cousin.

"I'm glad to see your safe return." The empress crooked her pale lips. "Rise, Lord Azriel Elkhart."

She fluttered open a fan embedded with jewels.

Azriel lifted his head and stood at attention, stepping back into his place in the brigade. My eyes watched him go as the box above his head floated with the same number as before. I was glad it hadn't gotten any worse than minus thirty, a small blessing compared to what I now faced.

Why, for the love of Vishka, did the empress have a meter?

"Soldiers of Zopan." The empress's resonant voice cut through the air like a knife. "Today you stand before me as the guardians of our great empire, sworn to protect its people and uphold its values. Your dedication and sacrifice do not go unnoticed."

The empress paused, her eyes scanning the faces of the assembled trainees. I wanted to shrink and hide away from her gaze. "I welcome those of you joining our army on this journey. But know this: the path you have chosen is not an easy one. The challenges that lie ahead will test your strength, your courage, and your unwavering loyalty. Only those who prove themselves worthy will earn the honour of serving the empire."

Right, we had to pass evaluations first.

"I have faith in each of you," the empress continued, her voice both stern and encouraging. "You have been chosen for this noble duty because you possess the potential to become true defenders of Zopan. It is up to you to rise to the occasion and prove yourselves worthy of the trust that has been placed in you."

As the empress's words echoed through the air, the weight of her expectations settled heavily. The thought of displeasing her, of failing to meet her standards, sent a surge of fear through my veins. I saw Teresa's determination and eagerness, but I couldn't help but feel a sense of dread.

Isn't three people enough? How the heck am I supposed to survive the empress?

The empress's piercing gaze scanned the faces of the trainees once more, and I instinctively averted my eyes, not daring to meet hers. Her mere presence commanded obedience, and I couldn't afford to risk her disapproval. Moreover, the meter above her head constantly reminded me of the consequences I could face. If I upset her, if her meter even as much as lowered . . . I dreaded to think what that meant for me. Just her dislike alone could spell my death sentence regardless of whether it reached minus fifty!

I had to stay away from her at all costs.

The empress's attention shifted to Azriel and the summoners, as she waved her fan in the sun's heat. "Congratulations on a successful return." She spoke with finality, raising her hand.

The sound of trumpets filled the air at her signal. "Hail the empress!" the summoners chanted again as she stepped back into the cover of the canopy. Relief washed over me like a tidal wave as the weight of her attention and daunting pressure released.

The chanting continued amongst the summoners, but Lieutenant Cragborn turned to face us, straining to be heard over the cacophony. "All right, detach with me. I will be taking you to Alinor Keep, your home for the duration of your evaluations," he announced, his words barely reaching our ears.

"March!" he shouted a little louder, stepping left, away from the brigade. I fell into formation alongside my fellow trainees, eager to get to our new destination and away from the empress.

The detachment moved forward, guided by Lieutenant Cragborn's commands. The second group of trainees followed, led by Lieutenant Sharpclaw. We marched, our footsteps echoing in rhythm as we left the imposing golden castle gates behind, entering deeper into the nobles' quarter. The crowd slowly faded into the background, replaced by a collective murmur of gossip amongst us.

"I can't believe we just saw the empress!" Teresa whispered. "She is just like the stories describe."

"Y-yeah. She definitely was intimidating," I mumbled, glancing back at the square we had left behind.

"Of course she is; the empress is the descendant of Carosel. The hero of Zopan," Garret said with a roll of his eyes. "What did you expect? Some weak-willed woman? She may have been lucky to inherit the throne as she didn't have brothers, but she earned her place. She is the most powerful summoner in the empire."

"Gifted with lightning aether, as all royals are." Harold nodded, rolling his shoulders to work out a knot that had formed.

"I wonder what she's like? Do you think we will ever get to meet her?" Teresa said with a thoughtful expression as she tapped her lip.

"Pfft." Garret laughed, amused. "Fat chance. Not even the majority of nobles get to meet her, let alone a commoner like you. She only meets people directly by invitation or when holding court."

"So you likely won't meet her either, then?" I said with a raised eyebrow.

Garret frowned. "Of course not; she only invites marquesses and dukes to her tea parties."

"That's good to know," I said, relaxing a little. I should be able to avoid the empress if that was the case; as the daughter of a viscount, I didn't have to worry about being invited directly at any point. Not that I had any idea why the empress would even entertain the thought of meeting me. I was the Crazy Cerue Lady. I doubted she even knew of my existence. So why did she have a meter?

The lieutenant led us along smooth paved roads as we passed by elegant town houses and mansions. A few carriages pulled by horses passed us, their curtains pulled aside as the nobles within snuck peeks at us with scrutiny and intrigue.

It was quiet here, a nice reprieve from our arrival in the capital. The farther we walked, the fancier the buildings became. Private guards stood at attention outside individual gates; they chatted amongst themselves with familiarity as they smiled at our passing. It was cleaner than the commoners' section had been; I spotted cloaked summoners walking towards posts of metal, aether streaming from their hands as they refuelled mage lamps in preparation for the night to come. We didn't have those in Talbour; mage lamps only existed inside the homes of nobles, not on the streets for guidance in the darkness.

A group of young women in elaborate pouffe dresses clustered together in a public garden. They giggled at our presence and waved handkerchiefs in impish teasing at some of the boys, making them blush. I saw Harold's ears turn a little red as he coughed in his hand when one called his name.

"Do you know them?" I grinned, seeing him flustered.

Harold startled a little at my comment but quickly restrained his posture. "She's a friend of my sister," he said quietly as the girls returned to a metal table where their servants poured tea.

Lieutenant Cragborn continued to guide us through the winding streets. I could sense the anticipation building amongst the trainees from their hesitant body language. Alinor Keep awaited us, our new home and the place where we would undergo further training.

I wondered what it was like.

We rounded a bend, and as we did so, yet another set of gates made from stone and metal made some of us halt our step. I looked at Teresa, and she shrugged, as clueless as I was as we approached the walled-off entrance to the east of the city. The gates were not as impressive as the palace gates, but they were still intimidating.

A smaller door built into the stone wall to the right of the gates opened at our arrival. A man dressed in a grey cloak with brown hem stitching stepped out. It contrasted against the bright orange shirt he wore. The man saluted Lieutenants Cragborn and Sharpclaw as we halted at the gates.

"Lieutenants, I heard the brigade had returned." The man grinned, happy to see them.

"It was a fruitful trip." Lieutenant Sharpclaw's pointed teeth showed as he clasped the man's hand and shook it vigorously. "Did you get it?" he asked eagerly.

"Yes, I sent it to your quarters." The man chuckled nervously. "Please don't ask me to get you dream clove again."

"What have you been doing, Myas?" Lieutenant Cragborn narrowed his eyes. "Guardsmen are not your errand boys."

"Oh, calm down, Igor, not like it's contraband." Lieutenant Sharpclaw rolled his eyes.

"Yes. It is." Lieutenant Cragborn sighed, rubbing his temple. "I have every mind to burn it."

"Don't you dare!" Lieutenant Sharpclaw exclaimed.

"Myas." Lieutenant Cragborn glared.

"Igor," he responded just as sternly.

They stared at each other, fighting a battle of wills, as we all stood aimlessly, watching. I raised an eyebrow at Lieutenant Sharpclaw. Dream clove was an herb used to induce a state of euphoria and relaxation. It was also somewhat addictive.

Lieutenant Cragborn's stern expression relaxed slightly as he sighed, relenting in the face of Lieutenant Sharpclaw's insistence. "Fine, but be careful with it," he warned, his voice laced with concern.

Lieutenant Sharpclaw grinned mischievously. "Of course, Igor. You worry too much."

"I don't worry enough," Lieutenant Cragborn mumbled. "Sir Pollard, if you please."

"Yes, Lieutenant." The man from the doorway saluted and rushed back inside the wall. As he did so, the large gates began to creak and open.

"Come on, trainees! Your quarters are this way!" Lieutenant Sharpclaw pointed at the gate, stepping towards it.

Lieutenant Cragborn sighed again at his eager colleague. "This way, trainees. This is Alinor Keep. The home of the army here in the capital. You will remain here until you have passed your evaluations to become soldiers."

My stomach fluttered as we passed the gates separating this place from the rest of the city. The atmosphere immediately changed as the streets and elegant buildings of the nobles' quarter were replaced by a more austere environment.

Immediately beyond the gate were large areas of open land. Each section was cordoned off with short wooden fencing. The air was filled with the sounds of clashing weapons, the grunts of exertion, and the occasional shout of an instructor. Gone was the peaceful atmosphere of the nobles' quarter.

Here was the power of the empire.

Lieutenant Cragborn didn't stop for us to linger and take in the surroundings; he led us forward through the training grounds, easily navigating the bustling environment. As we passed by the training dummies made of straw and cloth, I saw the intensity and precision with which the soldiers attacked them, honing their combat skills. I saw summoners and foot guards in training bearing weapons of all kinds as they swung or launched at their targets. None of them stopped to inspect us, all absorbed in what they were doing.

To our right, wooden poles stood tall, serving as a training apparatus for summoners practising their aerial manoeuvres. They used the power of air manipulation to propel themselves from one pole to another, displaying impressive agility and control. The difference in strength between foot guards and summoners was obvious. The foot guards seemed more agile with their weapons, whereas the summoners sparked their elements with their practice. Fire, water, wind, and earth spluttered all around us.

As we continued deeper into the keep, I noticed various other training areas, each dedicated to different aspects of combat and warfare. There were archery ranges where soldiers honed their marksmanship skills, and obstacle courses designed to test their speed, agility, and problem-solving abilities. The keep was a hub of constant activity and training.

I pinched my hand as I watched them; I had a lot of training ahead of me.

Lieutenant Cragborn took us through the open grounds, eventually leading us towards a set of buildings. Each of the buildings felt old yet well maintained. They varied in size and width, and the farther we went, the more it felt like we were entering another city. Summoners walked to their destinations, nodding to us as they passed or completely ignoring us. I smelled something delicious as we moved near a building in the centre of this second city. It stood out from the others, wider than the rest, its stone more faded. It had two large columns of stone at the entrance hiding aged oak doors, which swung open often as soldiers appeared to frequent it.

"This is the eatery," Lieutenant Cragborn informed us as we walked. "You can eat here using credits you earn as soldiers. You will all be provided with a stipend of fifty credits a month so you don't starve, but you are expected to contribute to the army in various tasks, which will earn you more."

Credits? Was that different from gold coins? I guessed I would find out.

We continued farther down the path, the ground giving way to stone as an open courtyard grabbed our attention. Many summoners were gathered here as they socialised, but what stood out was an unusual building at the centre of the courtyard. I had not seen one like it before; it looked more like an open stall one might see at a market, but it was made from stone. The front was open; no walls hid what lay inside. I could see desks of polished wood dividing the space, blocking entry to closed-off rooms beyond. Lines queued at different counters within the open building. Summoners gathered around the walls, pulling off paper flyers as they joined the queues.

"This is the task centre. Here you can acquire work to earn credits. It is first come, first served, so it is wise to visit early." Lieutenant Cragborn continued leading us farther.

We were taken away from the busy courtyard and passed more tall buildings that resembled visiting noble town houses in Talbour. It was quieter here in this section of Alinor Keep. The lieutenant weaved down a narrow path between the buildings and brought us to one at the very back of the city. He halted us at its double black-painted doors.

"This is the trainee quarters. You will each have a private room. I will not be giving you room assignments; you are not children. I trust you to choose a room that suits your taste. They are all the same regardless," the lieutenant said with disinterest. "Today, you can rest. Tomorrow, we will begin your training. I will meet you at the eatery at the first bell sharp. If you are not there, that is your own fault."

Teresa and I shared a smile as we clutched our bags. Finally, we could rest.

Vishka's Guidance System
Quest Update
Congratulations! You have reached the capital alive

Vishka's Guidance System
Quest received!
Grow your core to grade one

CHAPTER THIRTY-EIGHT

The lieutenant left us standing before the doors of the trainee quarters. We saluted his departure, all of us eager to explore our new residence.

"First come, first served!" a noble exclaimed, running towards the doors in haste the moment the lieutenant left our view. The action ignited a flurry amongst the trainees as they suddenly all rushed after the man, scrambling to be first into the tall building.

I held back, avoiding the stampede as the commoners joined in, eager to secure a room for themselves. The chaotic scramble reminded me of the hustle and bustle I had witnessed in the market of the city streets. I felt a mix of amusement and disbelief at the sight of the trainees scrambling to secure a room as if it would determine their fate; it was somewhat comical.

However, I understood the underlying desire for comfort.

"Didn't the lieutenant say they were all the same?" Teresa asked, her voice tinged with both confusion and mirth as she stood with me, wide-eyed at the commotion.

I nodded, a wry smile forming on my lips. "Yes, indeed. But no noble wants to be beat out of the 'better' room."

Garret, fuelled by the excitement in the air, plunged headfirst into the crowd, eagerly trying to push his way through the bodies vying for entry into the trainee quarters. The double doorway was not large enough to accommodate everyone at once, resulting in shoving and pushing amongst the crowd.

Harold, on the other hand, chose to wait out the initial wave with us, maintaining his calm demeanour. He raised an eyebrow at Garret's enthusiasm and shook his head disappointedly.

"I will be happy with any room," he said.

Rian, joining our small group, crossed her arms and let out a disapproving tut as she watched the scene unfold. "You would think they were worried about ending up in a barn instead of a room. It's just temporary until we pass our evaluations."

Teresa scrunched up her face thoughtfully. "Right, the lieutenant did say we would only stay here until then, huh? I wonder where we will live once we pass?"

Rian leaned in and shared her knowledge. "Most nobles have town houses here in the capital for the social season. The majority of them will reside in those estates."

Teresa's expression tightened with a hint of concern. "So, what about those of us who don't have fancy town houses?"

Rian shrugged. "I imagine you will be given lodging here in the keep or have the opportunity to earn enough to buy your own place. There are various ways to secure permanent residences outside the nobles' domain."

Teresa's shoulders sagged as she let out a moan. "Why does everything cost money?"

I smiled as she pouted. "Don't worry, Teresa, I won't let you suffer." I nudged her shoulder encouragingly. "We can find somewhere together."

"You won't stay in your family estate?" Harold asked, surprised. Rian shared a similar expression as she waited for my response.

My lips twitched at their gaze. "Probably not. I don't want to rely on my family's support forever." I did not want to depend on Roger Heversham's wealth, not this time. If I was to succeed in this life, the least I needed to do was to be able to survive without his aid. I also in no way wanted to stay in a house with my brothers for company. That wasn't happening if I could help it.

"A noble pledge." Harold nodded, happy with my statement. "I wish you luck when the time comes."

"Thank you, Harold," I replied, appreciating his support. It might not be my true reason for wanting a place of my own. But he didn't need to know that.

Rian, still wearing a curious expression, said, "It's admirable that you want to be independent. Many nobles cling to their family estates and wealth. It is our birthright." She paused with a knowing smile. "I can guess why you would think that way, though."

I nodded with a twist of my lips. Even if my choice was spurred by my desire to avoid Eduard and Callan, Rian was more perceptive than I thought.

"Yes. I want to prove that I can succeed on my own. I know that's probably weird to most nobles. But living in the keep or finding a place of my own will give me a chance to do just that."

Teresa's pout transformed into a small smile as she looked at me. "You always have a way of making things exciting, even when it comes to finding a place to live."

"I wouldn't have it any other way." I grinned as the crowd at the doorway thinned and the commotion around us began to settle.

"Looks like the frenzy has dispersed. Shall we?" Rian waved her hand towards the doors with a small smile, and we all nodded and followed her towards the trainee quarters. A few others who had also held back followed us; I noticed that Lord Caspian Landrick was amongst them.

He walked a short way behind us, his brown eyes roaming our surroundings as he tucked his long brown hair over his shoulder. He seemed the quiet sort, but Rian had described him as stubborn when we camped together.

The doors of our resident building opened smoothly inwards into a spacious foyer. We stepped inside, taking in the sight of the well-designed architecture and the sense of space that enveloped the area. Sets of armchairs and settees were nestled in the centre of the room, beckoning us to rest.

However, our attention was drawn to the staircase that spiralled upward, leading to the upper floors of the building. The balcony-like floors that clung to the walls provided a glimpse of the rooms on each level. As we looked up, we saw the towering roof above, giving the impression of a fortress within the keep.

The walls of the building were lined with closed doors, each bearing a painted number. Some doors had keys hanging from their locks, whilst others remained empty.

"I guess the ones with keys are still available?" Rian noted, observing the space.

She reached for one of the doors on the bottom floor, turned the key, and pushed it open, revealing the room beyond: a simple yet comfortable space furnished with a bed, a desk, and a small wardrobe. We gathered inside to check it out and found behind a partition a metal bathtub with strange crosslike stubs on one side.

"Looks like we have our pick," Harold remarked, noticing my curiosity about the bathtub. "Those are used to provide water, Lady Lynette. They are called taps," he said, placing a hand on one of the crosses and turning it. A spluttering noise gurgled as the metal groaned and water rushed out of the spout into the bathtub.

I stepped back instinctively, staring at the fresh water before Harold turned it off again.

"Water just like that?" Teresa exclaimed, dipping her hand into the water at the bottom of the tub.

"Yes. It is powered by summoners here in the capital. They have remarkable inventions here that have not yet reached the outer cities." Harold's calm façade broke for a moment as his lips edged into a smile at Teresa's enthusiasm.

"Oh my gosh, we can take a bath!" Teresa jumped up in glee.

We all laughed at Teresa's excitement, sharing in her joy. After days of travel and the chaos of the last few hours, the thought of a warm bath was incredibly appealing. An invention like this meant we didn't have to rely on maids to fill it with buckets like in Talbour.

Rian nodded, a mischievous glint in her eyes. "Indeed, we can. I think we all deserve it after everything we've been through."

"Choose whichever room suits you best." Harold smiled approvingly. "I think I will take this one if that is agreeable?"

"Fine with me! Let's explore the rest!" Teresa grabbed my hand and then Rian's, pulling us back into the foyer, as she urgently wanted to find her own room.

Rian and I exchanged a look as we were tugged along and laughed together.

With newfound energy, we quickly explored the other available rooms on the ground floor. Each room was similar in layout and furnishings. Some even had a window overlooking the training grounds, allowing a glimpse of the ongoing activities.

As we ascended the stairs, we continued to check the rooms on each floor, finding them all to be in good condition. The higher we climbed, the more breathtaking the view became from the small windows, offering a panoramic vista of the surrounding keep. Some, however, only had a view of stone reaching far into the sky. The residence was situated against the walls of the capital, it seemed. The majority of rooms left had such a view.

Finally we reached the top. The floor here was wider than the previous levels, allowing for a small common area. Large windows in the hallway allowed ample sunlight to fill the space, and comfortable seating arrangements were scattered around, inviting us to relax and enjoy the view.

"This is amazing," I exclaimed, taking in the sight before me. "I never imagined we would have such comfortable quarters during our training."

Rian nodded. "It's a pleasant surprise, indeed. I suppose they want to ensure we're well rested and ready for our rigorous training sessions."

Teresa stretched her arms above her head, letting out a satisfied sigh. "I could get used to this. It's quite luxurious compared to what I'm used to back home." She beamed as she plopped down onto one of the plush chairs. "I feel like a proper noble already!"

We all joined her in laughter, basking in the momentary respite from the future demands of our new lives as trainees.

In the end, Teresa seemed drawn to a room on the top floor with a window overlooking the pathway towards the building, allowing natural light to fill the space. Rian, on the other hand, preferred a room closer to the common area on the first floor, as she enjoyed the company of others during her downtime.

As for me, I chose a room on the second floor, near the staircase. It provided easy access to both the upper and lower levels and gave me a sense of proximity for a quick escape if I needed it. I didn't think I would, but knowing it was an option made me feel safer.

With our decisions made, we settled into our respective rooms.

I closed the door of my chosen room behind me, dropping my backpack onto the floor. This room was a little smaller than the rest, the window had a view of the city wall, and the bedpost had a notch in it as though it had been punched. But I didn't mind. It wasn't as large as my old room at the Heversham estate, but it was clean and suited me well enough. I had learned in my last life that clinging to luxury was not worth much if there was no happiness. The burnt-orange bedcovers were soft against my skin as I lay on the mattress and looked up at the ceiling.

"I made it, Vishka," I said to nothing, holding my hand above my face and gazing at the red tattoo that now laced my hand. "Now I have to make sure I stay alive."

My muscles had never felt so relaxed in months as I stepped out of the bathtub, satisfied. Wrapping my hair in one of the towels provided, I hummed in bliss from the warmth and cleanness of the bath. It had taken me a bit of trial and error to get the temperature right. It turned out one of the taps was for heated water and the other for cold. I marvelled at the device; if it had been available in Talbour, I would not have needed to rely on the maids so much.

Moving to the wardrobe, I found a set of garments inside it. They were unisex and had ties, so they would fit all sizes. I pulled out a grey cloak and held it between my fingers; the rough material symbolised a trainee's uniform. It was edged with black trim and had a small bronze badge pinned on it. The badge had an etching of a closed flower bud.

I gently placed the cloak back in the wardrobe and instead pulled out a simple set of white cotton garments with stretch in the waistline. They fit relatively okay but were quite large on me. Sitting down at the desk in the room, I opened the drawers and found neat piles of paper alongside a set of feathered quills and ink. The room was stocked with everything I could need, except there was a lack of books on the shelves. Only the bare minimum was provided.

Leaning my head on my hand, I tapped the desk, looking out at the window at the stone-walled view.

Our training would begin tomorrow.

I had to figure out how to improve my core to grade one for Vishka's quest. But there were more urgent matters to consider. I assumed Eduard was probably planning to present Roger's letter for my release from the blood contract as soon as possible. I doubted he would do it today; knowing Eduard, he would want to ensure that he was presentable first. Besides, it was already getting late, looking at the dimming sky.

I sighed, moving my gaze to the paper. I needed to present a reasonable argument against Roger's request, but that wouldn't be easy. As my adoptive father, Roger had the right to control my life to such a degree and I didn't have a strong enough core to argue my use as a summoner. I only had my herbology skills, which might not be enough to persuade the generals. Of course, then there was also Lord Azriel Elkhart. He had an interest in my ability to ride kreshna. Maybe I should have just told him about my beast-taming skill that day; my task might have been easier now if I had done so. But I couldn't change that now. If Vishka thought I should keep it hidden, I needed to trust her. She had got me this far.

What were my options?

I could try to grow my core to a usable level. Was that even possible in this short amount of time? I imagined that Eduard would present the letter first thing tomorrow. The technique Albus had given me hadn't made any changes for me so far. I didn't think that was something I could rely on happening in a day. Maybe if I could get some jabascus root?

Wait . . . my chest tightened as a sliver of an idea formed. I stared down at the paper and bit my lip. Perhaps there was one thing I could do, but I didn't know enough about the law to know if it was plausible. It was risky, more so than my scandal plan, but it might be my only choice.

Hesitantly, I picked up the quill and dipped it into the ink. I hovered the pen above the paper, my hand stilling as I considered this idea. After a moment, I swallowed my trepidation and began to write. I carefully crafted my argument, weaving together the threads of my reasoning and hoping that it would be strong enough to sway the decision in my favour. The ink flowed from the quill, forming words that danced across the page, each stroke carrying the weight of my hopes and fears.

As I delved deeper into my plan, I realised that I would need legal expertise to navigate the complexities of the law. I made a mental note to seek out someone knowledgeable in this area, but who could I trust to guide me through the intricacies of the system? Maybe I should try to find a textbook on it instead. I couldn't risk this reaching anyone before I needed it.

The room around me grew quieter, the oil lamp's soft glow casting a warm light. The night sky outside the window had darkened, and I knew that time was of the essence. The wheels of fate for my final life were turning, and I had to be prepared for any outcome.

Finishing the last sentence of my argument, I set the quill down and read over my words. Doubts and insecurities tugged at the edges of my mind, but I pushed them aside. I had made it here so far. I could do this.

With a sense of determination, I folded the paper neatly and placed it in a secure location, hidden away from prying eyes. It would serve as my backup plan, my last resort if all else failed. However, I hoped with all my heart that it wouldn't come to that. I didn't know what I would do if I had to use it.

Closing my eyes, I took a deep breath and reminded myself of my chosen path. It would be my backup. I would only use this if the generals took Roger's side.

I sat on the fluffy warmth of my bed. It felt wonderful to be on a mattress instead of the hard ground after a month of marching. Gazing at the blood sign on my hand, I crossed my legs and tried to sit comfortably. I remembered how Brendan had sat during my night with Eduard and his team as he cultivated, and I tried to copy it.

Taking one slow, deep breath, I closed my eyes and focused my attention towards my mindscape. Within moments I felt my body sensation change. Opening my eyes, I saw the familiar darkness that was my centre. I had managed to get there much faster than last time.

As expected, the tiny glow of my core bobbed in the air as the rune I had placed sucked in aether from the outside world. I approached its warm glow, my steps rippling through the darkness like ink. It hadn't grown in size since I last saw it, but upon closer inspection, as I followed the strands of aether soaking into it, I saw a swirl of pale white mixing within that hadn't been there before.

"Child of Vishka." A voice made me jump as I turned to my guest.

"A-Albus." I greeted the shadowy figure as he approached from the darkness. He was as creepy as he had been at our first meeting, his ethereal body blending into the space.

"I have not yet replenished fully, so I cannot remain long." He nodded towards my core. "You are unable to sustain me sufficiently without stunting your growth."

"Stunting my growth?" I asked, taking a step back from the man.

"Yes. The aether I require is greater than your current rate of gathering. If I were to take what you could gather at this moment, none would remain for you to grow your core with."

"It hasn't grown at all, has it?" I asked, looking back at the tiny orb. If I didn't have Albus, would I have seen a change by now?

"It has not. In order to grow, your core needs to be filled with aether. As of now, it is eight percent filled." Albus moved with a glide to stand beside me as he gazed at the swirling aether accumulating in my core.

"That's a little under half a percent a day." I sighed. There was no chance I could grow my core in time to argue my use as a summoner against Roger's request to have my blood contract revoked.

"Patience. It will grow in time." I swore from Albus's tone that he would have rolled his eyes if he had features.

"I'm worried I don't have time," I whispered, pulling my hands away from the orb in a slump. Maybe I was going to have to use my backup plan after all.

"Why are you so impatient?" Albus asked as he followed my movements.

I hesitated, looking back at the strange being that he was. I supposed he was the only person who knew the truth about Vishka and my repeated lives. Perhaps he was the only person I could truly confide in? He was the memory of a man who had experienced much of the same.

"Viscount Heversham wishes to have my blood contract to the army revoked. If that happens, I cannot learn to become a summoner, and I cannot follow Vishka's guidance." I pinched my fingertips.

"I see. That is troubling." Albus hummed as he raised his hand to stroke his chin. "I was not aware that such a requirement to become a summoner existed in this time."

"It is against imperial law for anyone to learn how to use their core if they are not a member of the imperial army or temple," I informed him. "There are no textbooks permitted for the public, and it is punishable by death for a summoner to teach another who is not enrolled."

Albus frowned, becoming still at this information. "Things have indeed changed," he mumbled as he began to pace in thought.

"It has always been this way, has it not?" I asked, my own curiosity piqued at his words.

"No," Albus responded. "I would not worry. I can teach you what you need."

I rubbed the back of my neck with a slight upturn of my lip as he avoided elaborating on my question. "I think that would possibly end up with my death." I laughed a little. "An unregistered woman who can suddenly use her core is definitely not something that would be permitted."

"Hmm. Your rules of this time are very restrictive."

"Yes," I sighed. They certainly were.

"It is unwise not to follow Vishka's will. What has she tasked you with?"

"To grow my core to grade one." I bit my lip, watching the rune as it thrummed. "I did have one idea about how I could do that, but it is not something I have done before."

"Tell me." Albus floated to me quickly, making me flinch.

"Jabascus root. In one of my previous lives, it was used with mistwood tea to increase one's core. Do you know anything about that?"

"What does this root look like?"

"It is a round green ball with three brown roots. It is used as a vegetable by most people."

"A vegetable?" Albus's voice rose in shock. "What you describe is a plant called ascious. It absorbs aether naturally as it grows. The size of a specimen indicates how much it has obtained. It is a lucrative plant that is rare to find."

I stood back a bit at Albus's sudden intensity. "It is very common . . ." I said as he raised his hands flippantly.

"It is used as a vegetable?" he exclaimed in outrage. "What has happened to this world?" He shook his head, resting it in his right hand. "Obtain this plant immediately."

"Yes?" I said, wide-eyed.

"Yes. I want to see what has become of this plant. If it has not mutated since my time, we can put it to use."

"All right, I'll get some mistwood tea as well." I nodded, feeling a sense of excitement.

"I have far better alchemic formulas than adding it to mistwood tea," Albus tutted.

"Alchemy? I'm not very good at that." I smiled hesitantly.

"No matter. You can learn." Albus crossed his arms, making me gulp. Was he going to be a tyrant teacher?

"I must go now. We have spoken longer than we should have. Do not come back without ascious." His form faded into the darkness, leaving me alone in my mindscape.

Right, so I should probably try to figure out when I could get to the market.

CHAPTER THIRTY-NINE

Glass separated me from the outside as I stared at the yard. Two young boys held wooden blades as they fought under the watchful eye of an older man under the bright sun. The boys sweated as they crossed their weapons, their smiles huge. They had arrived moments ago in a carriage from the capital. A young girl with blond hair happily watched them nearby.

A weight on my shoulder made me look up to the woman who had brought me to this house.

"They are your siblings, Lynette." Cassandra nodded to the two young boys who shared her grey eyes and the young girl with her ash blond hair.

"Siblings?"

"Yes, my dear. They are your family now. Would you like to meet them?" she asked warmly as I turned back to the window. A nervousness eased into the pit of my stomach.

"All right." I tucked my hand into the safety of Cassandra's as she led me out of the study and into the foyer. As we entered, the doors opened, and the four people I had seen outside entered the mansion, laughing happily as they spoke about their recent visit to the capital.

"Cassandra darling! I have missed you." The older man approached us, his arms wide, as he embraced Cassandra lovingly.

"I have missed you too, dear. I hope your trip to the capital was well?"

"It was splendid. The boys are more than eager to learn how to fight now that they have seen the capital's summoners. Kara is also excited to join the social season when she is old enough."

"I am pleased, Roger." Cassandra smiled. "I had a lovely trip to Wayward. My family passed on their regards to you."

"That's wonderful, but—" Roger released Cassandra and paused momentarily as I hid behind Cassandra's skirts. "What do you have there?" he asked.

"This is Lynette, your new daughter. I have decided to adopt her into our family."

"You . . . What?" Roger frowned and glared at me. I shrank further back as Cassandra scowled and lightly slapped his shoulder.

"Stop that. You are scaring the poor dear," she scolded.

"We have a new sister?" the young girl with blond hair piped up as she cocked her head towards me.

"Cassandra." Roger gritted his teeth. "What is the meaning of this?"

"Roger—" Cassandra raised her hand to cup Roger's cheek. "It is what I want."

The older man grimaced as he looked at me and back to his wife. "We will talk about this in my study."

"Very well." Cassandra nodded. "Eduard, Callan, Kara, this is Lynette. Your new sister." Cassandra stepped aside so her skirt was no longer hiding me, and I clutched my hands together, trying to settle my nerves.

"H-hi," I whispered, seeing the curious gaze of Kara and the frowns of Eduard and Callan.

"Sister! Oh, I have always wanted a sister." Kara beamed, rushing over to me. She held my clutched hands and brought them close to her chest. "Hi! I'm Kara; I can't wait to play with you! How old are you? Are you older than me or younger? Do you like to play tea time? Will you play it with me?"

I wanted to step back from this girl, but her friendliness made me smile shyly. "I am seven. I would love to play tea time with you."

"Seven! Oh, then you are older than me." Kara pouted. "I wanted a younger sister."

"Why do we have a new sister?" One of the boys with light brown hair stepped over, placing his hands on his hips. He looked down at me, scrutinising.

"Callan, staring like that is rude," the other boy with dark brown hair said as he approached. He was taller than the others. His gaze did not linger on me, though, and instead went to Cassandra, his mother, curious.

"Lynette is here by my will, children. She is now a Heversham. I want you to treat her as family," Cassandra said, leaning down to our height.

I glanced at Roger as he shook his head disapprovingly.

"Very well, Mother." Eduard nodded, accepting his mother's words. "Welcome to our family, Lynette," he said, bowing his head in greeting, causing the other boy, Callan, to copy him.

"We are so glad to have you." Kara giggled.

"Please take care of me," I whispered, mimicking their actions with the small curtsy Cassandra had shown me, hopeful for my new life as I joined this family.

* * *

An alarming ringing echoed throughout the room, making me leap up to clutch my ears. It was nothing like the soothing chime of the temple bells that signified the time of day. This echoed with a vengeance and sounded incredibly close. As swiftly as the sound came, it left me alone in my room's silence.

What the heck was that? Was that our wake-up call?

I shook my head from the shock and got out of the comfort of my bed. There was no way anyone would be going back to sleep after that. Moving to the partition in the room, I ran the tap, and fresh water streamed out, making me smile at the convenience. I washed my face and tied my raven hair into a high ponytail. It had dried wavy as it rested against my shoulders. I then opened my wardrobe and took out the grey cloak I had seen yesterday. It felt surreal in my hands.

I was really here. This hadn't been a façade. I was going to learn to become a soldier, possibly a summoner. I smiled, putting the cloak down on my bed to get out the rest of my uniform.

As I dressed in the remaining pieces of my uniform, I felt a surge of excitement mixed with a hint of nervousness. This was something I had never done before; it was all new to me. In all of my past lives, I had usually experienced some of the social events before. I had a semblance of what to expect, but I had no knowledge of what being in the army was like.

Once I was fully dressed, I took a moment to inspect myself in the small mirror hanging on the wall. The grey cloak was draped over my shoulders, the black trim framing the edges and the bronze badge glinting in the soft light. It was a visual representation of my new identity as a trainee, a symbol of the journey I was about to embark on.

Grabbing my jian and dagger, I attached them to the belt provided. As I was about to leave, I stopped my hand on the door. Looking back at the desk, I bit my lip, conflicted. If Eduard handed in the letter today, would they call upon me so quickly?

With a heavy sigh, I took out the letter I had written and tucked it safely into the pocket sewn into my chest garment. It was probably best not to leave without it, just in case.

Taking a deep breath, I opened the door and stepped out into the hallway. The quiet hum of activity filled the air as other trainees made their way through the corridors, their footsteps echoing against the stone walls. I spotted Lacey Weadall nervously flitting about near the stairs as she glanced around at us all. She was wearing the same uniform I was. We all were.

"Good morning, Lady Lacey." I waved to her as I made my way to the stairs. The small girl jumped, her frizzy auburn hair bouncing with her body at my voice.

"H-hi, Lady Lynette." She gulped at me, taking a step back. "H-have you seen Lady Rian?"

"Not yet. She chose a room on the first floor."

"Oh." Lacey meekly looked away from me.

"Would you like to come with me?" I hinted at the stairs as other trainees made their way down.

Lacey nodded, her eyes brightening with a mix of relief and gratitude. "Yes, please. I—I don't know anyone else here, and it's a bit overwhelming."

I smiled warmly, understanding her apprehension. "Don't worry, Lady Lacey. We're all in the same boat. Let's stick together." I smiled, trying to seem friendly. This girl probably had an opinion of me based on my actions in the past. We had never spoken much, but since Zachary was not very welcoming at my assessment, I could only presume that his sister also had reservations about me.

"Th-thank you," she whispered, moving closer to me, her eyes darting around at all the trainees passing us by.

We descended the stairs, joining the flow of trainees heading towards the common area. Most of the seats there had already been filled as groups gathered together. We looked around and eventually spotted Rian standing with Harold near his room's doorway. As we approached, Lacey quickly left my side and scurried towards Rian, clutching the hem of her grey cloak.

"L-Lady Rian," Lacey whispered, stepping closer to her.

Rian turned her attention to Lacey, her expression softening. "Oh, Lacey," she said, not surprised by the girl clinging to her. "Did you find a room?"

"Y-yes, on the second floor." Lacey glanced my way and quickly averted her gaze. "I'm a little nervous, but trying to stay positive."

Rian nodded understandingly. "Don't worry. I'm sure you will be fine."

Lacey managed a small smile, appreciating Rian's reassurance. "I'll do my best."

Rian glanced at me, and her features changed into a small smirk. "I see you enjoyed the bath?"

I nodded, returning her greeting. "Absolutely. It was a delight. I see you cleaned up as well."

"I do scrub up nice, Cerue." Rian winked, making me laugh.

"I'm eager to see what today has in store for us," I said, seeing some of the trainees leave the building.

"I imagine it's going to be lectures," Harold said, watching the trainees as well. "There is much they need to teach us about being in the army."

"Lectures?" Teresa's voice made us all turn. "Aren't we going to learn how to fight and stuff?" She made a motion with her hands, which I think was supposed to be manipulating aether. I couldn't be sure.

Harold chuckled softly at Teresa's enthusiasm, making us all pause. Rian raised an eyebrow at him, and I pursed my lips. I didn't think Harold had laughed once during our travels together. Hearing the deep chuckle from him was strange.

"Is something wrong?" Harold asked, looking at us confused.

"No, nothing," Rian said slowly. I think she was as surprised as I was. Harold was usually so sombre.

"Shall we head to the eatery?" I asked as quiet slipped between us. "We have until the first bell before Lieutenant Cragborn comes to get us."

"I hope it's as good as Rian's cooking," Teresa said with a smile, and Rian looked away, a little embarrassed.

"I'm sure it will be better than what I cook," Rian mumbled.

"Let's not waste time, then! My stomach needs nourishment!" Teresa joyfully walked ahead, making Rian frown at her easy acceptance.

We followed Teresa's lead and headed out of the building into the morning light. As we rounded the corner that led from the trainee quarters, I was shocked at how much busier it was. Summoners, trainees, and foot guards were sprawling throughout the keep. It was as though the number of people here had doubled since yesterday.

We carefully made our way through the crowd down the same lane where Lieutenant Cragborn had taken us. The crowd grew even thicker as we reached the task centre. Yesterday there had been lines and summoners gathered there, but it was thin enough that we could see the buildings at the centre of the courtyard. Today, it was so thick with bodies that seeing the task centre from the outer edges was impossible as we passed it.

We avoided bumping into a few summoners as they rushed towards the task centre. A shared glance between us at the flurry made us all nervous. The lieutenant had said it was first come, first served. I could see why so many summoners were panicking as it was already so full before the first bell.

Eventually, the large columns of stone that framed the eatery came into view. The crowd had lessened, but the noise was just as cumbersome as chatter and clanking of cups drifted into the space. We entered the large oak doors and were greeted with warmth and a tantalising aroma. The room was filled with long tables and benches, occupied by trainees and summoners engaged in lively conversations. To the right of the room was a queue moving swiftly along as soldiers placed orders with servers standing behind counters.

We joined the queue, eager to satisfy our rumbling stomachs. The aroma of sizzling meat and freshly baked bread grew stronger as we neared the counter. The servers worked efficiently, taking orders and swiftly assembling plates of food.

Finally, it was our turn to place our orders. A friendly server greeted us with a smile. "Good morning, how can I assist you?"

Teresa, as always, was the first to speak up. "I'll have a plate of eggs, bacon, sausages, and a side of toast, please. And a large glass of milk!"

The server noted down Teresa's order and turned to the rest of us. "And for you?"

"I'll have the same," Rian said with a nod, and the server scribbled it down.

"S-same for me," Lacey said quietly.

"I'll go with scrambled eggs and toast." Harold placed his order in his usual calm manner.

Turning to me, the server asked, "And for you, my lady?"

"I'll have a bowl of oatmeal and some fresh fruit, please," I replied, appreciating the healthy options available. I hadn't eaten any fresh fruit since before I died. I didn't want to overindulge just yet either; my body was still adjusting to eating more healthily.

The server thanked us and quickly began assembling our orders.

As the plates arrived, we found an empty table and settled down, eager to savour the delicious meal. That was, at least, until I saw a flash of red.

"Lady Lynette." With a snarky grin, Garret placed his plate of half-eaten food down on the table beside me just as Teresa was about to do so. Kit joined him, a little less enthused, as he chose to sit between Harold and Rian.

"I was going to sit there." Teresa narrowed her eyes at Garret, moving to sit on my other side instead, Lacey on her right.

"Tough, commoner; my place is beside Lady Lynette," Garret sniped at her.

I immediately lifted my plate and stood up. "I will eat elsewhere," I stated just as Garret grabbed my wrist. I felt my heart quicken at his touch as my mind flashed to the night at camp, which had begun similarly.

"Lady Lynette, do you not want to eat with us? Are we not worthy of your presence?" Garret frowned, his words insinuating that I didn't want to eat with the people at this table.

He was right. I did not want to be here.

"Let go of my wrist." My voice came out weak as I tried to control the fluctuating fear in my body.

"Lady Lynette, I meant no harm." Garret released me, acting puzzled at my response. He knew damn well why I did not want him touching me.

"Lord Garret, I wouldn't want to eat with you either." Teresa sighed, also standing. "Stop bothering Lynette already. Can't you take a rejection?"

"Shut your mouth." Garret's act faded momentarily as he growled at Teresa. "Nobody cares what you think, commoner. You shouldn't even be allowed to eat with us."

"I think that is enough, Garret." Rian sighed. "We aren't all advocates for the noble privilege."

"Oh? Does that make it any less a fact that a commoner should not be allowed to mingle with nobles? We are superior and have the power to prove it. It is our privilege whether you advocate for it or not."

"Then why do you obsess over Lynette?" Teresa raised an eyebrow. "She was born a commoner."

The table fell still at Teresa's words.

She looked back and forth, confused at this, as I took a deep breath.

It was a well-known fact that I was born a commoner, but it wasn't mentioned because of my history. In the past, I would have begun shouting at the insult by now. It was also a taboo topic for many nobles to bring up their birth heritage. Often children were adopted from distant family lines if an heir with a powerful core was not produced, so for this reason, it was not mentioned much in noble society. At least not openly; there were plenty of nobles who scorned others behind their backs for not being able to produce a child with a powerful core.

So why exactly was Garret so obsessed with me? I could not give him an heir with a guaranteed core like another noble could. Did he truly have feelings for me, or was there another motive I didn't understand?

"Teresa, shall we eat over there?" I pointed to an empty table nearby.

"All right." Teresa nodded worriedly at the silence.

"I hope you enjoy your meal, everyone, apart from you, Lord Garret." I cocked my head with a sweet smile as he frowned. "Please feel free to choke."

Garret's jaw fell open at my comment; Harold raised his hand to cover his mouth, but I saw his slight smile, and Rian grinned, leaning her head on her hand. Lacey and Kit stared at me, shocked, but I didn't care.

I waved goodbye to them as Teresa and I headed for the empty table.

CHAPTER FORTY

Trainees assembled and patiently waited outside the eatery, their anticipation growing with the sound of the first bell resonating throughout the city. True to his word, Lieutenant Cragborn arrived promptly, assuming the role of our guide, as he beckoned all of us to follow him away from the building. Scanning the area, I confirmed that most trainees arrived on time. However, as we embarked, I couldn't help but notice a young beast-kin boy chasing after us, a fluffy grey tail wagging behind him whilst he hurriedly devoured an apple. With Lieutenant Cragborn at the helm, we ventured deeper into the intricate compounds of Alinor Keep. Navigating through the bustling crowds, we manoeuvred into an expansive courtyard, our footsteps echoing against the grand architecture surrounding us.

The courtyard was unusually quiet compared to the rest of the keep. Here, a lush garden adorned the space, providing a serene atmosphere amidst the hubbub of activity. I spotted flowers of various species carefully pruned and well cared for. A large gazebo at the centre of the pathway joined an intersection as vines wrapped around the wooden structure. At the head of the garden was a large stone building two stories high, its weathered exterior giving it an air of timeless wisdom. It was evident that this courtyard held significance within Alinor Keep.

My attention was drawn to a secluded area beneath the shade of a towering oak tree. Soft rays of sunlight filtered through the leaves, casting gentle patterns on the ground. In the centre, a circular stone platform beckoned; it was an inviting spot. Nearby, a small pond took shelter under the trees. Water lilies floated on its calm surface, spotting the blue water with speckles of white and pink.

Another stone platform seemingly floated on the water at the pond's centre. As I looked at it, I quickly wanted to avert my gaze, but it was already too late.

Callan sat on the platform in meditation, his legs crossed as he breathed deeply. The sight of him so composed and serene caught me off guard. I didn't think I'd ever seen him so calm. However, he caught my gaze before I could turn away and strangely smiled.

His presence surprised me; I hadn't seen him since the night he had apologised. Amidst our chaotic parade into the capital, the empress's speech, and being shown my living quarters in Alinor Keep, our paths had diverged and I had lost sight of him. Callan and Eduard had likely returned to the Hevershams' town house yesterday rather than the keep.

But now, in this moment of quietude, Callan appeared different. His light brown hair was clean, and his attire seemed less formal without the weighty armour he had worn during our march. He wore a grey cloak that matched those of the trainees, but the deep blue of the trim on its edges and matching blue vest stood out, reflecting his connection to the element of water.

Vishka's Guidance System
Callan Heversham
Likeability: 19% (+7%)

I blinked at Callan's number. It had increased, but why? I hadn't seen him in order for it to have changed.

"This is the Garden of Reflection," Lieutenant Cragborn announced, dragging my attention back to him as we walked towards the building ahead. "Within these gardens, those of you who are able will learn to cultivate aether from your surroundings. Areas of the garden have been arranged with specific plants attuned to each element, which will aid in your growth as a summoner." I looked at the garden again and noticed the four paths that led to the gazebo, each splintering into different themed areas. Callan watched us as he remained on his stone platform at the pond's centre. In his area, I saw plants coloured various blues and whites that I realised required a damp atmosphere near bodies of water to survive. Beyond Callan, the garden path led to an area we could not see, but I suspected there would be more ponds for the section designed for water.

Besides the water garden, I saw many heavy trees standing tall and majestic. These trees seemed ancient, their gnarled trunks exuding endurance and strength. Their branches reached towards the sky, interlocking to form a dense canopy. Their shade created a mysterious ambience as if concealing ancient secrets beneath their protective embrace. The plants struggling for space beneath their shelter spoke of a fierce battle for survival as bushes and vines intertwined and competed for sunlight. That must be the earth garden.

On the opposite side, the fire garden blazed with vibrant hues of red. The flowers with thorns seemed to guard the fiery essence of the garden, their pointed blooms reaching skyward as if defying anyone who dared to touch them. Small coves held dimly burning coals amongst the flourishing flora, creating pockets of warmth and flickering light. The contrast between the intense red plants, the dark stems, and the presence of stone pedestals hinted at a connection to the element of fire, its power and transformation.

Beside the fire garden, the space opened and rocks were piled up, creating stepped paths to ground at different heights. Pale blooms of green sparsely poked through the gaps of the rocks, making themselves known with large petals that withstood a delicate touch. Some stone pedestals stood on the ground surrounded by white sand, whereas others were placed atop the peak of rock formations impossible to reach by climbing. The wind garden held an ethereal charm. The gentle rustling of leaves and the occasional breeze that swept through the area seemed to carry whispers.

My gaze returned to the courtyard's centre as we passed through the gazebo. Each garden had paths leading farther within, leaving much more to be explored. Each area held its own allure. I was a little excited to see what sort of plants were here up close. There must have been many I had only ever read about. I wondered how these gardens worked in aiding cultivation. Was there a method to get the plants sown?

As we reached the edges of the garden, Lieutenant Cragborn motioned for us to gather around him, drawing our attention back to the building ahead. As we walked towards it, I realised that its exterior showed signs of decay, and some areas had newer stones hinting at repairs.

"This is the library," Lieutenant Cragborn announced in a reverent tone. "Here you will find the accumulated wisdom of summoners who have come before us. These books and scrolls will be your guides, helping you deepen your understanding of the elements and refine your summoning skills."

"So we can get scrolls here?" Kit asked eagerly as he leaned forward towards the building.

"Yes, Lord Kit. However, they are not without cost. You must earn them with credits."

"Credits? I will use gold." Kit frowned, holding his step at the lieutenant's glare.

"Gold, Lord Kit, has no use within Alinor Keep. In order to maintain fairness, everything that is obtainable here must be purchased with credits, which you can earn at the task centre. We do not condone rewarding anyone who does not earn their place."

Kit's disappointment was evident as he absorbed Lieutenant Cragborn's explanation. It seemed the concept of earning credits instead of using gold didn't sit well with him. But I understood the reasoning behind it. Alinor Keep valued meritocracy and the idea of hard work and effort being rewarded. It was a place where one's abilities and dedication determined their progress. Teresa had tensed at the mention of gold, but I saw her slacken as she realised she would have the same chance to earn scrolls as the rest of the nobles. I patted her shoulder encouragingly, and she thanked me with a smile. We knew better than to speak after the lieutenant's previous reprimands.

"The library is one of many places you can spend credits. There is also the armoury, where you can request weapons, and training centres, where you can allocate sessions for private practice. I expect you all to utilise these, even those of you who cannot become summoners. A foot guard is required to learn how to fight just the same as a summoner. We do not keep slackers." The lieutenant's stern words made one of the commoners gulp.

Silently, I admired the lieutenant's commitment to upholding the principles of meritocracy. Knowing that our progress would be determined by our own efforts and abilities rather than external factors gave me hope. I wouldn't have to depend on Roger's wealth or my brothers' aid. It also meant that nobles would not be able to get a foothold against anyone who didn't have the same financial support.

"Before we can proceed any further"—the lieutenant paused and glanced across us all—"I will be giving each of you your evaluations."

I pinched my hands at a smooth wooden desk. The lieutenant had taken us all to a large building near the library he had called the lecture hall. The lecture hall was spacious, with high ceilings and rows of neatly arranged desks. The air carried a scent of aged parchment and the faint echo of past discussions. I found myself surrounded by my fellow trainees, each of us wearing a mix of anticipation and nervousness on our faces.

"Ouch, I don't think they got a good score." Teresa winced as a trainee shut the door to the lieutenant's private room. He slumped his shoulders and released a heavy sigh as he dragged his feet back to one of the desks.

The next trainee wiped some sweat from his brow before stepping inside.

"I'm dreading it." Lacey shook as she gripped her cloak tightly with anxiety.

"Try not to worry, we don't know what he was scoring us on." Rian tried to cheer her up, but it wasn't very successful.

Honestly, I shared Lacey's trepidation. The march had not been forgiving, the lieutenant had reprimanded me for not following orders to save Harold, and then Rian and I ended up separated from the brigade for a while. My score surely wouldn't be well received. I couldn't help but feel a knot of anxiety tightening in my stomach as I awaited my turn.

The lieutenant had given us each a number; my turn was after Lacey's. The trainee who had entered appeared, making Lacey freeze as she realised it was now her turn.

Lacey took a deep breath, trying to steady herself as she approached the door to the lieutenant's private room. Her grip on her cloak tightened even further, her knuckles turning white. We watched her with a mixture of sympathy and apprehension.

"You can do it!" Teresa raised a fist and saluted Lacey, making her break into a small smile.

The door creaked open, and Lacey disappeared inside, leaving the rest of us to exchange nervous glances. We could only imagine what was happening behind that closed door: the intensity of the lieutenant's gaze and the scrutiny to which he subjected each trainee.

"I'm sure she will be fine," Kit mumbled from his seat in front of our row.

"Probably just has to grow a backbone." Garret sighed, leaning back in his chair, tucking the back of his head into his hands.

I rolled my eyes at him, tempted to kick the leg of the chair he was balancing, but resisted the urge to engage in petty confrontation. I didn't need to be reminded that I wasn't approved of in the army.

Time seemed to stretch on as we waited anxiously for Lacey's return. The air in the lecture hall felt heavy with anticipation, and the silence was punctuated only by the distant sounds of shuffling papers and murmurs of conversation from outside.

"I hope she's okay," Teresa mumbled, leaning her head in her hands.

"It's not easy for Lacey." Rian sighed. "She didn't expect to have to join the army."

"I didn't think she had wanted to," I said, my own thoughts searching through my memories. I had never spoken much with Lacey in all my lifetimes. The girl was always quiet, but I didn't recall ever seeing her in a uniform or saying anything about it, so I had no idea she had enrolled.

"It was a last-minute decision, because of the decree," Rian said. "She had wanted to find a husband this year. I was rooting for her."

Decree?

"What dec—" I was about to ask when finally, the door swung open and Lacey emerged, her face a mix of relief and disappointment. Rian, Teresa, and I immediately got up from our seats and gathered around her, eager to hear about her evaluation. But before Lacey could utter a word, her shoulders slumped, and she sighed.

"I . . . I didn't do as well as I had hoped," Lacey confessed, her voice tinged with disappointment.

Rian stepped forward, offering a supportive smile. "Don't be too hard on yourself, Lacey. We're all still learning; these evaluations are meant as a starting point."

Teresa nodded, her eyes filled with empathy. "Absolutely, it can't be that bad. We haven't even begun training yet."

Lacey managed a small smile, gratitude shining in her eyes. "Y-yeah," she sighed, looking down at the sheet in her hands. "I n-need to learn how to fight . . ." She trailed off as her eyes began to water.

"We all do." I reached towards her, trying to offer her a little comfort, but Lacey stilled and stepped away, closer to Rian. I dropped my hand, a little hurt at her fear of me, but forced a smile. "Guess I'm next," I said, trying to push down the nerves in my stomach.

"Good luck, Cerue." Rian smirked, nodding towards the door.

"Yeah, I need all the luck I can get." I hesitantly raised my hand to the door and stepped inside.

CHAPTER FORTY-ONE

Lieutenant Cragborn stared at me with a raised eyebrow as if studying me. His piercing gaze made me shuffle on my feet as I gulped. Hesitantly I cleared my throat, steadying my voice as I stood before his dark mahogany desk.

His study, if that was what it was, was lined with bookcases filled to the brim with hardback books and rolled-up scrolls bursting from their confined spaces. The scent of aged parchment filled the room, with a little musk mixed in as a thin thread of sunlight poked through curtains hanging above a small window.

The lieutenant leaned back in his chair, his expression unreadable. His fingers tapped rhythmically on the polished mahogany surface of his desk as if he were contemplating something. Finally, he spoke, his voice deep and commanding.

"You've had quite an eventful journey so far, haven't you, Lady Lynette?" he remarked, with a hint of annoyance.

I nodded, my throat feeling dry. "Yes, Lieutenant. I suppose I have." I tried to force a smile, but my body language was too stiff from nerves.

"How do you think you handled yourself? I am curious what your perspective is," the lieutenant asked, leaning forward on the desk, lacing his hands together as he placed down the sheet of paper he had been reading.

"Y-you want my opinion? Of myself?" I asked, just to clarify; was this a trick question?

"Yes." He waved his hand to gesture that I get on with it, his patience slipping. "I haven't got all day, Lady Lynette," he sighed as I remained silent, scrunching up my face in thought.

Just what did he want me to say here?

I had barely kept up at the start of the march. My lack of stamina and strength were obvious in comparison to the rest of the trainees. They had been training since childhood for this; it was maybe only Lacey and I who were unprepared. Then there was the incident with the marsh snakes, and then when Rian and I fell into the cavern and got separated from the brigade.

I relaxed my stiff posture with a heavy sigh. "I would consider myself lucky, Lieutenant."

"Lucky?" the lieutenant responded after a pause.

"Yes, I was lucky to have survived my encounters with demonic beasts. I am acutely aware that I have no combat ability. I have never received formal training. I also lack physical strength compared to my peers. Without Rian, I would have died in the cavern if I had been alone."

The lieutenant nodded. "You most certainly would have against an agiluf."

"However," I continued, "I believe I have done my best. I trained most evenings to improve my combat skills. I pushed myself to keep walking despite my body's protests. I used my knowledge of herbology to help survive the fight with the agiluf. I believe I have performed well, all things considered."

The lieutenant's gaze narrowed as he listened to my words. Silence fell between us as he seemed to consider something. I felt my palms begin to sweat in anxiety.

"Your self-awareness is commendable, Lady Lynette." He finally broke the silence with a snarky smile. "Acknowledging your weaknesses is something many people find difficult to do. I am happy I do not have to convince you of them." His tone suggested he had maybe already had to do just that with others before me.

I felt a glimmer of relief wash over me at his reaction. Perhaps my honesty had been the right call here.

"I would add that you have an interesting, if not annoying, habit of inciting chaos around you. This is the first march where I have had to reprimand a trainee for not following orders during an attack. It is also the first march where I had a trainee supposedly die, to return riding none other than a demonic beast. It is also the first time I have had family members pester me about a trainee's safety."

"It isn't intentional," I mumbled, the small relief I had felt quickly fading away.

"Going from your history and the information I have pertaining to your character, you have a talent for upsetting the people around you. Intentional or not, you need to practise restraint in your actions."

"With all due respect, Lieutenant, my past actions in Talbour have not influenced my choices on the march." I bit the inside of my cheek. Had he researched the background of all the trainees? I hadn't thought my past would come up here.

"So you claim; I will take your word for it, Lady Lynette. However, your ability to unintentionally incite chaos is a cause for concern." He frowned firmly. "It is essential, not only for your own safety but the safety of those around you, that you learn restraint. Unpredictable actions can have dire consequences on the battlefield." Lieutenant Cragborn shook his head.

"You were indeed lucky when you disobeyed my order to gather during the marsh snake attack. That only one of the marsh snake beasts attacked you when you returned for Lord Harold was a relief. If it had been any more, neither yourself, Miss Garpson, nor Lord Harold would have survived. You put yourself and your friend in danger by going against orders."

"I—I understand." I swallowed, a lump forming in my throat.

"To make it clear, Lord Harold would have been rescued without your intervention. Marsh snakes do not devour a person's core until their poison has almost killed their target, which takes time."

"Y-yes, Lieutenant." I solemnly nodded at his reprimand.

"However," he continued, making me still. "Your efforts to save a fellow trainee were not unnoticed. The army values such traits as determination, which you have proven with your actions. You have also shown resilience in the face of adversity when separated from the brigade and your will to keep marching despite your lack of experience or skill." The lieutenant's tone softened as he picked up the paper he had been reading when I entered the study. "You would do well if you channel those qualities in a way that aligns with the needs of a unit and in your training."

"Th-thank you, Lieutenant," I said, surprised by his change in body language as he relaxed in his seat.

"To address my first concern, I recommend you begin training to improve your stamina and strength. There is a practice field you can use to run laps, which will help your stamina grow. In terms of expectations, you need to be at least level thirty-five, the threshold for journeyman, to be able to battle comfortably. Stamina is very important and can alter your success when battling demonic beasts. If you tire too quickly, they can overwhelm you."

"All right." I nodded, agreeing with his advice. "What about strength? I don't have a skill in that yet."

"No, I saw so on your evaluation sheet from your acceptance assessment. I would suggest you start with something simple, such as weightlifting. This will help give you the strength you need to wield weapons more easily. But depending on what weapon you resonate with, the level you need to reach may vary. For example, wielding a heavy battle axe will demand more physical power compared to a lighter sword or staff."

"Callan mentioned a weapon calling to you. Is that what you mean by resonate?" I asked as the lieutenant looked up at me from his sheet.

"Yes, once you have practiced a few different weapons, you will feel familiar with one particular type of weapon. You will find your level faster and more easily with it than anything else. That is the weapon you are resonated to. As a foot guard, you won't be able to feel the aether connection as a summoner can, so it will take some trial and error, but this method works just as well."

"A foot guard?" I furrowed my eyebrows.

"Yes? A foot guard." The lieutenant frowned with a look of confusion.

"Lieutenant, I was hoping to train as a summoner." I spoke with a slight hitch as worry began to settle into my stomach. I knew this was my likely outcome. But Vishka had granted me a quest to increase my core; I couldn't do that as a foot guard. I had grown hopeful that maybe I could be more than a mortal in this life.

"A summoner?" The lieutenant frowned. "Lady Lynette, you failed your examination for your core. You do not have a large enough core to become a summoner. You were only in my group for potential summoners rather than Lieutenant Sharpclaw's for future foot guards out of courtesy because you are a noble."

"Lieutenant, I wish to learn to become a summoner, not be a foot guard!" I protested. "I know my core is small, but I can grow it." I might not become powerful, as there was a limitation to how much a person could grow their core. I might not be able to reach grade eight, the limit for summoning an aether spirit, but surely there was a chance I could at least learn how to wield aether.

"Lady Lynette." The lieutenant's tone deepened as his expression turned serious. "Your core is so small that no average evaluation tool was able to detect it. No gathering techniques are safe for you to use with such a small core. You will only damage your body if you try to use them. Our lowest technique is for a grade one, and you are below that."

"What? But I have a technique for below grade one!" Albus had given me one. *How could there not be others?*

"I find that hard to believe, Lady Lynette." The lieutenant sighed.

His scepticism hung in the air, causing my heart to sink. I couldn't believe that my aspirations of becoming a summoner and learning to wield aether were being shattered so abruptly. The weight of his words settled heavily on my shoulders, and I felt a surge of frustration and disappointment welling up inside me.

"But, Lieutenant, I do have a technique," I insisted, desperation edging into my voice.

"If you do, I would insist you stop using it at once." The lieutenant quickly stood up and glared at me, making me jump in surprise. "Lady Lynette, all cores are unstable during the gathering stage. If you use a technique that you cannot withstand, then your core can be shattered, which will damage your ability to function. A shattered core leaks unfiltered aether into your body, poisoning it from the inside. Worst case, you will die from a shattered core. Your best case is you become immobile."

"G-gathering can kill you?" I stuttered, taken aback by this revelation.

"Of course it can. Why do you think it is banned for anyone to learn how to use aether outside of the army? Without safety measures and proper guidance, if any fool tried it on their own, they would only harm themself. Even transferring aether to someone without training can poison them if their body hasn't developed to handle it."

"I—I see." My eyes began to waver as fear tinged inside me.

Was the technique that Albus had taught me safe for me?

Was I the fool the lieutenant spoke of?

"Lady Lynette." The lieutenant's voice softened as he stepped around the desk to face me directly. "Sometimes life takes unexpected turns, and we find ourselves facing obstacles we never anticipated. It's how we respond to those obstacles that defines us."

"What am I supposed to do, then?" I asked, my voice trembling. "I joined the army to become a summoner, to be—to be stronger than I am now." His words had hit me like a blow, and I could feel tears pricking at the corners of my eyes.

"If a safe technique were available for someone with a core as small as yours, I would consider it. But as of now, such a technique does not exist within my knowledge, and I am very dedicated to categorising gathering techniques for my students." The lieutenant placed a hand on my shoulder, his deep red slitted eyes expressing sympathy.

Ah, he truly doesn't believe that there are techniques below grade one for gathering.

I couldn't show him the technique, though, not yet at least. That would reveal Albus, and something deep in my gut told me I should keep him a secret for as long as possible. But maybe . . . Maybe I could use this.

"Whilst becoming a summoner may not be a viable path for you, there are other roles within the army that you can excel in. You weren't given a blood contract so early because you lack the ability to become a summoner, Lady Lynette."

"It was because of my herbology skill." I sighed, rubbing my arms and trying to hold in my swelling anxiety.

"Precisely. Once you have learned combat, you will be able to consider a profession. I suspect a couple of departments will take an interest in you."

"They will?"

"Yes, our medical research team, for one; they are always looking for talented individuals to grow their herbology knowledge to lessen the strain on medic summoners."

"What—what if I can grow my core to grade one?" I had to ask. It was my task from Vishka. I had to grow it to grade one, regardless of my position within the army. But learning to become a summoner would make my growth much easier. With Albus teaching me, I wouldn't necessarily need the army to learn, but I couldn't explain any growth easily if I was labelled a foot guard.

I was going to have to be careful in how I approached this.

"Lady Lynette." The lieutenant's gaze darkened. "I have told you the risks involved. Even if you are able to grow your core to a grade one, it will still be considered small compared to that of the average summoner. Your growth will be limited early as your innate core is so small. I cannot, in good conscience, encourage you to pursue this."

I slumped at his words. I knew my growth would be stunted at some point, but surely I could become stronger and able to defend myself better if I grew it, even a little.

"However, if by some miracle you do figure out how to grow your core to a grade one despite my insistence on your safety, I will consider allowing you into my class," he said resignedly. From his tone, I could guess he didn't actually think I would be able to do it.

But I had Albus's technique, and I also had the advantage of knowing about jabascus root.

I was going to do it; I was going to prove to the lieutenant I could become a summoner, or at least strong enough to wield aether.

What other choice did I have?

CHAPTER FORTY-TWO

I stared at the paper in my hands as Lieutenant Cragborn returned to his desk. The sheet had a detailed overview of the intricacies of Alinor Keep. It included a list of the facilities available and the members in charge. A time schedule for the eatery and library alongside the rules expected as a member of the army. I also saw a list of lecture sessions I could attend.

"You will have a scheduled weapons training session you need to attend every two days. All trainees are expected to attend this. If you cannot learn to defend yourself by the social season, then you will not pass your evaluations." The lieutenant paused as he looked up at me from his seat. "At the evaluation, we will have trainee foot guards sign their blood pacts. Only summoner candidates will be signing a pact with me today."

His features creased with a frown as he looked at me, his eyes strained.

"However, in your case, even if you do not pass combat evaluation by spring, you will not be dismissed. Unfortunately"—he grimaced—"you will not be allowed the grace of dismissal if you cannot pass like the rest of the foot guards."

"Dismissal? I thought everyone had to sign when they reached the capital," I said, noticing the pile of parchment neatly placed on his desk. The red ink and familiar runes told me they were blood contracts.

"Summoner candidates do, as a requirement for learning to control aether. However, foot guards are not obliged to follow the same rules as they do not risk their lives with aether. If they cannot defend themselves in combat, they will be a risk and liability to the army, so we only have them sign if they pass final evaluations."

"I see," I quietly replied. That grace probably saved a lot of commoners' lives. Many joined only to have a safe roof over their head and a full belly. At least that was the case for many commoners from Talbour. Not everyone was cut out for battle, though.

I still had doubts about my own combat ability.

"General Saika is a brash man." The lieutenant sighed, somewhat aggravated. "I can only apologise for his actions."

"No, it's okay." I forced a smile. "I agreed to it as well." If I hadn't, I probably wouldn't be here now. Roger would never have allowed me to come.

"I doubt the general explained any of this to you. He knew you would not be able to become a summoner." The lieutenant pursed his lips. "His enthusiasm for your herbology skill clouded his better judgement."

"Really, it's okay." I waved my hand as I slowly began to notice the lieutenant's small facial fluctuations. He was a harsh, straightforward man, but I was learning from our conversation today that he seemed to worry a lot. In his own way, he had, in fact, shown concern for me.

"I see here that there are two summoner sessions?" I asked, trying to change the subject.

The lieutenant's frown deepened. "We have already discussed this, Lady Lynette."

"I know, I know!" I raised my hand in defence. "I was just curious about the aether theories you teach."

"That class is purely to discuss the applications of aether and our current understanding of it."

"So there isn't any practical knowledge?" I brightened as the lieutenant sighed.

"I see where you are going, Lady Lynette. No, nothing in that class can cause you any risk. It will have little relevance to you, though."

"Would I be able to sit in anyway? I am a noble; isn't this knowledge that I should at least have the privilege of acquiring?" I knew I was pushing his buttons here. I hadn't played my noble card in a long time, not since my second life.

"I see you are already applying your determination." The lieutenant shook his head. "Very well. You can join my sessions on aether theories."

The instant he agreed, I could feel the beam of my smile. "Thank you, Lieutenant."

My disappointment was hard to hide when I left Lieutenant Cragborn's study. Rian and Teresa had tried to cheer me up when I told them I didn't qualify to train as a summoner but as a foot guard. Rian didn't seem surprised when I told them. Her sympathetic look told me she had been expecting as much. Lacey gave me a comforting smile but didn't say anything, afraid to make eye contact with me still.

Honestly? I wasn't sure what I had expected.

I had somewhat predicted this. General Saika had warned me, after all, that I likely wouldn't be able to become a summoner at my assessment. I guessed I had held on to a glimmer of hope.

Maintaining a smile when Teresa and Rian returned from their assessments made it all the more difficult. They, of course, were enrolled in training as summoners. Teresa was apparently the only commoner with a core to have been accepted in years. I was happy for her, but a pang of envy gnawed in my gut. They would all learn how to control aether, whereas I had only Albus to rely on.

How far ahead would they get?

Was I going to be left behind, to be forever the weakest?

At least Lieutenant Cragborn had allowed me to join his aether theories lectures.

As the trainees received their evaluations, I sat at my desk in the lecture hall, reading the information sheet provided by Lieutenant Cragborn. The sheet contained detailed rules and regulations of the army. It outlined all trainees' expectations of conduct, appearance, and behaviour.

The first rule emphasised the importance of maintaining a neat and professional appearance whilst in public. We were representatives of the army and had to uphold its standards at all times. Additionally, trainees were required to request leave from the keep if they wanted to go to the capital.

The sheet also stressed the need for appropriate behaviour and adherence to the law. Breaking the law would result in severe reprimand, and disobeying orders from higher-ranking officers was not tolerated. It was mandatory for all recruits to take on jobs at the task centre, with a minimum of one job per month.

Respect and nonviolent conflict resolution were encouraged amongst the trainees. Antagonistic behaviour was frowned upon, and disputes were to be handled without resorting to violence. However, members could request duels if approved by a higher-ranking officer, though summoners were not allowed to duel foot guards using aether.

As I read through the rules, an angry voice interrupted my concentration. I looked up to see Garret scowling as he slammed his evaluation sheet onto the desk. Kit sat beside him.

"What a load of crap," Garret grumbled, causing a few heads to turn his way.

"What's wrong?" Kit asked, a little apprehensive.

"What do you think? He made me sign a blood contract! Of all things." Garret gritted his teeth in frustration.

"Well, duh, of course he did." Rian rolled her eyes beside me. "What did you expect?"

"I expected a delay." Garret scowled at her before his eyes shot in my direction. "I explained that I would be leaving as soon as Lady Lynette's contract was revoked. The stubborn fool wouldn't listen. Said it wasn't his problem."

I couldn't help the small smile on my lips. "How disappointing for you, Lord Garret."

"Very disappointing." Teresa smiled innocently on my left.

"Shut it, commoner," Garret snapped, casting a hesitant glance at his sheet on the table. "As soon as Viscount Heversham's letter has been delivered, I will request a delay in my training."

Rian raised an eyebrow, leaning on her hand. "You think they will allow that?"

"Of course." Garret waved his hand nonchalantly, nodding to himself. "It's been done before."

"You are placing a lot of trust in Viscount Heversham." I sighed, revelling in his predicament. My opinion of Lieutenant Cragborn continued to improve.

"Why wouldn't I?" Garret smirked, his confidence annoying me. "You've only been accepted as a foot guard. There is no worth in keeping you here."

"Foot guards are just as valuable as summoners." Teresa frowned, biting her cheek.

"Sure, they are useful to serve summoners." Garret grinned, leaning back in his chair. "A shame, really. If you were staying, Lady Lynette, perhaps you could serve me."

I felt a shudder run through me.

I hadn't even considered that possibility.

The information sheet provided by Lieutenant Cragborn explained that once summoners reached a certain level, a select few would train with foot guards to learn leadership skills. However, I highly doubted Garret would qualify for such a position of authority. But the mere thought of it . . .

"I wouldn't count on that." I narrowed my eyes at his red hair as my chest tightened. "Baron lineages are rarely promoted to leadership."

As expected, Garret's expression twisted upon hearing my words, though he struggled to restrain himself in front of our audience. I gave him my own smug smirk, further fuelling his hate. I purposely chose to demean his future noble rank. He was always sensitive about only being a baron when we were married.

"Lady Lynette," Garret said, his words gritted, aware of those around us. "I am saddened by your lack of faith in me."

"Faith has nothing to do with it, Lord Garret," I replied, offering him a saccharine smile. I swore I saw a vein bulge on his head in response.

Garret's face turned red with anger, his attempt to maintain his composure visibly failing. I could sense the boiling rage within him as he struggled to respond to my provocation. He most likely would have hit me in my last life married to him if I had said such a thing. Belittling his pride and skills was something he hated more than anything.

I usually would not have dared provoke him this way, but I couldn't help it. Something inside me bubbled at the thought of following his lead in any situation. Being a foot guard was such a terrifying prospect. He never did achieve any prestige in the army when we were married. He likely wouldn't in this life, either, but I had no guarantee of that.

Now?

The satisfaction that washed over me was undeniable. For once, I held the upper hand with our audience; he couldn't do a thing he wanted as we weren't alone, and Garret couldn't stand it.

"Lady Lynette," Garret finally managed to say through clenched teeth. "Have you no respect for a fellow noble's ambitions? As your fiancé, I am displeased by your words."

A chuckle escaped my lips; I was unable to contain the amusement I felt at his response. Rian and Teresa were tense beside me, and I could see Kit sweating. Harold looked away with a frown as Lacey shrank in her seat.

"Ah, Lord Garret, I think you are forgetting one very important fact." I tilted my head as I rested it in my hand.

Garret frowned, his eyes narrowing into fiery slits as the tension in the air grew. "And what might that be?"

"Respect is earned, Lord Garret, and I have seen nothing from you that merits my admiration or esteem." I met his gaze with a cool composure as my heart thumped.

Garret took a deep breath, visibly forcing himself to regain control. "Mark my words, Lady Lynette. I will prove you wrong. I will surpass your expectations."

"Unlikely, Lord Garret. I suggest you focus on honing your personality rather than your skills."

Garret's face exploded in emotion. "Personality?" he scoffed, his voice laced with disdain. "I have plenty of personality, unlike you, Lady Lynette. All I see is a spoilt noblewoman who thinks she is better than everyone else. You will do well to remind yourself you are lucky to have my interest."

A surge of irritation coursed through me, but I refused to let it show. Instead, I maintained my demeanour, my gaze steady and unwavering.

"Lucky?" I repeated, my voice calm and composed. "If being with you is what passes for luck, then I must have a very different understanding of the word. I have no desire to be tied to someone who lacks respect, humility, and the ability to see beyond their own inflated ego."

Garret's face twisted with anger, his fists clenched tightly by his sides. The tension between us was tight like a drawn string, and the room seemed to hold its breath, awaiting the next move. I could see his frustration and a flicker of disbelief that I would dare to challenge him.

"You think so highly of yourself, Lady Lynette," he spat, his voice laced with venom. "But mark my words. I will prove you wrong. I will make you regret doubting me."

I chuckled softly, with a glimmer of amusement. "Oh, Garret, how predictable you are. Always seeking to assert your dominance, to prove yourself superior. But the truth is, no amount of bluster or empty threats can change who you truly are."

His face contorted with rage, his control slipping further as his anger consumed him. I knew I had struck a nerve at the core of his insecurities. And as much as it pained me to stoop to his level, I couldn't help but revel in the satisfaction of exposing his true character.

A door slammed, making us all jump and turn to the study door. Lieutenant Cragborn glared across the room at us. I felt my body still at his hardened gaze towards me. However, his narrowed eyes quickly fell towards Garret, and I saw a flicker of displeasure.

"Trainees." The lieutenant spoke loudly, his voice stern. "Now that your evaluations are over, I will explain about the task centre."

I felt a soft warmth as my hand was gripped under my desk. Teresa forced a smile as I pulled my attention away from Garret, albeit with a lingering awareness of his eyes burning into me.

CHAPTER FORTY-THREE

The abrupt interruption from Lieutenant Cragborn served as a much-needed distraction from the tense confrontation between Garret and me. I shifted my attention to the stern figure at the front of the room, grateful for the opportunity to refocus and regain my composure.

I had let my emotions get the better of me again.

I shouldn't have argued with Garret like that in such a public space. I could already see the glances people were sneaking my way. I had probably been unreasonable to many eyes, doubting my supposed fiancé and belittling his ambitions. However, they did not know Garret as I did.

They had not suffered under his hands as I had.

As I took a deep breath, I reminded myself of the reasons why I had reacted the way I did. The pain of my experiences with Garret still lingered, and it influenced my words and actions at that moment. Whilst I understood that the public confrontation was not ideal, it was difficult to suppress my emotions entirely.

But now, in the presence of Lieutenant Cragborn and my fellow trainees, I knew I had to regain control and compose myself. I couldn't let my personal history with Garret dictate my behaviour during the training. This was a fresh start, an opportunity to redefine myself and prove my worth independent of my past lives.

"As you should have noted, it is mandatory for all recruits to take on jobs at the task centre. You must all take on at least one job per month," the lieutenant began as he folded his hands behind his back.

"As trainees, you will be limited to grade one tasks. These involve simple tasks such as gathering supplies, cleaning training yards, and organising documents. You are all quite capable of such tasks."

"Cleaning?" Kit raised his voice with a complaint. "Nobles don't clean."

"They do here, Lord Kit. Either do these tasks or have your core stripped."

"Wait, what?" Kit exclaimed, his eyes widening.

"Yes, I thought it best to tell you all this at once rather than individually. If any of you training to become summoners break the law, cause harm to innocents, or do not uphold your blood contracts, you will be reprimanded. Any deemed unworthy will have your core stripped of aether and a block placed on your core."

"Isn't that extreme?" another noble called out.

"Not at all, Lord Garn. A summoner without restraint is dangerous to the population. It would be irresponsible of us not to do so if anyone posed a threat."

The lieutenant's words caused a collective unease amongst us. The severity of the consequences for breaking the rules and causing harm was apparent.

It sent a chill down my spine.

It was a drastic measure to block someone's core. They would be rendered powerless. Essentially a noble's nightmare; they would be the same as a commoner. The same as I had been in my past lives. They would have to live under the rules of their family. They would depend on them for survival. A small bitter smile creased my features. They would be treated as many of the women in high society. Nothing but pawns for marriage connections.

The nobles in the room seemed particularly taken aback by the notion of performing menial tasks like cleaning. Their privileged upbringing had shielded them from such responsibilities, but it was clear that the rules applied to everyone, regardless of their noble status.

I glanced at Kit, who appeared flustered by the lieutenant's statement. It seemed he had never considered the potential consequences of breaking the rules or refusing to perform the assigned tasks. The reality of the situation was starting to sink in for him.

"What about those in the temples? They have summoners serving the gods. Do they get their cores stripped?" Another hand rose.

"Trained summoners who choose to join the temple as guardians do so because they have unique talents that suit temple life. Those who are unable to successfully learn aether transfer, or fail to grasp control of their aether, often become monks instead of having their core stripped. All summoners who serve the gods originally trained here, in the army. They are held to the same values and rules as we are."

I perked up at the mention of the temples. I had heard about the prestige of being chosen to serve as a temple summoner. They were often sent overseas to the neighbouring kingdoms under the Zopan Empire to establish the gods and protect the priests. Maybe that was something Vishka wanted for me?

She was a god, after all.

The lieutenant explained the importance of the task centre. Only one job was required each month, but completing a job meant credits. Credits were essential to life in the keep. It was the only accepted currency, and we would need them if we wanted to eat the more luxurious meals at the eatery. Today our meal was free, but that was no longer the case. We would each receive fifty credits monthly as a stipend, but this was only enough for bread and eggs daily. We needed credits to book out personal training slots, practice equipment, and scrolls to learn new techniques. Though I wouldn't be able to access scrolls as a foot guard.

The importance of credits was made very clear. Without them, we would be fighting for resources and time. However, there were only so many jobs available, so it was imperative to try to obtain a desirable job as soon as possible.

The badges provided with our uniforms were inscribed with runes. We all took them off our cloaks and inspected the tiny enchantments etched into the back of the bronze. They were enchanted to keep count of our credits. Touching them with another could transfer credits and also pay for facilities. We each were given our stipend by the lieutenant, who also had us prick our fingers to drop blood onto them, sealing them as ours. This provided an identity to each badge so anyone else could not use it.

The lieutenant then also explained about our rooms. Our room keys worked similarly. We repeated the process of sealing them as ours with our blood. They were each attuned to each room. By sealing the key as belonging to us, we prevented any access to our room from anyone else. It was a relief to know that no one would be able to enter my room without my permission. Maybe I could have left my letter in my room rather than tucking it into the pocket of my chest garment.

Our six-day week was scheduled for us. On fire days, we would train to improve our skills or attend the lecture on the theories of aether. On water days, we would have our session training with weapons. Earth day was a personal choice. We could train as we wanted, complete a job, or request permission to go into the capital. Wind day was more weapons training, darkness day was skills or practical aether manipulation, and light day was another personal choice, but there was a lecture to teach numeracy and how to write for commoners.

Finally, the lieutenant explained that we would be free to explore the keep today. Tomorrow, on water day, we would begin our training with weapons and physical combat with Lieutenant Sharpclaw. All trainees were required to pass combat evaluations, summoner and foot guard. We were expected to pass at different intervals, as our skills would vary. Once we passed, we would be entered into a ranking system of recruits.

I gulped as the ranking system was explained. Combat was our primary skill to train for at the gathering stage, and our ranking would be focused on that. It was a way of encouraging individual competition and a will to improve amongst the trainees. Duels could be requested to try to increase your ranking. It was also a way for the lieutenants to decide who would work best on a team.

For summoners, the ranking system would help determine the compatibility of their skills with others, even before they gained their elemental abilities at foundation. It was a way to assess who would work best together in the future, as teamwork was crucial for summoners in fulfilling their roles.

On the other hand, foot guards would be more interchangeable, placed where needed without necessarily forming a set team. The duels and rankings would help the lieutenants determine the appropriate professions and summoners under whom the foot guards would later serve.

Garret's smirk towards me made me flinch. I could read the thoughts he was no doubt thinking. He was excited to have an opportunity to publicly duel me when given the chance. If he would have the chance.

I turned away from his gaze, a frown plastered on my lips. I had to make sure I was able to fight. I couldn't remain useless. Not if I wanted to stay here.

After the lieutenant brought our welcome lecture to an end, he dismissed us with a wave of his hand before returning to his study.

"Do you think they have any jobs in the eatery?" Teresa pondered as she gazed at the bronze badge in her hand, tracing the pattern of the flower bud inscribed on it.

"Maybe, but I didn't think . . . you liked cooking?" I asked hesitantly, remembering our numerous meals of burnt food during the march.

Teresa pinned her badge back onto her grey cloak with a heavy sigh. "It's not that I don't like it. It's more that I suck at it."

"So why would you want a job at the eatery?" Rian asked as she stood up from her desk with us.

"I don't want to suck at it any more." Teresa pouted. "Figured a job there may teach me? Maybe?"

Rian and I shared a glance with small smiles. "I think it's worth a try. You never know." I followed them both down the rows of desks.

"It is an interesting outlook on the task system." Harold nodded beside me. "Choosing a task that will also grant you a skill is intriguing. I will choose carefully."

"Anything that makes me clean up after someone is preposterous." Garret scowled ahead of us as he interjected into our conversation.

"Agreed. I refuse to do anything that demeaning," Kit mumbled, displeased.

"M-maybe there will be a task for organising research documents?" Lacey stumbled a little on the length of her cloak, blushing red at the act.

"If there is, I will be taking that." Garret raised his head high. "Sorting documents is far preferred to anything servants should be doing."

"Of course you would think that way." I rolled my eyes at Garret's ego. I imagined that many of the nobles thought the same way. They were above the work of servants and commoners. In my past lives, I maybe would have thought the same. However, now I had little care for such things. My only goal was to survive in this life.

"Lady Lynette." Garret stopped at the end of the desk rows, allowing other nobles to pass him by.

"Yes?" I narrowed my eyes as I got closer.

"May I have a word, alone?" he asked with a tint of grit in his voice.

I froze in my step, meeting his dull brown eyes as he stared at me. Rian and Teresa tensed beside me, blocking the exit from the desks. My skin prickled at the look in Garret's eyes. I knew that look. He was angry. Fuming even.

"I—I have other matters to attend to." I swallowed the nerves that erupted throughout my gut. I had been brazen before, confident, as we had not been alone together.

Garret shot out his hand to block my way as I tried to leave. "This cannot wait." He glared at me. "You cannot refuse this request, Lady Lynette, my *dear* fiancée."

"Lord Garret, this is inappropriate." Rian frowned as she gently placed a hand on my shoulder and stood in front of me. "You cannot force Lady Lynette to meet with you."

"Lady Rian, with all due respect, you have no say in when a man wishes to speak with his partner," Garret retorted snidely.

Rian flinched a little. I could see her frustration as she gripped her sheet of paper tighter.

Sadly, Garret was correct.

As Rian was not my family, she could not stop Garret from requesting to speak with me. It was an old misogynistic etiquette rule that allowed a man of close relation to request a private audience with a woman. Only a family member could refuse on my behalf, and I had no luck with that happening. Because I was Garret's supposed fiancée, he was unfortunately considered a close relation since Roger had accepted his proposal against my wishes. In the past, many women had been exploited by such means by their supposed fiancés, so it was now heavily frowned upon.

Garret, however, did not care about this fact. He was a traditionalist.

I could refuse him, but that would only incite him to drag this out longer. *Maybe I could finally get him to leave me alone if we talked.*

"It's okay, Rian," I said weakly, removing her hand from my shoulder. "I will speak with him." I didn't have a choice. If I did not comply, Garret would only make things worse. I couldn't implicate Rian in my feud with Garret. It was my issue, not hers. I knew disrespecting him like that would have its consequences. Garret was not a forgiving man.

Rian grimaced as Garret grinned triumphantly at my reluctant agreement to his request.

With a small nod from Rian and a concerned gaze from Teresa and Harold, I stood aside as the rest of the nobles and commoners left the hallway, leaving me alone with Garret.

CHAPTER FORTY-FOUR

The lecture hall felt ominous as I stood alone with Garret. My eyes flicked to the doorway that was Lieutenant Cragborn's study. He had shut himself away in there; knowing he was nearby was somewhat comforting. I wasn't entirely alone.

Garret stood before me with a look that would have frightened a child. As he stepped closer, I quickly backed away, folding my arms across my chest as I regarded him warily. "What is it that you wanted to discuss, Lord Garret?" I bit out my words, trying to calm my thumping heart.

The last time we were alone like this, he had assaulted me.

He couldn't do anything this time, though; now that he had signed a blood contract, if he harmed me, he could face dire consequences for breaking the rules.

Garret dropped his arm as he approached. Seeing my body language, he sneered before opening his mouth, his voice laced with barely concealed anger. "I won't tolerate your disrespect, Lady Lynette. It was humiliating for me to endure your outburst earlier."

My lips upturned at his words. "Humiliating? Exactly how do you think your actions towards me aren't humiliating? You had no right to lay your hands on me, but you did anyway." I furrowed my eyebrows as my unease swirled with a mix of rage.

"Hah," Garret sneered. "I have every right to you as your fiancé. I can do what I want." He immediately stepped towards me, and my heart quickened.

There's that uptight traditionalist mindset again.

I stepped away from him, avoiding his attempt to grab my arm again, which only upset him.

"Lady Lynette, you are treading on thin ice," Garret growled as he stepped towards me again. I quickly sidestepped once more, avoiding contact, inciting a furious snarl from his lips.

"I am your fiancé!" Garret shouted, his hands balled into fists. "You will learn to show me the respect I deserve."

"Fiancé?" I laughed with no emotion. "A title you claim to hold by virtue of an arrangement made by our families. It means nothing to me, Lord Garret. I have not agreed to any such thing. You cannot force me to show you any respect."

Just why was he so insistent on this?

Garret's face twisted in anger as he glared at me. The room seemed to grow colder as I held his gaze. He took a step closer, his voice low and dangerous. "You will regret crossing me, Lady Lynette. I have power and influence and won't hesitate to use it against you." He clenched his fists tightly by his side. "Why won't you just accept the proposal?" he shouted, his voice a little desperate.

I held my ground, refusing to let his threats intimidate me.

Not this time.

I pushed down the fear crawling in my skin. I couldn't let myself become the woman I had been as his wife. This life had to be different.

"I'm not afraid of you, Lord Garret. I've endured far worse than you can ever imagine. I will not be silenced or controlled by you, a mere baron's son." I lied a little. My fear of him was still ingrained in my body. "I simply do not want to marry you."

Garret's eyes narrowed, a mix of frustration and anger flickering in his gaze. "You think you're so smug, but you will be nothing without me. You will remain a worthless token noble. I can ruin you, tarnish your family's name."

"Ruin my family name?" I couldn't stop my mocking laughter. Garret hesitated, a little surprised at my tone. "I could not care less about that. You can do nothing that will threaten me in that regard, Lord Garret." What did I care if Garret created rumours to tarnish my name? It was already bad enough with my past actions. I also had absolutely no care anymore for my family's reputation.

"You little bi—" Garret raised his hand so quickly I didn't register what was happening. A memory flashed in my mind of this very act, and fear punctured my courage.

My body flinched and stiffened in an automatic response, as it always did when Garret was about to hit me. I quickly shut my eyes, readying for the impact, unable to move.

But no pain followed.

Hesitantly, I opened my eyes in a squint and quickly widened them at the box now in my vision.

> **Vishka's Guidance System**
> Callan Heversham
> Likeability: 24% (+5%)

"C-Callan?" I stuttered as he stood beside me, his hand gripping Garret's outstretched wrist with an intense fury that sent a shiver through me.

"You little shit." Callan furrowed his lips as he stared daggers at Garret. "What do you think you are doing to my sister?"

Garret trembled as Callan tightened his grip on his shaking wrist. "L-Lord Callan. I—I was merely trying to t-tuck Lady Lynette's hair behind her ear." Garret lied reflexively.

Callan's grip on Garret's wrist tightened even further, his voice dripping with disbelief. "Do you take me for a fool, Lord Garret? You were about to strike her."

Garret's face flushed with anger, but there was a glimmer of fear in his eyes as he gulped under the weight of Callan's gaze. "Y-you misunderstand. I would never harm my fiancée."

Callan's eyes narrowed. "Yet you would force her to meet with you alone, knowing she could not refuse easily? You reek of lies, Lord Garret."

Garret's composure wavered, his façade crumbling under Callan's unwavering scrutiny. His voice trembled as he struggled to maintain his lie. "I . . . I love Lynette. I would never lay a hand on her."

My name coming out of Garret's mouth made me want to hack in repulsion. Yet a bitter laugh escaped my lips as I took in my situation.

Never would I have thought I would see a day where Callan defended me.

"Love? Is that what you call it?" I shook my head, stepping away from the two as my heart squeezed tightly. "You have a messed-up ideal of love, Lord Garret." Not that I knew what love really was. That was something that had eluded me all of my lifetimes.

Garret's expression contorted with a mix of frustration and desperation. "Lady Lynette, you don't understand. I—"

Before he could finish his sentence, Callan released Garret's wrist, but his stance remained solid as he stood between us, a silent warning hanging in the air.

"Leave. Now, Lord Garret." Callan's voice was cold and piercing. "You will stay away from my sister. If I ever hear of you demanding to be alone with her again, I will make sure you face the consequences."

Garret stumbled back, his face pale as he cupped his wrist with a mixture of anger and defeat. He glanced between Callan and me before speaking bitterly. "I assure you, Lord Callan, this is a misunderstanding." Garret forced a polite smile. "I will respectfully do as you ask, though, and forgo my right as her fiancé to spend time alone with Lady Lynette." He straightened and performed an awkward bow.

"Leave." Callan spoke calmly, his irritation with Garret's remaining presence not showing in his body language.

"As you wish," Garret gritted out as he turned on his heel and exited the lecture hall without uttering another word. The air seemed to lighten as the door slammed behind him, leaving behind a heavy silence that was eventually broken by a deep exhale from Callan.

The stiffness in my body slowly relaxed a little as Callan turned to face me, his grey eyes searching me with a look of concern so much like Cassandra's once did. "I'm sorry I didn't get here sooner," Callan said, the cold edge to his voice softening.

"How did you know I was here?" I asked quietly as I unfolded my arms, my heart slowly calming down.

"Lady Rian rushed over to me whilst I was gathering. She told me what Garret had requested of you." Callan spat Garret's name with a purse of his lips. "That little swine. How dare he invoke such an old etiquette request? Nobody does that anymore."

"Th-thank you," I said, still processing.

"I promised I would not leave you alone with him. I want to keep my word." Callan looked at me with what I could only regard as sympathy—something I had not experienced often. "I—" He paused as his expression tightened.

"What is it?" I pried, a little uncertain. Callan had promised me such, but I had never truly thought he would do so. His presence here, now, was surprising. As my brother, only he or Eduard could have refused Garret's request. Yet I never expected that either of them would.

"I am sorry, Lynette." Callan sighed with a look of guilt.

"Why are you sorry?" I frowned, a little confused. It was not Callan who made Garret so despicable.

Callan gently reached for my hand, and I allowed him to take it. "I tried to speak with Eduard about Lord Garret, but he refused to listen." He looked away. "Eduard did not trust what you told me."

I resisted the snort that wanted to escape my lips. "I wouldn't worry. Eduard has never had much faith in me." So Callan had told Eduard of my interaction with Garret and his assault. It was no surprise that Eduard did not believe me, and even less so that he did not believe Callan.

"He is stubborn, but no matter what I said, he would not listen." Callan frowned. "Lynette, he has handed Father's letter to the generals for your blood contract to be revoked this morning."

My hand in Callan's froze for a moment.

Despite my expectation of Eduard doing this, my heart still sank. The small sliver of hope I had buried that maybe he wouldn't do as Roger wished was broken.

"I see," I said sullenly, my own letter tucked in my chest pocket, burning with its presence.

"Lynette, I promise, I wouldn't say this if I didn't think it the best option for you. But maybe you should accept it being revoked. I heard you are only being admitted as a foot guard, and well, I worry about you. You aren't exactly the best with a jian." Callan spoke softly, but the calm that had washed over me faded as a wave of new anger replaced it.

I ripped my hand out of Callan's and stepped back as he reached out, concerned.

"So you think I won't be able to make it as foot guard?" My voice turned cold as I looked at my brother. I thought maybe he was changing, having come to save me from Garret. Perhaps I was wrong.

"Lynette, I'm only being realistic." Callan used a soothing tone. "As a foot guard, you will eventually be deployed somewhere to assist summoners. You will be at risk. You could die. You barely survived the march."

"I am here to train, aren't I? There are plenty of other weapons than the jian I could be good at." I bitterly clenched my teeth as I saw Callan's box flicker. "I haven't resonated with one yet."

"That may be so." Callan raised his voice a little. "But staying in the army is a death trap for you. You aren't suited to battle. They could send you out at any moment, no matter your profession."

"Who are you to determine what I am suitable for?" I argued.

"I am your brother, Lynette," Callan replied, his voice tinged with a mix of exasperation and genuine worry. "I only want what's best for you. I've seen the hardships you've endured, the struggles you've faced on the march. I don't want you to be put in further danger."

I crossed my arms, my anger boiling beneath the surface. "And what do you think is best for me, Callan? To be trapped in a life dictated by an arranged marriage, where I am at the mercy of a man like Garret Asher? To surrender my agency and live as a prisoner in my own existence?"

Callan's expression softened, a flicker of remorse in his eyes. "I understand your anger, Lynette. I do. But the army, the life of a foot guard . . . It's not the only path for you. There are other ways to find freedom and happiness."

I scoffed, bitterness seeping into my words. "Tell me, Callan, what are these other ways? Enlighten me. Are there options that don't involve me being shackled to a man I despise? Are there alternatives that allow me to go against Roger's wishes?"

Callan sighed. "I don't have all the answers, Lynette. But I won't let that happen. I will do everything in my power to stop your marriage. But believe that there are paths out there for you, ones that don't involve the army."

I knew better. I had lived those other paths already and died.

"Where is Lord Nathaniel?" I spoke resignedly as Callan scrunched up his face.

"He will be in his office. Why?"

"Can you show me where that is?"

"Sure, but . . ." Callan's hesitation to bring me to the man from my scandal was obvious. Likely, his conversation with Eduard was what had sparked this argument between us. Eduard was adamant that I was not suitable for the army; he had said as much.

"Please, take me to Lord Nathaniel. I have something to discuss with him," I told Callan, glancing at the box above his head as he frowned.

"All right," he agreed reluctantly.

Vishka's Guidance System
Callan Heversham
Likeability: 21% (−3%)

CHAPTER FORTY-FIVE

Callan walked beside me as he took me through the hallways of the audi-torium. We passed a few other trainees as they explored the building that contained the lecture halls. Each of them hesitated as we passed them by, Callan's expression one of dour frustration.

I studied his features for a moment as we walked. "Did something happen?"

"What?" Callan turned to me, a little puzzled.

"Your face. It looks a little red on your left side." I raised my hand towards him on instinct, my fingers gently brushing the light swelling, making Callan flinch.

He took my hand and shoved it away quickly as his ears reddened. "It's nothing for you to worry about."

"You should put something cold on it. It will help reduce the redness faster." I shrugged at his actions. Had he gotten into a fight again? He often did that when we were kids.

"Why do you want to see Lord Nathaniel all of a sudden?" Callan asked as we rounded a corner. The hallway's constriction opened into a large courtyard. Pillars of stone edged our walkway, separating it from the small square garden beside it. I gazed at the circular water fountain at the centre of the garden, eerily similar to the fountain I had died beside when Callan had stabbed me.

"It's a private matter I do not wish to discuss with you." I pressed my lips together as Callan glowered at my response.

"So, you really did get cosy with him then," he sneered, tightening his fists.

"What I did or didn't do really isn't your concern." I sighed as he slowed his pace to allow a group of summoners to pass us.

"Not my concern? I think, as your brother, I have a right to know if Lord Nathaniel is going to be my new brother-in-law."

"Brother-in-law? Now, that is presumptuous. I'm supposedly an engaged woman, Callan." I rolled my eyes, a little sarcasm leaking into my voice.

"If that's presumptuous, then what you did is immoral." Callan stopped at the end of the walkway to face me. The sun peered around the pillars to cast a pattern of shadow on his face as he frowned with a look of irritation. "I get why you did it, to cancel your engagement with that twit. But your relationship with Lord Nathaniel is going to make others question your intentions."

"My intentions?" I raised an eyebrow, folding my arms. "Callan, I don't see what my intentions have to do with you, or anyone else for that matter." Was he really suddenly deciding to care about my life? I know he had said he wanted to be a better brother to me. But still, this was strange.

I saw his eyebrow twitch as Callan took a deep breath. "Lynette, I swear you are dense sometimes," he said, a little strained. "Everyone knows you sullied yourself in the tavern that day, but it's not common knowledge who it was with. If you keep clinging to Lord Nathaniel, they will figure it out, and that will put him in a bad position, as well as you. It will create expectations for both of you. If you really don't intend to marry Lord Nathaniel, then stop going to him for 'private' discussions."

"You almost sound jealous." I smirked at him. Of course, I knew that, but Nate was the only person I had any semblance of trust towards. I had to ask someone about my plan before I was summoned by the generals for the revocation of my blood contract. If Eduard had handed in Roger's letter this morning, then I didn't have much time. Searching the library for legal books was out of the question. I was left with having to ask someone directly. I couldn't discuss it with Callan as he would likely try to stop me.

Nathaniel was my only option.

"Take this seriously, Lynette," Callan retorted as his voice rose at my comment. "Lord Nathaniel is the heir to Marquess Hudson. We can't involve him in our affairs. His father won't stand for any blemish on their reputation that you may bring them. It's better for you and Lord Nathaniel that you stay away from him from now on."

"I—" I pinched my fingers and cast my gaze away. I hadn't forgotten Nathaniel came from a marquess's lineage. He had said there would be complications now that I was coming to the capital; maybe it was his father. I had no idea what the marquess was like; perhaps this was risky. With their higher rank, his family could easily inflict damage on us. Maybe Callan truly was worried about this. He must have known the marquess's reputation, as he attended the events of the social season every year.

"I will be careful," I mumbled, stepping forward to pass Callan and the pillared walkway. I could see the hallways converging on this small open court-yard ahead of us.

"Lynette, did you hear what I said?" Callan exclaimed, following me, his voice raised with disbelief as I continued forward despite his warnings.

"I did, Callan. But I have something I must discuss with Lord Nathaniel. It cannot wait." I had no choice; I had no one else I trusted. I was sure a conversation with Nathaniel wouldn't put too much pressure on his social standing. However, Callan was probably right. I shouldn't involve Nathaniel too much in my personal issues; they were mine to deal with. It was only his advice I needed, nothing else.

"Is it really that important?" Callan shuffled beside me as he bit his cheek.

"It is," I sighed as I realised I had no idea where I was supposed to go now that we were back in the hallways of the auditorium.

"Fine." Callan scowled. "His office is this way; all of the senior-ranked members of the army have their offices on this side of the building."

"Thank you, Callan." I truly was thankful. Despite his clear irritation at doing this, he had taken me to Lord Nathaniel. He didn't have to do that; he could have walked away and left me to try to find Nathaniel myself, which would have taken up valuable time. I was lucky he was close by, in all honesty; if his office at been on the other side of Alinor Keep, I might not have made it in time before the generals summoned me.

"Just promise me you won't get him involved any further." Callan stopped by a doorway in the middle of the hallway. Other similar-looking doors surrounded it, but each of them had names carved into the wood in elegant writing.

"I don't intend to." I smiled with a small nod as I raised my hand to the door and knocked.

Vishka's Guidance System
Callan Heversham
Likeability: 19% (−2%)

I stared up at the man with honey-blond shoulder-length hair who opened the door. Striking deep orange eyes looked down at me through glass spectacles as he raised an eyebrow in thought. The orange tone contrasted exceptionally with his light-toned face.

"I—um," I spluttered, trying to speak as my gaze drifted from his square jaw to the tips of his hair, dyed the same dark orange as his eyes. His features were incredibly similar to Nathaniel's, but this man was not him.

"Who is it, Soren?" Nathaniel's voice called from behind the man in the doorway.

"No clue. Some woman," Soren said as he leaned his hand on the doorway.

"I—I am Lady Lynette. I wish to speak with Lord Nathaniel." I shook myself out of my stupor. I felt my cheeks redden as I realised I had been staring. This man was incredibly handsome.

"Lady Lynette?" Soren's eyes narrowed as though something had dawned on him. "What do you want exactly?" His tone changed from curious to apprehensive.

"Lynette? What a pleasure to see you." Nathaniel's joyful tone interrupted Soren's gaze as he bounded from behind and moved Soren aside.

"Lord Nathaniel." Callan bowed beside me and discreetly grabbed the material of my cloak to pull me down with him. I quickly followed suit and bowed as expected of someone of a viscount's lineage in the presence of the son of a marquess. We were no longer on the plains marching; we had to show proper decorum in the capital.

"Oh, Lord Callan, you are here too . . ." Nathaniel seemed surprised to see Callan. "What brings you here?"

"I wished to speak with you, Lord Nathaniel." I rose from my bow as Nate cocked his head. "Callan was kind enough to show me where I could find you. I apologise for this sudden request. However, I must speak with you as a matter of urgency."

"I was going to come find you on earth day, but now is fine." Nathaniel smiled warmly. "I told you to call me Nate, remember?" He chuckled as Callan frowned beside me, clearly unhappy with our familiarity.

"Of course, Nate." I mirrored his smile, feeling tense as both Callan and Soren looked at me, displeased.

"Come inside, Lynette. Is Lord Callan joining us?" Nate asked, looking at Callan's stiff figure. Callan opened his mouth to respond, and I could tell that he wanted to join us rather than leaving me alone with Nate.

"If it is quite all right, may we speak alone, Nate?" I said quickly, causing Callan to shoot a look at me as his box began to blur again.

"Nate, is this appropriate?" Soren mumbled as he pushed the bridge of his glasses closer to his eyes. His action was so graceful for such a simple thing. Wait, was I staring again?

"It's fine, Soren." Nate waved his hand nonchalantly. "Lynette and I are well acquainted. Besides, a captain may speak with a trainee alone." His grin was wide. If I were not a trainee, speaking alone with Nate right now would probably be inappropriate for a lady.

"Very well," Soren sighed as he moved to leave the office. "We will continue our conversation at a later date. Lady Lynette, Lord Callan." Soren bowed slightly to us both, and we returned the etiquette as he moved to leave. His footsteps echoed on the hard floors as his red summoner cape fell into place with his steps.

I watched Soren leave, still a little mesmerised by his beauty. I had never seen orange eyes like his before. I wondered if they were normal. Was he human or daemon like Lieutenant Cragborn? His hair also had a tinge of the same orange as his eyes, like daemons' features often did.

"I will wait here for your conversation to conclude," Callan gritted out, straightening his posture. "I intend to escort my sister around Alinor Keep today."

"How very gracious of you." Nate hummed as I stepped into his office. They were both being civil with one another. However, I could see Callan's struggle not to raise his voice. There was little he could do to go against someone from a marquess's lineage. No matter how much he did not want me to be alone with Nate, he could not refuse it.

"We won't be long." I smiled at Callan, trying to calm him. I didn't want to risk him overhearing my conversation with Nate. I couldn't let him suspect anything about my plan. If he had even the smallest hint, it wouldn't bode well for me. For that reason, I wasn't going to object to Callan's desire to escort me. It would only irritate him.

"After you, Lynette." Nate directed me to a plush leather chair in the centre of the room in front of a black wooden desk as he closed the door on a scowling Callan.

Vishka's Guidance System
Callan Heversham
Likeability: 18% (−1%)

CHAPTER FORTY-SIX

Nathaniel's office was very different to Lieutenant Cragborn's. Instead of bookshelves, various halberds hung on the walls as decoration. A large window behind his desk let sunlight fill the room, showing off the intricate pattern woven into a large round rug. His desk was made of black-dyed wood with silver handles and edges adorned in silver triangles. A collection of ink bottles was scattered on the right side, atop a sheet of ink-stained cloth.

Everywhere I gazed, I spotted a sign of his wealth as heir to a marquess. The curtains hanging in the window were embroidered with lions in golden thread matching the pattern on the rug. The porcelain cup in which he served me tea was whiter than snow, and the tea itself was spectacular, with a fragrant hint of lemon. It was refreshing and warming all at once.

Now that I looked closely, I saw that lions were etched into the handles of the halberds on the wall. Was the Hudson family crest a lion?

"I have to thank you, Lynette." Nate chuckled as he settled down into his chair behind his large black desk.

"Thank me?" I asked, sipping my tea.

"Yes, you got me out of a conversation I really didn't want to have with Soren." He sighed, rather pleased.

"Soren . . ." I stared, a little hesitant to ask. "Is he a Hudson?" The man shared so many features with Nate that it was hard to believe they weren't family.

"Yes, my younger brother. He's a bit prickly but soft as a lamb once you get to know him."

"Right . . ." I blinked at that description. He really didn't come across as soft.

"How are you settling in? It's your first time in Zromore, isn't it?"

"The capital is grander than I had imagined," I said nonchalantly, noticing the view from Nathaniel's window. He had a direct view of the small courtyard Callan and I had walked through to get here. The small square garden seemed to be built at the centre of this auditorium, surrounded by offices and lecture halls.

"It does take a little getting used to. Alinor Keep works separately from the rest of the capital, though. You will have to explore the city on earth day; I can take you to a great restaurant I know if you'd like?"

"That would be wonderful, Nate." I smiled. Having a meal with my first friend in this life would be nice. Maybe I could bring Teresa and Rian? Wait, no, I was supposed to be limiting my time with Nate. He was the son of a marquess. I didn't want to tarnish his reputation.

"Now that you are here, we should probably discuss . . . those complications." Nate sighed reluctantly.

"Ah, right, you did mention there would be an issue after our . . . event." I blushed, thinking back to the day in the tavern. I had approached Nate because of my selfish desire to be with a handsome man. I hadn't expected him to be kind and not at all interested in me that way. Was it the luck of Vishka that I chose Nate that day?

"Yes." Nate leaned over and poked my cheek.

"Ah!" I jumped, holding my hand against my cheek as he pulled away.

"You were redder than a tomato." Nate grinned mischievously, no doubt making me grow redder.

"Please don't tease me." I pouted as embarrassment set in, making Nate laugh and hold up his hands.

"All right, I won't tease you anymore," he said, but a glint in his eyes made me suspicious.

"The issue is my mother," he continued as I tried to forget about my embarrassing appearance.

"Your mother?" I widened my eyes. I thought the issue would have been Marquess Hudson.

"Yes, she is insistent that I marry, has been for a while now. If she finds out about our rumour, she will likely hook onto it. Not to mention"—he paused and grimaced—"there are some noble ladies who will be displeased with you for stealing *their chance.*" He said the last part with disgust.

"You have admirers? That is no surprise. You are a handsome man, Nate." I didn't hesitate to compliment my friend, making him blush this time. Ha, revenge.

"Lynette." Nate covered his face with his large hands. "Don't tell me you fell for this face as well?"

"It's hard not to," I said innocently. "You are dazzling. It must run in your family."

"Oh?" Nate raised his eyebrows with a smirk. "You find Soren dazzling too, then?"

"I—" I felt a rock form in my throat. I had just admitted that, hadn't I? Crap. "It would be unfitting of me to lie," I mumbled, sipping some more tea.

"I suppose." Nate had a cheeky look that made me purse my lips.

"What is it I should be wary about in regard to your mother?" I said, changing the subject.

Nate saw through me, but shrugged and went along with it. "It's the social season you will need to worry about. I know you haven't attended before, but if you are staying in the capital, you will come spring. I suspect you may be approached by my *admirers*, and they won't be too cordial with you. Then there is my mother. If you cancel your engagement, she will try something with you. I haven't shown interest in any other women, to her knowledge."

"I see." I sighed. It would not be my first time dealing with snooty women. My second life had given me plenty of experience in that as a socialite. "That may or may not be an issue, as I may not be staying in Zromore."

"Oh?"

"It is in regard to what I wished to speak with you about."

"Is that what you wanted to talk about so urgently? Your brother didn't seem all too pleased," Nate mused as he leaned back into his chair. He had cut his blond hair since I last saw him. It was shorter now and styled with a flick across his forehead. It suited him.

"It's nothing pleasant," I sighed, placing my cup down on his desk. "Roger Heversham has written a request to have my blood contract revoked. Eduard handed it in this morning."

"What?" Nate paused in shock as his eyes widened. "Why on earth would your father do that?"

"Roger believes I should be a reserved woman. He wants me to marry Lord Garret and be a good housewife," I said sullenly. "He doesn't believe women belong in the army." Or anywhere other than a bedchamber, for that matter. As a traditionalist, Roger would be happy for all women to birth heirs and do nothing else.

"Gosh, I knew he had a reputation for being traditional, but that's a bit much." Nate frowned, tapping his finger on the desk. Roger would be aghast with a man like Nate.

"I have only been accepted as a foot guard, so Roger's request is likely to be accepted."

"Oh, I see." Nate's expression faltered for a moment as his eyes searched me. "The generals probably will revoke your blood contract if you joined without your father's permission. If you have no aether, and you are just a foot guard, they won't see a reason to go against his wishes. Foot guards are not supposed to sign a contract until they pass their weapons exam, so your case is unusual."

"I know." I tried to hold the knot that was forming in my stomach. There was no time for me to grow my core to become reviewed as a summoner. I wouldn't be able to get my hands on any jabascus root until earth day, two days from now.

"Lynette . . ." Nate looked at me with sympathy. "There's nothing I can do to change the generals' decision when they make one."

"I know, Nate; that's not why I am here." I forced a smile as I reached into the chest pocket that held my letter. "I have an idea, but I don't know enough about the law to know if it is feasible. I was wondering . . . hoping you would be able to advise me on this?"

Nate leaned his head on his hand, curious, as I placed the letter on the desk between us.

"If this isn't an option, I would be grateful if you . . . didn't mention it to my family."

"Of course, though I will be irritating Eduard when given the chance." Nate grinned as he took my folded letter.

"Please, maybe refrain from that." I smiled, remembering how irritated Eduard had been with Nate in the past. Nate really did know how to get on Eduard's nerves.

"No promises," Nate mused. "Now, what is this?" He unfolded my letter and began to read. I watched his expression change to shock as he paused and looked at me.

"Lynette . . . are you sure about this?"

"Very sure." I gripped the material of my grey cloak. I had come so far in this life, my last life. I would do anything if it meant I could stay.

"There is a way you can do this, but I—"

A knock pounded on Nate's office door, making us jump.

Was that Callan? Why was he knocking so loudly?

"Lord Nathaniel, I understand Lady Lynette is with you. She has been summoned to the tribunal. We have come to escort her." A deep voice I did not know spoke loudly through the door.

Nate pursed his lips at the interruption. "Talk about timing," he muttered. "One moment," he shouted louder so the man behind the door could hear.

Quickly, he stood up from his desk, my letter in hand, grabbing one of the round wooden stamps. Nate plunged it into a bowl of red ink and then stamped the base of my letter. He then opened a drawer, grabbed some fresh paper, and began writing something. His quill moved swiftly as he wrote with a furrowed brow. It was short, but he sealed it with the same stamp he had used on mine and then folded them both into an envelope.

"Here; it's a sound plan, but are you really sure about this, Lynette?" Nate held out the envelope and I gingerly took it from him.

"I am. If it's possible, I will use it only if I have no other choice." I didn't know what decision the generals were going to make. Nothing was set in stone yet. I still had my chance to argue my opinion.

"It is indeed possible. I have added a note of my own should anyone question it. My seal will be enough to know it comes from my hand, not yours. That should provide legitimacy for you."

"Thank you, Nate." I felt a bubble of emotion welling inside me. "You really are too kind to me." No one I knew would do this. It was a crazy plan. Some would say it was stupid, but Nate had accepted it and stamped it with his own seal. I hadn't wanted to get him involved, only his advice, but his seal would make it difficult not to involve him now.

I had already inadvertently broken my promise to Callan not to get Lord Nathaniel involved.

"Lynette, it's hard not to want to help you." Nate smiled as he placed his large hand on my shoulder. "I worry about what you intend to do, but I trust you know what you are doing. It's not a decision someone would make lightly. If you truly do want to stay in the army, I will support you the best I can."

"I could not ask you for anything more than what you have already done for me, Nate. Thank you." I bowed and lifted the hem of my cloak, as if I were wearing a dress, in my utmost respect for this man.

My first friend.

CHAPTER FORTY-SEVEN

The auditorium halls felt even more enclosed as four summoners escorted me. They surrounded me tightly in formation like a caged animal that could go wild at any moment. I peeked behind me and saw Nathaniel following us at a distance with Callan beside him. It was strange seeing the two of them walking together so calmly, not a pair I would ever think moved in the same social circles much.

"Lady Lynette, are you aware of the decorum in a tribunal?" A summoner in front of me spoke, his voice mature with age as his white hair betrayed his once youthful vigour.

"I am aware. I must not speak until questioned." I smiled ruefully. I had learned this during the trial of my third life, which resulted in my apparent guilt and beheading.

"Correct. However, this trial is not one to determine guilt. It is merely a means to come to a decision about your status in the army. Please do not fret. You are not under arrest." The older man turned to face me with a smile. Apparently, he was attempting to comfort me. I supposed this sort of escort would be scary for a normal noblewoman. I was certainly terrified the first time.

"I understand. I am aware of why I have been summoned to a tribunal." I bit my cheek, trying to hold back my nerves. It might not be a trial to determine whether I was guilty of treason, but it was a trial that would affect my future. If this ended badly, I could wind up married to Garret again.

If that happened . . . well, would there be any point in reliving that life?

"I see. You will need to stand on the podium at the centre of the room when you are called. I will introduce the three generals to you when we arrive." The older man concluded our conversation.

My escorts led me out of the auditorium. We passed the Garden of Reflection, the nearby library, and a number of trainees. Their gazes upon me made me want to shrink. This was not how I wanted my peers to see me. My escorts seemed to sense my unease at their stares and tightened their formation around me, blocking my body from view. It was a small kindness I highly appreciated.

I was taken down a path I had not yet explored. The buildings grew tighter and appeared newer than I had seen so far. Eventually, I was taken towards a set of large stone steps guarded by foot guards.

"Captain Stewart." One of them saluted at our approach. "The generals are ready and waiting."

"Thank you, Sir Ratchet. I will take Lady Lynette straightaway, then. They won't want to be kept waiting." The older man who had spoken to me before nodded to the foot guard as my escort cage dispersed. The other three summoners saluted Captain Stewart before entering the foreboding building I had been taken to.

"I wish to witness the tribunal, if allowed?" Nate sauntered up the steps, his hands folded behind his back, followed closely by Callan.

"Only family members can bear witness, Lord Nathaniel, as you know." Captain Stewart raised an eyebrow at Nate.

"Right, right, of course," Nate sighed with a knowing look. "I suppose I will wait here, then."

"My apologies, Lord Nathaniel." Callan bowed to Nate with a smug smirk. "I will watch over my sister as her *brother*." Callan seemed to be calling himself my brother rather frequently recently.

"Certainly, Lord Callan," Nate calmly responded, ignoring Callan's apparent jest at our friendship. Though I guessed from Callan's perspective, Nate, and I were more than just friends, thanks to our scandal.

He must be concerned about pulling Nate into our family affairs.

"This way, Lady Lynette, Lord Callan." Captain Stewart raised his arm towards the double doors, his green cloak slinking over his arm. I braced myself, my heartbeat steadily rising, and picked up the hem of my cloak to ascend the rest of the steps towards the doors.

The captain pushed them open for us, revealing a wide-open hall. It was split at the centre by a large partition, with glass at the top and a wooden counter at the bottom. The walls were painted stark white, and our feet tapped against matching white stone. It looked identical to the stone the temples used. Summoners milled around in groups on this side of the partition. A few of them glanced our way, but most were engrossed in their conversations. All of them wore an emblem of a gavel at the centre of a laurel wreath. The captain took us forward to the far left of the room, opening yet another doorway.

"The tribunal halls are down here," the captain explained as we left the large hall.

"Where are we exactly?" I asked as the painted walls became stone in a hallway similar to the auditoriums. Windows lined the right side, with a doorway directly opposite each.

"The enforcement building; every profession has a specialised building." The captain slowed his pace a little as he noticed that I was curious about my surroundings. "Summoners who join enforcement are responsible for upholding the law of the Zopan Empire. Here, we train them in the laws and how to enforce them before sending them to the cities of the empire."

"It is also where many members of the council consult before approaching Congress," Callan mumbled beside me as we moved farther down the narrow hallway.

"Yes, an enforcer is responsible for ensuring order in the empire. Many summoners go on to become advisors in the palace or are assigned to a marquess of each city. However, there are always disputes amongst nobles and commoners alike that we resolve."

"I see. You must come across some interesting arguments," I said absently as we approached the end of the hallway. A doorway larger than the rest was, again, guarded by two foot guards at the end.

"Captain Stewart." They saluted before conversing with the captain quietly as Callan and I waited some steps away.

"Eduard will be in there." Callan spoke beside me.

"I figured he would be," I said, my eyes fixated on the door. My fate was behind it.

"Kara will be happy to have you home with her again. I will speak with Father about Lord Garret and try to sort something out."

"Maybe," I said, barely paying him attention. Callan assumed I was going to have my blood contract revoked, then? I supposed that was a fair conclusion.

"Lynette—" Callan began, but the captain turned from his conversation.

"You may enter now, Lord Callan. Please join the stands for witnesses. Lady Lynette, remain with me." The captain pushed against the large door.

The tribunal room was round like the temple in Talbour. Dark stone contrasted against the white of the rest of the building as I stood upon a raised wooden podium. Before me were even higher podiums, forcing me to raise my head upwards to see the three generals sitting leisurely in high-backed chairs. The whole setup was designed to make the accused feel small and insignificant against their power of authority.

It was indeed working.

I felt pitiful before their bored gazes. The captain had introduced them before showing me the podium to stand upon.

General Mullins wore a deep blue cloak. He had hard eyes, one of which was white from the scar that marred his face as it blended into the wrinkles on his forehead. He was the general of enforcement.

General Drew tapped a quill repetitively against the arm of his chair, adorned in a green cloak of wind. His shaven head looked polished against the scruff of his long brown beard. He was the general of administration.

Finally, General Fleming. He was younger than the others, without a wrinkle in sight. His brown cloak was untidy, with a rip running up its side; his shaggy brown hair hid his eyebrows as he leaned on his hand. He was the general of healing.

My eyes flitted to the witness stands on the left side of the room.

Eduard watched me intently with eyes as cold as the grey they were. His expression was firm, resolute. I hadn't seen him since I returned from my detour during the march. He had shaved the little stubble he had, and he wore a new tunic of dark blue and silver thread. A snake, the symbol of our house, was stitched on the chest. He looked as immaculate as he usually did in Talbour.

I pressed my lips together when I saw the box above his head.

Vishka's Guidance System
Eduard Heversham
Likeability: −10% (+2%)

Still in the minus; I wasn't surprised. Though it was strange, it had increased since I last saw him. Did Eduard's and Callan's opinions of me improve when I didn't speak with them? Or was I doing something that they approved of?

It was no use contemplating it right now.

Callan was beside Eduard, watching me with a softer tone. Maybe it was worry? I couldn't be sure as I wasn't used to him caring about me yet. Oddly, from their postures they didn't appear to be comfortable around each other.

What had happened between them?

"Shall we begin, then?" General Drew said, his voice reverberating in the room.

"Let's. I have a meeting scheduled shortly." General Mullins sounded impatient.

"Are we sure he should be here?" General Fleming asked, nodding towards a man in the witness stands I had assumed was meant to be here.

"He won't leave even if we ask him to," General Drew sighed. "Yamu, be sure to stay quiet, would you? You've caused enough grief already, handing out a blood contract before assignment."

"I stand by my decision." General Saika, the man who had assessed me in

Talbour and given me my blood contract, pouted on the witness stand. "I should be up there, not you, General Fleming."

"That would be biased, Yamu." General Mullins frowned. "Tribunals must be impartial. As the party responsible for this mess, you cannot make a decision on this."

"Tch." General Saika folded his arms in defiance. "This is why I don't like you enforcers. The girl has skills we can use!"

"General Saika!" General Mullins's voice rose. "You will refrain from speaking further."

As the discussion amongst the generals continued, I took a deep breath, trying to steady my nerves. The weight of the situation pressed down on me, knowing that my fate rested in their hands. It was a shame General Saika wasn't allowed to weigh in on the decision. By the sound of his frustration, he might have been a vote I could count on.

"Lady Lynette," General Drew called, pulling my attention to him. "You have been summoned here today as your father, Viscount Heversham, has expressed his displeasure about your decision to join the army. He informs us that you joined without his permission and are, in fact, to marry in the spring. Do you refute this?"

I gulped, finally able to speak as I had been addressed. "I do not, General Drew."

"So he writes the truth of the matter, then?" General Mullins asked.

"He does, General Mullins. However, I did not agree to any such engagement, and I do not intend to uphold it." As I spoke, I caught a glimpse of Eduard's frowning face from the corner of my eye.

"Bold words, Lady Lynette. However, it is commonplace that a parent may arrange their child's marriage. That is the way of the nobles," General Fleming said with a raised eyebrow.

"That may be, General Fleming. However, I still stand by my wish to cancel my engagement."

"Is that why you joined the army? To run away from your responsibilities?" General Mullins frowned down at me.

The tension in the tribunal room seemed to escalate as my response was met with disapproval from the generals. I felt my nerves rocket in my stomach. This wasn't going so well.

"I did not join the army to run away from my responsibilities, General Mullins," I replied, trying to keep my voice steady despite the nerves gnawing at me. "I joined because I want to use my skills to serve the Zopan Empire. As a loyal subject, I want to do my part as a dutiful citizen. Viscount Heversham's decision to arrange an engagement without my consent does not change this choice."

I was lying a bit. I wasn't as loyal to my country as I was eager to avoid my previous lives. I wouldn't mention that it was also Vishka's guidance that moved me. That was truly the only reason I joined.

General Drew leaned back in his chair, scrutinising me. "You claim loyalty and duty yet defy your father's wishes. How do you reconcile that?"

I blanched at this question. He was right, of course. How should I approach this?

"I do not seek to defy the viscount." I forced the lie from my mouth. "However, I believe in having the right to make choices that align with my own beliefs and aspirations. It is not an act of disrespect but rather a declaration of my desire to follow my own will."

Again lies. I did not respect Roger Heversham in any form. But saying that wasn't going to get me anywhere. Telling the truth in my trial last time only got me killed. I wouldn't make that mistake again. Luckily, these generals did not know me. They wouldn't be able to notice my lies like Eduard and Callan probably could. Although they often presumed I was lying when I wasn't.

General Fleming raised an eyebrow, seemingly intrigued by my response. "Your convictions are admirable, Lady Lynette, but you must understand the implications of your actions. Arranged marriages strengthen alliances and maintain social harmony. By rejecting this engagement, you risk upsetting the balance between the noble families involved."

"I understand the consequences, General Fleming," I replied. "But I cannot sacrifice my own happiness and aspirations for the sake of political alliances."

The generals exchanged glances, and I noticed that General Drew's expression had softened somewhat. General Mullins, however, still appeared stern and unyielding.

"Lady Lynette, you speak passionately, but emotions cannot always guide important decisions," General Mullins said gruffly. "You may have your reasons, but your father's wishes cannot be dismissed lightly. This matter requires thoughtful consideration and respect for tradition."

"I do respect tradition, General Mullins," I replied quickly, trying to maintain my composure as I began to grow irked by this man. "But I do not believe my engagement should impact my blood contract."

"No impact? Is that not the reason your father petitioned for your revocation?" General Drew asked.

"Viscount Heversham believes I am incapable of being in the army," I said, making eye contact with General Mullins. "I refute that opinion."

"I understand you have been assigned as a foot guard, Lady Lynette?" General Fleming asked, knowing my answer.

"That is correct," I confirmed.

"Then is his opinion not substantiated? I know of no noble who is a foot guard," General Mullins responded, but it was clear to me his mind was made up from the roll of his good eye.

Of course, it was probably embarrassing for a noble to have a child join as a foot guard.

"I intend to become a summoner once I have grown my core, General Mullins."

"Grow your core?" General Mullins scoffed. "You barely have one, Lady Lynette. You won't be able to use a gathering technique to do so."

"You seem confident in your statement, Lady Lynette," General Fleming said, his brown eyes narrowing. "Why?"

I braced my heart against the tension. This was it. I had to prove myself. "I have a technique that allows gathering for a core as small as mine."

"Impossible, no such thing exists," General Mullins exclaimed.

I pinched my fingers. I had been expecting that response; Lieutenant Cragborn had reacted similarly.

"Consider me intrigued, Lady Lynette." General Drew stroked his long beard. I felt my heart flutter; he had taken the bait.

"You can't be serious." General Mullins glared at General Drew.

"What? It's not impossible now, is it? We have aether researchers for a reason," General Drew replied.

"You think a young woman from Talbour knows a miraculous gathering technique for a core below grade one? Your head is in the clouds, Drew." General Mullins shook his head in exasperation.

"Regardless," General Fleming said, interrupting them both. "Results would be proof enough."

"True enough, Fleming." General Mullins withdrew his argument with General Drew.

I felt a small hope rising. Maybe I wouldn't need to use my backup plan. They would need to let me stay in order to see such results, just as I had hoped.

"I can't see any reason to go against Viscount Heversham's request at this point. If the young lady truly has such a technique, she can grow her core at home and redo the assessment at a later date." General Mullins waved his hand as my skin prickled.

"That could get her killed, Mullins. If her technique is not suitable for her core, she will only end up poisoning herself with aether." General Fleming frowned. "It is best that she stay so we can monitor her results."

Two decisions were made, and there was only one left. I watched General Drew in anticipation as my heart raced. His features scrunched as he contemplated a decision. I held my breath as he looked to the other two generals, appearing torn.

"Considering her lack of approval and arranged marriage, I am inclined to agree with Vis—"

"I request your attention to my declaration!" I shouted desperately to stop those last words from leaving General Drew's mouth. All three of the generals paused at my outburst, and I quickly rushed to pull out my envelope.

I had no choice.

"What is your declaration?" General Fleming nodded to Captain Stewart, who approached the podium and took the envelope from my hands. He brought it over to the generals. They opened it and began to read my written request.

I glanced at Eduard and Callan. They looked at me in confusion as I swallowed the pit that hardened in my throat. I wondered how badly this would affect them.

I'm sorry, Cassandra. I will have to go back on the kindness you gave me.

"I wish for the immediate revocation of my legal adoption!"

CHAPTER FORTY-EIGHT

No sooner than the words left my mouth, chaos ensued in the tribunal room. Voices rose over one another as I flinched at the familiar shout directed my way.

"Lynette! What are you doing?" Callan's outrage overpowered the generals' confused chatter. He gripped the witness stand's railing so tightly his hands were turning white.

Eduard's body was as still as ice, his gaze fixed on me with an emotion I didn't know he could feel. I met his eyes and stiffened as my heart pounded tightly against my chest.

"Lynette!" Callan cried again as I swallowed my anxiety at the blurring boxes above both of their heads.

Vishka's Guidance System
Eduard Heversham
Likeability: −30% (−20%)

Vishka's Guidance System
Callan Heversham
Likeability: −2% (−20%)

In the stands, General Saika slapped his hand onto Callan's shoulder and pulled him back from running to me.

My lips twitched into a strained smile in response to my brothers. I hadn't wanted it to come to this, but there was no other way. It felt like I was discarding all Cassandra had gifted me, betraying her generosity. Pain thrummed in my heart as I tried to hold back my guilt for my actions.

I had no choice.

"Quiet down!" General Mullins beckoned to the room, forcing a silence to descend. His one good eye narrowed at Callan as he tapped the arm of his chair. Callan shoved General Saika's hand away before Eduard stepped forward and whispered something to him to calm him down.

"Lady Lynette," General Drew began, addressing me amidst the turmoil. "Are you indeed requesting the annulment of your adoption?" he asked me with a face of confusion and shock.

"I am, General Drew," I affirmed, keeping my voice steady. "I have written a formal request for this and—" I paused, glancing back towards my brothers. "I have had my request legitimised by a higher-ranking noble."

"What?" A voice shouted out in shock and I jumped at its tone. Eduard frowned at me, but his grey eyes were wide with concern and anger. I gulped as the numbers in his box led me closer to my potential death.

Vishka's Guidance System
Eduard Heversham
Likeability: −35% (−5%)

"She has indeed." General Fleming smirked as he passed my letter towards General Drew. "I suggest we request their attendance at once."

"I concur. If anyone was mad enough to go along with this, they should speak for themself." General Mullins shook his head in disbelief. "In all my years in enforcement, I have never known anyone to petition to annul their adoption."

"I must say, I am rather shocked myself." General Drew took a deep breath as he passed my letter to General Mullins. "Captain, please bring the notary here."

Captain Stewart, who had been staring at me, blinked in stupor at the mention of his name. "Right, of course." He bowed to the generals before pausing. "Who might that be?"

I saw both my brothers swivel their heads to the generals as they anticipated the name that had backed me in dishonouring the Heversham family.

"Lord Nathaniel Hudson." General Fleming smiled as he relaxed in his chair. It almost looked like he was enjoying this turn of events.

Captain Stewart rose at once to do as he had been commanded. However, I did not miss the look of realisation on his face. It probably mirrored my own as I came to the same conclusion. This must be why Nate chose to wait outside the enforcement building. He must have known he would end up attending.

Eduard's chin jutted at Nate's name, his attention quickly returning to me. "Why would you do this, Lynette?" he said in disbelief.

I wanted to laugh out loud at his shock, but instead, I smiled awkwardly as I gazed at the box above his head. I knew this would be a risk. I had to choose my words carefully so the numbers didn't fall too far. I didn't want to be killed again. I had to have faith; Vishka had said I risked death below minus fifty percent. Not a definite.

The generals all watched me expectantly for a response. I wouldn't usually be able to respond to anyone but them, but it seemed they wanted to ask the same question as Eduard.

"Is this really so much of a surprise, Eduard?" I said coldly as he frowned. "I have told you what I want. Yet you never listened. You never do."

Eduard's expression shifted from disbelief to frustration as he tried to grasp my words. "I know you're headstrong, Lynette, but this . . ."

Vishka's Guidance System
Eduard Heversham
Likeability: −40% (−5%)

Callan's voice broke through, laced with disappointment. "You involved Lord Nathaniel in this? You went to him behind our backs?"

I sighed, my heart aching at the hurt in his eyes. The effort and progress we had made this past month had been shattered. I knew it would be. "I told you both that I want to be here. Yet you both told me to do as the viscount demands. Is it really so hard to see that I trust Lord Nathaniel more than I do both of you, my brothers?"

They froze in place, their expressions pained. The boxes above their heads blurred fast as the numbers refused to settle into place.

General Mullins cleared his throat, breaking the tension. "Lady Lynette, we must hear from Lord Nathaniel Hudson directly before proceeding."

"Of course, General Mullins." I nodded at his request for my silence.

Callan slumped into his seat, gripping his hair with both of his hands. Eduard refused to remove his grey eyes from me as his chest moved slowly, trying to calm his emotions.

A silence beckoned in the room as we waited. It was deafening.

General Drew shuffled uncomfortably as he rubbed his shaven head. "You do realise, if we agree to this, you will be stripped of your noble rank?" he probed, attempting to break the atmosphere.

"I am aware, General Drew." I smiled. Of course, I knew that. "I am, and always will be, a mere commoner." I had known this would be a consequence. I would no longer be Lynette Heversham, just Lynette. I would no longer have any power to protect myself with my status. I would be all on my own. If it was the price I had to pay to keep my place here, I would pay it. It would be better to face life with nothing than to return to repeat a miserable life I had already lived once.

Besides, being demoted to commoner would also annul my engagement with Garret. An incredible bonus.

Perhaps that would also be best if I was to follow Vishka's will.

The doors to the tribunal room opened. Captain Stewart returned, looking flushed, and quickly ran over to the generals. As he opened his mouth to speak, the door boomed open as clattering footsteps interrupted my trial.

"Why is it I was only informed of this mere moments ago?" A hardened voice made my skin prickle in panic as two figures entered.

Vishka's Guidance System
Azriel Kamil Elkhart
Likeability: −29% (+1%)

What the heck was the Lord Azriel of the Frozen South doing here? My eyes bulged as I watched him march towards the generals, barely sparing me a glance. I made a face at Nate as he casually strolled behind him, his hands behind his back. Nate noticed and winked at me with that cheeky of grin of his.

What was going on?

"Y-Your grace," General Drew stuttered, as shocked as I was. "This is a trial to determine the continuation of Lady Lynette's blood contract. You do not take an interest in them usually."

"Does that mean I do not wish to be informed when it concerns a person of interest to me?" Azriel's voice was clear despite the metal mask that covered most of his features.

"Consider it our mistake, your grace." General Fleming sighed with a wave of his hand. His attitude towards Azriel was so laid back compared to General Drew. "As I am sure Lord Nathaniel has informed you, there have been developments that have changed this trial anyway."

"I have indeed been informed, Duke Fleming." Azriel's form of address shocked me again. General Fleming was a duke? Wait . . . Fleming . . . ah! I widened my eyes as realisation struck me; the dukedom of the Viridian North belonged to Fleming. He was the duke who overlooked the nobles in Ingalham and Talbour! How had I not realised . . .

"Your grace, respectfully, are you going to put a stop to this farce?" General Saika piped up from the witness stands with a smug expression towards General Mullins as he folded his arms. He had patiently been watching with an irked attitude this whole time and seemed to revel in this disruption.

"Saika." General Mullins chastised him with a glare. "Quiet down."

Eduard and Callan had moved closer to the exit from their stands, itching to intervene if given the opportunity. Callan desperately tried to meet my eyes, but I couldn't pull away from Azriel Elkhart as my heart hammered.

"Lady Lynette has yet to resolve a declaration made to me regarding an ability of hers." Azriel frowned towards me, making me flinch as his purple eyes narrowed. "I understand Lord Nathaniel has also backed her request for an annulment of adoption?"

"Th-that is correct," General Drew gulped. "We were awaiting Lord Nathaniel for confirmation of this."

"Very well." Azriel nodded as he moved around the podiums to join the generals directly on their stand. He stood beside General Fleming and gave him an expectant look I did not comprehend. However, General Fleming seemed to understand as he rolled his eyes, taking out a pouch from his pocket. Opening it, he clicked his fingers, and soil spurted out of the pouch. It expanded at an exceptional rate before forming into a solid earthen chair.

Azriel sat down and leaned back into the high-backed chair. "Lord Nathaniel, have you used your seal for this request of Lady Lynette's?"

Nate smiled ruefully, sauntering over to stand beside me as I stood on the podium, still absorbing this new development.

"I have, indeed, agreed to back Lady Lynette in her request," Nate stated proudly.

"What are your reasons for doing so, Lord Nathaniel?" General Mullins asked, displeased. "Lady Lynette's reasons are lacking, to say the least."

I tightened my hand into a fist.

Nate's eyes remained steady as he addressed the sceptical general. "General Mullins, I simply believe Lady Lynette would not ask for such a thing if she did not have her reasons. I trust her judgement."

General Mullins's brow furrowed as he exchanged a brief glance with the other generals. The room seemed tense, as if everyone was awaiting an explanation.

Eduard and Callan paled slightly, and I couldn't help but feel a warmth float inside me. Nate had agreed to my request by faith in me alone, a woman he did not know very well. It was more than either Eduard or Callan had given me growing up.

"I see." General Drew nodded slowly, processing Nate's response. "Lady Lynette, can you provide further clarity on the matter?"

I swallowed the lump in my throat, aware that Azriel's unwavering gaze was fixed upon me. The presence of the Lord Azriel and his unexpected involvement had shifted the trial dynamic entirely. I would not put Nate's trust in me to shame.

"I appreciate your willingness to understand, General Drew," I began, my voice steady despite the turmoil of nerves growing within me. "To truly grasp my motivations, I believe it's necessary to delve into the circumstances that surrounded my adoption."

Callan and Eduard exchanged a tense glance, uncertainty etched on their faces, bracing themselves for what was to come.

"Please proceed," General Fleming said encouragingly, his curiosity piqued.

"When I was a child of seven, the late viscountess, Cassandra Heversham, rescued me from the brink of starvation in Wayward Town," I recounted, my voice carrying a mixture of gratitude and pain. "She brought me into her home and treated me with kindness beyond measure. It was an act of generosity that I've always been deeply grateful for."

"Then how can you justify what might be seen as a betrayal of that generosity?" General Mullins's tone held a note of accusation. "Your father arranged a respectable marriage for you, despite your limited core, and your own safety led to the request for the blood contract's revocation. Yet, in response, you're seeking the annulment of your adoption—a drastic step."

I met General Mullins's gaze head-on, the conflict within me mirrored in his eyes. "I understand how my actions might be perceived as ungrateful," I admitted, my voice tinged with a hint of sadness. "And truthfully, there is a part of me that feels as though I'm betraying Cassandra's memory."

It sickened me that I was betraying her kindness like this.

"Then why proceed?" General Mullins's voice held a trace of scepticism, a hint of challenge.

"I acknowledge that perspective, General Mullins," I replied, my gaze unwavering. "But the warmth and kindness I once knew ceased to exist after Cassandra's passing."

"Lynette . . ." Callan spoke softly, with mild regret, as he met my eyes. He understood the pain I was referring to, the pain that he had taken part in creating with his lie. Eduard's tense posture beside Callan was strange; it was almost as though he wanted to protest but was fighting internally with himself.

"I fail to see how her passing has any bearing on your request," General Drew interjected, his expression puzzled.

"The circumstances changed drastically after Cassandra's death," I explained, my voice steady despite the memories that threatened to overwhelm me. "The truth is, if my adoption were up to Viscount Heversham today, I believe he would choose not to adopt me."

General Drew's brows furrowed, and I pressed on, determined to lay bare my reasons. At least, enough of what I was willing to share. "He has never treated me as a daughter, and he has often gone out of his way to remind me that I am a burden," I continued bitterly as I recalled the painful moments. "Considering this, I believe that the annulment of my adoption would be in both his interest and mine."

A heavy silence settled in the room as my words hung in the air, emotions echoing in the space between us. Callan's expression softened, his regret palpable, whilst Eduard's initial apprehension seemed to shift to confusion and frustration. He desperately wanted to speak to me but knew he couldn't.

Azriel's presence seemed to loom larger than life, his intent scrutiny obvious even through the mask that covered part of his face. He leaned back in the make-shift earthen chair, fingers intertwined.

Azriel broke the silence, his tone measured and authoritative. "I do not believe this can be decided without Viscount Heversham's input."

"I agree," General Fleming sighed, but I caught his small smirk. "Perhaps, in the interest of all here, we should postpone a decision on revocation of the blood contract and adoption until the spring social?"

"The spring social?" General Drew leaned forward in his chair. "That's two seasons away."

"It makes sense." General Mullins nodded reluctantly. "The viscount usually travels midwinter. Despite my opinion that Lady Lynette is being foolish, we cannot make such a decision without the viscount's input."

"This will also allow you to confirm Lady Lynette's ability with demonic beasts, your grace." General Fleming's tone was mocking towards Azriel. "It will also allow us to see if Lady Lynette's claim to have a gathering technique is truthful."

"Indeed, she can train as a recruit, and we can monitor her results for her safety." General Drew stroked his beard, nodding.

"Very well, it is decided, then. We will reconvene this matter in the spring when Viscount Heversham is here to speak."

"Do you agree to this, Lady Lynette?"

"I do," I said as relief poured into every fibre of my being.

It was the best I could have hoped for. Time was all I needed. I would have the entirety of autumn and winter to train, grow my core, learn how to fight, and prove that I could survive in the army. If I could become a summoner, they wouldn't be able to revoke my blood contract so easily. It wasn't going to be easy; I still had to get my body stronger, and I would have to catch up with the other trainees as they trained to become summoners. Until I could join them, I would be the best foot guard trainee I could be.

I was determined to change my fate.

Vishka's Guidance System
Eduard Heversham
Likeability: –25% (+15%)

Vishka's Guidance System
Callan Heversham
Likeability: 15% (+17%)

Vishka's Guidance System
Azriel Kamil Elkhart
Likeability: −18% (+11%)

EPILOGUE

Zachary's Assessment

Heat poured onto the back of the summoner's neck as he waded through the growing crowd of Talbour. Zachary had been away from Talbour for quite some time. He hadn't attended the annual demonic culling of the deadlands in a few years, so he hadn't had a chance to return home. A small smile passed his lips as he spotted his baby sister arriving at the square centre. Zachary's family carriage stood out to him, adorned with his family crest of an owl, its wings spread wide perched on a branch.

The carriage pulled to a halt as Zachary approached, its white doors flinging open to reveal its occupants.

"Brother!" A usually quiet voice rose as a young girl with frizzy auburn hair filled the entry. The girl wasted no time hopping down the carriage steps as she leapt towards Zachary, arms open wide. Zachary caught his baby sister in a strong embrace, twirling her around in laughter.

"Lacey, I have missed you!" he chuckled, placing her feet back onto the ground and gently cupping her cheek. "You have grown since I last saw you."

"I have, haven't I?" Lacey beamed with a flattering smile as she turned back to the carriage, "Mother, see, Zachary says I've grown."

A figure stood up from the carriage seats, her auburn hair braided into a ring around her head, her frilly dress wide as she raised a pale yellow fan above her lips and held out her hand. Zachary took it and helped his mother descend the carriage steps. She studied Zachary, her eyes roaming over his figure as she inspected him for his health and well-being. Seeming satisfied, she lowered the fan.

"I am glad to see you, Zachary. It has been some time." Uma Weadall patted her son's hand affectionately. "I trust you have been growing in the capital?"

"Yes, Mother," Zachary said proudly. "I have built on my foundation and strengthened my skin meridians recently." As a summoner, Zachary had reached foundation stage a little over a year ago. He was now focusing on strengthening his body to withstand the ascension into solidification. Many summoners failed to strengthen their bodies sufficiently in foundation. They either lacked a core large enough or had severed a meridian in the attempt, forever ending their chances of ascending into solidification. It was a precarious stage for a summoner.

"That is excellent news." Uma praised her son as she tucked her arm into his. "Your father is busy assisting the commoners today. There was a beast breach into the northern fields. He was very disappointed he could not be here to greet you." She frowned, worried that her husband's absence might upset her son.

Zachary nodded. "I will see him this evening. It cannot be helped. I will have the same responsibility someday." He was slightly disappointed about his father's absence. However, the commoners would not be able to withstand a demonic beast attack. His family was responsible for protecting the northern fields of Talbour, just as the Hevershams protected the southern fields. Without them, commoners could not safely plant their crops or tend to livestock beyond the walls. Some day, Zachary would take up his father's mantle and command the barons into battle to protect Talbour.

"He is very excited to see you." Uma giggled as she reached her daughter and gently tucked a strand of her frizzy hair behind her ear, making her blush. "Just as he is saddened to see our dear Lacey leave." She sighed heavily with regret.

Zachary shared his mother's grimace as he turned his attention back towards Lacey. It had always been intended for Lacey to enter the social season this year, to find her a potential husband and keep her safe from having to learn to fight. She had always been a weak-natured child. Her strength was her mind, not her bravery.

"Are you sure there is no way out of this? She has to join?" Zachary said as Lacey glumly looked down at her feet.

"There is no other way," Lacey whispered, rubbing her arm in a mix of fear and nerves.

"Sadly, there is not. At least not without ruining our reputation." Uma squeezed her daughter's shoulder reassuringly, seeing her familiar habit of withdrawing within herself. "The empress has demanded a larger enlistment of suitable recruits. If we withhold Lacey, the marquess will question us."

"As you wrote in your letters." Zachary scrunched his eyebrows. Normally, women were not expected to join the army. When they joined, it was by their own choice, not out of responsibility like the future heirs of houses. However, the empress's recent pressure on the marquess of each province had forced many houses to have their daughters enrol this year for mere lack of sons.

Each noble household was now expected to provide at least two children for enlistment. For houses like Zachary's, that meant it had to be Lacey as they were the only two children of the viscount. They could not argue against it either, because of the considerable size of Lacey's core.

Even for a viscount's lineage, Lacey's core was exceptional. At grade six, she had the same as an earl's untrained core. She was guaranteed to become a full-fledged summoner who could wield an aether spirit, unlike many barons. Withholding her enlistment because of her timid nature would only have repercussions from the Marquess of Talbour.

"You must take care, Lacey." Uma lowered her stance a little, her pale yellow dress spilling onto the ground. "You will always listen to Zachary, follow your orders, and take every precaution to be vigilant of your surroundings."

"Y-yes, Mother." Lacey nodded, inching closer to Zachary as she gripped the hem of his green cloak. Her eyes watered as she took deep breaths, seeing that more nobles were arriving and forming a queue for the recruitment test.

Zachary's lips thinned in anger as he wiped away the tears that were forming on his baby sister's cheeks. He hated this, sincerely wishing that he had been graced with another sibling, a brother.

Zachary stood in his assigned role at the tables for the recruitment test. He glanced at the queue of potential recruits as Lacey's face paled at the final table. She had been accepted, and her fright at the prospect was obvious. He tightened his hand around the pen he held as he sent away a commoner he had just tested. He was frustrated at his inability to help his sister get out of this. He could do nothing to go against the marquess or the empress's demand. He could only help Lacey whenever he could.

A set of footsteps alerted him to his next visitor. Raising his eyes, Zachary immediately frowned as he recognised the unusual long black hair and jade-green eyes of the woman standing before him.

"Crazy Cerue Lady. Never thought I would see you here," Zachary scoffed, scratching the light dirty-blond stubble on his chin. Of all people, why was she here? There was no way she was being forced to join like Lacey was. Lynette had no core to be useful as a summoner, and her two brothers had already enrolled, meeting the empress's decree.

"Zachary." Lynette Heversham greeted him, making him purse his lips. He was not friendly enough with Lynette for her to use his name so casually. He might be her brother's friend, but he was not hers.

"What on earth made you attempt to sign up for the army? Don't you cause enough hassle at home? We don't need you," Zachary chided her, his own frustration for Lacey leaking through his tone. He had no ill will towards Lady Lynette, but he did not care for her. She caused nothing but headaches for Eduard. It was likely she would do the same for Lacey.

"I have my reasons. Do I need to explain them as part of the assessment?" Lynette asked with a tone of superiority. Zachary narrowed his pale blue eyes, his short, curly blond hair blown in the wind. She was always hostile towards the people around her.

"No", he said curtly. There was no point in arguing with her. "Let's get on with it, then. Show me your skills." He held up the board along with his pen.

Zachary was surprised to learn that Lynette did not know what a blood sign was. Eduard often spoke about how dealing with his sister's actions pained him. She was brash and obnoxious and acted above the people around her. Zachary had witnessed her treatment of commoners on more than one occasion. He even saw her threatening to burn a commoner's stall last year because of some dispute. He did not know the details of what had upset her so much, but such a threat was below the nobility. The woman was supposed to uphold the dignity of a viscount's lineage. Even if they weren't related by blood, her actions affected not only the Hevershams' reputation but also that of his own family.

That was why, when Zachary placed the red aether ink onto her hand and spoke the activation phrase, "Blood of this one, gods, reveal their truth," he didn't at all feel guilty about the pain she was about to feel. She had dealt emotional pain much worse than this to people who did not deserve such treatment. Fortunately, the pain was brief as the blood sign imprinted smoothly onto Lady Lynette's skin. Zachary remembered doing the same for Lacey when she turned eighteen and frowned as he glanced back to the tent she was waiting in.

"What?" Zachary asked as he heard Lady Lynette mumble something.

"Uh, nothing." Lynette blushed, her cheeks growing pink as she rubbed the new mark on her hand thoughtfully.

"Whatever." Zachary rolled his eyes at her actions. Why was she suddenly embarrassed? The woman was an enigma. "Say 'Show skills' whilst holding up your palm. It will show me if you have achieved any skills that may be worthwhile to the army. I doubt it, though, with your recklessness." He shook his head.

As far as Zachary knew, Lynette had grown up pampered in her household. Eduard and Callan were always irritated by her pompous attitude, but they had never trained her in weaponry as she had no core. Instead, they allowed her to do as she wished. She had even avoided having a governess to teach her after the viscountess passed. It was common for children to dislike education, but to completely neglect it was shameful. He had never understood why Eduard and the viscount allowed such a thing. It was doubtful Lynette had any skills of worth to the army. Not to mention, this girl had the luxury of avoiding the army. She could live the life that Lacey should, safe and away from danger. In fact, he recalled that she was already engaged. She had no reason to be here.

"Show skills!" Lynette shouted, making Zachary roll his eyes at her eagerness.

"Why do they always shout?" he grumbled at the box that appeared between them. Everyone always shouted when they said those words for the first time.

"Let's see now . . . name, yes . . . rank, yes . . . aether core null, as expected." Zachary's lip upturned. Of course, it was as Eduard had told him. Lynette's core was nonexistent, a mere pinprick. She couldn't become a summoner. She was lucky to avoid the empress's decree.

"Now skills, what *wonderful* skills do you have?" Zachary exaggerated the word, his expectations low. However, as he read the list of skills she possessed, he couldn't help but pause in his writing.

"What . . ." he said absently, narrowing his eyes at Lynette's blood sign, then returned his gaze to Lynette's hesitant expression. "Just how . . ." he mumbled as he quickly jotted down what he saw.

How in the world does she have pain and poison resistance?

It made absolutely no sense for her privileged upbringing.

He scrunched his fist around his pen as he continued to read and saw Lynette's unusual herbology skill. He looked at her briefly in surprise before returning to Lynette's blood sign. Wasn't she uneducated? When did she have the time to grow her level so high? Could that be connected to her poison resistance? Was Lynette secretly interested in poisons?

Yet even Lacey didn't have pain resistance. Lacey had avoided learning combat, as she hated any aspect of violence. Lynette Heversham was the same, wasn't she? Eduard had said she had never trained with weapons. She had no reason to have pain resistance if she hadn't trained in anything. Of course, it could be gained as a skill if someone. . . .

Zachary felt his heart tug as he furrowed his brows. No, there was no way. Lynette was a noble. There was no way she could have earned such a skill from . . .

Raising his hand, he pointed at the box and then flicked his finger upwards. The text of her skills quickly changed into a diagnostic of her health—a section of the blood sign often overlooked by many. It listed Lynette's blood type, cholesterol, blood glucose, weight, and other aspects of her health. It was information that only trained medical experts knew how to interpret.

Zachary widened his eyes as he inspected Lady Lynette's health readings. He expected as much from many of the skinny commoners who had already come to his table. They were underfed, lived in poor conditions, and did not have a varied, balanced diet.

But a noble . . .

Zachary frowned. He looked back at Lady Lynette with an expression of sympathy, guilt, and puzzlement.

Before he made any conclusions, he had to check for himself. His aether would be able to determine her true state.

"Give me your wrist," Zachary said quietly as he contemplated everything he knew about Lady Lynette. She was defensive and brash and avoided people if possible. She often overreacted to silly comments and irked Eduard and Callan.

"All right." Lynette was clearly perplexed by Zachary's request as she held out a hand. He gripped her wrist, being careful to be gentle now that he knew how fragile the lady was. Lynette's blood sign vanished as he dropped his board and enclosed her hand with his left. He frowned as he did so. Lynette's hand felt very small in his.

"You will feel a tingling, but it's normal and won't hurt, so don't worry," Zachary said softly, seeing her apprehension as her hand stiffened within his. She had flinched when he touched her. Why hadn't he noticed that before?

"What are you doing?" she asked tentatively, her eyes wavering upon his hands.

"Just checking for something, don't worry." Zachary scrunched his features as he calmed his mind to concentrate. He didn't want to reveal his true intentions. Lynette might pull away before he could confirm his suspicions.

Focusing on the aether running through his meridians, Zachary directed it to travel through to his fingertips. His aether slithered through his skin, hesitant at first, but then flowed smoothly towards his palms, embracing Lynette's hands. Zachary's hands began to glow a pale green as his aether congregated into them. It pushed against the barrier of Lynette's skin, foreign and alien to the aether within Zachary. With a mental forceful shove, the aether broke through Lynette's skin, which was powerless to defend against him. With a rush of power, Zachary's aether plummeted through Lynette's body. It spread like tendrils, poking at her organs, her heart, and her skin before pulling quickly back to the safety of its owner's body.

As the aether returned, it brought back all it found, its inspection of his patient complete. Information flooded Zachary's mind as he interpreted the findings to match up with what he had suspected.

Zachary pulled his hands away from Lynette's, gazing at her with a pained expression as his fears were confirmed. Lynette Heversham was suffering from a degree of malnutrition. Her muscles were weakened, and she was not as fit as a girl her age should be. Paired with her pain resistance and a lack of weapons skills, it didn't make sense. The only possible conclusion was that something had happened to Lynette Heversham, something no one should experience. It left a sour taste in his mouth. He had been so caught up in his feelings for Lacey that he hadn't even considered that Lynette had her own issues. She was not living a life of luxury and safety if she was like this.

"You . . . I didn't . . ." He began to speak but paused at the look in Lynette's eyes as she blinked in confusion up at his face. *She must know. Doesn't she?* Zachary frowned, shaking his head as he picked up his check board. This was a sensitive matter. He should speak with Lynette about this privately. There were too many eyes and ears here in public. She might not be comfortable speaking with him about such matters in such a place.

Just what had happened to her since Eduard and Callan had been away in the capital? He knew that Roger Heversham was not the most pleasant of people, but he doted on his daughters, didn't he?

"You have passed this assessment," Zachary said, scribbling.

"I have?" Lynette said, astonished, which only upset Zachary further.

"Yes. But . . ." He paused, looking at Lynette with a pained expression as he considered what she must have been living with to end up like this.

"Would you come to see me if you pass the next test?" He really needed to speak with her about this. Zachary didn't want to let his mind run loose, but did Eduard know that Lynette Heversham was in this shape?

Perhaps not.

They only ever returned for a few days at a time these past few years because of the increase in demonic beast attacks. Eduard might not have seen the changes in Lynette, as he wasn't a medical officer. Zachary should speak with Eduard as soon as possible.

"I—I guess?" She hesitated, but her acceptance was enough. Zachary nodded, knowing he would find her even if she did not come to him. It was his duty as a medical officer.

"Good. I suspect you will, with those skills." Zachary hadn't seen anyone with a herbology skill that high in years. She was no doubt going to be accepted. They desperately needed people who understood how to make medicines even commoners could produce. Too often there were more injured than summoners who could heal.

"What skills?" Lynette asked, very confused.

Zachary paused, then smiled. She truly had no idea how high her skill was in herbology? Had she been holed up at home all this time researching? Was that why she only rarely appeared in public?

"You will find out soon enough. The next table is your final assessment. They will talk to you about it and ask you some questions." He should let it be a surprise for her.

"All right," she sighed reluctantly. "Are you going to tell Eduard about . . . you know . . . me being here?" Her tone changed as she nervously shuffled her feet.

Zachary considered her words and everything he had just learned about Lynette. Had she decided to join the army without the viscount's or Eduard's knowledge? Why did she feel the need to keep this from them?

No, of course, they wouldn't want her to join.

Zachary didn't want Lacey here. Why would Eduard and Roger Heversham want Lynette here? It wasn't safe for them.

"Does he not know?" Zachary asked, rubbing his chin. Eduard was going to be furious. Zachary would be if Lacey did this without their parent's knowledge or consent.

"Not technically . . . no . . . no, he doesn't," she whispered, looking down at her feet. Zachary saw her reaction, her nerves, how she looked away from him, not wanting to make eye contact and the slight tinge in her expression. He frowned deeply, a wrinkle forming on his head.

Lynette was . . . afraid of Eduard?

"I won't mention it unless he asks," Zachary said, his mind spinning. Something was going on in the Heversham household. Something he himself feared. He tightened his grip into a fist, trying to hold back his feelings. Zachary wanted to immediately grab Lady Lynette and take her to one of the medical tents. He wanted to ask her about her treatment, why she was so unwell, why she was so afraid of Eduard.

But he could not do that.

She was already afraid. He couldn't stress her out any more than she clearly already was. She might have acted unreasonably at times, but what caused her to act in such a way? Her defensive attitude might have been out of desperation if this was her normal state. Anger began to creep into Zachary's heart.

"Really?" Her surprise was upsetting.

"As I said, I won't tell him unless he asks. I can't lie to my friend," Zachary answered, shaking his head. No, he would not say a thing. If Eduard truly knew that something was wrong, he would ask Zachary himself for his medical opinion. Surely, if he didn't pick up on it, well . . . That only made him question Lynette's fear even further. Just what was being hidden in the Heversham household? What had Eduard done to cause her to be so afraid?

"Thank you, I appreciate it. I will be sure to come to see you when I can." Lynette bowed.

"Please do." Zachary nodded as he watched the lady leave for the final assessment.

EPILOGUE

Callan's Discussion

As always, the empress's visage had a powerful and intimidating aura. A young man looked up at her authority as she glanced across the gathering brigade. Summoners stood in neat rows below her shrill purple eyes as they inspected her army. Her gaze lingered on the trainees for a moment, as though she was counting their number. As she ended her greetings, releasing the brigade from their duties, the summoners saluted, their hands forming fists against their hearts as they bent their opposite arms behind their backs.

Shuffling the backpack that had gained a rip in its side, a young water summoner brushed a strand of his tawny brown hair out of his grey-ash eyes. A shuffle of movement and shouts and the brigade began to disperse in organised formation. Callan's attention drew towards the trainees as they scrambled after their lieutenant. Only one stood out to him, a mess of black wavy hair amongst a mass of lighter colours, the point of his interest. Lynette Heversham hurried after her comrades as she was led out of the noble quadrant square of Zromore, the capital of the Zopan Empire.

"What ya looking at?" a young woman asked in an airy voice as she tilted her head his way with a bright smile. Her ginger hair was plaited into a bun.

"Nothing." Callan broke away from watching his sister as he regarded his teammate. "Leave it, Felicity." He tightened his lips at the glint in her eyes.

"Ooooo, struck a nerve, did I?" Felicity Goodwin giggled, rocking back on her heels as she gripped the straps of her backpack. "You know, you could just strike up a conversation with her, maybe go out to eat, try a new hobby together, watch the sunset . . ." She rolled on, irritating Callan with her insistence on poking her nose into his life.

"I am not discussing this with you," Callan snarled, whipping his head to move away from her.

"Felicity, stop it." A tall man with dark brown hair and a neatly trimmed beard touched Felicity's shoulder, pulling her back. "This isn't easy for him."

"Ugh, fine." Felicity rolled her eyes at their team leader, Calbert Cavendish. "Spoilsport," she muttered under her breath, and she twirled on her heels.

"Don't mind her, Callan," Calbert sighed as he watched Felicity skip towards their other teammate, Shane Cooper. Shane nodded to the girl demurely as he listened to her vibrant discussion regarding the best types of meat and what vegetables were best paired with them.

"What? You think she bothered me?" Callan frowned defensively as they began to walk away from the noble square. He had done this many times after returning from the deadlands.

"Not at all." Calbert smiled knowingly, causing Callan to glare at him.

"Let me guess, you have your own opinions." Callan rolled his eyes with a shake of his head. He glanced back towards the trainees, but they were no longer there. He hadn't spoken with Lynette since the previous night, when he had apologised for his actions. He likely wouldn't see her today, as she would be staying in Alinor Keep. New recruits always stayed there until they passed their combat evaluations. Then she could come back to the Heversham town house with him.

"Of course, but it is not my place to get involved in your family affairs. I can only make suggestions." Calbert shrugged beside Callan as they walked under the stone archway to the left of the square, entering the cobbled pathway that led to the visiting nobles' plateau.

Zromore was divided into quadrants within three stone rings. The commoners occupied the first ring; three quadrants made up the area, encompassing homes, markets, and workplaces, and finally there was a section for warehouses and city storage.

The second inner ring was only for nobles and commoners within the army, with the rare exception of commoners, usually merchants, who could afford to purchase a home within this ring. The first quadrant was occupied by Alinor Keep, the home and training grounds for the army. The second quadrant was for the estates of nobles from Zromore. Grand mansions, lush gardens, and private parks could be found there. The third quadrant was similar, only for the homes of visiting nobles and rich merchants. Rather than mansions, many town houses were packed tightly together to provide the amount of housing required. There was simply not enough space for the lush gardens here. The final quadrant was the shopping district. Many businesses catering to nobles flourished there.

The third inner ring was for royalty. The palace towered above the white stone walls that kept out all except those who were permitted to enter, a set of golden gates standing proudly. It was an honour for any to step through those gates, a privilege that all nobles took advantage of during the social season.

Callan and his team wandered amongst others as they entered the visiting nobles' plateau. Their families each owned a town house here, preferring to live in the comfort of luxury rather than the small rooms Alinor Keep provided.

"I would prefer you keep your suggestions to yourself." Callan scowled at his friend.

"That's why I haven't said anything." Calbert smirked, folding his hand behind his back, supporting the bottom of his backpack. It was filled with numerous small fire aether cores they had gathered from killing flame scorpions in the deadlands. The enchantment on his bag was struggling to safely secure them all, threatening to break.

Callan paused his step at his friend's response, opening his mouth to respond before closing it and rethinking. He had been trying to do that more lately, thinking about what he would say before he actually did.

"Fine. What would you suggest," Callan finally said, his curiosity getting the better of him. He knew he would probably regret asking.

"Well, I would start with trying to connect with her more." Calbert grinned at his stubborn friend.

"Easier said than done." Callan looked ahead as his features tightened.

He had been furious to find out that his team had followed him last night. They had seen the whole messy apology he had given to his sister. After he escorted her back to her camp, all three pounced on him with insistent questions about what happened. Felicity had punched him in the gut before he even had a chance to try to shut them up. Her anger at hearing his apology and what he had done to his sister was justified. But Callan was enraged that they had intruded on a private moment between him and his sister. They had no right to do that. He hadn't wanted his dirty laundry to be aired so publicly. Yet he knew he probably deserved it.

He had been an arse.

"What's so difficult about it? She's your sister, isn't she? Surely you have something in common you can talk about."

"We have nothing in common. She's stubborn, she never listens, and she goes out of her way to make things difficult for us. Do you know how often my father had to pay off someone for the stuff she broke?"

Calbert silently raised an eyebrow at Callan in amusement.

"What?" Callan scowled.

"You have plenty in common, Callan." Calbert laughed at his friend's obliviousness. "Who do you think pays for the stuff you break all the time?"

"What . . . well . . . hmm." Callan started to argue but found his words dead in his throat. "Maybe you're right," he finally mumbled, annoyed. He knew he had a quick temper, and there were plenty of things he had broken himself in rash actions.

"Of course I'm right. I always am," Calbert said smugly. "I would say your biggest obstacle is getting her engagement dissolved."

Callan's fist tightened before he dropped it back to his side. "I want to drown that bastard."

"I would love to roast his arse on a fire spit, but we can't do that. That would be considered murder, Callan." Calbert gave a pointed look at Callan.

Callan bit his cheek. Calbert knew him rather well. It was no surprise that he knew Callan had been considering the numerous ways he could make Lord Garret disappear. He had sat up all night in their shared tent, imagining how he might be able to have that little twerp die. His favourite was having him accidentally fall into a pond in the Garden of Reflection, then using his water aether to drag him down. Callan might not be a full-fledged summoner yet, but he was certainly no pushover in using aether.

"Pfft. I know that, Calbert, I wasn't going to do anything," Callan said, but he wasn't convincing. "I am going to speak with Eduard about it tonight."

"Do you think he will help?" Calbert said as they turned off the main pathway and headed down a narrower street. Felicity and Shane were matching pace some distance behind them.

"He will. Nobody threatens our family and gets away with it," Callan said with a huff as a hot rage flared, causing him to grind his teeth.

The setting sun cast shadows through the windowpanes as Callan marched down the hallway of the Heversham town house. He had stayed here every year since turning twelve. The hallways were just as familiar to him as the manor back in Talbour. At first, it had only been a couple months of the year as he accompanied his father and brother during the social season. Then Kara had joined them in her twelfth year, when he turned sixteen. After joining the army at eighteen and passing his combat evaluation, he grew more settled in the town house than in Talbour, now only visiting Talbour for a couple months a year. Last year Callan hadn't even gone back when he hadn't joined the expedition to the deadlands.

Callan's expression pinched as he stopped at a vase resting on a stand in the hallway. Kara had bought it to brighten the place up when she visited. He touched the fragile porcelain gently. Lynette had never been here. Roger Heversham had never wanted to bring her on the journey, worried she would disgrace them in some way publicly like she did in Talbour. Callan had understood his judgement, having heard the sordid stories of her actions whilst he and Eduard were away in Zromore.

Now?

He pulled his hand back and continued onwards. Lynette's actions were probably his fault. He had acted like a jealous, ignorant fool when he lied to his father about his mother's necklace. Callan clenched his teeth as he thought about Lynette's expression when they were on the cliff. Self-hatred creased into his heart.

Raising his hand, Callan knocked on his brother's door. The servants had informed him that Eduard had returned. It had surprised Callan that Eduard had arrived a little over two hours after he did. Usually, they arrived at the same time. What had Eduard been doing after the empress's greeting?

No answer came from behind the door, disgruntling Callan. He wasn't going to wait. He wasn't some servant who had to await his brother's beckon. Rather heavy-handedly, Callan pushed open the door and stormed into his brother's room.

"Eduard, we need to talk!" he called as he shut the door behind him, but he found himself faced with an empty room. "What . . . where . . ." He began to look around before spotting the steam floating out of a door on the right of the room.

"Oh." Callan straightened as he realised he had just barged in on Eduard whilst he was bathing. "Hmm. May as well wait, then." He shrugged and pulled out the chair from under Eduard's desk. The chair scraped against the hardwood floors as he slumped into it, leaning back and letting his arms dangle over the arms. Callan felt a little deflated, having been prepared to argue with his brother, but now found himself waiting patiently.

Eduard's room was similar to Callan's. They were all the same in these town houses. Not many of them varied in structure, having been mass-built from the same designs. It made it easier for the servants to navigate, as they often changed houses if they were empty for some time when nobles returned to their home cities. Each had a private en suite bathroom with a working aether-tapped bath, shower, and lavatory. The rooms had double four-poster beds with patterned screens separating the area from a small sitting space.

Most had a table and padded chairs for guests in their sitting areas. However, Eduard had removed his years ago and instead installed an office of sorts. A desk, a shelf filled with books, and two chairs were all he had. Eduard was never fond of guests.

The steam and the sound of running water stopped, perking Callan up from his slouch. After a moment, the bathroom door opened. Eduard stepped out into his room, rubbing a white towel on his tousled dark brown hair, glaring at Callan.

"Callan. It's rude to enter someone's room without permission," Eduard chided as he tightened the belt on his trousers.

"You didn't answer. I wasn't going to wait at your door like an idiot." Callan rolled his eyes, picking up a dark blue shirt from on the desk and throwing it at his brother. "Put this on, will you? We need to talk." Callan averted his gaze from his brother's bare skin. It always made Callan uncomfortable to see his brother's scars.

Eduard grabbed the shirt with a heavy sigh, dropping the towel into a basket of laundry for the servants to collect. He raised his hand over his scarred arms, sluicing the water off his skin with a flick of his wrist. The dozens of pairs of equidistant puncture scars lightened their tone as his skin dried with the use of aether. It was rare to see them, as Eduard always covered them with his clothes.

"What is it that has you so impatient?" Eduard crossed the room towards Callan, pulling his shirt on before pulling out the second chair behind his desk.

"It's about Lynette," Callan said, shifting to face his brother. Eduard narrowed his eyes at the mention of Lynette's name.

"What did she do?" he said in a lower tone of apprehension.

"Nothing." Callan frowned at his brother's first reaction. Did Eduard always react like this?

"Then why are you here?" Eduard sighed, the tension from his shoulders relaxing.

"It's about—" Callan hesitated, closing his eyes and taking a deep breath. "It's about what I did to her."

Eduard released a heavy sigh, raising his hand to his temple as he worked a knot that was beginning to form. "Callan, I'm sure whatever you did, Lynette will soon forget about it."

"No!" Callan raised his voice, making Eduard pause at his intensity. "She won't. She said she can't trust me yet. I need to make amends to her."

"What in Urish's name did you do that you need to make amends for? Lynette has caused us enough trouble that you should have nothing to apologise for."

Callan looked away from Eduard, studying his hands as he flexed them. "I lied about Mother's necklace."

Silence fell as Eduard absorbed what his brother had confessed to him.

"Mother gave Lynette her necklace?" Eduard asked, his voice quiet.

"Yes," Callan said, ashamed as his eyebrows knitted. "Kara needs to give it back."

A loud thump sounded.

Callan fell backwards in his chair with a clatter, clutching his left cheek. Eduard stood over him, his hand squeezed tightly into a fist as he glowered down at his brother.

"How dare you!" Eduard shouted with a rage Callan had not experienced from his usually well-polished brother. "Do you know what that made Father think of her, what I thought of her after that!"

"I know!" Callan stumbled over the chair as he picked himself up. "I know, all right? I was an idiot, I didn't think! I just didn't want her to have Mother's necklace when she didn't even give me anything!" Callan screamed back at his brother, his face numb where he had been struck.

"And you think that petty jealousy gave you the right to take it away from Lynette?" Eduard gritted his teeth. "It's no wonder she doesn't trust you!"

"That's why I'm trying to make amends to her!" Callan lifted his arms in frustration. "I didn't know that Father resented her so much after that. I didn't know the servants started to give her that foul shit because of that! I thought she was just acting out. I thought she was just acting spoilt whilst we were in Zromore!"

"Then pray tell me, Callan. What made you suddenly realise that what you did had consequences?" Eduard glared at him.

"She told me herself!" Callan exclaimed, causing Eduard's eyes to widen.

"She told you?" he replied, his voice lowered in surprise.

"Yes." Callan sighed, picking up the chair. He slowly sat back down, rubbing his cheek. "She told me during the march."

"She didn't say anything about it to me." Eduard frowned as he also sat back down, his rage simmering down.

"She tried to tell us before," Callan mumbled as he felt a pit of guilt.

"What do you mean?" Eduard probed.

Callan bit the inside of his cheek. He had been going over many things in his mind since Lynette had told him what his petty lie had done to her.

"Remember when we were still kids? She flipped that table, complaining about the food. Father was going to . . ." Callan paused, glancing towards Eduard's arms. "You stepped in and sent her to her room as punishment."

Eduard froze, his hand stilling on his head as he rubbed his temple. His memory flashed back to the event. She had practically destroyed the dining room that day. Her outrageous behaviour had infuriated Father. She had broken dozens of plates and splintered the wood table when she flipped it over. She had said something about the food, but she had lied so many times before that neither Eduard nor their father had believed her.

"I remember," Eduard said sullenly.

"I need to make amends to her, Eduard." Callan pursed his lips. "Her engagement needs to be dissolved."

"What?" Eduard shook himself out of his stupor. "Why? Lord Garret was gracious enough to keep the engagement despite what she did with Lord Nathaniel." His eyes twitched. "There won't be many other offers for her."

"Maybe not, but she can't be with that sick little man. Lynette told me what he tried to do to her."

"What did she tell you?"

"How he tried to force himself on her during the march. He's a wretched man," Callan spat, his anger flaring just thinking of Garret Asher.

Eduard found himself pausing for the third time during this discussion. He looked at his brother's irritated face as Callan started to tap his foot, the telltale sign that he was struggling to hold back his emotions. Eduard couldn't help feeling jealous. Why was Lynette opening up like this to Callan?

"That is not something for us to decide," Eduard replied as he looked at the letter on his desk. Lynette's crying face when she shared his tent repeated itself in his mind. "I will hand in Father's request for her blood contract revocation tomorrow morning. Once she is safely back in Talbour, I will discuss this matter with Father."

"You can't seriously still want to send her back to Talbour?" Callan sat up straight, his hand slamming against Eduard's desk.

Eduard folded his arms and leaned back in his chair. He took a deep breath as he focused on himself. "You would rather she die on assignment? Use your head, Callan. Lynette doesn't have the capacity to become a summoner. They will be making her a foot guard. She hasn't got the temperament for battle. She won't survive for long once they send her to an assignment."

"But then she will have to marry that bastard!" Callan flung his hand out, knocking a pile of paperwork and an ink pot onto the floor. "I promised her I wouldn't let that happen!"

"Then you were foolish." Eduard tamped down his emotions, deep within his gut. He had to maintain control. He was the heir of the Hevershams. He had to do as his father had taught him. He had to keep his family safe, first and foremost.

"You have no say in her marriage, Callan. We also have no evidence of what she insinuated Lord Garret did to her. She had made it clear she did not want to marry Lord Garret before we left on the march. This could be another ruse of hers, just like what she did with Lord Nathaniel."

"You still doubt her?" Callan said, shocked. "After everything I just said?"

Eduard's temple twitched at Callan's statement. "I can only help when I know she is safe. That is in Talbour, not here. I will be handing in Father's request."

"Hah." Callan chortled as he flopped back into his chair, deflated. "I see. This must be what she has been dealing with."

"What are you spouting now?" Eduard was slowly losing control as he tightened his arms closer to his chest.

"You know, since we left Talbour, did you notice?" Callan said numbly.

"Notice what?" Eduard replied.

"Lynette hasn't once called Roger Father."

EPILOGUE

Garret's Desperation

The halls of the Asher town house were dark. The curtains were drawn tightly, blocking all view from the outside to protect the secrets of the house. A maid stood near a door as Garret paced back and forth, biting his fingernails. His grey cloak flourished as his steps followed the worn path on the hardwood floors where many before him had paced as they waited.

Garret was anxious; his first day as a trainee had not gone as he had hoped. Despite his persistence, that damn woman was still stubbornly refusing his hand in marriage. She irked him like a persistent, low-grade irritation dancing beneath his skin. Lynette Heversham, how dare she think herself above him.

She was tainted goods now, and he had graciously still been willing to accept her. He had to, despite how much he hated that woman. If she weren't beautiful, it would be even more difficult to carry out this task. She was just a woman; why wouldn't she comply with her father's wishes?

The maid standing guard moved as a slight knock disrupted Garret's pacing. The old woman, with a worn-out expression and her eyes lidded with wrinkles, bowed to Garret. "You may enter now, Lord Garret."

Garret straightened, patting down his ginger hair nervously. "Move aside, then, maid," he spat at her, clenching his hand to hide its shaking.

The maid nodded, ever obedient, as she stepped aside. Garret stepped forward, raising his hand to the door with a gulp.

"Come in, boy." An older voice dripping with disdain summoned him. Garret hesitantly opened the door as he entered his uncle's study.

"Uncle, how pleasant to see you. I hope you have been well this past year," Garret said, holding back a lump in his throat as cold brown eyes studied him.

"Sit." Tarlon Asher spoke curtly; he had no patience for small talk.

Garret nodded, clenching his fists tighter as he moved further into the dark room. A small mage lamp hung above his uncle, illuminating only his thin figure, casting shadows against the furniture.

Tarlon's eyes followed Garret as he took one of the high-backed chairs placed before the desk. It was intentionally uncomfortable, not designed to keep guests long. The moment Garret sat, Tarlon slammed his hand onto the desk before him, causing Garret to startle.

"Why are you dawdling?" Tarlon said in a low voice.

"I—I am not, Uncle. That woman is just so stubborn. She refuses me even though she has no other prospects."

"Pathetic," Tarlon snarled. "You can't even complete such a simple task."

"I am trying, Uncle! I promise." Garret pleaded under the heavy, angry gaze of his uncle. "Her joining the army was unexpected. As soon as her blood contract is revoked and she returns to Talbour, there won't be a delay. The viscount has already agreed to the marriage; she is just a woman. She can't go against it."

"Oh? Do you truly think so?" Tarlon's voice deepened, his eyes narrowing, creating a panic in Garret's throat.

"Wh-why do you say that?" Garret said as his hand began to shake again.

"Her blood contract revocation has been delayed until the spring. Lynette Heversham has requested an annulment of her adoption."

"She what?" Garret widened his eyes in disbelief. What had that insane woman done?

Frustration welled like an unwelcome storm. Lynette had brought nothing but complications to Garret's task. Everything had been going so smoothly after he had met her at Sarah Gangley's ball. It was the first time Garret and his father had laid eyes upon her. They had both been shocked to see that the recluse adopted child of the Hevershams was in fact Dramorian. She had been described to them a few times, but they had never imagined such a dramatic reason. No Dramorian stepped foot in the Zopan Empire unless it was to make war.

It was essential that they make her a part of their family.

Roger Heversham had accepted the marriage proposal; it was easy to get his acceptance. Luckily Lynette was born without a strong core, so there were no other nobles to fight with for her hand. It was a discerning choice that Garret had made. He knew he deserved better, a woman with a core who could give the Ashers a powerful heir, but Lynette was necessary. He was the only male member of his family who was unmarried.

Yet that blasted woman had spent the night with Lord Nathaniel. Then she joined the army to add further complications, delaying any marriage. When

Garret married her, he would be shamed to have a sullied wife. Now that she was advocating to become a commoner, he would be demeaned even further.

"We must not allow that to happen. We cannot force her hand if she is no longer a noble." Garret bit his lip as he tried to think of way to stop it. If he had to marry that woman, the least she could do was bring the honour of connecting the viscounts to their barony.

Tarlon tapped his aged, wrinkled fingers against the dark wood of his desk. The rings that adorned them glinted under the mage lamp. He watched his nephew with a dim gaze. "If she is a commoner, she will have no way to fight us, foolish boy."

Garret stilled in his seat at his uncle's words. Did he truly mean to make him marry a commoner with no noble backing? A hot hatred simmered; Garret did not even want to marry this woman. But he could not refuse his uncle's or father's command. Why was she making his life more miserable?

"You mean we can force her to marry me?" Garret asked hesitantly. He didn't like the idea of having a wife so repelled by him that they would have to force her into it.

"I'm surprised you understood that." Tarlon sneered at his nephew, making Garret's lips twitch. "No matter what she does, we must have a Dramorian connection. Our backer has insisted upon it, boy; you know what that means, don't you?"

"Y-yes." Garret slumped in the tense, hostile atmosphere. He could not fail, or their backer would kill them.

Acknowledgments

To my ever-patient husband,

For enduring my late-night typing frenzies, my endless writerly rants, and my insistence on repeated cups of tea, this book is dedicated to you. Thank you for your unwavering support, your gentle reminders to take breaks, and your nagging—I mean, loving encouragement. Without you this book might still be a chaotic mess of half-formed ideas. Here's to many more chapters of emotion, laughter, and, yes, occasional nagging.

And to my dear granddad,

As this story gained followers, you embarked on your final journey, leaving cherished memories and profound wisdom behind. Your belief in me echoes throughout these pages. Though you're gone, your encouragement remains. This book is a tribute to you and the love you bestowed upon me.

With love and laughter,
J. L. Rabone

About the Author

J. L. Rabone is a British author who is deeply passionate about fantasy's enchanting realms. Through a childhood immersed in the wonders of reading, she developed a profound appreciation for diverse books and genres. Having transitioned from avid reader to aspiring writer, she now channels her imagination into crafting her own captivating fantasy tales, seeking to enchant readers with her narratives. When she's not weaving tales of magic and adventure, Rabone can be found lost in the pages of a book, cuddling her cats, or losing herself in a new game.

Podium
DISCOVER
STORIES UNBOUND
PodiumAudio.com